Maisey Yates is a *Ne...* of more than thirty r... habit she has no in... Pinterest addiction. S... children in the Pacific... writing she can be found singing in the grocery store, shopping for shoes online and probably not doing dishes. Check out her website: maiseyyates.com.

Lucy Gordon cut her writing teeth on magazine journalism, interviewing many of the world's most interesting men. She's had many unusual experiences, which have often provided the background for her books. Once, while staying in Venice, she met a Venetian who proposed in two days. They were married for 45 happy years, until his sad death. Naturally this has affected her writing, in which romantic Italian men tend to feature strongly. Two of her books have won a Romance Writers of America RITA® Award. You can visit her website at lucy-gordon.com

USA Today-bestselling author **Jennie Lucas's** parents owned a bookstore and she grew up surrounded by books, dreaming about faraway lands. A fourth-generation Westerner, she went east at 16 to boarding school on scholarship, wandered the world, got married, then finally worked her way through college before happily returning to her hometown. A 2010 RITA® finalist and 2005 Golden Heart® winner, she lives in Idaho with her husband and children.

Postcards
COLLECTION

January 2019

February 2019

March 2019

April 2019

May 2019

June 2019

Postcards from Rome

MAISEY YATES

LUCY GORDON

JENNIE LUCAS

MILLS & BOON

First Published in Great Britain 2019
By Mills & Boon, an imprint of HarperCollins *Publishers*
1 London Bridge Street, London, SE1 9GF

POSTCARDS FROM ROME © 2019 Harlequin Books S.A.

The Italian's Pregnant Virgin © 2017 Maisey Yates
A Proposal from the Italian Count © 2017 Lucy Gordon
A Ring for Vincenzo's Heir © 2016 Jennie Lucas

ISBN: 978-0-263-27570-4

0419

Printed and bound in Spain
by CPI, Barcelona

THE ITALIAN'S PREGNANT VIRGIN

MAISEY YATES

To my parents, who actually are great and have always supported me. In spite of what 90% of my characters' parents might suggest.

CHAPTER ONE

"THE THING IS, Mr. Valenti, I'm pregnant."

Renzo Valenti, heir to the Valenti family real estate fortune, known womanizer and chronic overindulger, stared down at the stranger standing in his entryway.

He had never seen the woman before in his life. Of that he was nearly one hundred percent certain.

He did not associate with women like this. Women who looked like they had spent a hot, sweaty afternoon traipsing through the streets of Rome, rather than a hot, sweaty afternoon tangled in silk sheets.

She was red-cheeked and disheveled, her face void of makeup, long dark hair half falling out of a bun that looked like an afterthought.

She was dressed the same as many American college students who flooded the city in the summer. She was wearing a form-fitting black tank top and a long, ankle-length skirt that nearly covered her dusty feet and flat, unremarkable sandals that appeared to be falling apart.

Had she been walking by him outside, he would never have paid her any notice. Except she was in his home. And she had just said words to him no woman had said to him since he was sixteen years old.

But they meant nothing, as she meant nothing.

"Congratulations. Or condolences," he said. "Depending."

"You don't understand."

"No," he said, his voice cutting through the relative silence of the grand antechamber. "I don't. You practically burst into my home telling my housekeeper you had to see me, and now here you are, having pushed your way in."

"I didn't push my way in. Luciana was more than happy to *let* me in."

He would never fire his housekeeper. And the unfortunate thing was, the older woman knew it. So when she had let a hysterical girl into his home, he had a feeling she considered it punishment for his notorious behavior with the opposite sex.

Which was not fair. This little *creature*—who looked as though she would be most at home sitting on a sidewalk in the vicinity of Haight-Ashbury, playing an acoustic guitar for coins—might well be some man's unholy punishment. But she wasn't his.

"Regardless, you're not drawing this out and making a show, and I have no patience for either."

"It's *your* baby."

He laughed. There was absolutely no other response for such an outrageous statement. And there was no other way to remove the strange weight, the strange tension that gripped him when she spoke the words.

He knew why it affected him. But it should not.

He could imagine no circumstance under which he would touch such a ridiculous little hippie. And even so, he had just spent the past six months devoted to the world's most obscene farce of a marriage.

And though Ashley had been devoted to the pleasure of both herself—and other men—during their union, he had been faithful.

A woman with a small baby bump, barely showing

beneath that skin-tight top, claiming to be carrying his child could be absolutely nothing but ridiculous to him.

He'd had nothing at all but six months of fights, dodging vases flung in a rage by his crazy wife—who seemed to do her best to demolish the stereotype that Canadians were a nice and polite people—and then days on end of ridiculous cooing like he was some kind of pet she was trying to tame again after a sound beating.

Little realizing that he was not a man to be tamed, and never had been. He had married Ashley to make a point to his parents, and for no other reason. As of yesterday, he was divorced and free again.

Free to take this little backpacker in any way he wanted to, if he so chose.

Though, she would find the only place he wanted to take her was out the front door, and back onto the streets she had come from.

"That, you will find, is impossible, *cara mia.*" Her eyes went round, liquid, shock and pain visible. What had she imagined would happen? That he would fall for this ruse? That she would find her salvation in him? "I can see how you would build some strange fantasy around the idea I might be your best bet for help," he said, attempting to keep his tone calm. "I have a reputation with women. But I have also been married for the past six months. So whatever man is responsible for knocking you up in a bar crawling with tourists and never calling again? He is not me, nor will you ever con me into believing it is. I am divorced now, but in the time I was married I was faithful to my wife."

"Ashley," she said, blinking rapidly. "Ashley Bettencourt."

He was stunned, but only momentarily, by her usage of his wife's name. It was common knowledge, so of course if she knew about him, she would know about Ashley. But if she knew he was married, why not choose an easier target?

"Yes. Very good," he said. "You're up on your tabloid reading, I see."

"No, I *know* Ashley. She's actually the person I met in a bar crawling with tourists. *She's* the one who knocked me up."

Renzo felt like he'd been punched in the chest. "Excuse me? None of what you're saying makes sense."

The little woman growled, lifting her hands and gripping her head for a moment before throwing them back down at her sides, curling her fingers into fists. "I am… I am trying. But I thought you would know who I was!"

"Why would I know who you are?" he asked, feeling at a loss.

"I just… Oh, I should never have listened to her. But I was… I am just as stupid as my dad thinks I am!" She was practically wailing now, and he had to admit, this farce was inventive even if it was damned disruptive to his day.

"Right at this moment I'm on your father's side, *cara*, and I will remain so until you have offered me an explanation that falls somewhere short of being as stupid as my *ex-wife* getting you pregnant."

"Ashley hired me. I was working at a bar down by the Colosseum, and she and I started talking. She was telling me about the issues in your marriage and the trouble you were having conceiving…"

The words made his gut twist. He and Ashley had never attempted to conceive. By the time they'd gotten to a place where they might discuss giving him an heir to his empire, he'd already decided that no amount of shock value made her worth it as a wife.

"I thought it was weird, her talking to me like that. But she came back the next night, and the next. We talked about how I ended up in Italy and how I had no money…" She blinked. "And then she asked me if I would consider being her surrogate."

Pressure built in Renzo's chest until it exploded. English deserted him entirely, a string of vulgar Italian flowing from his lips like a foul river. "I don't believe it. This is some trick that bitch has put you up to."

"It's not. I promise you it isn't. I had no idea that you didn't know. No idea at all. It was all very… What she said… It made sense. And…and she said it would be easy. Just a quick trip to Santa Firenze, where the procedure is legal, and then I just have to…be the oven. I was supposed to get paid to make the bread, so to speak, and then… well, give it to the person I…baked it for. Someone who wanted the baby desperately enough to ask for help from a stranger."

Panic tore through Renzo like a wild beast, savaging his chest, his throat. Making it impossible to breathe. What she was saying was impossible. It had to be. Mostly.

Ashley was…unpredictable. And God knew how that might manifest. Especially since she'd been enraged by the divorce—made simple because of their marriage in Canada, which she had felt was calculated on his part. It was, of course.

But she wouldn't have done this. She couldn't have. Still, he pressed.

"It made sense to you that a woman pursued surrogacy, and claimed to have a husband whom you never saw?"

"She said that it would be impossible for you to come to the clinic. She could only do it because she wore large sunglasses and a hat. She said that you were far too recognizable. She said you were very tall." She swept her hand up and down. "You are. Obviously. You don't blend. Not even sunglasses would disguise… You know what I mean."

"I know nothing. It has become apparent to me over the past few minutes that I know less than I thought. That snake talked you into this. How much did she pay you?"

"Well, she hasn't given me everything yet."

He laughed, the sound bitter. "Is that so? I hope that final price is a high one."

"Well, the problem is that Ashley said she doesn't want the baby anymore. Because of the problems that you're having."

"Problems?" The question was incredulous. "Does she mean our divorce?"

"I...I guess."

"So, you did some cursory research on us, and then no more?"

"I don't have internet at the hostel," she said flatly.

"You live in a hostel?"

"Yes," she said, her cheeks turning a darker shade of pink. "I was just passing through. And I ran out of money. Took a job at a bar, and I've been here longer than I anticipated. Then I met Ashley about three months ago."

"How far along are you?"

"Only about eight weeks. I just... Ashley decided she didn't want the baby anymore. And I don't want to...I don't want to end the pregnancy. And I thought that even though she said you didn't want to handle any of this, because it damaged your view of the whole thing...I wanted to come to you. I needed to make sure."

"Why is that? Because you fancy that you will raise the baby if I don't want it?"

It was her turn to laugh. There was no humor in it, only hysteria. "No! I'm not going to raise a baby. Not now. Not *ever*. I don't want children. I don't want a husband. But I was involved in this. I agreed to it. And I feel like...I don't know. How can I not feel responsible? She became a friend to me almost. I mean, she was one of the first people in forever who talked to me, told me about her life. She made sure I knew how much she wanted this baby and…now she doesn't. She might have changed her mind, but I can't change my feelings about it."

"What will you do?" he asked. "What will you do if I tell you I don't want the baby?"

"I'll give it up for adoption," she said, as though it were the most obvious thing. "I was going to give birth anyway. That was part of the agreement."

"I see." His thoughts were racing, trying to catch up with everything that the woman in front of him—the woman whose name he still didn't know—was saying to him. "And was Ashley planning on paying you the rest of the fee if you continued with the pregnancy?"

The woman looked down. "No."

"So, you had to make sure that you could still collect your fee? Is that why you came to speak to me?"

"No. I came to speak to you because it seemed like the right thing to do. Because I was becoming concerned about your lack of involvement in the whole thing."

Anger built inside him, reaching its boiling point and bubbling over. "Allow me to paint a clear picture for you of what exactly happened. My ex-wife went behind my back to hire you. I still don't understand how this happened. I don't understand how she was able to manipulate both you and the doctor. I don't understand how she was able to accomplish this without my knowing. I don't understand what her endgame was, as she is now clearly backing out. Perhaps now that she has seen she will get no money from me, and I'm not worth the effort anyway, she does not wish to be saddled with my child for the rest of her shallow existence. Or, perhaps it is simply Ashley. Who decided to do something on a whim, thinking that something of this magnitude would be a delightful surprise she would drop in my lap like the purchase of a new handbag. And much like my ex feels about handbags, she has decided she is bored of this one and moved on to the next shiny thing. Regardless of her motivation, the end result is the same. I didn't know. I did not want this baby."

At that, she seemed to deflate. Her shoulders shrunk inward, some of her defiant posture diminishing. "Okay." She blinked rapidly, lifting her chin and staring him down. "If you change your mind, I'm at the hostel Americana. You can find me there. Unless I'm working at the bar across the street." She turned on her heel and began to walk away from him, toward the front door. Then she paused. "You claim you've been in the dark this whole time. I just didn't want you to have that excuse anymore."

Then she walked out of his house. And just like his ex-wife, he determined that he would think about her no more.

It nagged at him. There was no escaping it. For three days he'd attempted to ignore and dismiss the events that had occurred earlier. He did not know the woman's name. He didn't even really know if she was telling the truth. Or if she was another of his ex-wife's games.

Knowing Ashley, that was it. Just a game. A weird attempt to try to draw him back into her web. She had been far too content with the dissolution of their union. Particularly after she had been so bitter about it in the first place. She had claimed he had always known it would end this way. Which was why they had sought marriage outside the country. Divorce in Italy was far too complicated. And, he supposed, the fact that he had covered his bases in such a manner was in some ways indicative of his commitment. Or at least, his faith in the mercurial Ashley.

But then, he imagined Ashley had gotten her revenge. Surrogacy was not legal in Italy. Undoubtedly why she had sought to have the procedure done in neighboring Santa Firenze.

More the pity that his sister, Allegra, had dissolved her agreement with the prince of that country and married Renzo's friend—Spanish duke Cristian Acosta, who would be no help to him in this situation—instead.

He should let it go. Likely the woman was lying. Even if she weren't…what should it matter to him?

A sharp pang in the vicinity of his heart told him he clearly hadn't had enough to drink. So, he set out to remedy that. But for some reason, grabbing a hold of the bottle of Scotch reminded him of what the stranger had said before she'd left.

She worked at a bar. She worked at a bar near the Colosseum, and if he wanted to find her he could look there.

He took the stopper out of the Scotch bottle. That would all be very well and good if he in fact wanted to find her. He did not. There was no point in searching for a woman who was—in point of fact—probably only attempting to scam money out of him.

But the possibility lingered. It lingered inside him like an acrid smell that he couldn't shake. One that remained long after the source of the odor was removed. He couldn't let it go because of Jillian. Because of everything that had happened with her.

He gritted his teeth, setting the bottle back down. Then, he strode toward his closet, grabbing a pair of shoes and putting them on quickly. He would get his car, he would go down to the bar, and he would confront this woman. Then, he would be able to come back home and go to bed, sleeping well, knowing with full confidence that she was a liar and that there was no baby.

He paused for a moment, taking a deep breath. Perhaps he was being overly cautious. But given his history, he felt he had to be. He had lost one child, and he would not lose another one.

CHAPTER TWO

ESTHER ABBOTT TOOK a deep breath as she cleared off the last table of her shift. Hopefully, she would have a decent amount of money in tips when she counted everything up, then, she would finally be able to rest easy. Her feet hurt. And she imagined that as early on as she was in the pregnancy, she couldn't exactly blame it on that.

It was just the fact that she had been working for ten hours. But what other choice did she have? Renzo Valenti had sent her away. Ashley Bettencourt wanted nothing to do with her or the baby. And if Esther had any sense in her head she would probably have complied with the other woman's wishes and pursued a termination. But she just couldn't do it.

Apparently, she had no sense in her head. She had a lot of feelings inside her chest, though. Feelings that made all of this seem impossible, and painful, and just a bit too much.

She had come to Europe to pursue independence. To see something of the world. To try to gain perspective on life away from the iron fist of her father. That brick wall that she could no more reason with than she could break apart.

In her father's world, a woman didn't need an education that extended beyond homemaking. In her father's world, a woman didn't need to drive, not when her husband should accompany her everywhere at all times. In her father's world a woman could have no free thought or independence. Esther had always longed for both.

And it was that longing that had gotten her into trouble. That had caused her father to kick her out of the commune. Oh, she'd had options, she supposed. To give up the "sinful" items she'd been collecting. Books, music. But she'd refused.

It had been so hard. To make that choice to leave. In many ways it had been her choice, even if it was an ultimatum. But the commune had been home, even if it had been oppressive.

A place filled with like-minded people who clung to their version of old ways and traditions they had twisted to suit them. If she had stayed any longer, her family would have married her off. Actually, they would have done it a long time ago if she hadn't been such a problem. The kind of daughter nobody wanted their son to marry.

The kind of daughter her father eventually had to excommunicate to set an example to the others. His version of love. Which was really just control.

She huffed out a laugh. If they could see her now. Pregnant, alone, working in a den of sin and wearing a tank top that exposed a slim stretch of midriff whenever she bent over. All of those things would be deeply frowned upon.

She wasn't sure if she approved of her situation either. But it was what it was.

Why had she ever listened to Ashley? Well, she *knew* why. Because she had been tempted by the money. Because she wanted to go to college. Because she wanted to extend her time in Europe, and because she found that waiting tables really was kind of awful.

There was nothing all that romantic about backpacking. About staying in grimy hostels.

It was more than that, though. Ashley had seemed so vulnerable when they'd met. And she had painted a picture of a desperate couple in a rocky place in their marriage, who needed a child to ease the pain that was slowly breaking them apart.

The child would be so loved. Ashley had been adamant about that. She had told Esther about all her plans for the baby. Esther hadn't been loved like that. Not a day in her life.

She had wanted to be part of that. Even in just a small way.

Finding out that was a lie—the happy-family picture Ashley had painted—was the most wrenching part of it all.

She laughed and shook her head. Her father would say this was her punishment for being greedy. For being disobedient and headstrong.

Of course, he would probably also expect this would send her running back home. She wouldn't do that. Not ever.

She looked up, looked at the view in front of her. Looked around her at the incredible clash of chaos that was Rome. How could she be regretful? It might be difficult to carry the baby to term with no help. But she would. And then after that she would make sure that the child found a suitable home.

Not one with her. But then, it wasn't her baby, after all. It was Renzo's. Renzo and Ashley's. Her responsibilities did not extend beyond gestation. She felt pretty strongly about that.

The hair on the back of her neck seemed to stand on end, a rush of prickles moving down her spine. She straightened, then slowly turned. And through the crowd, across the bar that was teeming with people, tables crammed together, the dark lighting providing a sense of anonymity, he seemed to stand out like a beacon.

Tall, his dark hair combed back off his forehead, custom suit tailored perfectly to his physique. His hands were shoved in his pockets, his dark eyes searching. Renzo Valenti.

The father of this baby. The man who had so callously sent her away three days earlier. She hadn't expected to see him again. Not when he had been so adamant about the fact that he would have nothing to do with the child. That he didn't even believe her story.

But here he was.

A surge of hope went through her. Hope for the child. And—she had to confess internally, with no small amount of guilt—hope for her. Hope that she would be compensated for the surrogacy, as she had been promised.

She wiped her hands on her apron, stuffing a bar towel in the front pocket and striding across the room. She waved a hand, and the quick movement must have caught his attention, because just then, his gaze locked on to hers.

And everything slowed.

Something happened to her. A rush of heat flowed down through her body, pooling in her stomach, and slightly lower. Suddenly, her breasts felt heavy, her breath coming in short, harsh bursts. She was immobilized by that stare. By the fathomless, black depths that seemed to pin her there, like a butterfly in one of the collections her brothers had had.

She was trembling. And she had no idea why. Very few things intimidated her. Since she had stood there in front of her father—in front of the whole commune, like a bad movie or something—refusing to recant the "evil" things she had brought in from the outside, there wasn't much that bothered her. She had clung to what she wanted, defying everything she had been taught, defying her father, leading to her expulsion from the only home she'd ever known. That moment made everything else seem mundane in many ways.

Perhaps, she had imagined, the world would turn out to be every bit as scary and dangerous as her mother and father had promised her it would be. But once she had purposed in herself that she was willing to take that chance to discover herself, to discover her freedom, she had made peace with it. With whatever might happen.

But she was shaking now. Was intimidated. Was maybe even a little bit afraid.

And then he began to close the space between them. And it felt as though there was a connection between the two of them. As though there was a string tied around her waist, one he was holding in his hands. And even though he was the one drawing nearer to her, she felt the pull to him.

It was loud in the bar, but when he spoke it cut through like a knife. Effortless, sharp and exceedingly clear. "I think you and I need to have a little chat."

"We tried that," she said, shocked at how foreign her voice sounded. How breathless. "It didn't exactly go like I planned on it going."

"Well, you walked into my home and dropped a bombshell on me. So, I'm not entirely certain how you expected it to go."

"Well, I didn't know it was a bombshell. I thought we were just going to discuss something you already knew. A bombshell you were complicit in."

"Sadly for you, I was not complicit. But if what you're saying is true, we definitely need to come to an agreement of some kind."

"What I'm saying is absolutely true. I have the documentation back at the hostel."

He narrowed his eyes. "And I'm supposed to believe that this documentation is factual?"

She laughed. "I wouldn't know where to begin forging medical paperwork like that."

"That means nothing to me. Your word means nothing to me. I don't know who you are. I don't know anything about you. All I know is that you showed up at my house earlier and are now asking me to believe the most fantastical of tales. Why should I?"

"Well," she said, looking down at her sandaled feet, "I suppose because you're here." She looked back up at him, her breath catching in her throat when she met with his furious gaze. "That means you must think it could be true. And if it could be true, why wouldn't it be? Why would I target you? Why would I…I don't know. It's just… Trust me. I would never have cooked this up on my own."

"Take me back to your hostel."

"I'm just off shift. I need to go write down my time."

He reached out, grabbing hold of her bare arm. The contact between his fingers and her skin sent an electric crackle down through her body. She had to think. Really think if she had ever been touched like this by a man. Other than a doctor or her family members, she'd had very little physical contact with anyone. And this seemed… It seemed more than significant. It burned her all the way down to the soles of her feet. Made her feel like her shoes might melt.

Like *she* might melt.

"I will speak to your boss later if need be. But you're coming with me now."

"I shouldn't."

A smile curved his lips. It was not kind. It did nothing to dispel any of the tension in her chest. If anything, it made everything feel heavier. Tighter. "But you will, *cara mia*. You will."

After that statement of declaration, she found herself being propelled out of the open-air bar and onto the busy street. It was still teeming with people, humidity hanging in the overly warm air. Her hair was sticking to the back of her neck, her tank top sticking to her skin, and his body was like a furnace beside her as they strode purposefully down the street.

"You don't know where I live."

"Yes I do. I am fully capable of looking up the name of a hostel and finding the directions. And I know the streets well."

"This isn't the way back," she said, feeling the need to try to find some power in the situation. She despised feeling helpless. Despised feeling controlled.

"Yes," he said, "it is."

Much to her dismay, this alternate route seemed to put them back at the front door of the hostel much more quickly than the one she typically took. She pursed her lips together, frowning deeply.

"You're welcome," he said, pushing the door open, his entire posture and tone radiating a kind of arrogance she had never before come into contact with.

"For what?"

"I have just showed you a better route home. Likely I will save you time in the future. You're welcome."

She scowled, ducking her head and walking past him into the narrow hallway. She led him down the hall, to the small room that she had in the back. There were four bunk beds in it, with two other women currently occupying the space. It was fairly private, all things considered. Though, as Esther began to feel more symptomatic of her pregnancy, it began to feel more and more crowded.

She kicked her sandals off, making her way across the pale, uneven stone floor, and headed to the bottom bunk, where all of her things were kept when she wasn't sleeping. Her backpack was shoved into the corner by the wall, and she grabbed hold of it, dragging it toward her.

When she didn't hear footsteps following her, she turned to see Renzo standing in the doorway. His frame filled the space, and when he took that first step inside, he seemed to bring something with him. Tension. A presence that filled not only the room, but any empty space in her chest.

"Welcome," she said, her tone flat.

"Thank you," he responded, his words carrying a level of disdain that was almost comical. Except, it was difficult to find much of anything funny at the moment.

She tugged on the drawstring that kept her backpack cinched shut, then hunted around for the tightly folded papers that were down in the bottom. "This is it." She held it out to him and he took it. His fingertips didn't brush hers, and she found herself preoccupied by the realization that she had almost hoped they would.

"What is all of this?" he asked, unfolding the documents.

"Medical records of everything and the signed agreement. With both mine and Ashley's signature. I suppose you would know if it looked different from your wife's actual signature. And I think we can both agree that the likelihood of me randomly being able to forge it is slim."

He frowned, deep lines forming between his dark brows. "This seems… It seems like perhaps there could be some truth."

"Call Ashley. Call her. She's mad at me. I'm sure she'll be more than happy to yell at you, too."

"Ashley wants you to end the pregnancy?"

Esther nodded, swallowing hard. "I can't. I agreed to

this. And even though the baby isn't mine, without me, maybe it wouldn't exist. And I just… I can't."

"Well, if this is in fact my child, that isn't what I want either."

"You want the baby?"

She tried to read his expression, but she found it impossible. Not that she was exceptionally adept at decoding what people were thinking. She had spent so many years growing up in a closed community. Seeing any faces at all that were unfamiliar was a shock. Going out into the wide world after an entire life being cloistered was… There were so many sights. So many sounds and smells. Different voices, different accents. Different ways of expressing happiness, sadness.

While she often felt at a disadvantage, sometimes she wondered if she actually read people a bit better than those who didn't have to look as closely at the people around them. She always felt that if she released hold on her vigilance—even for a second—she would find herself lost in this endless sea of humanity.

But there were no clues at all on Renzo's face. It was as though he were carved from granite. His lips pressed into a firm line, his black eyes flat. Endless.

"I will take responsibility for my child," he said, which was not the same as wanting the child. But she supposed, it didn't matter.

"Well…I suppose that's…" She didn't want to ask about payment. Except, she desperately wanted to ask about payment.

"But the first thing we must do is get you out of this…" He looked around the room, his lip curling slightly. "This place. You cannot stay here. Not while you are carrying the heir to the Valenti fortune."

She blinked rapidly. The baby that she was carrying

was the heir to a fortune? She knew that Renzo was rich. Of course she did. She had seen the way that Ashley was accustomed to living after their stay at the lavish hotel the other woman had insisted they stay in when they'd gone across the border for the procedure.

Still. This revelation seemed different. "But we've been fine for the past couple of months," she said.

"Perhaps. Though, I imagine our definition of 'fine' may be sharply different from one another's. You are not to work at that bar, not anymore. And you will come with me. Back to my villa."

Esther felt like she had been punched in the chest. She found that she couldn't breathe. She felt immobilized. Utterly and completely weighted down by that dark, uncompromising gaze.

"But what if I… What if I don't want to?"

"You don't have a choice," he returned. "There is a clause in this agreement that says Ashley can choose to terminate it should she decide she no longer wants the pregnancy carried to term. That has happened. That means unless you comply with my demands, with my word, you will get nothing. And you will have no recourse. Not—I assure you—in Italy. I will pay you more than the sum my wife agreed on, but only if you do exactly as I say."

Her head was spinning. She felt like she needed to sit down or she was going to fall down. She found herself doing exactly that before she even realized it, her weak legs folding, plopping her down roughly onto the edge of the thin mattress, the wood frame digging sharply into her thighs.

The noise from outside filtered through the single-pane windows, joining the thoughts in her head, swirling around, making her feel dizzy. "Okay," she said, only because she could think of no discernible reason to refuse him.

She knew there were other consequences to consider. Concerns for her safety, perhaps? She didn't know him. Didn't know him in any way beyond a brief understanding of his reputation as a businessman.

She also knew that he had been married to Ashley. Ashley, who had proved to be untrustworthy. Manipulative and—if Renzo was to be believed—a liar.

So, she imagined that said something about his character.

But she didn't see another option. Not one beyond putting herself through something that would undoubtedly be both physically and emotionally demanding without any kind of recourse. Not for the first time, she felt a deep sense of guilt and regret.

She tried not to traffic too much in guilt. Mostly because she had spent so much of her life neck deep in it. Every time she found a book at the local book exchange and slipped it into her bag—one she knew she shouldn't have. Every time she figured out a way to smuggle in a CD she shouldn't have had.

When she'd been kicked out after the discovery of her smuggled items, she'd become determined to live life on her own terms. To shamelessly adore pop music, and sugared cereal and movies. To read all the books she wanted, including books with dirty words and dirty scenes. And to feel not even a hint of shame.

But on this score, it was difficult for her to feel anything but a creeping sense of shame. She had seized this opportunity because it had seemed like a chance for her to make her dreams come true. To go to school. To continue to travel. To start a life that would remain completely separate from where she had come from.

She had been so single-minded, so focused, so determined to keep herself from ever returning to her family, to that small, claustrophobic existence, that she had ignored any and all twinges of discomfort over this arrangement.

But now, it was impossible to ignore. Impossible to wave her hand over the fact that she was carrying a baby. That she had some kind of responsibility in all of this. That it would be incredibly hard on her body. That it would likely wreck her emotionally. And that if she didn't comply with what Renzo was asking her to do…

There was a very good chance she would come out of it diminished. That the strength she had gained, strength enough to strike out on her own, would be gone. And for what? For money she wouldn't even be able to get.

So, she found herself cinching her backpack back up. Slipping her feet into her sandals, and turning to face Renzo.

"Okay," she said, her lips feeling slightly numb. "I'm going with you."

CHAPTER THREE

ADRENALINE AND ANGER coursed through Renzo in equal measure on the car ride back to his villa. It did not escape him that the woman—whose name he had read in the documents, but whom he had yet to be formally introduced to—was looking around the Italian-made vehicle with an expression akin to a country mouse. But he found he could spare little thought to it.

Not when the reality of the situation was so sharp. When his pulse was beating a steady tattoo in his throat, when his blood was running hot and fast beneath his skin. A baby. Esther Abbott, this American backpacker, was pregnant with his baby. Yes, he would have to verify all of this with Ashley, but he was forced to believe Esther. Though he had no real reason to.

Nothing beyond gut instinct. The idea of trusting his gut nearly made him laugh. But then, he rarely trusted his gut. Usually, he trusted in parts lower. And his own quick intellect, which he often allowed himself to imagine was above reproach.

In matters of business, it was. When he was consulted on where a certain business should be built, when he was tasked with seeing to a major bit of real estate development, he never failed. Instincts, inherited from his father, drove him in that arena.

Apparently, in other matters he was not quite so discerning. Or so unerring. His ex-wife was one of the very prominent examples of that truth.

Jillian being another.

Women. It seemed he had a tendency to be a fool for women. No matter that he kept his heart out of any such entanglements, he seemed to have a knack for finding women who got him in other ways.

He looked sideways at Esther, then quickly turned his focus back to the road. He would have no such issues with her. She was plain. Pretty, he supposed. But her wide brown eyes were unlined, unenhanced in any way. Her dark eyebrows a bit heavier than he typically liked on a woman. There were vague bruised-looking circles beneath her eyes, and he couldn't work out if that was because of exhaustion, or if it was simply part of her coloring.

He was so accustomed to seeing women with a full face of makeup that was near enough to airbrushing in real life that he found it very hard to say.

Her lips were full, dusky, and he thought probably the most attractive thing about her. Though, her body was also nice enough. Her breasts weren't large, but they were beautiful shaped, and it was clear she wasn't wearing a bra beneath that black tank top of hers.

But her breasts were immaterial. The only thing that mattered was her womb. And whether or not his child currently resided inside it.

He turned sharply into his driveway, leaving the gate wide open, and not particularly caring. Then, he got out of the car, rounding it and jerking open the passenger door. "Welcome to your new home," he said, knowing that his tone sounded anything but welcoming.

She bit her bottom lip, gathering her backpack from the floor of the car, and getting out, holding the offensive canvas bag to her chest. She looked around, eyes wide, a sort of sickly pallor appearing beneath her tan skin.

"You were just here a couple of days ago," he said. "You can stop looking so intimidated."

"Well," she said, directing her focus to him, "you're intimidating. A house like this… One that is practically a castle… That's intimidating." She took a deep breath. "And I know I was here earlier. But this is different. I was focused on telling you about the baby. I wasn't thinking I would stay here."

"Are you going to pretend that you would prefer the hostel? There is no need to pretend with me. You agreed to carry a child for money. It isn't as though you can suddenly make believe you have no interest in material things."

She shook her head. "I don't. I mean, not the way that you think. I want to go to college."

He frowned. "How old are you?"

"Twenty-three."

He held back a curse. She was the same age as his sister, Allegra. Possibly a bit younger. Had he been the sort of man who possessed the ability to feel sympathy for strangers, he thought he might feel some for her. But those softer feelings had been bled from him long ago, empathy replaced by a vague sense of concern.

"And you couldn't access any scholarships?"

"No. I had to pay to take the SATs. I didn't exactly go to high school. But my scores are good enough to get into a few places. I think. I just need to get my financial ducks in a row."

"You didn't go to high school?"

She pursed her lips together. "I was homeschooled. Kind of. Anyway, it isn't like I was trying to get myself a yacht. And even if I was, nobody does surrogacy for free for a stranger."

He lifted a shoulder. "I suppose not. Come this way."

He led the way into the villa, suddenly completely at a loss. His housekeeper had already retired to her quarters, and here he was with an urchin whom he suddenly had to manage. "I imagine you're tired," he said.

"Hungry," she replied.

He gritted his teeth. "The kitchen is this way."

He led her through the expensive house, listening to the sound of her shuffling footsteps behind him as they made their way to the kitchen. The house itself was old. Stonework dating back centuries. But inside, all of the modern conveniences had been supplied. He made his way to the large stainless steel fridge and opened it. "You may have your pick of what's inside."

As soon as he said that, he realized that most of the food was still ingredients, and not exactly a meal. But surely, there would be something. Then he remembered that his housekeeper often left portions in the freezer for him just in case.

He didn't often eat at home, and he would just as soon go out if there was no staff on hand to make him something. But he was not going back out tonight.

He looked until he found what looked to be a container of pasta. "Here you go," he said, setting it down in front of a wide-eyed Esther.

He didn't stay to see what she did after that. Instead, he strode from the room, taking the stairs two at a time and heading toward his office. He paced the length of the room for a moment, then turned to his desk, taking hold of his phone and dialing his ex-wife.

It took only two rings for Ashley to answer. That didn't surprise him. If she was going to answer, of course she would do it quickly. Otherwise, had she intended to ignore

him, she would have done so steadfastly. She was nothing if not extreme.

"Renzo," she said, sounding bored. "To what do I owe
the pleasure?"

"You may not find it such a pleasure to speak to me,
Ashley. Not when you hear what I have to say."

"I have not actually found it a pleasure to speak to you
for quite a few months."

"We were only married for six months, so I hope that's
an exaggeration."

"It isn't. Why do you think I had to find other men to
satisfy me?"

"If you are talking about emotional satisfaction, I have
several answers for that. However, if you mean to imply
that I did not satisfy you physically, then I'm going to have
to call you a liar."

Ashley huffed. "There's more to life than sex."

"Yes indeed. There is, in fact, the small matter of the
woman who is currently downstairs in my kitchen."

"We're divorced now," Ashley said, her voice so sharp
it could cut glass. "Who is or is not in your kitchen—or
bed—is none of my concern."

"It is when it's Esther Abbott. A woman who claims that
she had an agreement with you. For her to carry *our* child."

There was a pause. He was almost satisfied that he
had clearly succeeded in rendering Ashley speechless. It
was such a difficult thing to do. Even when she had been
caught in bed with someone else, she had done her best
to talk, scream and cry her way out of it. She was not one
to let it rest. She was never one to let someone else have
the last word.

Her silence now was telling. Though, of her absolute surprise, or of her chagrin at being found out, he didn't know.

"I thought it might save us. But that was before…

Before the divorce was final. Before you found out about the others."

"Right. The five other men that you were with during the course of our marriage?"

Ashley laughed. "Seven, I think."

It didn't matter to him. Five, seven or only the one he had actually witnessed. He had a feeling the truth didn't matter to Ashley either. It was all about scoring points.

"So this is true," he said, his tone harsh.

"Yes," she replied, her voice tight.

"How?" he bit out.

She huffed out an impatient-sounding laugh. "Well, darling, the last time we were intimate you used a condom. I just…made use of it after you discarded it. It was enough for the doctor."

He swore. At her. At himself. At his body. "Is there nothing too low for you?"

"I guess that remains to be seen," she said, her tone brittle like glass. "I have a lot of living left to do, but don't worry, Renzo, you won't be part of it. My depths will not be of any concern to you."

"This woman is pregnant with *our* child," he said, trying to bring it back around to the topic at hand. To the reason he had some creature-ish backpacker in his home.

"Because she is stubborn. I told her she didn't have to continue with it. In fact, I told her I refused to pay the remainder of the fee."

"Yes," he bit out. "I have had a discussion with her. I was only calling you to confirm."

"What are you going to do?"

That was a good question. An excellent question. He was going to raise the child, naturally. But how was he going to explain it? To his parents. To the media. These would be headlines his child would read. Either he would have to be honest about Ashley's deception, or he would have to concoct a story about a mother abandoning her child.

That would not do.

But surrogacy was not legal in Italy. No agreement would be binding within these borders. And he would use that to his advantage.

"There is nothing to be done," he said, his tone swift, decisive. "Esther Abbott is pregnant with my child. And I will do the responsible thing."

"Renzo," she said, her voice fierce, "what do you intend to do?"

He knew. There was no question. He had been in a situation similar to this before. Only then, he had had no power. The woman involved, her husband, his parents, had all made the decisions around him. His ill-advised affair with Jillian costing much more than his virginity.

At sixteen, he had become a father for the first time. But he had been barred from having anything to do with the child. A story carefully constructed to protect her marriage, her family, that child and his reputation had been agreed on by all.

All except for Renzo.

He would not allow such a thing to happen again. He would not allow himself to be sidelined. He would not put him, or his child, in such a precarious position. There was only one thing to do. And he would see it done.

"I shall do what any responsible man would do in this situation. I intend to marry Esther Abbott."

Esther had never seen anything quite like Renzo's kitchen. It had taken her more than ten minutes to figure out how to use the microwave. And even then, the pasta had ended up having cold spots and spots that scalded her tongue. Still, it was one of the best things she had ever tasted.

That probably had more to do with exhaustion and how long she'd gone without eating than anything else. Pasta was one of her favorite newly discovered foods, though. Not that she'd never had noodles in some form. It was just that her mother typically made them for soups, and not the way she'd had it served in Italy.

Discovering new foods had been her favorite part of travel so far. Scones in England with clotted cream, macarons in France. She had greatly enjoyed the culinary adventure, nearly as much as the rest of it.

Though, sometimes she missed brown bread and stew. The kinds of simple foods her mother made from scratch at home.

A swift kick of loneliness, of homesickness, punched her low in the stomach. It was unusual, but it did happen sometimes. Most of her home life had been difficult. Had been nothing at all like the way she wanted to live. But it had been safe. And for most of her life, it had been the only thing she'd known.

She blinked, taking another bite of her pasta, and allowing the present moment to wash away the slow-burning ache of nostalgia.

She heard footsteps and looked up. Renzo strode into the kitchen, and that dark black gaze burned away the remaining bit of homesickness. There was no room for anything inside her, nothing beyond that sharp, cutting intensity.

"I just spoke to Ashley."

Suddenly, the pasta felt like sawdust in Esther's mouth. "I imagine she told you the thing you didn't want to hear."

"You are correct in your assessment."

"I'm sorry. But it's true. I really didn't come here to take advantage of you, or to lie to you. And I really couldn't have forged any kind of medical documents. I had never even been to a doctor until Ashley took me for the procedure."

He frowned. She could tell that she had said something that had revealed her as being different. She did that a lot. Mostly because she didn't exactly know the line. Cultures were different, after all, and sometimes she thought people might assume she was different only because she was American.

But she was different from typical Americans, too.

"I lived in a small town," she said, the lie rolling off her tongue easily. She had always been a liar. Because if ever her parents asked her if she was content, if ever her mother had asked her about her plans for the future, she'd had to lie.

And so, covering up the extent of just how strange she was became easier and easier as she talked to more people and picked up more of what was expected.

"A town so small you did not have doctors?"

"He made house calls." That part was true. There had been a physician in the commune.

"Regardless of your past history, it seems that you were telling the truth."

"I said I was."

"Yes, you did. It is an unenviable position you find yourself in—or perhaps it is enviable, depending on your perspective. Tell me, Esther, what are your goals in life?"

It was a strange question. And never once had she been asked. Not really. Her parents had spoken to her about what she would do. About what her duty was, about the purposes of women and what they had to do to be fulfilled. But no one had ever asked her if it would fulfill her. No one had ever asked her anything at all.

But he was asking. And that made something warm glow inside her.

It made her want to tell him.

"I want to travel. And I want to go to school. I want to get an education."

"To what end?" he asked.

"What do you mean?"

"What do you wish to major in? Business? History? Art?"

"Everything." She shrugged. "I just want to know things."

"What do you want to know?"

"Everything I didn't before."

"That is an incredibly tall order. But one that is certainly possible. Is there a better city in the world to learn about history? Rome."

"Paris and London might have differing opinions. But I definitely take your point. And yes, I agree I can get quite an education here simply by being here. But I want more."

He began to pace, and there was something in that stride, attention, a purpose, that made her feel a bit like a small, twitchy little field mouse standing in front of a big cat. "Why shouldn't you have more? Why shouldn't you have everything? Look around you," he said, sweeping his hand in a broad gesture. "I am a man in possession of most everything. For what reason? Simply because I was born into it. And yes, I have done all that I can to ensure I am worthy of the position. I assumed the helm of the family business and have continued to navigate it with proficiency."

"That's very nice for you," she said, mostly because she had no idea what else she was supposed to say.

"It could be very nice for you," he said, leveling his eyes on her. Her skin prickled, somewhere beneath the surface, where she couldn't tamp it down, not even by grabbing hold of her elbows and rubbing her forearms vigorously.

"Could it?"

"I am not going to be coy. I am a billionaire, Ms. Abbott. A man with a limitless supply of resources. Ashley was not as generous with you as she might have been. But I intend to give you the world."

She felt her face growing warm. She cleared her throat, reaching up and tucking a strand of hair behind her ear, just so she had something to do with the reckless energy surging through her. "That's very nice. But I only have the one backpack. I'm not sure the world would fit inside it."

"That is the catch," he said.

"What is?"

"You will have to give up the backpack."

She blinked. "I'm not sure I understand."

"I am a man with a great deal of power—that, I should think, is obvious. However, there are a few things I am bound by. Public perception is one of them. The extremely conservative ideals of my parents are another. My parents have gone to great lengths in my life to ensure that I became the man that I am today." His jaw seemed to tighten when he said that, a muscle there twitching slightly. "And while I was certainly pushing the edges of propriety by marrying Ashley, I did marry her. Marriage, children, that is what is expected of me. What is not expected? To have a surrogacy scandal. To have it leak out to the public that my wife conspired against me. I will not be made a fool of, Esther," he said, using her first name for the first time. "I will not have the Valenti name made foolish by my mistake."

"I don't understand what that has to do with me. You're going to have to be very direct, because sometimes I'm a little bit slow with shorthand."

He frowned. "Just how small is that town you're from?"

"Very small. Very, very small."

"Perhaps the size of the town makes no difference. Admittedly, we are in a bit of an unprecedented situation. Still, my course is clear."

"Please do enlighten me."

He paused, looking at her. Which shouldn't have been significant. He had looked at her before. Lots of times. People looked at each other when they talked. Except, this time when he looked at her it felt different.

But this was different. Whether or not that made any sense, it was different. His gaze was assessing now, in a different way from what it had been before. As though he were looking deeper. Beneath her clothes, the thought of which made her feel hot all over, down beneath her skin. As though he were trying to see exactly what her substance was.

He looked over her entire body, and she felt herself begin to burn everywhere his gaze made contact. That strange, restless feeling was back between her thighs, an intense heaviness in her breasts.

She sucked in a sharp breath, trying to combat the sting of tears that were beginning to burn there. She didn't know why she wanted to cry. Except that this felt big, new and completely unfamiliar. Whatever this was.

"Esther Abbott," he said, his words sliding over her name like silk, "you are going to be my wife."

CHAPTER FOUR

ESTHER FELT LIKE she was dreaming. She had a strange sense of being detached from her body, of looking down on the scene below her, like it was happening to somebody else and not her. Because there was no way she was standing in the middle of a historic mansion, looking at the most beautiful man she had ever seen in her entire life, his proposal still ringing in her ears.

Beautiful was the wrong word for Renzo, she decided. He was too hard cut. His cheekbones sharp, his jaw like a blade. His dark eyes weren't any softer. Just like the rest of him, they were enticing, but deadly. Like broken edges of obsidian. So tempting to run your fingers over the seemingly smooth surface, until you caught an edge and sliced into your own flesh.

It struck her just how ridiculous it was, fixating on her mental use of the word *beautiful*. Fixating on his appearance at all. He had just stated his intention to make her his wife. *His wife.*

That was her worst nightmare. Being owned by a man again. She couldn't stand it. Never. Yes, Renzo was different from her father. Certainly this was a different situation. But it felt the same. It made her feel like her throat was closing up, like the walls were closing in around her.

"No," she said, panic a clawing beast scurrying inside

her. "That's impossible. I can't do that. I have goals. Goals that do not include being your... No."

"There is not a single goal that you possess that I cannot enable you to meet with greater ease and better style."

She shook her head. "But don't you see? That isn't the point. I don't want to stay here in Rome. I want to see the world."

"You have been seeing the world, have you not? Hostels, and dirty bars. How very romantic. I imagine it is difficult to do much sightseeing when you are tethered to whatever table you are waiting at any given time."

"I have time off. I'm living in the city. I have what I want. Maybe you don't understand, but as you said, you had very much of what you possess given to you. Inherited. My legacy is nothing. A tiny little house with absolutely no frills in the middle of the mountain range. And that's not even mine. It's just my father's. And it never would've passed to me. It would've gone to one of my six brothers. Yes, *six* brothers. But not to any of my three sisters. You heard that number right, too. Because there was nothing for us. Nothing at all for women. Though, I'm not entirely certain that in that scenario the boys have it much better." She took a deep breath. "I'm proud of this. Of what I have. I'm not going to allow you to make me feel like it's lacking."

"But it is lacking, *cara*." The words cut her like a knife. "If it were not lacking, you would not have goals to transcend it. You wish to go to school. You wish to learn things. You wish to see the world. Come into my world. I guarantee you it is much more expansive than any that you might hope to enter on your own."

The words reverberated through her, an echo. A promise. One that almost every fiber of her being wanted to run from. Almost. There must have been some part of her that was intrigued. That wanted to stay. Because there she was, as rooted to the spot as she had been when he entered the bar earlier that night. There was something about him that did that to her, and it seemed to be more powerful than every terrified, screaming cell in her brain that told her she should run.

"That's insanity. I don't need you, I just need the payment that was agreed upon, and then I can better my circumstances."

"But why have a portion of my fortune when you can have access to the entire thing?"

"I wouldn't have the first idea what to do with that. Frankly, having anything to call mine is something of a new experience. What you're talking about seems a little bit beyond my scope."

"Ah, but it does not have to be." His words were like velvet, his voice wrapping itself around her. Her mother had been right. The devil wasn't ugly. That wouldn't work when it came to doling out temptation. The devil was beautiful. The devil—she was becoming more and more certain—was Renzo Valenti.

"I think you might be crazy. I think that I understand now why your wife left you."

He chuckled. "Is that what she told you? One of her many lies. I was the one who threw that grasping, greedy shrew out onto the streets, after I caught her in bed with another man."

Esther tried not to look shocked. She tried not to look as innocent and gauche as she was. The idea that somebody would violate their marriage vows so easily was foreign to her. Marriage was sacred, in her upbringing. Another reason that what Renzo was suggesting was completely beyond the pale for her.

"She cheated on you?"

"Yes, she did. As I said to you earlier, I, for my part, was faithful to my wife. I will not lie and say that I chose Ashley out of any deep love for her, but initially our connection was fun at least."

Esther turned that over for a moment. "Fun?"

"In some rooms, yes."

The exact meaning of what he was saying slipped past her slightly, but she knew that he was implying something lascivious, and it made her face get hot. "Well, that is…I don't…I'm not the wife for you," she finished. Because if she couldn't exactly form a picture to go with what he was trying to imply here, she knew—beyond a shadow of a doubt—that she could never be in that kind of relationship with him.

She had never even been kissed. Being a wife… Well, she had no experience in that area. Not only that, she had no desire to be. Oh, probably eventually she would want to be with someone. It was on the list. Way far down.

Sex was a curiosity to her. She'd read love scenes in books, seen them in movies. But she knew she wasn't ready for it herself, not so much because of the physical part, but the connecting-to-another-person part.

And for now, she was too busy exploring who she was. What she wanted from life. She had never seen a marriage where the man was not unquestionably in control. Had no experience of male and female relationships where the husband did not rule the wife with an iron fist.

She would never subject herself to that. Never.

"Why is that? Because you harbor some kind of childish fantasy of marrying for love?"

"No. Not at all. I harbor fantasies of never marrying, actually. And as for love? I have never seen it. Not the way that you're talking about it. What I have seen is possession and control. And I have no interest in that."

"I see. So, you are everything that you appear to be. Someone who changes with the wind and moves at will."

He spoke with such disdain, and it rankled. "Yes. And I never pretended to be anything else. Why should I? I don't have any obligation to you. I don't have any obligation to anyone, and that's how I like it. But I got myself into this situation, and I do intend to act with integrity. At least, as I see it. I wanted to make sure you knew about the baby, I wanted to make sure that your wishes were being met."

"And yet, you saw no point in checking in with me in the first place?"

She let out a long, slow breath. "I know. I should have. But that was part of why I came to find you after Ashley said she no longer wanted the baby. Because she had made it so clear that you wanted a child desperately in the first place, and I could not believe that you would suddenly change your mind. Not based on everything she had said."

"A convincing liar, is my ex-wife."

"Clearly. But I don't want to be tangled up in any of this. I just want to have the baby and go on my way."

"That… That can be discussed. But for all intents and purposes, we are going to present you to the world as my lover. What happens after the birth of the child can be negotiated, but we will conduct ourselves as an engaged couple until then."

"I don't understand… I don't want…"

"I am a very powerful man. The fact that I'm not throwing you over my shoulder and carrying you off to the nearest church, where I have no doubt I could bring the clergy around to my way of thinking, shows that I'm being somewhat magnanimous with you. I am also not overly enticed to jump back into marriage, not after what I have just been through. So, it is decided. You will play the part of my fiancée, at least until the birth of the child, at which point your freedom—and the parting price—can be negotiated."

"We will be in the news?" The idea of her parents seeing her with him… It terrified her.

"Tabloids most likely. Perhaps some lifestyle sections of respectable papers. But that will mostly be contained to Europe."

She let out a slow breath, releasing some of the tension that had built in her chest. "Okay. Maybe that isn't so bad."

He frowned. "Are you hiding from someone? Because I need to know. I need to know what might put my child in danger, *cara*."

"I'm not hiding from anyone. And, trust me, I'm not in danger. I mean, I'm kind of hiding. But not because I'm afraid somebody will come after me. My parents were… strict. And they don't approve of what I'm doing. I just don't want them to see me written about in the paper, with a man. Pregnant. Not married." In spite of the fact that she had long since given up hope of pleasing her parents—in fact, she had come to terms with the fact that her leaving home would mean cutting ties with them forever—she felt sick shame settle in her stomach.

"They are traditional then."

"You have no idea." The shame lingered, wouldn't leave. "They never even wanted me to wear makeup or anything."

"Well, I fear you will be defying that rule, as well."

"Why?" She had the freedom to wear whatever she wanted now, but she hadn't bought makeup yet. There had not been an occasion to.

"Because my women look a certain way."

That forced a very specific image into her head. A *certain* kind of woman. The kind of woman her mother often talked about. Fallen, scarlet.

She had a difficult time wrapping her head around the

idea that she would be presented to the world like that. Not because she felt ashamed, but because it just never occurred to her. The idea that she might be made up, and dressed up, on the arm of a man like Renzo Valenti.

"You go to… You go to a lot of events, don't you?"

"A great many. As I said to you before, the world that I will show you is far beyond anything you could access on your own. If you want to experience, I can give you experiences you didn't know to dream of."

Those words made something hot take root at the base of her spine, wrap around low and tight inside her, making her feel both hot and empty somehow.

"All right," she said, the words rushed, because they had to be. If she thought about it any longer, she would run away. "I'll do it."

"Do what exactly?" he said, his eyes hard on hers.

"I will play the part of your fiancée for as long as you want me to. And then after that… After the baby is born… I go."

He took a step forward, reaching out and taking hold of her chin between his thumb and forefinger. His touch burned. Caught hold of her like a wildfire and raged straight through her body. "Excellent. Esther," he said, her name like a caress on his lips, "you have yourself a fiancé."

Renzo knew that he was going to have to tread extremely carefully over the next few weeks. That was one of the few things he knew. Everything else in his life was upended. He had a disheveled little street urchin staying in one of his spare rooms, and he had to present her to the world as his chosen bride soon. Very soon. The sooner the better. Before Ashley got a chance to drop any poison into the ear of the media.

He had already set a plan in motion to ensure she would

not. A very generous payout that his lawyer would be offering to hers by the time the sun rose in Canada. She would not want to defy him. Not when—without this—she would be getting nothing from him due to the ironclad prenuptial agreement they had entered into before the marriage.

Ashley liked attention, that much was true. But she liked money even more. That would take care of her.

But then there was the small matter of his parents. And his parents were never actually a small matter.

He imagined that—regardless of the circumstances—they would be thrilled to learn that they were expecting a grandchild. Really, they would only be all the happier knowing that Ashley was out of the picture.

But Esther was most certainly a problem he would have to solve.

With great reluctance, he picked up his phone and dialed his mother's number. She picked up on the first ring. "Renzo. You don't call me enough."

"Yes, so I hear. Every time I call."

"And it is true every time. So, tell me, what is on your agenda? Because you never call just to make small talk."

He couldn't help but laugh at that. His mother knew him far too well. "Yes, as it happens, I was wondering if you had any plans for dinner."

"Why yes, Renzo. I in fact have dinner plans every day. Tonight, we are having lamb, vegetables and a risotto."

"Excellent, Mother. But do you have room at your table?"

"For?"

"Myself," he said, amused at his mother's obstinance. "And a date."

"Dating already. So soon after your divorce." His mother said that word as though it were anathema. But then, he supposed that was because for her it was.

"Yes, Mother. Actually, more than dating. I intend to introduce you to my fiancée, Esther Abbott."

The line went silent. That concerned him much more than a tirade of angry Italian ever could. Then, his mother spoke. "Abbott? Who are her people?"

He thought of what she'd said about the mountain cabin her rather larger-than-usual family lived in, and he was tempted to laugh. "No one you would know."

"Please tell me you have not chosen another Canadian, Renzo."

"No, on that score you can relax. She is an American."

The choking sound he heard on the other end of the line was not altogether unexpected. "That," she said finally, "is even worse."

"Even so, the decision is made." He considered telling her about the pregnancy over the phone, but decided that it was one of those things his mother would insist on hearing about in person. She did like to divide her news into priorities like that. She had never gotten over Allegra's pregnancy news filtering back to her through the gossip chain.

"So very typical of you." There was no real condemnation or venom in her tone. Though, the simple statement forced him to think back to a time when it had not been true. When he had allowed other people to force his hand when it came to decision making. He tried very hard not to think about Jillian. About the daughter who was being raised by another man. A daughter he sometimes caught glimpses of at various functions.

Just one of the many reasons he worked so hard to keep his alcohol intake healthy at such things. It was much better to remember very little of it the next day, he found.

He had been sixteen when his parents had encouraged him to make that decision. And since then, he had changed the way he operated. Completely, utterly. He was not bitter at his mother and father. They had pushed him into making the best decision they could see.

And hell, it had been the best decision. He had proved that fifty times over in the years since. He had not been ready to be a father. But he was ready now.

"Yes, I am typical as ever. But will we be welcome at your table tonight, or not?"

"It will be an ordeal. We will have to purchase more ingredients."

"When you say 'we,' you mean your staff, whom you pay handsomely. I imagine it can all be arranged?"

"Of course it will be. You will be there at eight. Do not be late. Because I will not wait, and the one thing you do not want, Renzo, is for me to be one glass of wine ahead of you."

He felt his mouth turn upward. "That," he said, "is very true, Mother, I have no doubt."

He disconnected the call. Then, he made another call to the personal stylist his mother had used for years, asking that she clear her schedule and bring along a team of hair and makeup artists.

He was not sure if Esther had enough raw material to be salvageable. It was very difficult to say. The women whom he involved himself with tended to be either classic, polished pieces of architecture, or new constructions, as it were. He had no experience with full renovations.

Still, she was not unattractive. So, it seemed as though he should be able to fashion her into something that looked believable. The thought nearly made him laugh. She was pregnant. She was pregnant with his child. And while it may take a paternity test on his end to prove that to the world—or his parents—they would never ask for a test to prove maternity.

Therefore, by that very logic, people would believe their connection. But he would like to make it slightly easier.

When he went downstairs and found her sitting in the dining area, on the floor by the floor-to-ceiling windows, her face tilted up toward the sun, a bowl of cereal clutched tightly in her hands, he knew that he had made the right decision in bringing in an entire team.

"What are you doing?"

She squeaked, startling and sloshing a bit of milk over the edge of her bowl, onto the tile floor. "I was enjoying the morning," she said.

"There is a table for you to sit at." He gestured to the long, banquet-style piece of furniture, which had been carved from solid wood and was older than either of them, and was certainly more than good enough for this little hippie to sit and eat her cereal at.

"I know. But I wanted to sit by the window. And I could have moved a chair, but they're very heavy. And I didn't want to scuff the tile. And anyway, the floor is fine. It's warm from the sun."

"We are going to my parents' house for dinner tonight," he said, because it was as good a time as any to broach that subject. "And I trust you will not sit yourself on the floor then." The image of her crouched in a corner gnawing on a lamb shank was nearly comical. That would upset his mother. Though, seeing as she had been prewarned that Esther was an American, she might not find the behavior all that strange.

He regarded her for a moment. Her hair was caught up in that same messy bun she'd had it in yesterday, and she had traded her black tank top for a brown one, and yesterday's long, flowing skirt for one in a brighter color.

She frowned, her dark brows locking together. "Of course not." He had thought her face plain yesterday, and now, for some reason, he thought of it as freshly scrubbed. Clean. There was something… Not wholesome, for this exotic creature could never be called something so mundane, but something natural. Organic. As if she had materialized in a garden somewhere rather than being born.

Which was a much more fanciful thought than he had ever had about a woman before. Typically, his thoughts were limited to whether or not he thought they would look good naked, whether or not they would like to get naked with him, and then, after they had, how he might get rid of them.

"Good. My parents are not flexible people. Neither are they overly friendly. They are extremely old, Italian money. They are very proud of their lineage, and of our name. I told them that we are getting married. And that you're American. They are amused by neither. Or rather, my mother is amused by neither, and my father will follow suit."

Her dark eyes went round, the expression on her face worried. It was comical to him that she might be concerned over what his parents thought. Someone like her didn't seem as though she would concern herself with what other people thought.

"That doesn't sound like a very pleasant evening," she said, after a long pause.

"Oh, evenings with my parents are never what I would call pleasant. However, they are not fatal."

"I have an aversion to being judged," she said, her tone stiff.

"Oh, I quite enjoy it. I find it very liberating to lower people's expectations."

"You do not," she said, "nobody does. Everybody cares about pleasing their parents." She frowned. "Or, if not their parents, at least somebody."

"You said yourself, you left your parents. And that they weren't happy with you. Obviously, you don't worry overly much about pleasing your parents."

"But I did. For a long time. And the only reason I don't now is out of necessity. I mean, I would've never had any freedom if I hadn't let go of it."

There was a strange feeling in his chest, her words catching hold of something that seemed to tug on him, down deep.

About freedom. About letting go.

"Well, on that same subject, there is some work to be done if we are going to present you at dinner tonight."

"What sort of work?" She looked genuinely mystified at that statement, as though she had no idea what he might be referring to.

As he stood before her in his perfectly pressed custom suit, and she sat cross-legged on the floor looking like she would be more at home at a Renaissance fair than in his home, it occurred to him that she really was a strange creature. The differences between the two of them should be obvious, and yet, she did not seem to pick up on them on her own. Or rather, she didn't seem to care.

"You, Esther."

"What's wrong with me?"

"What did you plan on wearing to dinner tonight?"

She looked down. "This, I suppose."

"You do not see perhaps a small difference in the way that you are dressed, compared with the way that I am dressed?"

"Did you want me to wear a tux?"

"This is not a tux. It's a suit. There is a difference."

"Interesting. And good to know."

He had a feeling she did not find it interesting at all. "I have taken the liberty of having some clothing ordered for you." He lifted his hand and looked at his watch. "It should be here any moment."

Just then, his housekeeper came walking into the room, a concerned expression on her face. "Mr. Valenti, Tierra is here."

His stylist went by only one name. "Excellent."

"Should I have her meet you upstairs with all of her items?"

"Yes. But in Esther's room, if you don't mind."

Esther's eyes widened. "What exactly are you providing me with?"

"Something that doesn't look like it came out of the bottom of a bargain bin at some sort of rummage sale for mismatched fabrics."

She frowned. "Is that your way of saying there's something wrong with what I'm wearing?"

"No. My way of saying that is to say what you're wearing isn't suitable. Actually, it's perfectly suitable if you intend to continue to wait tables at a dusty bar crawling with tourists. However, it is not acceptable if you wish to be presented to the world as my fiancée, and neither is it acceptable for you to wear on the night you are to meet my parents."

At that, his housekeeper's face contorted. She began to speak at him in angry, rapid Italian that he was only grateful Esther likely wouldn't be able to decode. "She is pregnant with my child," he said. "There is nothing else to be done."

She shook her head. "You have become a bad man," she huffed, walking out of the room. That last part she had said in English.

"Why is she mad at you?"

"Well, likely because she thinks I impregnated some

poor American tourist while I was still married. You can see how she would find that upsetting."

"I suppose." She blinked. "But doesn't *she* work for *you*?"

"Luciana practically came with the house, which I purchased more than a decade ago. It's difficult to say sometimes who exactly works for whom."

She frowned. "And now what? You're going to…buy me new clothes?"

"Exactly. And take your old clothes and burn them."

"That isn't very nice."

He raised his brows, affecting his expression into one of mock surprise. "Is it not? That is regrettable. I do so strive to be nice."

"I doubt it."

"Don't snarl at me," he said. "And, remember, you have to pretend to be my fiancée. In front of Luciana, and in front of Tierra."

She scowled, but allowed him to direct her up the stairs, depositing her cereal bowl on the dining room table as she went. He watched the gentle sway of her hips as she began to ascend the staircase. When she was in motion, her clothing seemed less ridiculous. In fact, the effect was rather graceful.

There was an otherworldly quality to her that he couldn't quite pin down. Something that he had difficulty describing, even to himself. She was very young, and simultaneously sometimes seemed quite old. Like a being who had been dropped down to earth, knowing very little about the customs of those around her, and yet, somehow knowing more than any human could in a lifetime.

And that was fanciful thinking that he never normally allowed himself.

So instead of that, he focused on the rounded curve of her rear. Because that, at least, he understood.

When they reached the bedroom, the stylist had already unveiled a rack of clothing. She was fussing around with the hanging garments, smoothing pleats and adjusting the long, complicated skirts on the various gowns.

"Oh, my," she said, turning and getting her first look at Esther. "We do have our work cut out for us."

CHAPTER FIVE

FOR THE NEXT two hours, Esther was pulled, prodded, poked with pins and clucked at. Well and truly clucked at. As though this woman, Renzo's stylist, was a chicken. And as though Esther was a naughty chick rather than a woman.

Renzo had left them to it, and she was thankful. Since the moment he had walked out, the other woman had begun stripping Esther's clothes off her body and forcing new undergarments, new dresses and new shoes onto her.

Esther had never felt fabrics like this. She had never seen styles like this on her spare curves. She had been all about experiencing new things since she had left her home, but she hadn't gotten around to the clothing and makeup. Or hair. That all required a disposable income that she simply didn't possess. She was more concerned with keeping food in her belly. And clothing herself in the basics, rather than exploring the world of fashion.

But now she felt as though she had been well and truly educated in which colors looked best on her, which shapes best suited her figure. Of course, most of it had happened in abrupt Italian that Esther could understand only parts of, but still. She could see herself.

In fact, right at the moment, she couldn't take her eyes off herself. She was wearing a dark green gown that had little cap sleeves and a plunging V neckline that showed off acres of skin around her neck and down farther. The kind of daring look that would never have been allowed in her family home.

The skirt was long, falling all the way down to the tops of the most beautiful pair of shoes Esther had ever seen. Of course, they were also the tallest pair of shoes she had ever worn, and she had serious doubts about her ability to walk in them.

Somewhere in the middle of the clothing frenzy, two men had arrived to work on her hair and makeup. And work they had. Her hair was tamed into a sleek, black curtain, a good half a foot cut off the near-unmanageable length.

Her eyes, which she had always thought were almost comically large, didn't look comical now. Though, they still looked large. They had been rimmed with black liner, the corners of her eyes highlighted with gold. They had brushed something onto her cheeks, too, making them glow. And her lips... A bit of pale, burnished orange gloss colored them, just slightly, highlighting them, just enough.

She looked like a stranger. She couldn't see so many of the defining features of her face, not the way she usually did. Those dark circles that had permanent residence beneath her eyes were diminished, her nose somehow appearing more narrow, her cheeks a bit more hollow, thanks to a technique they had called contouring.

And then there was her body. She had never thought much about it. She didn't have overly large breasts, and for convenience, she typically opted not to wear a bra, sticking to plain, high-necked tops in dark colors that she always hoped concealed enough.

Even though this gown still didn't allow for a bra, it created an entirely different effect on her bustline than the simple cotton tank tops she preferred. Her breasts looked rounder, fuller, her waist a bit more dramatically curved, rather than straight up and down. The shape of the skirt enhanced the appearance of her hips, making her look like she almost had an hourglass figure.

It was strange to see herself this way. With all her attributes enhanced, rather than downplayed.

The bedroom door opened and she froze when Renzo walked in. She felt hideously exposed in a way that she never had before. Because for the first time in her life she was aware that she might look beautiful, and that there was a man who was most certainly beautiful looking her over. Appraising her as he might a work of art.

"Well," he said, turning his focus to the team of people who had accomplished the effect, and away from her, "this is a very pleasant surprise."

"She is a dream to dress," Tierra said. "Everything fits so nicely. And that golden skin of hers allows her to pull off some very difficult colors."

"You know all of that is lost on me," he said. "However, I can see that she is beautiful."

Warmth flooded her. Such a stupid thing. To feel affected by this charade. But she wasn't entirely sure if she cared at all that it was a charade. What did it matter, really? Even playing a game like this was new. Feeling like she was the center—the focus—of male attention was something that she had scarcely gotten around to dreaming about.

She had been grappling with freedom. Both the cost of it and the gains. With who she wanted to be, apart from everything she'd been taught. Apart from the small rebellions she'd waged hidden in the mountains behind her house, listening to contraband music while reading forbidden books.

To find it especially appealing to link herself up to a

man, even in a temporary way. But now, beneath Renzo's black gaze, she found something deliciously enticing in it.

A swift, low kick of temptation hit her hard, making it difficult for her to breathe. And she couldn't even quite work out what the temptation was. It reminded her of walking past the bakery down in the town she'd grown up adjacent to, and seeing a row of sweets that looked delicious. Treats she knew she wouldn't be allowed to have.

That same feeling. Of wanting, feeling empty. Of that intense, unfair sense of deprivation that always followed.

Except, no one controlled her life now. If she wanted a cake, she could buy it and then she could eat it.

Which made her deeply conscious of the fact that if she wanted Renzo, she supposed she could have him, too.

But for the love of cake, she didn't know what she would do with him. Or what he would do with her if she reached out and tried to get a taste.

She took a deep breath, craning her neck, straightening her shoulders and doing her best to make herself look even more statuesque. She didn't know why. Maybe to inject herself with a little bit more pride, so she wasn't just standing there being subjected to the judgment of every person in the room.

It was so strange being the center of attention like this. She wasn't entirely certain she disliked it.

"That dress is spectacular. However, it is a bit too formal for dinner," Renzo said, sitting down in one of the armchairs that were placed up against the back wall. "What else is there?"

"Oh," Tierra said, turning around and facing the rack, pulling out a short, coral-colored dress that Esther had tried on earlier. "How about this?"

Renzo settled even deeper into the chair, his posture like that of a particularly jaded monarch. "Let's see it."

"Of course."

Esther found herself being turned so that she was facing away from Renzo, and then she felt the zipper on the gown give. She gasped, then froze, not quite sure what she was supposed to do next. If she should protest the fact that she was being undressed in front of a man who was a stranger to her, or if that would ruin the charade.

And then it didn't matter, because the green dress was pulling down at her feet, and her bare back and barely covered bottom were now fully exposed to Renzo.

"Very nice," he said, his voice rough. "Part of the new wardrobe?"

She knew he meant the black pair of lace panties she was wearing, and she wanted to turn around and tell him off for making this even more uncomfortable. Except, then she would have to turn around. And expose herself even further, and she wasn't going to do that. Instead, she decided that she would do her best to show him that she wasn't so easily toyed with.

"Yes," she said simply.

A few moments later the next dress was on and firmly in place. Then, she turned back to face Renzo, and her heart crawled up into her throat. Because as intense as he always looked, as much impact as those dark eyes always had on her, it was magnified now.

"Come closer," he said, his tone hard-edged, the command clearly nonnegotiable.

She swallowed hard, taking one unsteady step toward where Renzo was sitting. His dark gaze flicked away from Esther, landing on the style team. "Leave us," he said.

They did so, quickly and without a word. And when they were gone, it felt as though they had taken all the air out of the room with them.

"Do people always do what you ask?"

"Always," he said. "Closer."

She took another step toward him, trying to disguise the fact that her legs were shaking and that she had no idea how she was supposed to walk in heels that were tantamount to stilts.

He rested his elbow on the arm of the chair, propping his chin on his knuckles. "Of course, some people obey more quickly than others."

"Did you want me to break an ankle? Because I guarantee you if I walk any faster I'm going to."

He moved swiftly, his movements liquid, his grace making a mockery of her own uncertain clumsiness. He stood, reaching across the space between them and sweeping her up into his arms. Then he turned, depositing her in the chair he had occupied only a moment ago.

She pressed her hand to her heart, feeling the rapid flutter beneath her palm. Her throat was dry, her head feeling dizzy. Her body felt warm. As though she had been burned all over. His arms had been wrapped around her, her shoulder blades pressed up against that hard, broad expanse of his chest.

That was what stunned her most of all. Just how hard he was. There was no give in him at all. His body was as unbending as the rest of him.

He turned away from her, facing the rack of clothing and the stack of shoes that was beneath it. "If you cannot walk then you will not present a very convincing picture. We don't want you to look as though you were only polished today."

"Why? Why does it matter?"

"Because I associate with a very particular kind of woman. I do not need my parents thinking that I swooped in and corrupted some innocent, naive backpacker."

It took her a moment to process that. She wondered if

he really believed that she was naive and innocent. She was. It was just that he had never seemed particularly sold on that version of her.

"They would believe that?"

He laughed, not turning to look at her. "Oh, yes. Easily." Then he bent, picking up a pair of bejeweled, flat shoes before facing her again. He moved back to where she was sitting, dropping to his knees before her and making a seeming mockery of her earlier thought that he was unbending.

"What are you—"

He said nothing. Instead, he reached out, curling his fingers around the back of her knee. The warmth shocked her. Flooded her. He let his fingertips drift all the way down the length of her calf, the touch slow, much too slow. Something about it, about that methodical movement, seemed to catch her at the site of their contact and spark through the rest of her. Reckless. Uncontrollable.

She fought the urge to squirm in her seat. To do something to diffuse the strange energy that she was infused with. But she didn't want to betray herself. To betray that his touch made her feel anything.

He grabbed hold of the heel on her shoe and pulled it off slowly, those searching fingertips dragging along the bottom of her foot then as he removed the shoe.

She shivered. She couldn't help it.

He looked up then and a strange, knowing smile tilted the corner of his lips upward. It was the knowing that bothered her more than anything else. Because she was confused. Lost in a sea of swirling doubts and uncertainty, and he seemed to know exactly what she was feeling.

You do, too. You aren't stupid.

She gritted her teeth. Maybe. She really wished she were a little bit more stupid. She had tried to be. From the first moment she had laid eyes on him, and he had looked back at her, she had done her very best to be mystified by what all of the feelings inside her meant.

She wasn't going to give a name to them now. Not right now. Not when he was still touching her. Slipping the ornate flat shoe onto her foot, then moving on to the next. He repeated those same motions there. His fingertips hot and certain on her skin as he traced a line down to her ankle, removing the next stiletto and setting it aside.

"A little bit like Cinderella," she said, forcing the words through her dry throat.

Not that she'd been allowed to read fairy tales growing up, but a volume of them had been one of her very first smuggled titles.

"Except," he said, putting the second shoe in place, then straightening, "I am not Prince Charming."

"I didn't think you were."

"Good," he returned. "As long as you don't begin believing that I might be something I'm not."

"Why would I? I'm actually not just a stupid backpacker. I already told you that my family situation was difficult." She took a deep breath, trying to open up her lungs, trying to ease the tension in her chest. She wasn't bringing up her family for him. She was bringing them up for her. To remind her exactly why being bound to someone—anyone—was exactly what she didn't want.

She wanted freedom. She needed it. And this was a detour. She wouldn't allow herself to become convinced it was anything else.

She would enjoy this. The beautiful clothes, the expertly styled hair. She would enjoy his home. And maybe she would even allow herself to enjoy the strange twisting sensation that appeared in her stomach whenever he walked into a room. Because it was new. Because it was different. Because it was something so far removed from where she had come from.

But that was all it was. It was all it would ever be.

"But now," he said, looking down at her feet, "you will be able to walk into my parents' home tonight without falling on your face. That, I think, will be a much nicer effect."

He stood completely and held his hand out. She hesitated, because she knew that touching him again would reignite that burning sensation in the pit of her stomach she had when he'd touched her leg. But resisting would only reveal herself more. And she didn't want to do that.

And—she had to admit—she had perversely enjoyed it. Even though she knew it could never come to anything. Even though she knew there was nothing she could do beyond enjoying it as it was, as the start of a flame and nothing more, she sort of wanted to.

And so, she reached out, her fingertips brushing his palm. Then, his hand enveloped hers completely, and she found herself being pulled to her feet with shocking ease. In fact, he pulled her to her feet with such ease that she lost her footing, tipping forward and moving her hands up to brace herself, her palms pressing flat against that rock-hard chest.

He was so… He was so hot. And she could feel his heartbeat thundering beneath her touch. She hadn't expected that. She wondered if it was normal for him. For his heart to beat so fast. For it to feel so pronounced.

And then she had to wonder if it was related to her. Because her own heartbeat was thundering out of control, like a boulder rolling down a hill. It wasn't normal for her. It was because of him. And she couldn't pretend otherwise, not even to herself.

Was that why? Was that why his heart was beating so

fast? Because she was touching him? And if so, what did that mean?

It was that last question that had her pulling away from him as quickly as possible. She smoothed the front of her dress, doing her best to take care of any imaginary wrinkles that might be there, pouring her focus into that, because the alternative was looking at him.

"Yes," he said, his voice hard, rough, infused with much less ease than seemed typical for him. "Tonight will go very well, I think." And then he reached out, taking hold of her chin with his thumb and forefinger. He forced her to look at him, stealing that small respite she had attempted to take for herself. His eyes burned, and she wasn't sure if she could still somehow sense his heartbeat, or if it was just her own, pounding heavily in her ears. "But you will have to find a way to keep yourself from flinching every time I touch you."

Then, he dropped his hand, turning away from her and walking out of the room, leaving her alone. Leaving her to wonder if she had imagined that response in him because of the strength of her own reaction, or if—somehow—she had created movement in the mountain.

CHAPTER SIX

DINNER AT HIS parents was always infused with a bit of dramatic flair. Tonight was no exception. They were greeted by his parents' housekeeper, their coats taken by another member of staff and then led into the sitting room by yet another.

Of course, his mother would not make an appearance until it was time to sit down at the table. He had a feeling it was calculated this time, even more than usual. That she was preparing herself for the unveiling of Renzo's new fiancée.

His father would go along with his mother's plan. Mostly because he had no desire to have something thrown at his head. Not that his mother had behaved with such hysterics for a great many years. But everyone knew she possessed the capacity for such things, and so they tended to behave with a bit of deference for it.

He turned to look at Esther, who was regarding the massive, Baroque setting with unconcealed awe. "You will have to look a bit more inured to your surroundings. As far as my parents know you have been with me for at least a couple of months, which means you will have been at events like this with me before."

"This place is like a museum," she said, keeping her tone hushed, her dark eyes glittering with wonder. It did something to him. Something to his chest. Unlike earlier, when she had done something to him in parts much lower.

"Yes," he said, "it is, really. A museum of my family's achievements. Of all of the things they have managed to collect over the centuries. I told you, my parents were very proud of our name and our heritage. Of what it means to be Valentis." He gritted his teeth. "Blood is everything to them."

It was why they would accept Esther. Why they would accept the situation. Because except in extreme circumstances, they valued their bloodline in their heritage.

He deliberately kept himself from thinking of the one time they had not.

"Renzo." He turned at the sound of his sister's voice, surprised to see her standing there with her husband, Cristian, at her side, Renzo's niece held securely in her father's arms.

"Allegra," he said, standing and walking across the room to drop a kiss on his younger sister's cheek. He extended his hand for Cristian, shaking it firmly before touching his niece's cheek. "I did not know you would be here."

"Neither did we."

"Did you fly from Spain for dinner?"

Cristian lifted a shoulder. "When your mother demands an audience, it is best not to refuse, as I'm sure you know."

"Indeed."

He turned and looked at Esther, who was still sitting on the settee, her hands folded in her lap, her shoulders curved inward, as though she were trying to disappear. "Allegra, Cristian, this is my fiancée, Esther Abbott."

His words seemed to jolt Esther out of her internal reclusion.

"Hello," she said, getting to her feet, stumbling slightly as she did. "You must be… Well, I'm not really sure."

Allegra shot him a questioning glance. "Allegra Acosta. Formerly Valenti. I'm Renzo's younger sister. This is my husband, Cristian."

"Nice to meet you," she said, keeping her hands folded firmly in front of her but nodding her head. He was hardly going to correct her, or direct her to do something different from what she had done, but he could see that coaching would be required in the future.

"It seems the family will all be here," he said. "Such a surprise."

"Engaged. You're engaged. That's why Mother called us and told us to get on Cristian's private jet, I imagine."

"Most definitely," Renzo returned.

"You didn't tell me," Allegra said.

"In fairness to me, you did not tell me that you were expecting my best friend's baby until it became unavoidable. You can hardly lecture me on not serving up a particular piece of news immediately."

His sister's face turned scarlet, and he looked back at Esther, who was watching the exchange with rapt attention. "Don't pay attention to him," Allegra said to Esther. "He very much likes to be shocking. And he likes to make me mad."

"That seems in keeping with what I know about him," Esther said.

Cristian laughed at that. "You two can't have been together very long," he said. "But it does seem you have a handle on him."

Esther looked down. "I wouldn't say that."

Renzo poured himself a drink, feeling slightly sorry for Esther that he could not offer her the same. Especially given what he was about to do. "Since Mother didn't tell you the great news of my engagement, I imagine she didn't tell you I have other news."

"No," Allegra and Cristian said together.

"Esther and I are expecting a baby." He reached out, putting his arm around Esther's shoulders, rubbing his thumb up and down her arm when he felt her go stiff. That didn't help, but he knew that it needled her. So, he would have to take that as consolation.

Allegra said nothing, Cristian's expression one of almost comedic stillness. Finally, it was Cristian who spoke. "Congratulations. Start catching up on your sleep now."

Allegra still said nothing.

"I can see you're completely stunned by the good news," he said.

"Well, yes. I know you've made many declarations to me about how you intend to be shocking at all times, so I don't know why I'm surprised. Actually, I heavily resent my surprise. I should be immune to any sort of shock where you're concerned."

Of course, she wasn't. Being his younger sister, Allegra always seemed to want to believe the best of him. Which was a very nice thing, in its way. But he was a constant disappointment to her. He knew that his marriage to Ashley had been something more than a shock. Although, why, he didn't know. He had told her, in no uncertain terms, that he intended to marry the most unsuitable, shocking woman that he could find.

That was one that had backfired on him.

"Truly, little sister, you should know me better than that by now. Anyway, let us refrain from speaking of the other ways in which I've shocked you in front of Esther. She's still under the illusion that I'm something of a gentleman."

Esther looked at him, her expression bland. "I can assure you I'm not."

Cristian and Allegra seemed to find that riotously amusing. Mostly, he imagined, because they thought she was being dry. In fact, he had a feeling Esther was being perfectly sincere. She was sincere. That was something he was grappling with. Because he didn't know very many sincere people.

He was much more accustomed to those who were cynical. Who approached the world with a healthy bit of opportunism. It was the sincere people who dumbfounded him. Mostly, because he couldn't figure out a way to relate to them. He couldn't anticipate them.

Seeing her earlier today trying on all of those clothes, the way she had looked at him when he had touched her leg, when he had bent down to change her shoes, had been something of a revelation. Until then he had still been skeptical of her. Of her story, of who she claimed to be.

But who she seemed to present was exactly who she was. A somewhat naive creature who was from a world entirely apart from the one she was in now. Her reaction to his parents' house only reinforced that. He had watched her closely upon entry. If she were a gold digger, he felt he would have seen a moment—even if it was only a moment—where she had looked triumphant. Where she had fully understood the prize that she was inheriting.

Frankly, the position he had put her in gave her quite a bit of leverage for taking advantage. Yes, DNA tests would prove that the child wasn't hers, but who knew how a ruling might go in Italy where there were no laws to support surrogacy. She was the woman who carried the child, and she would give birth to the child. He imagined that legally there was no way she would walk away with nothing.

And he had offered to marry her. Another way in which she could take advantage of him and his money. And yet she had not seemed excited by that either.

That didn't mean things wouldn't change, but for now,

he was forced to reconcile with the fact that she might be the rarest of all creatures. Someone who was what she said.

"Excellent," Allegra said to Esther. "I would hate for you to marry my brother while thinking he was well behaved."

Spurred on by his earlier ruminations, he turned his head, nuzzling the tender skin on Esther's neck, just beneath her jawline. "Of course," he said, allowing his lips to brush against her, "Esther is well aware of how wicked I can be."

He looked up, trying to gauge her response. Her burnished skin was dark pink beneath, a wild, fevered look in her eye. "Yes," she said, her voice higher than usual. "We do know each other. Quite well. We are... We're having a baby. So..."

"Right," Allegra said.

Just then, a servant came in, interrupting the awkward exchange. "Excuse me," the man said. "Your mother has asked me to 'come and fetch you for dinner.'"

Likely, those were his mother's exact words.

Keeping his hand on Esther's lower back, he led the charge out of the room and toward the dining hall. He could feel her growing stiffer and stiffer beneath his touch the closer they got, almost as if she could sense his mother. He wouldn't be surprised. His mother radiated ice, and openly telegraphed her difficulty to be pleased.

"Take a breath," he whispered in her ear just before they walked in. She complied, her shoulders lifting with a great gasp. "See that you don't die before dessert."

And then he propelled her inside.

His mother was there, dressed in sequins, looking far too young to have two grown children, one grandchild and another on the way. His father was there, looking every bit his age, stern-faced and distinguished, and likely a portrait of Renzo's own fate in thirty years.

"Hello," his mother said, not standing, which Renzo knew was calculated in some way or another. "So nice to meet you, Esther," his mother said, using Esther's first name, which he had no doubt was as calculated as the rest. "Allegra, Cristian, so glad you could come. And that you brought my favorite grandchild."

"Your only grandchild," Allegra said, taking her seat while Cristian set about to setting their daughter in a booster seat that had already been put in place for her.

All of this was like salt in a wound. He loved his niece, but there was a particular kind of pain that always came when he was around small children. And when his parents said things like this…about their only grandchild… that pain seemed insurmountable.

"Not for long, though," Allegra continued. "Unless Renzo hasn't told you?"

"He has not. Good. Well, at least now we're all up to speed." His mother gave Renzo a very pointed look. "Do you have any other surprises for us?"

"Not at the moment," he said.

Dinner went on smoothly, their mother and father filling up most of the conversation, and Renzo allowing his brother-in-law to take any of the gaps that appeared. Cristian was a duke, and his title made him extremely interesting to Renzo and Allegra's parents.

Then suddenly, his father's focus turned to Renzo. "I suppose we will see both you and Esther at the charity art exhibit in New York in two weeks?"

Damn. He had forgotten about that. His father was a big one for philanthropy, and he insisted that Renzo make appearances at these types of events. Not because his father believed firmly in charity in a philosophical sense, but because he believed in being seen as someone who did. Oh, he wasn't completely cold-blooded, and truly, it didn't matter either way. A good amount of money made it into needy hands regardless.

But bringing Esther to New York, having her prepared to attend such a land mine–laden event with very little preparation was… Well, just thinking about it was difficult.

More than just the Esther complication, there was always the Jillian complication. Or worse, Samantha. They split their time between Italy and the States, so the probability of seeing them was…high.

But he'd weathered that countless times. Esther was his chief concern. She would probably end up hiding under one of the buffet tables, or perhaps eating a bowl of chocolate mousse on the floor. Thankfully, it would be at night, so there would be no sunbeams for her to warm herself beneath.

"Of course," he said, answering as quickly as possible, before Esther opened her mouth. He had to make it seem as though they had discussed this. That he had not in fact forgotten about the existence of this event—one that he attended every year—due to the fact that he had been shocked by the news of a stranger carrying his child.

"Excellent," his father said. "I do find that it's much better for a man such as yourself to attend with a date."

"Why is that?"

"So you aren't on the prowl for women when you should be on the prowl for business connections."

That shot from his father surprised him. Especially in front of Esther. His father was typically the more restrained of his two parents. Still, he was hardly going to let the old man see that it had surprised him. "You live in the Dark Ages, Father," he said. "Sometimes, women are in high-powered positions of business, in which case, my being single helps quite a bit. However, Esther will not be an impediment, on that you are correct."

"Certainly not," his father said. "If anything, she will be something of an attraction to those jaded big fish you intend to catch."

"Are you going to be there, Father?"

"No. When I said I hoped to see you there, I meant only that I hope to see your photograph in the newspaper."

Renzo couldn't help but laugh at that. And after that, conversation went smoothly through dessert. At least, until they were getting ready to go. A staff member waylaid Esther, a maneuver that Renzo fully took notice of only when his father cornered him near the front door.

"I do hope this isn't some sort of elaborate joke like your last relationship seems to have been," his father said.

"Why would it be?"

"She is a lovely girl. She's a far cry from the usual vacuous model types you choose to associate yourself with. I had to cut ties with one of my grandchildren already, Renzo, lest you forget."

"You didn't have to. You felt it was necessary at the time and you convinced me the same was true. Don't pretend that you have regrets now, old man," Renzo said, his tone hard. "Not when you were so emphatic about the need for it all those years ago."

"What I'm saying is that you best marry this girl. And that marriage best stick. A divorce, Renzo. You had a divorce. And a child outside of wedlock that none of us can ever acknowledge."

"What will you do if I disappoint you again, Father? Find the secret to immortality and deny me my inheritance?"

"Your brother-in-law is more than able to take over the

remainder of the business that is not yet under your control. If you don't want to lose dominion over the Valenti Empire upon the event of my death, I suggest you don't disappoint me."

His father moved away from him swiftly then, and Esther came to join him standing by the door. She looked like a deer caught in the headlights, blindsided completely by the entire evening.

And he knew he now had no choice in the matter. This farce would not be enough. It had to be more. His father was threatening his future, and not just his, that of his child.

Esther Abbott was going to have to become his wife, whether she wanted to or not.

And he knew exactly how to accomplish it. He had seen the way she had reacted to his touch back at his villa. He knew that she wasn't immune to him. And a woman like her, naive, vulnerable, would not be immune to the emotions that would come with the physical seduction.

It was ruthless, even for him. He preferred honesty. Preferred to let the women he got involved with know exactly what they were in for. Preferred to let them know that emotion was never going to be on the table. That love was never going to be a factor.

But he would offer her marriage, and she could hardly ask for more than that. In this instance, what would the harm be?

There was no other option. He was going to have to make Esther Abbott fall in love with him. And the only way to accomplish that would be seduction.

"Come on, Esther," he said, holding out his arm, "it is time for us to go home."

CHAPTER SEVEN

ESTHER WAS USED to the breakneck pace of working in the bar. Going out every night and working until closing time was demanding. But the routine of getting ready, polishing herself from head to toe, so that she could go out with Renzo for a dinner in Rome, was something else entirely. And it was almost no less exhausting.

Being on show was such a strange thing. She was used to being ignored. Invisible.

But two nights ago they had gone to his parents' house, and the scrutiny she had been put under there had been unlike anything she'd experienced since she'd lived at home and it had always seemed as though her father was trying to look beneath her skin for evidence of defiance, sin or vice.

Then, last night they had gone out again to a very nice restaurant, and Renzo had explained to her exactly what the charity event in New York was, and how she would be accompanying him.

Tonight, they were going to another dinner, though Renzo had not explained the purpose of this one. And it made her slightly nervous. He had also made her a doctor's appointment at a private clinic, not the one that Ashley had used. But one that he had chosen himself. Based on, he claimed, the doctor's reputation for discretion.

It seemed ridiculous to have to get dressed up for a doctor's appointment, but Renzo had explained that they would be going out afterward, so she would have to dress appropriately for dinner beforehand.

So, here she was now, sitting in the back of a limousine, being driven out to her appointment where Renzo was supposed to meet her. She was wearing lipstick.

The limo came to a stop, and she was deposited in front of a building that seemed far too polished to be a simple medical clinic. But then, Ashley had been aiming for a different kind of discretion when they had gone to the surrogacy clinic.

The driver opened the door for her, and she realized that she had to get out. Even though she just wanted to keep sitting there. For one horrifying second she wondered if she was going to go into the clinic, lie down on the doctor's table, and he was going to tell her the baby was gone.

For some reason, in that moment, the thought made her feel bereft. She wasn't sure why it should. Maybe for Renzo? Because he was rearranging his life for this child?

Or maybe, it's because you aren't ready to let go of the baby?

No, that was unthinkable. She wasn't attached to this. She just felt natural protectiveness. It was a hormone thing. She was sure of that. But she couldn't remember feeling sick for the last couple of days, not even a little bit of nausea, and she wondered if that was indicative of something bad. She wondered that even while she spoke to the woman at the front desk and was ushered into a private waiting room.

She wrung her hands, jiggling her leg, barely able to enjoy the opulence of the surroundings. She tried. She really did. Because she had purposed to be on this journey.

To enjoy this little window into something that would always and forever be outside her daily experiences.

She didn't know when she had started to care. At least not in a way that extended beyond the philosophical. That extended past her feeling like she had to preserve the life inside her out of a sense of duty. She only knew that it had.

Thankfully, she didn't have a whole lot of time to ruminate on that, because just then, Renzo entered the room. There was something wild and stormy in his gaze that she couldn't guess at. But then, that was nothing new. She didn't feel like she could ever guess what he was thinking.

"Where is the doctor?" He didn't waste any time assessing the situation and deciding it was lacking.

"I don't know. But I imagine it won't be much longer."

"It is a crime that you have been kept waiting at all," he said, his tone terse.

She hugged herself just a little bit more tightly, anxiety winding itself around her stomach. "You weren't here anyway. It didn't matter particularly whether or not the doctor materialized before you, did it?"

"You could have been preparing for the exam."

Esther didn't say anything. She could only wonder if Renzo was experiencing similar feelings to hers. It seemed strange to think that he would, but then, also not so strange. It was his baby. It actually made more sense than her being nervous.

"Ms. Abbott," a woman said, sticking her head through the door. "The doctor is ready to see you now."

Esther took a deep breath, pushing herself into a standing position. She was aware of walking toward the door on unsteady legs, and then hyperaware of Renzo reaching out and cupping her elbow, steadying her. "I'm fine," she said.

"You look like a very light breeze could knock you over."

"I'm *fine*," she reiterated. Even though she wasn't certain if she was.

Renzo let the line of conversation go, but he did not let go of her arm. Instead, he held on to her all the way down the private hallway and into the exam room.

"Remove your clothing and put on this gown," the nurse said. "The doctor will be in in just a few moments."

Esther looked at Renzo, her gaze pointed. But he didn't seem to take the hint.

"Can you leave?" she asked, the moment the nurse was out of sight.

"Why should I leave? You are my fiancée, after all."

"Your fiancée in name only. You and I both know that this child was not conceived in the…in the…the usual way that children are conceived. You don't have any right to look at me while I'm undressing. I couldn't say that in front of the stylist the other day, but I will say it now."

"I will turn," he said, his tone dry. And he did.

She took a deep breath, her eyes glued to his broad back, and she began to remove her clothing. It didn't matter that he couldn't *see* her. The feeling of undressing in the same room as a man was so shockingly intimate.

Everything had happened so quickly during her little makeover the other day. And while she had been embarrassed that he was looking at her body, she hadn't fully processed all of her feelings. Right now, she could process them all a bit too well.

From the dull thud of her heart, to the fluttering of her pulse at the base of her throat. The way that her fingers felt clumsy, numb, but everything else on her body felt hypersensitive and so very warm, tingly.

She could sense him. More than just seeing him standing in front of her, he felt all around her. As though he took up every corner of the room, even though she knew such a thing wasn't possible.

Finally, she got all of her clothes off, and stood there for a moment. Just a moment. Long enough to process the fact that she was standing naked in a room with this powerful man, who was dressed in a perfectly tailored suit.

It was such a strange contrast. She had never felt more vulnerable, more exposed or…stronger, than she did in that moment. And she could not understand all of those contrasting things coming together to create *one* feeling.

She picked up the hospital gown and slipped it onto her shoulders, then got up onto the plush table that was so very different from the other table she had been on just a few months ago. "This is different," she said. "From the clinic in Santa Firenze."

He turned then, not asking if he could. But she had a feeling that Renzo was not a man accustomed to asking for much. "In what way?"

"Well, I get the feeling that Ashley was doing her best to keep all of this from getting back to you. So, she opted for discreet. But not like this. It was…rustic?"

His lip curled. "Excellent. She took you to a bargain fertility clinic." His hands curled into fists. "If I ever get my hands on her…"

"Don't. The fact that she is who she is is punishment enough, isn't it?"

He laughed. "I suppose it is."

There was a firm knock on the door, followed by the door opening quickly. Then, the doctor—a small woman with her hair pulled back into a tight bun—walked into the room. "Ms. Abbott, Mr. Valenti, it's very nice to meet you. I'm very pleased to be helping you along with your pregnancy."

After introductions were made, and Esther's vitals were

taken, the woman had Esther lie down on the table, then she placed a towel over Esther's lap and pushed the hospital gown up to the bottom of her rib cage.

"We're going to do an ultrasound. To establish viability, listen to the heartbeat and get a look at the baby."

Anxiety gripped her. This was the moment of truth, she supposed. The moment where she found out if those prickling fears she'd had in the waiting room were in any way factual. Or if they were just vague waves of anxiety, connected to nothing more but her general distrust of the situation.

She really hoped it was the second.

The doctor squirted some warm gel onto her stomach, then placed the Doppler on her skin. She moved the wand around until Esther caught sight of a vague fluttering on the monitor next to her. Her breath left her body in a great gust, relief washing over her. "That's the heart," she asked, "isn't it?"

"Yes," the doctor said, flipping a switch and letting a steady thumping sound fill the room. "There it is."

It was strange, like a rhythmic swishing, combined with a watery sound in the back. The Doppler moved, and the sound faded slightly.

"I'm just trying to get a good look." She kept on moving the Doppler around, and new images flashed onto the screen, new angles of the baby that she carried. But Esther couldn't make heads or tails of any of it. She had no experience with ultrasounds.

"Do either of you have a history of twins in your family?"

The question hit Esther square in the chest, and she struggled to come up with any response that wasn't simply *why*.

She didn't. But she knew that the question didn't actually pertain to her, since the child she was carrying wasn't hers. "I…"

"No," Renzo said, his tone definitive. "However… The baby was conceived elsewhere through artificial means. If that has any impact on what you're about to say."

"Well, that does increase the odds of such things," the doctor said. "And that is in fact what it looks like here. Twins."

All of the relief that had just washed through Esther was gone now, replaced by wave after wave of thundering terror. Twins? There was no way she could be carrying twins. That was absurd.

Here she had been worried that she had lost one baby, that they would look inside her womb and see nothing, when they had actually found an extra baby.

"I don't understand," Esther said. "I don't understand at all. I don't understand how it could be twins. I've been to the doctor before to have the pregnancy checked on…"

"These things are easy to miss early on. Especially if they were just looking at heartbeats with the Doppler."

She felt heat rush through her face. "Yes," she confirmed.

"I understand that it's a bit of a shock."

"It's fine," Renzo said, his tone hard, belying that calm statement. "I have more than enough means to handle such things. I'm not at all concerned. Of course we are able to care for twins."

"Everything looks good," the doctor said, pulling the Doppler off Esther's stomach and wiping her skin free of gel. "Of course, we will want to monitor you closely as twins are considered a more high-risk pregnancy. You're young. And all of your vitals look good. I don't see why you shouldn't have a very successful pregnancy."

Esther was vaguely aware of nodding, while Renzo

simply stood there. Like a statue straight from a Roman temple.

Seeing that neither of them had anything to say, the doctor nodded. "I'll leave you two to discuss."

As soon as the doctor left, Esther sagged back onto the table, flattening herself entirely, going utterly limp. "I can't believe it."

"You can't believe it? You're the one who intends to leave. Why would it concern you?"

"*I'm* the one who has to carry a litter," she shot back.

"Twins are hardly a litter."

"Well, that's easy for you to say. You're not the one gestating them."

He looked stunned. Pale beneath his burnished skin. "Indeed not." He turned away from her. "Get dressed. We have reservations."

"I know I do. I have several reservations!"

"For dinner."

"You're not seriously suggesting that we just go out to dinner as though nothing's happened?"

"I am suggesting exactly that," he said through gritted teeth. "Get dressed. We are leaving to go to dinner."

She growled and got off the table, moving back over to her clothes on unsteady legs. She picked up the lacy underwear that had been provided by Renzo's stylist and slipped them up her legs, not even bothering to enjoy the lush feel of the fabric as she had been doing every other time before.

There was no pausing for lushness when you'd just found out you were carrying not one, but *two* babies.

She made quick work of the rest of her clothes. At least, as quick work as she could possibly make of them with her trembling fingers. "I'm ready," she snapped.

"Very good. Now, let us cease with the dramatics and go to dinner."

He all but hauled her out of the office, taking her to his sports car, where he yanked open the passenger-side door and held it for her.

She looked up at him, at his inscrutable face that was very much like a cloudy sky. She could tell a storm was gathering there, but she couldn't quite make out why. Then, she jerked her focus away from him and got into the car, clasping her hands tightly in her lap and staring straight ahead.

He closed the door, then got in on his side, bringing the engine to life with an angry roar and tearing out of the parking lot like the hounds of hell were on his heels.

"You dare call me dramatic?" she asked. "If this isn't dramatic, I don't know what is."

"I only just found out that I'm having two children, not one. If any of us is entitled to a bit of drama…"

"You seem to discount my role in this," she fired back. "At every turn, in fact, you treat me as nothing more than a vessel. Not understanding at all that there is a bit of work that goes into this. Some labor, if you will."

"Modern medicine makes it all quite simple."

"That is…well and truly spoken only like a man. What about what this is going to do to my body? It's going to leave me with stretch marks and then some." She didn't actually care about that, but she felt like poking him. Goading him. She wanted to make him feel something. Because for whatever reason this revelation had rocked her entire world, made her feel as though she herself had been tilted on her very axis. She didn't think he had a right to be more upset than she was. And maybe that wasn't fair. Maybe it was hormones. But she didn't particularly care.

"I will get you whatever surgery you want in order to return your body to its former glory. If you're concerned about what lovers will be able to get afterward, don't be."

That statement was almost laughable.

"I am not concerned about lovers," she said. "My life is not dependent on what other people think. Been there, done that, got rid of the overly starched ankle-length dresses. But what about what *I* think?"

"You are *impossible*. And a contradiction."

He drove on with a bit too much fervor through the narrow streets, practically careening around every corner, forcing her to grip the door handle as they made their way through town.

They stopped in front of a small café, and he got out, handing the keys to a valet in front of the door. It took her a moment to realize that he was not coming around to open the door for her. She huffed, doing it herself and getting out, gathering the fabric of her skirt and getting herself in order once she was fully straightened.

"That was not very gentlemanly," she said, rounding the front of the car and taking as big a step as her skirt would allow.

"I am very sorry. It has been said that I am perhaps not very gentlemanly. In fact, I believe it was said recently by you."

"Perhaps you should listen to the feedback."

He wrapped his arm around her waist, the heat from his hand shocking. His fingertips rested just beneath the curve of her breast, making her heart beat faster, stronger.

"I'm *very* sorry," he said, his voice husky. "Please say you'll forgive me. At least in time for the paparazzi to catch up with us. I would not want pictures of our dinner to go into the paper with you looking stormy."

"Oh, perish the thought. We cannot have anything damaging your precious reputation."

"Our association is entirely for my reputation. You will not ruin this. If you do, I promise I will make you pay. I will take money out of our agreement so quickly it will make your head spin. You do not want to play games with me, Esther."

He whispered those words in her ear, and for all the world he would look like a lover telling secrets. They would never guess that it was a man on the brink issuing threats.

It galled her that they worked.

He walked them inside, without being stopped by anyone, and went to a table that he had undoubtedly sat at many times before. He did pull her chair out for her, making a gentlemanly show there as he had failed to do at the car.

"Sparkling water," he said to the waiter when he came by.

"What if I wanted something else?" she asked, just to continue prodding at him.

"Your options are limited, as you cannot drink alcohol."

"Still. Maybe I wanted juice."

"Did you want juice?" he asked, his tone inflexible.

"No," she said, feeling defeated by that.

"Then behave yourself."

He took control like that with the rest of the dinner, proceeding to order her food—because he knew what the best dishes were at the restaurant—and not listening to any of her protestations.

She didn't know why she should find that particularly surprising. He had done that from the beginning. She had tried to come to him, had tried to do things on her own terms, but he had taken the reins at almost every turn.

Suddenly, sitting there in this restaurant that was so far outside her experience—would have been outside her scope for imagination only a few weeks earlier—she had the sensation that she was being pulled down beneath the surface. That she was out in the middle of the sea, unable to grab hold of anything that might anchor her.

She was afraid she might drown.

She took a deep breath, tried to disguise the fact that it was just short of a gasp.

Finally, their dessert plates were cleared, and Esther felt like she might be able to approach breathing normally again. Soon, they would be back at the villa. And while she still found his palatial home overwhelming, it was at least a familiar sort of overwhelming. Or rather, it had become so over the past few days.

Then, she looked up at him, and that brief moment of sanity melted into nothing. There was a strange look in his eye, one of purpose and determination. And if there was one thing she knew about Renzo it was that he was immovable at the best of times. Infused with an extra sense of purpose and he would be all-consuming.

She didn't want to be consumed by him. Not in any capacity. Looking into his dark eyes now, an answering twist low in her stomach, she wasn't certain she could avoid it.

He reached into the interior pocket of his jacket then, his dark eyes never wavering from hers, and then he got out of his chair, kneeling in front of her. She couldn't breathe. If she had had the sensation of drowning before, it had become something even more profound now. Like being swept up in a tide that she couldn't swim against. The effect those eyes always had on her.

The effect he seemed to have on her.

She was supposed to be stronger than this. Smarter than this. Immune to the charms of men. Especially men like him. Men who sought to control the world around them, from the people who populated their surroundings, to the homes they lived in, all the way down to the elements. She imagined that if a weather report disagreed with Renzo, he would rail at that until it changed its mind.

She knew all about men like that. Knew all about the importance of staying away from them.

Her mother had been normal once. That was something Esther wasn't supposed to know. But she had found the pictures. Had seen photographs of her mother as a young girl, dressed in the trends of the day, looking very much like any average girl might have.

She had never been able to reconcile those photographs of the past with the woman she had grown up with. Quiet. Dowdy. So firmly under the command of her husband that she never dared to oppose him in any way at all.

It had been a mystery both to her father and her mother that Esther had possessed any bit of rebelliousness at all. But she had. She did. And if there was one thing Esther feared at all in the world, it was losing that. Becoming that drawn, colorless woman who had raised her.

Love had done it to her. Or more truthfully, control carefully disguised as love.

It was so easy to confuse the two, she knew. She knew because she'd done it. Because she'd imagined her father had been overbearing out of a sense of protectiveness.

Those thoughts flashed through her mind like a strobe light. Fast, confusing, blinding, obscuring what was happening in front of her.

She blinked, trying to get a grip on herself. Trying to get a grip on the moment. It wouldn't benefit her at all to lose it now.

"Esther," he said, his voice transforming itself into something velvet, softening the command that had been in it only moments before. Brushing itself against her skin, a lush seduction rather than a hard demand.

He was dangerous. Looking at him now, she was reminded of that. She told herself over and over again as he opened the box he had taken out of his coat pocket and held it out to her. As he revealed the diamond ring inside.

He was dangerous. This wasn't real. This was something else. A window into a life she would never have. This was experience. Experience without consequence. She was pregnant. She was having twins. And she was playing at being rich and fancy with the father of those twins. But they weren't her babies. Not really. And he wasn't her fiancé. Wasn't her man at all.

That was a good thing. A very good thing. She didn't want anything else. Not from him. Not from anyone. She couldn't sustain this.

But she had to go along with this. And she had to remember exactly what it was, all the while smiling and doing nothing to disrupt the facade. Which, he had reminded her, was the most important thing. She could understand it. On a surface level, she could understand. But right now, she felt jumbled up. And she hated it.

Still, when he took the ring out of the box and then took her hand in his, sliding the piece of jewelry onto her fourth finger, she felt breathless. Felt like it was something more than a show, which proved all the weakness inside her. All the weakness she had long been afraid was there.

"Will you marry me?" he finished finally, those last words the darkest, the softest of all.

This was a moment she had never even fantasized about. Ever. She had never seen marriage or relationships as anything to aspire to. But this felt... This felt like nothing she had ever known before. And the question Renzo was asking seemed to be completely different from the one her father had undoubtedly asked her mother more than twenty years ago.

Of course it was. Because it was a ruse. But more than

that, this whole world might as well exist on another planet entirely.

But that doesn't make him less dangerous. It doesn't make him a different creature. He's still controlling. Still hard.

And he doesn't love you.

Her heart slammed hard against her rib cage. "Yes," she said, both to him and to the voice inside her.

She knew Renzo didn't love her. She didn't want Renzo to love her. Not like that. Love like that wasn't freedom. It was oppression.

She was confused. All messed up because of the doctor's appointment today. Because of the revelations that had resulted. Because of her hormones and because she was—frankly—in over her head.

That was the truth of it. She, Esther Abbott, long-cloistered weirdo who knew very little about the outside world and a very definite virgin, had no business being here with a man like Renzo. She had absolutely no business being pregnant at all, and she really shouldn't be on the receiving end of a proposal.

It was no great mystery that she felt like a jumble of feelings and pain while her head logically knew exactly what was happening. Her brain wasn't confused at all. Not at all.

But there was something weighty about the diamond on her finger. Something substantial about her yes that she couldn't quite quantify, and didn't especially want to.

It was the confusion inside her, tumbling around like clothes in that rickety old dryer at the hostel, that kept her from preparing herself for what happened next. At least, that was what she told herself later.

Because before she could react, before she could catch her breath, move or prepare herself in any way, Renzo brought his hand up and cupped her cheek, sliding his thumb over her cheekbone. It was like putting a lit match up against a pool of gasoline. It set off a trail of fire from that point of contact down to the center of her body.

And while she was grappling with that, added to everything else, he closed the distance between them and his mouth met hers.

Everything burned to ash then, bright white and cleansing. Every concern, every thought, everything gone from her mind in a flash as his lips moved over hers. That was what surprised her the most. The movement.

She hadn't imagined there was quite so much activity to being kissed. But there was. The shift of his hand against her face, sliding back to her hair, his lips learning the shape of hers and giving to accommodate that.

Then, his lips, lips she had never imagined could soften, did. And after that they parted, the shocking, wet slide of his tongue at the seam of her mouth undoing her completely. It set off an earthquake in her midsection that battled through her, leaving her devastated, hollowed out, an aching sense of being unfulfilled making her feel scraped raw.

She didn't know what to do. And so, she did the one thing she had always feared she might do when facing down a man like this. She gave. She allowed him to part her lips, allowed him to take it deeper.

Another tremor shook her, skating down her spine and rattling her frame. She didn't even fight it. She didn't even hate it.

When she had left home, when she had decided that she was going to go out into the world and see everything that was there for her to take. When she had decided finally to sort through what her parents had taught her and what was true, when she had decided to find out who she was, not who she had been commanded to be, this had never factored in.

She had never imagined herself in a situation like this. In the back of her mind she had imagined that someday she would want to explore physical desire. But it had been shoved way, way to the back of her mind. It had been a priority. Because so much of her life had been about being bound to a group of people. Being underneath the authority of someone else.

So, she had wanted to remain solitary. And at some point, she had imagined she might make a group of friends. When she decided to settle. At some point, she had imagined she might want to find a man for a romance. But it had been so far out ahead of what she had wanted in the immediate.

Freedom. A taste of the world that had always been hidden from her. Strange food and strange air. Strange sun on skin that had always been covered before.

Suddenly, all of that was obscured. Suddenly, all of it paled in comparison to this. Which was hotter than any sun, more powerful than any air she'd ever tasted—from the salted tang of the Mediterranean to the damp grit of London—and brighter than any flavor she'd ever had on her tongue.

It was Renzo. Pure, undiluted. Everything that gaze had promised her from the moment she had first seen him. The way he had immobilized her with just a glance had been only a hint. Like when a sliver of sun was just barely visible behind a dark cloud.

The cloud had just moved. Revealing all of the brilliance behind it. Brilliance that, she had a feeling, would be permanently damaging if she allowed herself to linger in it for too long.

But just a little while longer. Just a moment. One more

breath. She could skip one more breath for another taste of Renzo's mouth.

He pulled back then, dropping one more kiss on her lips before separating from her completely. And then he curled his fingers around hers, pulling her from her chair and up against his chest. "I think," he said, a roughness in his voice that had been absent only a moment ago, "that it is time for us to go home, don't you?"

"Yes," she said. Because there was nothing else to say. Because anything more intelligent would require three times the brain cells than she currently possessed.

And then he took her hand and led her from the restaurant. The car was waiting against the curb when they got back, and she didn't even ask how he had made sure they wouldn't have to wait.

He hadn't made a phone call. She hadn't caught any sort of signal between himself and a member of the restaurant staff. It looked like magic. More of the magic that seemed to shimmer from Renzo, that seemed to have a way of obscuring things. At least, as she saw them.

She had to get herself together. She told herself that, all the way home from the restaurant, and as she stepped into the house. And then she told herself that again when she realized that she had just referred to Renzo's home as her own in her mind.

She wanted to look at the ring on her finger. To examine the way the landscape of her own body had changed since he had put it on. She had never owned a piece of jewelry like that. She had bought a few fake, funky pieces when she had left home. Because she liked the way they jingled, and she liked the little bit of flash. Something to remind her of her freedom.

But diamonds had been a bit outside her purview.

She stole a quick glance down, the gem glittering in the light.

Then, it was as though a bucket of water had been dumped over her head. Suddenly, the haze that she had been under diminished. And once it did, she was angry.

"What were you thinking? Why didn't you warn me?"

CHAPTER EIGHT

RENZO DID NOT have the patience to deal with Esther and her pique right at the moment. His world felt like it had been completely turned on end. He was not having one child, but two. He could hardly sort through that.

He had opted to carry on with his plan, as though there had been no surprises at the doctor's today. He had continued on with his plan to propose to her at one of the more high-profile restaurants in Rome, where they would be sure to have their picture taken, so they could be splashed out on the tabloids. The same tabloids that had covered his incredibly public divorce from Ashley just recently.

It had been calculated. Very specifically. To set the stage so the people would believe this relationship was real. So that they would believe this pregnancy had come about in a natural way.

What he had not counted on was the kiss. Or more specifically, how it had affected him. Yes, he had known that Esther was beautiful. He had also known that he was not immune to that beauty. When he had watched Tierra dress her just the other day, he had been captivated by the smooth curve of her waist, her hip, the way that black lace underwear had barely covered her shapely rear.

But that big attraction still hadn't prepared him for what had transpired in the restaurant. She was unpracticed. Much less experienced than he had even imagined, judging by that kiss. She had barely moved.

But somehow, she had lit him on fire inside. He had tasted every female delicacy the world had to offer. Had delighted himself in feminine company after his first heartbreak. Seeing no reason he could not satisfy his body since he was bound and determined never to involve his heart again.

But she had broken through that jaded wall that surrounded him. She had done something to him. And now, she was yelling at him.

"I could not warn you, *cara*," he said. "That would have spoiled the surprise."

"I didn't like the surprise," she said.

"Still, I needed you to look surprised. You are aware that most women do not know when they're going to be proposed to, are you not?"

She sniffed audibly. "Maybe I'm not."

"I think you are. I needed it to look real."

"Is that why you…pawed at me afterward?"

"That's a very elegant way to describe what transpired between us. Though I do believe, you did some pawing of your own."

She huffed. "I did not. Like I said, you surprised me. I feel as though you could have warned me. About all of it. And you would not have lost the element of surprise. I could have acted."

"Sadly, you're a terrible actress. I hate to be insulting, but it's true. You have no artifice." As he said it, he realized how very true it was.

"You were trying to control me," she said, her tone hard, the anger behind it indicative of a deeper wound. One that had existed long before he'd arrived in her life.

"That wasn't it," he said, although he imagined it was

semantics at this point. "You have no… You're very soft. You seem to have no way of protecting yourself from any of this at all. You sit in sunbeams with bowls of cereal. And I do not know what to do with you. I do not know what you might do next. I do not like it."

She breathed in deeply, and if a breath could be called triumphant, then this one certainly was. "Good. I don't live my life to please people anymore. I am my own person."

"Yes. So you've said."

"It's the truth. I know that I told you my parents were difficult. But you have no idea."

"Well, you have met my parents. Assume I have some idea of difficult parents."

She snorted. "Trust me. Your parents seemed delightful to me."

"Your frame of reference is off."

"Undoubtedly." He began to pace the length of the room, all of the unquenched fire and unspent energy inside him threatening to boil over. "You must remember that you are not in charge here. This thing that we're doing is important only to me. Therefore, I will direct all actions. If I decided that this was the best way to go about confirming our engagement for the public, then you must accept that my way is law."

"You keep saying this is only important to you. But that isn't the case. I care. You may not understand it—I don't even understand it. But it matters. I'm linked to it. Physically. I know that these babies aren't mine, but it's all jumbled up. Biology and ownership, what it means… I don't know. I just know that I don't feel like a womb for rent. I feel like a person, a person who is going through something big and terrifying. A person who is carrying a baby. *Babies*, even. There is no divorcing my emotions from it. There is no detaching myself, not completely."

He regarded her closely. "Have you changed your mind about leaving?" She would. He would make sure of it. But if she was leaning toward a change of heart now, that would make his job all the easier.

Her reaction to that kiss would seal things completely.

"No," she said, her tone muted. She looked away, biting that lush lower lip that he had tasted less than an hour ago. "I can't. I have too much to do. I know that...I know that. But stop telling me that what I want doesn't matter. That what I feel isn't like what you feel."

"But," he said, unable to let that comment slide, even if he should for the sake of harmony. For the sake of manipulation. "It is the truth. I'm going to be a father to these babies. To these children. I'm going to be the one who raises them. I know what that entails. It is going to require sacrifice. Change." Until he spoke those words he had not realized that he intended to change it all. Somewhere in the back of his mind he had imagined that he would throw the raising of these children over to nannies. But now, he realized that was not the case.

He thought of his daughter. The daughter whose name he could barely stand to think, even after all these years. The daughter he sometimes saw across the room, through crowds of people, growing from a child into a young woman. Without him. Without ever knowing.

The idea of being a distant father again, even if his children were in the nursery and he was downstairs seeing to his routine while they were cared for by others, was too much.

"My life will change." He reiterated that, as much for himself as for her.

"I have a feeling mine will, too."

"Yes. Because of all the money that I will pay you."

"No," she said, her tone fierce now. "Because I was

naive. Because I was foolish to think that I could do this and feel nothing. That I could do this and simply walk away with a check at the end. This experience is never going to go away. I... I'm going to be changed," she said, sounding sad now, broken. "I thought that everything would be fine because I was committed to having this life or I didn't have ties and strings and any of those things that I was trying to avoid. But that's not true. Everything has consequences." She laughed. "I think I pushed that out of my mind. Because it was something that my father used to talk about. Consequences for actions. How everything you do will come back to you. How distressing to find out that not everything my parents taught me is wrong."

"That is usually the case," he said, her words hitting him in an uncomfortable place yet again. "Tragic though it may seem, no matter how difficult the situation, no matter how unreasonable your parents can be at times, they are often not entirely incorrect."

She shook her head. "I'm going to bed."

She turned away from him, and he reached out, grabbing hold of her arm and stopping her from going. "Remember," he said, not quite sure what he was going to say. For a moment, he just stood there holding on to her, not certain of why he had prevented her from leaving. "Remember that we have to go to New York in two weeks. If you thought tonight was public, then what you encounter there will surprise you. If you need any kind of preparation in advance, I suggest you speak to me about it. Otherwise, I will assume that you know what you're getting yourself into and I will expect you to behave accordingly."

He released his hold on her. He knew he was being an ass, but he couldn't quite bring himself to correct the behavior. Why should he?

Seduction, perhaps?

He gritted his teeth. Yes, that might have been the better path. To kiss her again, to soften her fears while he claimed that soft mouth of hers. And yet, he found he needed more distance from that initial kiss than another. More than he would like to admit.

"I think I can figure it out," she said, her tone soft.

"See that you do."

There were only a couple of weeks left until he would present her to the world as his fiancée. And at that point—his father was correct—it needed to be permanent. But Esther was hungry for experience. To see the world, to see all that life had to offer. And if there was anything that he possessed, it was access to what she craved.

He could give her glamour. He could give her excitement. He could—quite literally—show her the world.

And there was one more thing. Yet another that she would get from no other man, not in the way that he could give it. Passion. The two of them were combustible, there was no denying that after the kiss they had shared tonight. It was not a common kind of chemistry. He was a connoisseur of such things, and he should know.

Yes. New York would be the perfect place to spring his trap.

He would take her to the finest hotel, show her the finest art, take her to unsurpassed restaurants. And then when he took her back to that plush hotel and laid her on that big bed… He would make her his.

In the weeks since their engagement, they had settled into an odd sort of routine. They ate meals together—and she had none of them on the floor—and they shared polite conversation where he never once tried to kiss her.

He was interesting, and that was perplexing, because

she found herself seeking him out in the evenings just so she could talk to him.

Then there were the books. Every day after work he brought her a new one. Small, hardbound travel guides. Paperback novels. Extremely strange history books that focused on odd subjects such as uniforms for different armies and the types of women's clothing through the ages.

She'd asked him why, and he'd responded that it was so she could learn all the things she didn't know. Just as she'd said she wanted to.

It made her feel…soft. She wasn't sure she wanted that. She also wanted things to stay the same. In this strange, quiet lull where she felt like they were poised on the brink of something.

She liked being on the brink. It felt safe. Nothing too big, or too outside her experience.

Of course, it had to end. And she got her big shove over the brink when he came home from his office one day and swept her and all of her clothing up in a whirlwind of commands, packed her into his car and then summarily unpacked her on his private plane.

A private plane. Now, that she had not managed to imagine with any kind of accuracy. The horrors of traveling economy over the Atlantic had been something she hadn't quite anticipated, but on the opposite end of the spectrum.

The long flight to New York seemed to pass quickly with her enveloped in the butter-soft leather of the recliner in the living area of Renzo's plane. There was food that bore absolutely no resemblance to the meal she had been served on her crossing from the United States, and all manner of fresh juice and sparkling water.

Then, there was some kind of light, sweet cream cake that she could have eaten her weight in if she hadn't been stopped by the landing preparation.

Renzo had spent the entire flight buried in work. That was neither completely surprising nor unwelcome. At least, it shouldn't have been unwelcome. Except she had craved conversation but had instead settled for reading the book he'd gotten her for the flight, which strangely felt like him talking to her in some way.

She didn't know why she was being weird about it. They were connected by the babies she was carrying, and that was it. They didn't need to form more of a personal connection than they already had. More than that, it was probably best if they didn't.

She did her best not to think about that kiss. She did her best not to think of it as she was ushered off the plane and into another limousine. She did her best not to think of it as they made their way down the freeway, the famous Manhattan skyline coming into view.

That helped take her focus off Renzo and the strange ache in her chest.

New York. She had never been to New York. She had hoped to make it there someday, but her first inclination had been to get as far away from her parents as she possibly could, and that had meant taking a little sojourn around Europe.

But this was amazing. The kind of amazing that she hadn't imagined she would experience in her lifetime. At least, not when you combined it with the flight over. In some ways it was a relief to see that Renzo was making good on his promise. To show her a part of the world that she couldn't have seen without him. The way that people with money lived. The way that they traveled, the sorts of sights and foods that they saw and ate.

In another way, it was disquieting.

Because it was just another way Renzo might have

changed her. What if she got used to this? What if she missed it? She didn't want that.

She shook that thought off immediately as the city drew closer.

This was what mattered. The experience. Not the lushness of the car. But where she was. She wasn't going to change in that regard. Not that much. She had been sort of distressed when she had realized fully that her parents might have had some points when they'd lectured her about consequences.

And what she had already known was that the way they had instilled the lack of materialism in her really had mattered. It really had made a difference. And it made it a lot easier for her to pick up and travel around. While a lot of her various roommates in the different hostels had been dismayed by conditions, she had been grateful for a space of her own.

Independence was the luxury. She would remember that.

She and Renzo completed the ride down into Manhattan in silence. She remained silent all through their arrival at the hotel. It was incredible, with broad stone steps leading up to the entry. The lobby was tiled in a caramel-color stone, shot through with veins of deeper gold. It wasn't a large room. In fact, the hotel itself had a small, exclusive quality to it. But it was made to feel even more special as a result.

As though only a handful of people could ever hope to experience it.

The room, however, that had been reserved for herself and Renzo was not small. It took up the entire top of the building, bedrooms on one end and a large common living area in the center. The windows looked out over Central Park, and she stood there transfixed, gazing at the green square surrounded by all of the man-made grit and gray.

"This is amazing," she said, turning back to face him, her throat constricting when she saw him.

He was standing there, deft fingers loosening the knot on his black tie. He pulled it through his shirt collar, then undid the top button. And she found herself more transfixed by the view before her than by the one that was now behind her.

The city. She was supposed to be focusing on the city. On the hotel. On the fact that it was a new experience. She was not supposed to be obsessing on the man before her. She was not supposed to be transfixed by the strong, bronzed column of his throat. By the wedge of golden skin he revealed when he undid that top button. And not just skin. Hair. Dark chest hair that was just barely visible and captured her imagination in a way that stunned her.

It was just very male. And she knew from experience that so was he. His kiss had been like that. Very like a man. So different to her. Conquering, hard. While she had softened, yielded.

No. She would not think about that. She wouldn't think about yielding to him.

"What do you think of your first sight of New York?"

"Amazing," she said, grateful that he was asking about the city and not about his chest. "Like I said. It's big and busy like London, but different, too. The energy is different."

He frowned slightly, tilting his head to the side. "The energy is different." He nodded slowly. "I suppose that's true. Though, I had never thought of it quite that way."

"Well, you've never sat on the floor and eaten your cereal in a sunbeam either."

"Correct."

"Noticing energy is more the sort of thing someone who'd eat their cereal on the floor in a sunbeam would do."

"I would imagine that's true."

"You're too busy to notice things like that. The real estate development business is…busy, I guess."

"Yes. Even during slow times in the economy, it's comparably busy if you've already got a massive empire."

"And you do," she said.

"I would think that was obvious by now."

"Yes. Pretty obvious." She forced herself to turn away from him, forced herself to look back at the view again. "I find cities so very interesting. The anonymity of them. You can be surrounded by people and still be completely alone. Where I grew up, there were less people. By far there were less people. But it felt like you were never alone. And not just because I lived in the house with so many other people. But because every time you stepped outside you would meet somebody you knew. You could never just have a bad day."

He lifted a shoulder. "I am rarely anonymous when I go out."

She frowned. "I suppose you aren't. I mean, I would never have known who you were. I'm not metropolitan enough."

"You're certainly working on it."

She looked down at the outfit that had been chosen for her to travel in. Dark jeans and a white top. She supposed she looked much more metropolitan than she had only a few weeks ago. But it wasn't her. And none of this belonged to her either.

"The appearance of it at least." She regarded him more closely. "I suppose you can't exactly have a public bad day either."

He chuckled, the sound dark, rolling over her like a

thick summer night. "Of course I can. I can do whatever I like, behave as badly as I like. I'm Renzo Valenti, and no one is going to lecture me on decorum."

"Except maybe your mother."

He laughed again. "Oh, yes, she most definitely would. But there is nothing my parents can do to me." He looked past her, at the city visible through the large windows. "They gave me too much freedom for too long, and now I have too much power. All they can do is direct their disapproval at me with as much fervor as humanly possible. A pity for them, but rather a win for me, don't you think?"

"In some ways approval and disapproval is power, isn't it?" She thought of her own family. Of the fact that what had kept her rooted in her childhood home for so long was the knowledge that if she should ever leave she would never be able to go back. That if she ever stepped foot out of line her father would disown her. Would turn all of her siblings against her, would forbid her mother from having any contact with her. It was the knowledge that the disapproval would carry so much weight she would be cut off completely, and in order to make even one decision of her own she would have to be willing to accept that as a consequence.

"I suppose."

"You don't believe me. But that just means that your parents' approval doesn't come with strings."

That made him laugh again, and he wandered over to the bar, taking out a bottle of Scotch and pouring himself a drink. She wouldn't have known what the amber-colored alcohol was only a few months ago, but waiting tables had educated her.

"Now, that isn't true. It's only that I possess a certain amount of string-pulling power myself. So what you have is a power struggle more than a fait accompli."

"That's what I needed," she said, "strings."

Of course, that was what actually hurt, she concluded, standing there and turning over what he said. The fact that she wasn't a string. Her presence in their life wasn't a string. Control mattered to her father, not love. And he couldn't have anyone around to challenge that control because it might inspire the other people in his household to do the same.

Parental love wasn't strong enough to combat that. If there was any parental love coming from his direction at all.

"You should probably get some rest. You will have to start getting ready for the gala tonight as soon as possible. So a short nap might be in your best interest."

She wasn't exactly sure what had inspired the abrupt comment, but she would be grateful for some distance. Grateful for a little bit of time away from Renzo and his magnetic presence, and all of the feelings and emotions he stirred up inside her.

"I think I will have a nap. Is... Is someone going to come and help with my makeup and hair?"

"Of course. I'm hardly going to leave that to chance on the night of the most important professional event of the year."

"Good. I'm too relieved to be offended." And then she turned and walked away from him, heading into the first bedroom that she saw. Without another thought, she threw herself across the plush mattress and closed her eyes.

And if it was Renzo she saw behind her closed lids rather than the brilliant city skyline, she chose to ignore that.

Renzo had a plan. And he had a feeling it would be one that was quite simple to complete. He was intent on seducing Esther tonight. Judging by the way she had looked at him this afternoon, the seduction was halfway complete. He was not a vain man, but he was also not a man given to false modesty.

Esther was attracted to him. She had been affected by that kiss, and he would be able to overtake her senses yet again when he touched her tonight. More than that, she was affected by all of this. By the luxury of the travel, by the places in the world that he brought to her fingertips by virtue of his money and connections.

He wasn't angry that she had an interest in these things; rather, he found it to be a boon to his cause.

If she had been as unaffected by these things as she had claimed that she would be, then he would have lost some leverage. But she wanted to go to school, she wanted to see the world, and whether she knew it or not, she craved his touch. He could give her all of those things. He could satisfy her in a way that no other man could, in a way no other man had.

All she would have to do was agree to marry him. Beyond that, she would have to present a respectable front in public. But that was it. He could see no reason she would find that objectionable.

He had lied to her, of course, when he said that his parents had no leverage with him. His father had presented incredibly hard leverage at his home only two weeks ago. And dammit all, Renzo was not immune. He would not have control in his stake of the family business given up to his brother-in-law. He would not have it given to anyone. He had given up enough.

In order to maintain the status quo, he had already given up a child. He would not lose anything more.

Rage burned in his chest, the kind of rage he had not felt for years. He hadn't realized it was quite so strong still. He had thought he had accepted that decision. His parents had been acting in his best interest. But it burned. In fact, the more the years passed, it seemed to burn even brighter.

The older he got, the more control he assumed of his life, the angrier he was about the lack of control he'd had at sixteen.

His line of thinking was cut off completely when the door to Esther's room opened and a flash of slender leg caught his gaze. He turned his focus to her, a hot slug of lead landing in his gut and making his body feel heavy.

Her dark hair was hanging loose, in glossy waves around her shoulders. The bright blue dress she had in place showed off her curves, enhancing her modest bust with the heart-shaped line.

The shimmering, fluttering fabric hung loose over her stomach, a stomach that was showing subtle changes brought about by the pregnancy.

Gold shadow enhanced her eyes, and her cheeks were the color of poppies, matching her full lips.

She was an explosion of color, of shimmering light, and he could not take his eyes off her. Not for the first time, he wondered who might be seducing whom. Perhaps the idea of staying with him was in her plans already. Perhaps all of this was an elaborate ruse to gain access to his wealth and power.

Looking at her now, combined with the incontrovertible evidence of her pregnancy from the scan, he wasn't sure if it mattered. If she was every bit as innocent as she claimed, and appeared to be, or if she was calculating.

He should care. He just found that he didn't.

"You look amazing," he said, closing the space between them and curving his arm around her waist. The stylist he had hired was behind her in the room, and he knew that he could use that as an excuse later for what he was about to do.

He leaned in, brushing his lips against hers. A taste, a tease for them both.

It became apparent immediately that he had not imagined the heat and fire between them. In fact, just that brief touch ignited something inside him that was hotter than anything he'd felt in his memory.

It was nothing. Just lips. Just a hand on the curve of her waist.

And it left him shaken.

"Come," he said, his voice rough, "*cara*, let us go to the ball."

CHAPTER NINE

THE VENUE WAS packed full of people, lavish and expensive, money dripping from every corner of the place. From the diamonds that hung in women's ears, to the chandelier that hung overhead. It was the perfect example of the kind of opulent lifestyle that Renzo could offer her if she chose to stay with him. The perfect piece of manipulation, and one he had not even planned for.

But it would do. It would do nicely. Esther clung to his side, her delicate fingers curved around his biceps. And even though there were layers between them—his coat and his shirt—he could still feel the heat from her skin.

Yes, this was a very nice diversion, and one that would work to his advantage, but he couldn't wait till after. Till he would finally strip her bare and hold her in his arms. It had become a madness over the past few weeks. To resist her, to wait.

To speak to her over dinner when he'd wanted to pull her over the table and have her there. To bring her books to read in bed, when he wanted to keep her occupied with other things in bed.

He had thought so many times of going into her room and breaking the door down, laying his body over hers and kissing her until neither of them could breathe.

Of taking full possession of her without any of this

pretense. Without any of this delicacy. Because he had a feeling that it wasn't needed. He had a feeling that the fire burned as hot in her as it did in him. And he desperately wanted to find out if that was true.

However, he could not afford to allow impetuousness to make his decisions for him. He could not afford to make a wrong move simply because his libido was ratcheted up several notches.

He shifted, her hip brushing against him. The reaction was immediate. Primal.

He wanted to hold on to those hips, hold her steady as he thrust into her. As he made her cry out. Thankfully, he had thought to call the doctor before they left Rome. Under the guise of discussing safe travel. And he had of course asked her about what sort of intimacy would be all right, given that the pregnancy was considered a slightly higher risk.

She said that normal intercourse would be fine.

A smile curved his lips. Yes, he was going to have her. Tonight.

"There are so many people here," Esther said, "and they all seem to know you."

"Yes, but I do not know them."

"What must that be like?" she asked, as though he hadn't spoken. "To be...famous."

"*Infamous*, more like. I'm not going to lie to you, I'm mostly well-known because men know they have to watch their women around me." Now she stiffened, and he was pleased with himself for that well-timed comment. It was a risk, but there was no hiding his reputation from her. However, using it to fire up a little jealousy in her couldn't hurt, certainly.

"Is that so?" she asked.

"Yes," he said. "I was single for a very long time, Esther. And I didn't see any point in living with restraint. As I told you earlier, I don't have to watch the way that I behave. I have a certain amount of immunity granted to me because I am both male and very rich."

"That must be nice."

"I don't know any differently."

"My father was big on the men-having-whatever-they-wanted thing," she said, the tone of her voice disinterested, casual, but he sensed something deep beneath the surface.

"Traditional, was he?"

She shook her head. "I don't know. Maybe that's one word for it. One of the things I've been working on is recognizing that whatever my father and the other men like him believed, it isn't necessarily connected to anything real. It's not about other people who believe similarly to them. They took something that was all right and twisted it to suit their own ends. And I do understand that."

"You had…a religious upbringing?"

She shrugged. "I'm hesitant to call it that. I'm not going to put the blame on religion. Just the people involved."

"Very progressive of you."

She shrugged both shoulders this time. "Isn't that the point of life? To progress? That's what I'm trying to do. Move forward. Not live underneath the cloud of all of that." She looked up, refracted light shimmering across her face from the chandelier above them as she did. "I'm not under a cloud at all right now." She smiled then, and all of the thoughts he had earlier about her potentially calculated behavior faded. It was difficult for him to imagine somebody who was simply genuine. Because it was outside his experience. Yet, Esther seemed to be, and if he looked at her from that angle, if you looked at her now, he felt slightly guilty about what he intended to do. Because that really did make it a manipulation, rather than a simple seduction.

But still, she would get everything that she wanted in the end, just in a slightly different format. So, he should not feel guilt.

He turned, and suddenly it felt as though the chandelier had detached from the ceiling and come crashing down around him. It was everything he'd been afraid of, and yet no amount of forward thinking could ever prepare him for it.

There she was.

Samantha.

His daughter.

Seeing her like this, closer to being a woman than a girl, always shocked him. But then, everything about this had always been shocking, horrifying. Seeing her was always something like having his guts torn out straight through his stomach. Having his heart pulled out of his mouth.

It was a pain that never healed, and for a man who avoided strong emotion at all cost it was anathema. He controlled the world. He controlled more money than most people could fathom. He had more—would have more—than many small countries ever would. And yet he did not have her, and there was nothing he could do about it. Nothing he could do short of destroying what she thought her life was. Who she thought she was.

In this, he was helpless. And he despised it.

But there was very little that could be done. In order to be a good man in this situation, in order to be a controlled man, he had to go against everything his instincts told him to do. He had to honor the life that he had chosen to give to his daughter. Even if he had been coerced into it, the ultimate result was the same. There were things she believed about herself and her parents that he could not shake, not now.

He knew it. He knew it, but he despised it.

Fire burned inside him, rage, intensity. He couldn't go to her. All he could do was hold even more tightly to Esther. And as he did, he held even more tightly to his conviction. He had to make her his. At all costs. Because he would never take a chance that he might lose his children, not again.

He had lost one daughter. And the pain never faded. He doubted it ever would. There was nothing that could be done about it. It was a red slash across his life that could never heal. A mistake that would not be undone.

Oh, her existence wasn't a mistake. It never could be. The mixture of grief and pride that filled him when he saw Samantha was something that defied description. It was all-encompassing, overwhelming. She was not a mistake. She was destined for a life that was better than the one he could have given her at the time. Than the one she would have had if she had been raised by an angry, bitter woman whose marriage was destroyed because of her existence and a sixteen-year-old boy who could scarcely take care of himself, let alone a little girl.

Yes, there was no doubt she was living a better life than he could have given at the time.

But now... Now he had no excuses. Now he had resources, he had experience, maturity. He had already lived an entire existence trying to prove that he was unsuitable to raise the child he'd had at far too young an age.

Now he was going to have to fashion a new existence. One where he became everything these children would need.

He would give them everything. Starting with a family. One with no room for Ashley, who had engineered their existence for the sole purpose of manipulating him. One that consisted of a mother and a father. Esther. She was the one. She was going to give birth to them. She was the one the public would consider theirs, and so, too, would they.

He was renewed in his purpose. As he stood there, his insides being torn to shreds piece by piece as he looked at the beautiful young woman whom he would never know, who shared his DNA but would always remain a stranger, his purpose was renewed.

He turned away from Samantha. He turned back to Esther. "Dance with me," he said.

She blinked. "I don't know how to dance."

"Don't tell me, dancing was forbidden?"

She laughed, but the sound was uncomfortable, and it made him feel guilty. "Yes," she said. "Dancing was definitely something that was off the table. But…I did a lot of things I wasn't supposed to."

Something about that admission made his stomach tight, made his blood run hotter. "Is that right?"

"Yes," she said, her cheeks turning pink. "But I didn't dance. I might embarrass you."

"You're the most beautiful woman in the room. Even if you step all over my feet I will not be embarrassed to be seen with you."

A warm flush of color spread up her cheeks, her dark eyes bright. She liked that. This attention, the compliments. He reached out, sliding his thumb over her cheekbone, tracing that wash of color that had appeared there. "Do you know that you're beautiful?"

"It's nothing that I ever gave much thought to. I mean, I've probably given it much more thought ever since I met you."

He drew her close to him, guiding her to the dance floor, curving his arm around her waist and taking her hand in his. "In a good way, I hope?"

She looked down. "Meeting you has made me think a lot about people."

"I'm not sure I follow you."

She moved easily along with him as he guided her in time with the music. But she kept her eyes downcast. "Just…people. Men, women." She looked up then, something open and naked in her gaze. It held him fast, hit him square in the chest. "How different we are. What it means. Why it matters. My beauty never mattered until I wanted you to see it. And then, well, since then I've wondered about it. If I had it, and if I did, if it was the kind that you noticed. It's a weird way to think about it, maybe. But I never spent much of my life thinking about how I looked except in the context that being vain about it was wrong." She shook her head, her dark hair rippling over her shoulders. "That's quite liberating in a way. If vanity is wrong, then you simply push thoughts of your appearance out of your mind. You don't worry about it, and neither does anyone around you. But that isn't the way the rest of the world works."

"Sadly not."

"I guess that's another thing about how I was raised that maybe isn't so bad. Because now I have worried about it. How my dresses fit, how they look, what you think. But then… Feeling beautiful isn't so bad. And when you tell me that I am…"

"You like it," he said.

"I do."

His stomach tightened, and a smile curved his lips, a feeling of anticipation lancing him. He was very close to having her in the palm of his hand. To having all that glorious skin under his hands. "Vain creature," he said, injecting a note of levity into his voice.

"Is that a bad thing?" she asked, her tone tentative.

"I find it somewhat charming. Though, I have to ask you now… What have you been thinking about me? You said you had been thinking about our differences."

The undertone of pink in her cheeks turned scarlet. "That's silly. Juvenile. You don't want to hear about that."

"Oh, I assure you I do."

He examined the lush curve of her mouth, the dramatic high cheekbones and her dark lashes. She was the epitome of glorious feminine beauty, but there was an innocence there, and part of him wondered just how much.

"You're just very…" Her lashes fluttered "…big. I'm small. I feel like you could overpower me if you wanted to, and yet, you never have. There's something incredibly powerful about that. It feels dangerous to be near you sometimes, and yet I know you won't hurt me. I don't how to describe that. But sometimes the realization washes over me and it makes me shiver."

He did something then that he could not quite fully reason out. He released his hold on her hand, sliding his fingertips up her arm and resting his thumb against the hollow at the base of her throat as he curved his fingers around the back of her neck. Demonstrating that power, perhaps.

He could feel her pulse beginning to throb faster beneath his touch, and he felt an answering pounding within his own body.

"What else?" he asked, keeping his tone soft and his touch firm.

"You're very…hard."

"Am I?" he asked, lowering his voice further.

She had no idea. He was getting harder by the second. This little flirtation, something he hadn't quite anticipated enjoying, was adding fuel to the fire of his determination.

"Yes," she said, doing something completely unexpected, taking her free hand and pressing it against his chest, sliding her palm down to his stomach. "Much harder than I am."

"You seem like you would benefit from the chance to explore that."

Her breath caught in her throat. "I don't…"

He reached down, catching hold of her wrist and pressing her hand more firmly against his chest. "I want you."

He wanted her. Needed her. And not just because he needed her to marry him, because he needed to ensure that she was bound to him. But because he needed something to blot out the unending pain that was coursing through him—had been coursing through him for sixteen years.

Her eyes widened, an innocent stain spreading across her cheeks. "Want me to…what?"

He pulled her even closer, pressing his lips against her ear. "I want you naked," he said, feeling her shiver against him. "I want to lay you down in my bed and strip that dress from your body. Then I want to touch every inch of you. And then I want to taste you."

He barely recognized his own voice. It was rough, hard. And he was somewhere past control.

Esther trembled, and he could feel her shaking her head. "No, you don't."

"Of course I do. I said you were beautiful. I meant it."

"But that doesn't mean…" Her cheeks looked like they were on fire beneath her golden skin. "There are plenty of other women you could have. You don't have an obligation to me. We might be engaged publicly, but we both know that privately…"

"Of course I can be seen with no other woman but you," he said, "but that is beside the point. You're the one that I want. You, Esther Abbott. Not anyone else."

"But I'm not…I don't know… You can't. Not me."

The fire in him burned even hotter, and he was surprised by the strength of his conviction. Yes, it was all tangled up in the need to keep possession of his children, the need to give them the best life possible, and he believed he needed Esther for that, but there was more. In this moment, there was more. It would not be a hardship to convince her that he wanted her. Because he did.

"Yes," he returned, "you. I love your skin. I want to know if it's smooth like this all over." He moved a fingertip over her arm, relishing the tremor that racked her frame. "Your lips." He moved his fingertip around the lush line of her mouth then, that softness doing something to all of the hard, jagged places inside him. The seduction working better on him than he had intended. This was supposed to be about an end goal, one that extended far beyond finding himself between her beautiful thighs tonight. But it was difficult to remember that with lust pounding through him like a drumbeat.

"Your hands," he said, moving to curve his fingers around her wrist, caressing her palm slowly. "I want to feel them all over my body. And yes, I could have another woman. I have had them. More than I can count, I won't lie to you. But I don't want them now. I couldn't." It was the truth in his words that surprised him more than anything else. The fact that this wasn't simply a calculated statement. The fact that the strange creature in front of him had bewitched him in some way.

That she had compelled him to give her books, of all the ridiculous things. A new one every day because he passed a shop on his way home from work, and he thought of her every time he did. Because she wanted to learn and he wanted her to.

And, *Dio*, what he would teach her tonight.

"You haunt me," he ground out, losing hold of the carefully scripted line of compliments that he had put together moments before, going off into the dark parts of himself, where he could scarcely see an inch in front of him, much less guess at what might come out of his mouth next. "My dreams," he said, the words rough, "and every moment I lay in bed not dreaming because I'm thinking about you."

Her entire body was shaking like a leaf in a storm, and he felt nothing but triumph. His vision was a blur, a haze of everything but Esther. His mind blank of everything except what would happen in the moments immediately following this one.

She would say yes. She had to.

She pulled away slightly, and he wondered if he had gone too far. If he had been too intense, if he had been too honest.

He made a decision then.

He took firm hold of her arms and dragged her forward, closing the distance between them and claiming her mouth with his own. He wrapped her up in him then, folding her in his arms, gripping her chin tightly as he braced her firmly against him and forged a new, intimate territory between them.

He had kissed her before. But not like this. This wasn't a show for the people around them. It was not designed for cameras. And it wasn't designed to end here.

It was a beginning. A promise. A precursor of what was to come. An echo of the act that he intended to follow.

As he thrust his tongue in and out of the sweet, hot depths, as he felt her moan and shake beneath him, he knew that he had won. Because if he could reduce her to this—reduce them both to this—here in the presence of all these other people, then there would be no resisting him once he had her alone.

His father would be angry. Because Renzo had not taken this opportunity to forge new business deals as he had promised. But his father had no idea about the other war that was being raged. The war to keep Esther close, the war to defend the family that was growing inside her even now.

It took all the strength that he possessed to pull away from her. To keep himself from pushing her into the nearest alcove, shoving her dress up her hips and taking her then and there. Claiming her. But that would only further the cause of satisfying his desire. It would not further the cause of seduction.

He doubted if Esther had ever been taken up against a wall in a public place. And he also doubted if she would find that overly romantic.

As much as his body didn't care, the rest of him had to. He managed to find his focus in that. And when he turned back around and saw his daughter standing at the back of the room chatting with friends and taking no notice of what had been happening with him—why would she? She had no idea who he even was—it brought him crashing down to reality with an extreme sense of purpose.

"Come," he said.

She blinked. "We haven't been here that long. We came all the way to New York for this."

He laughed, every jagged thing inside him brought to the surface because of what had happened tonight stabbing through him. "No, *cara*. I came all the way to New York for you. To seduce you. To have you."

She looked shaken by that, her dark eyes filled with confusion. "You could have had me in Rome," she said finally, her tone muted.

"But I will have you here," he said, smoothing his thumb over her swollen lower lip. "With this city in the background, on that big bed in a beautiful hotel. In this place that you've never been before, where no other man has ever had you. And I swear to you, you will never forget it."

She looked away from him, hesitating for a moment as though she were about to say something. But then, she didn't. Instead, she simply nodded and took his hand.

CHAPTER TEN

THERE WAS A wild thing inside Esther. She had always been afraid of it. From the moment she had first suspected that it was there. Of course, it was that very wild thing that had inspired her to rebel against her family in the first place. That had inspired her to break the strict code she'd been raised in to seek out other things.

That had gotten her thrown out of the only home she'd ever known.

But even when she'd left, she'd hoped to control it in some way. Had never imagined she would give it free rein.

She had told herself that she wasn't going to find a man, because she needed freedom. She had told herself she didn't care about making herself look more beautiful, because she had a world to see, and who cared what it saw when it looked back at her.

But there was more to it than that. This was what she had always been afraid of. That the moment she met a beautiful man, the moment that he touched her, she would be lost. Because that wild thing inside her wasn't simply hungry for the beauty of the world, wasn't simply hungry for a taste of food.

It was hungry for the carnal things. For the sensual things. For the touch of a man's hands on her bare skin.

For the hot press of his lips against hers, and on her neck, and down lower.

Renzo had ripped the cover off all her pretense. He had exposed her. Not to him—she had a feeling she had been exposed to him from the moment she'd seen him. It was the fact he had exposed her so effectively to herself that had her shaken.

But she wasn't turning back. Not now. There was no way. Not now that she knew. Not now that she wanted. With such a sharp keenness that it could not be denied.

She didn't want to deny it.

There was a conversation they would have to have. After this. They would have it after. She didn't want to say anything that would make him stop now. She had a feeling that he had some suspicions about her lack of experience, but what he had said just a few moments earlier about having her in the city where no other man had ever been with her before made her think that he perhaps didn't know just how inexperienced she was.

That he hadn't guessed yet that he was the first man to kiss her. That he would most certainly be the first man to...

She shivered as the limousine pulled up in front of the hotel. She could tell him no. She knew she could. And he would stop.

She thought back to the fierce way he had taken her mouth in that room full of people. It had been something more than a kiss, something so intimate it made her catch fire inside to think about other people seeing it.

He had been beyond himself then, all of that icy control that she had witnessed in him from the first time she'd seen him burned away. Scorched by the fire of the attraction between them.

She swallowed hard, looking over at him, at the hard carved lines of his face that seemed to look even more intimidating now than they ever had. She was fairly certain that he would stop if she asked him to.

Yes, of course he would. He was a man, not a monster. Even if he was a man she could scarcely recognize now. There was an intensity to him that she had never witnessed before. A desperation, a hunger. It mirrored her own and stoked the flames inside her so that they burned brighter, hotter.

He didn't touch her during the elevator ride up to the penthouse. She was afraid, for a moment, that it might give her too much time to think. That it might allow the heated passion inside her to begin to cool.

But once the doors closed behind them and they were ensconced in the tight space, she found it to be entirely the opposite. She could scarcely breathe for wanting him. For needing him.

The seconds in the elevator stretched between them tight and thick, wrapping around her neck, constricting her throat. By the time the doors opened into the hall, she let out a great gasp, a sigh of relief that she knew he had heard.

He still didn't touch her as they approached the door and he used the key card to undo the lock. But then he placed his palm on her lower back, ushering her in, the contact burning through the thin fabric of her dress.

And when he closed the door behind them, she was the one who closed the remaining distance between them. She was the one to kiss him. Because she didn't want him to change his mind. Didn't want whatever madness he was beholden to to fade. She kissed him with all of that desperation. That need for satisfaction.

She began to frantically work at the knot on his tie, clumsy fingers then moving to the buttons on his shirt.

"Slow down," he said, his voice a low, gravelly command.

"No," she said, between kisses, between desperate grabs for his shirt fabric. "No," she said again, "I can't."

He reached up, taking hold of her wrists, his hold on her like irons. "There is no rush," he said, leaning in slowly, brushing his cheek against hers. It was much more innocuous contact than the kiss from before, and yet it affected her no less profoundly. "Some things are best when they're taken slowly."

Taken slowly? She felt like there was a wild creature inside her trying to break out, desperate for release, and he wanted to talk about taking it slowly? She had waited twenty-three years for this moment. To be with a man. To want a man like this. And now, with satisfaction so close, he wanted to take it slowly.

She wanted it done now.

That certainty surprised her, especially after the small attack of nerves that she'd had right before coming into the hotel. There were no nerves now, not in here.

What she said to him out on the dance floor, it had been true. His strength, the way that he kept it leashed, all the while with her totally conscious of how easily he could overpower her, was a powerful aphrodisiac.

"I don't want slow," she said, leaning back into him.

And now, he used that strength against her, holding her fast, not allowing her to kiss him again. "Wait," he said, his tone firm.

He shifted his hold, gathering both of her wrists into one hand, then lowering his free hand to her back, grabbing hold of her dress's zipper tab and pulling it down slowly. The filmy fabric fell away from her curves, leaving her standing there in nothing more than a pair of lace panties.

It was similar to what had happened that day he'd come to her fitting. But also, like something completely different. She had been facing away from him then, and though she had been able to feel his eyes on her, she had not seen the expression on his face. She could see it now.

All of that lean hunger directed at her, the intensity of a predator gleaming in those dark eyes. He looked her over slowly, making no effort to hide his appreciation for her breasts as he allowed himself a long moment to stare openly at them.

They felt heavier all of a sudden. Her nipples tightening beneath his close inspection. An answering ache started between her thighs, and she felt herself getting slicker, felt her need ratcheting up several notches without him putting a hand on her.

"See?" he asked, the knowing look in his eye borderline humiliating. "Slow is good. It will be better for you. I don't know what kind of experiences you've had before, but I can guess at the sort of men a woman traveling alone and staying in hostels meets. I can guess the sort of sex those kinds of semipublic quarters necessitate. But we have all night, and we have this room, we have a very big bed. And you have me. I am not a man who rushes his vices, *cara*. Rather, I prefer to linger over them."

"Am I a vice?" she asked, her voice trembling.

"The very best kind."

He leaned in, scraping his teeth across her chin before moving upward, kissing her mouth lightly before catching her lip in a sharp bite. The sensation hit her low and deep, unexpected and sharp, and not unpleasant at all.

He tightened his hold on her, reinforcing his control as he angled his head and kissed her neck, tracing a line down her vulnerable skin with the tip of his tongue. Her nipples grew even tighter, begging for his attention. She knew what she wanted, but she was much too embarrassed to say. She didn't even know enough to know for sure if it was a reasonable thing to want.

But, thankfully, he seemed to be able to read her mind.

He moved his attentions lower then, tracing the outline of one tightened bud before sucking her in deep, the sensation sending sparks down low in her midsection that radiated outward. She struggled against his hold, because she needed to grab on to something, rather than simply stand there helpless, with her wrists captured by him.

If he noticed, he didn't respond. If he cared, he didn't show it. Instead, he continued on his exploration of her body. Turning his attention to her other breast and repeating the motion there. She seemed to feel it everywhere, over every inch of her skin. It made everything far too sensitive, made everything far too real. And not real enough all at the same time.

Part of her felt like she was hovering above the scene, watching it happen to someone else, because this couldn't be happening to her. It was safe, though, to view it that way. Because the alternative was to exist in her skin all while feeling it was far too tight for her body.

Then, he released his hold on her, planting his hands tightly on her hips and pulling her up against him before sliding them around to her rear and letting his fingertips slip beneath the lace fabric of her panties, cupping her bare flesh.

And then she wasn't divided at all. Then, she wasn't hovering over the scene. She was in it, and everything was far too sharp, far too close. She felt too much, wanted too much. The hollow ache inside her was as intense as a knife's cut, slicing unerringly beneath her skin and releasing a hemorrhage of need.

He squeezed her, pulling her more tightly against his body, allowing her to feel the evidence of his need for her. He was so big, so hard, everything she had never known to fantasize about. And yet, it was terrifying, too, even as it was the fulfillment of her every need.

Because she didn't know what to do with this. Didn't know what to do with a man such as him. But she had a feeling she was about to find out.

Slowly, so very slowly, he pushed her panties down her legs and slipped them over her feet—still clad in the jeweled flats she'd put on earlier. Then, he knelt before her, removing her shoes as he had done that day in her room.

Only this time, when he was finished and he looked up at her, she knew that there was no barrier between her body and his gaze. She shivered, relishing being his focus, wanting to hide herself from him, as well.

He gripped hold of her legs, sliding his hands firmly up the length of them, to her thighs, where he paused in front of her, looking his fill at her exposed body. She pressed her knees tightly together, as though that would do something to hide her from him. As if it would do something to stop the pounding ache.

He looked up at her, a smile curving his lips. Instinctively, she struggled to get away from him, but he held her fast. And then he leaned in, the hot press of his lips against her hip bone making her jerk with surprise.

"Don't worry, *cara*," he said, tracing a faint line inward with the tip of his tongue. "I'm going to take care of you."

Surely this was wicked. That was the predominant thought she had when he moved unerringly to her center, his tongue hot and wet at the source of her need for him. Surely this was the height of her rebellion. The furthest that she could fall.

He tightened his hold on her, the blunt tips of his fingers digging into the soft skin on her rear as he took his sampling of her body deeper, as he slid his tongue all the way through her slick folds and back again, a rumbling sound of approval vibrating through his massive frame.

And then she simply didn't care. If it was wrong, if they were wrong. She didn't care about anything, anything at all except for the exquisite sensations he was lavishing her body with. She shivered as his tongue passed over the sensitive bundle of nerves again and again, establishing a rhythm that she thought might crack her into tiny pieces.

She planted her hands on his shoulders, and she didn't push him away. Instead, she braced herself as he stole her control with each pass of his tongue. As he worked to reduce her to a puddle of nothing more than shock and need. Oh, but the need won out. And if it was shocking, if she felt scandalized, it only made all of it that much more delicious.

Because this was the dark secret thing inside her allowed to come out and play. This was the piece of herself she had most feared, and here she was living it. She had always been afraid that she was wrong. That she could never, ever be the person her parents wanted her to be, no matter how her dad yelled at her. No matter how they tried to control her. She was proving it right. She had started on this journey more than a year ago, and this was the logical end.

But it didn't feel like a disaster. If anything, it felt like a triumph.

Suddenly, he shifted positions, taking hold of one thigh and draping it over his hip before he wrapped an arm around her waist, keeping the other firmly planted on her rear as he stood, bracing her body against his as he walked them through the main room of the penthouse toward one of the bedrooms.

She clung to his shoulders, shivering as his hot breath fanned over her flesh, as shock and anticipation continued to fire through her with a strength that seemed beyond reality.

When they came into the bedroom, he moved to the end of the bed, setting her down on the edge before going to his knees again, gripping her hips and bringing her to his mouth. He settled her legs over his shoulders, her heels pressed against his shoulder blades as he tasted her deeper, adding his fingers now, pressing one deep inside her. The unfamiliar invasion making her gasp.

But any discomfort was erased as he moved the flat of his tongue over her again and again in time with that finger, before adding a second, pushing her higher, harder than she had imagined it was possible to go. She was moving toward a goal she didn't even recognize. All she knew was need, but she didn't know what it was she needed.

He increased the pace, the pressure, and she forgot to breathe, forgot to think. She threw one arm over her eyes, moving her hips in time with him, not caring if that was wrong. Not caring if she should be embarrassed. She didn't care about anything but satisfying that need. And she knew this was it, she knew that he possessed the power to do it, and she would give him anything, allow him any liberty, in order to see it done.

Then suddenly it all broke apart, the tension that was screaming inside her bursting into shards of glass, shimmering inside her, bright and deadly and much more acute than anything she'd ever known before.

He continued to trace the shape of her with his tongue as aftershocks rolled through her, taking his time, satisfying himself even as she lay there assaulted by the shock of her own satisfaction.

"Renzo," she said, feeling unsteady, trembling all the way through. "I need…"

"I'll give you what you need," he said. "Patience."

She didn't even know what she needed. She shouldn't need anything more than what he'd already given. And yet, she could sense that something was missing. That she wouldn't be fully satisfied until she had him—all of him—inside her.

But then he moved away from her, standing and picking up where she had left off with his shirt, undoing each button slowly, revealing more and more golden skin, hard-packed muscles and the perfect amount of dark hair sprinkled over them.

She ached to touch him. To taste him. But she was boneless, and she found that she couldn't move. Her throat went dry as she watched his slow removal of clothing, the maddeningly methodical reveal of his body. And when his hands went to his silver belt buckle, everything in her froze.

She had never seen a naked man before. She wasn't sure if she was glad then, or if she regretted that she had no other experience to fall back on.

She licked her lips as he lowered that zipper, slowly, everything so very slow, her attention undivided. And then he pushed them down his lean hips—taking his underwear along with them—revealing every inch of his masculinity to her hungry gaze.

Her stomach clenched tight, seizing with desire and no small amount of virginal fear when she saw him.

In the back of her mind she tried to placate herself, tried to say things about new experiences and all of that. Except, it didn't work. It didn't work because he was more than just a new experience. Because she wasn't just having sex with him for the sake of experiencing sex. She wanted him. She wanted him in spite of her nerves, she wanted him more than she could ever remember wanting anything.

It was terrifying in its way. You want someone so much, in spite of any and all hints of fear or doubt. To know that it might end badly and to not care at all. It was also fascinating and about the best reason to do something that she could even think of. Because she couldn't help herself. Because she felt there was no other option.

"You don't have to worry about me. My health," he clarified. "I was extensively tested post-Ashley. And I haven't been with anyone else since."

"I'm good," she said, before she could even fully sort through what he was saying.

"Good," he said.

He joined her on the bed, placing his hand on her head and moving his palm down her thigh, then back up again, to the indent of her waist, to her breast. He cupped her, moving his thumb over her nipple. She gasped, arching against him, shocked at the ferocity with which she wanted him so soon after that soul-shattering release.

He kissed her, and as he did he settled between her thighs, the blunt head of his arousal pressing against her slick entrance. She let her head fall back, everything in her sighing *yes*. She wanted him. There was no doubt now. None at all.

And if there was fear? It was all part of it. All sacrificed on this altar. She was giving him her fear, her body, her virginity. It was what made it matter. It was what made it feel so immense. And that immensity was what made her embrace it so completely.

She would never be the same after this. Her eyes met his as the thought clicked into place, as he began to press inside her. The enormity of that filled her as he did, blotting out the brief, sharp pain that accompanied his invasion.

She reached up, touching his face, not able to tear her gaze away from him. He was… He was inside her. Part of her. They were joined together. And she knew that changed everything. She knew that—for her—there was no experiencing this on a casual level. That for her sex would always be deep like this, something that echoed inside her and resonated through to her soul.

He flexed his hips forward, and she saw stars as he moved even deeper, as he butted up against that sensitive bundle of nerves there. She clutched his shoulders as he established a steady rhythm, pushing them both to the brink, his rough, uneven breathing the soundtrack of her desire.

Knowing that he was so close to the edge, knowing that he was as affected as she was, only pushed her arousal to an even higher place. Impossible. It was impossible to think she could contain so much. So much need, so much of him. She would break apart completely if she didn't find release soon, and yet, she almost didn't want to come. Almost wanted to stay like this, poised on the brink of pain, and closer to anyone than she had ever been in her life.

She moved her hands down from his shoulders, her fingertips skimming over his muscles, feeling his strength as he braced himself above her, as he thrust into her harder and harder. She loved that. This feeling that consumed all of her, that was too much and not enough.

This was life. Life unfiltered, unprotected. Raw and intense, and no doubt every bit as dangerous as she had always been taught.

But it was real. Real in a way nothing else had ever been.

He growled, and it was that sound, that show of intensity, that sent her over the edge. Orgasm rocked her, this release going deeper, hitting her harder than the one that had come before it.

She clung to him long after the release passed, held him while he tensed, and then shattered, his muscles trembling as he gave in to his own pleasure. As powerful as it had been to find climax with him, it was his that undid her. To have him shake and shudder over her body, in her body, this man who was so much more experienced than she was, who was larger than life and seemed to be built out of stone… To have him lose his control because of her was altering in every way.

In a way it never could have been if he weren't the man he was. If he were an easy man, one who gave easily to the environment around him, then she would have simply been one more element that changed the shape of him.

Instead, this made her different. It made her matter. She had moved a mountain, and only a few hours ago she would have said that wasn't possible.

He was different from her father. Who controlled her because he was afraid of what she could be. That wasn't Renzo. It made her wonder if Renzo controlled everything around him because he was afraid of himself.

And that, she supposed, was the difference between a man who acted from a place of weakness and a man such as Renzo, who was coming from a place of damaged strength.

She didn't know why she thought that, why she imagined he was anything other than perfect and beautiful and whole as he presented himself.

Maybe it was because she had seen him in pieces just now. Just like her.

He moved away from her then, levering himself into a sitting position and pushing his hand through his dark hair. "You could have told me you were a virgin."

CHAPTER ELEVEN

"I genuinely thought it was self-evident," she said, not sure how she felt that he was leading with that. "And I kind of thought that after the procedures at the fertility clinic it might not be obvious. I do think that it would be obvious given the fact that I clearly don't know how to kiss."

He shook his head. "A lot of people have sex without knowing what they're doing, Esther. A lack of skill can speak to the fact you've been with men who didn't handle you correctly."

"Well, there were none. I dropped enough hints about my childhood that… Anyway. It doesn't matter. Are you saying you wouldn't have slept with me if you'd known?"

"No," he returned, his voice rough.

"Well, then I suppose this is a fight that isn't worth having."

"I might have been a little bit gentler with you."

"All the more reason for me to not tell you. Because… I liked how you did it."

He treated her to a hard look. "You don't know better."

She shrugged, suddenly feeling small and naked. "That's true of me and a lot of things."

"Explain yourself to me."

She scrambled into a sitting position, grabbing the blankets and holding them over her chest. "That doesn't exactly make me feel inspired to share."

"I want to understand you," he said, clearly deciding that there had to be a better way to approach this. "Tell me about yourself. Everything."

"I feel like if you had been paying closer attention you would have deduced the fact that I hadn't been with anybody."

"I assumed you would have found somebody as part of your world travel. Backpacking and staying in hostels generally lends itself to casual hookups."

She drew her knees up to her chest. "You know that from your time spent backpacking?"

"*Everyone* knows that," he said, his tone definitive.

"Okay. Well, I guess this is where I tell you that I'm not like other girls." She laughed. "I mean, obviously. I wasn't raised in a small town. That was misleading. Not entirely a lie, but not entirely the truth. I was raised in a commune."

That was met with nothing but silence.

"You see," she said, "I've learned not to lead with that."

"Do you mean you were raised in a cult?"

"Kind of. I guess. We weren't allowed to watch TV, I wasn't allowed to listen to the radio. I wasn't exposed to any pop culture, any popular music. Nothing. I didn't know anything my family, or the leaders in the community, didn't want us to know."

"That…strangely makes you make more sense." The way he spoke, slowly, as though he were putting all the pieces together and finding out that they did in fact fit, would have been funny if it didn't make her feel like such an oddity.

"I imagine it does." She took a deep breath. "But I never fit. I started…rebelling. Secretly, though, when I was a child."

He stared at her. "When you're raised in one way, believing one thing, exposed to nothing else, what makes you question your surroundings?"

No one had ever asked her that before. Most people didn't want to talk about her past because they found it uncomfortable. Or, they wanted to ask her if she had been a child bride or if she had shaved her head.

"I don't know. I just know that it never felt right. So I started...collecting things. There was a book exchange in the little town we lived near. A wooden kind of mailbox that had free books. And I used to stick them in my bag and sneak them back home when my mom was distracted with her grocery shopping. Then I would take them home and hide them in the woods. I did the same later, with music. But that was harder because I never had much in the way of money. But between rummage sales and the library, I managed to get a portable CD player and some CDs."

"Not a huge rebellion," he said.

"Well, maybe not for everyone. But for me it was. For... for my father it was. My youngest brother is the one who told on me. I know he didn't mean for it to be as bad as it was. I know he didn't mean to... He was just being a brat." She laughed, shaking her head and trying to hold back tears. "He found my books and my music, and he showed my mom. Who in turn showed...my dad. He said I had one chance to say I would never read or listen to anything unapproved again or I...I would have to go."

"And you didn't?" he prompted.

"I wouldn't. So there was a meeting. A meeting with everyone, and I thought...my father loved me. I asked him, I asked him then in front of everyone. If he loved me, how could he send me away just because I liked different books and different music? Just because I was different."

She pressed her hand to her chest, trying to ease the ache. "But he said…he said that if I wouldn't change I couldn't be his daughter anymore. He said it in front of everyone. He said that it was for the good of everyone else. That it was real love to require that I change and…and I don't think it is. It's control. And if he couldn't control me, he didn't want me."

Even though she would never go back, even though she would never make a different decision, it hurt all the same. Her life had changed for the better because she'd left, but she could still never give her father credit for that.

Not when the rejection hurt so much.

"That must have been hard," he said, his voice rough.

"It was," she said. "I felt sorry for myself for a while, then I got a job at a diner in town. Saved up my money for a year. I took the SATs. I got a passport. I went to Europe and started working wherever I could and…"

"And you met Ashley."

"And you," she said, the words settling strangely in the air, tasting strange on her tongue. Settling strangely in her chest. It felt so significant, meeting him. Being here with him. Even though she had decided to have sex with him, knowing that it wasn't about simply experiencing sex, she was still processing the implications of that.

"Yes," he said, something strange coloring his tone. "You got a bit more than you bargained for with all of this, didn't you?" There was something soft in his voice now, and she was suspicious of it. Mostly because there was nothing soft about him.

"You are a lot," she remarked. "A lot of a lot."

"We get along well, don't we?"

"I'm not sure what context you mean that in. You mean, when you're calling me strange and commenting on my habit of eating cereal on the floor?"

"Mostly I mean in bed," he said, "but that is the place I most often try to relate to women."

She frowned. "I'm not sure that was the most flattering thing for you to say."

"I am divorced. You have to consider that there may be a reason for that."

"Well, I met the other half of your marriage. So, I am not terribly mystified as to why that didn't work out. However, I have asked myself a few times why you ended up with her."

"Because she was unsuitable. Because she was a nightmare. And I knew it."

"I don't understand."

"I imagine growing up in a strict household, you received quite a bit of punishment when you did things wrong, or things that your parents thought were wrong."

"Yes," she said, "of course."

"Ashley was my punishment." He laughed, the sound containing no humor at all.

"For what?"

He shook his head. "It doesn't matter." Except, she had a feeling that it mattered more than just about anything else. "But I knew it was doomed. Somewhere, part of me always knew. But you... I feel like with you perhaps things might not be so hopeless."

It felt, very suddenly, as though her stomach had been hollowed out. "What?"

"What if we tried, Esther?"

"Tried what?" She wasn't thinking straight. It was impossible to think straight right now, with their lovemaking still buzzing through her system, with her heart pounding so hard she could scarcely hear her own brain over it.

"Us. Why do we need to separate at the end of this?" He moved closer to her, touching her face, that simple gesture warming her in a way that nothing else ever had. That connection, so desperately needed after being so intimate with him.

"Because," she said, no conviction behind that word whatsoever, "you didn't choose this. Neither did I. We just… We're making the best out of this. And of course we are attracted to each other, but it doesn't make any sense to start in a way that we can't go on."

"That's what doesn't make sense to me. Why can't we go on?"

"You know why. Because I just got away from a restrictive existence. One that made it so I couldn't decide who I was or what I wanted. I can't do that to myself," she said, but still not even she could believe the words coming out of her mouth. She knew in her head that she should, knew that there was truth in them, and that there was importance and weight to what she was doing. Finding herself out here in the real world when before she had been so isolated from it.

And that it was dangerous to feel that everything of importance had shrunk down to this hotel room. To the space between their naked bodies, and the need for there to be less of it.

That her anticipation of what was to come had become small, focused. On where his hand might travel next, what point on her body his fingertips might make contact with next.

So dangerous. So very dangerous.

"Has anything about your life with me been restricting? I have taken you more places than you could have gone on your own. You're not bound to waiting tables in order to stay alive. You have days you could devote to studying, and there is no reason you can't be with me and go to school."

What he was saying… It was so tempting. So bizarrely

clear and easy in appearance in that moment. A life with him, where they could travel at will, where she could still get the schooling that she wanted. It was just that she would be with him. And she couldn't even see that as a negative. Not now, not while her entire being was still humming from his touch.

"But we can't start something that we can't…keep going. I know these babies aren't mine. I went into this knowing that I would give them up. Things are getting muddled, and I don't know if it's hormones or what. I just know that as it gets more real, it gets more difficult. And I just keep telling myself that I can't do it. But do you know what I really can't do? I can't be their mother for a little while and then walk away. I have to either stay as I am, with absolutely no intention of raising them, or I have to have them forever." The very idea made her stomach seize tight with a strange kind of longing.

It was as though a dam had been destroyed and a flood of emotions was suddenly washing forward. Things she hadn't allowed herself to imagine pushing forward in her mind. What it would be like to see the babies once they were born. If she would hold them. And what it would feel like when she did. When they were in her arms rather than in her womb.

What it would feel like to hand them to Renzo and then walk away forever.

Or, even more insidious, what it would feel like to hold them forever. To become a mother.

That thought made her feel like she was being torn in two. Part of her was desperately afraid of having another human life under her care. What did she know? She was practically a child herself, still learning about the world, discovering all of these things that had been hidden from her for so long.

But there was another part of her… Another part of her that craved it in some ways. That craved real connection. Love. In a way she had never before received it in her life. It would be a chance to love someone unconditionally. A chance at having that love returned.

She looked up at Renzo. And that made her feel like she had been shot straight through the heart. Because there was another person involved in all of this, someone other than the children.

She realized then that she wasn't entirely sure what he was suggesting. "Are you suggesting that I stay as the… the nanny? Your mistress? Or…"

"Of course you will be my wife, Esther."

Her stomach tightened painfully. "You want to marry me?"

"We can give our children a family. We can be a family. I made a terrible mistake when I married Ashley. I was angry at the world, I cannot lie to you about that. I was trying to prove something. To prove my lack of worth. But the reality that I am having two children makes me want to do just the opposite. I want to take this situation and turn it into something that could be wonderful for everyone."

This was the first she had heard him express a sentiment like this. But then, this was also the first time they had ever made love. Maybe it had changed things for him, too. She knew that she felt altered. Utterly and completely. Why wouldn't it be the same for him?

But there was one thing she couldn't overlook. She had lived in a household where there was no love, and she knew beyond a shadow of a doubt that she could never do it again. He was promising her things. Promising her freedom, promising her that she could still see to her dreams.

But she needed to know if there was something behind it. If there was insurance. Something to ensure that it wouldn't all break apart, the way that things had broken apart with Ashley and him. Sure, there was the fact that she was not Ashley, but he was still himself. And even though she had feelings for him, deep feelings, there was so much about him she didn't know.

What she felt was much more instinctual than it was logical. There had been something about him, something electric from the moment she had first laid eyes on him. Maybe it was biology. Maybe it had something to do with the fact that she was pregnant with his babies.

But she had a feeling it was deeper.

She wished it weren't deeper. It would make all of this so much simpler. She could evaluate it a bit more coldly. With the sort of distance that it required.

She had no distance.

And she needed to know something, one thing. Because she had learned something important once already. That control was destructive. It had destroyed her mother. Broken her down from the normal woman she'd once been— vibrant and full of life—into a gray and colorless creature. It had very nearly broken her, too. But she'd found the strength to stand.

If she found herself in the same situation again…would she be able to stand strong? Or would she be too damaged, too broken down this time?

No. She couldn't let it. So she had to know.

"Renzo," she said, speaking the words as soon as she could form them in her mind. "I need to know something. I mean, I need to tell you something. I feel like…I've been happy with you these past few weeks. And I didn't expect to be. I didn't even want to be. Because I wanted to feel nothing for you, to feel nothing about this pregnancy. I wanted to be able to walk away. I don't think I can do that now. Not easily. Not the way that I intended. No matter what my intentions were, I know that something has been building between us. That there's a connection there that wasn't before. I think…I think I might love you. And that's why I'm hesitating to say yes to you now. I've lived in a home where I wasn't loved, and I can't do that again. So I need to know. Do you love me? Do you think you could at least grow to love me?"

There was no hesitation. Instead, he leaned forward, kissing her deeply, with all of the lingering passion that still existed between them even after their crashing releases earlier.

"Of course I love you," he said when they parted, his dark gaze intense, as affecting as it had been from the very first moment they'd met. "I want to spend my life with you. Say yes, Esther. Please, say yes."

She looked at him, and she realized that there was only one answer she'd ever given to Renzo, and that would remain true now, too. "Yes," she said, "yes, Renzo. I'll marry you."

CHAPTER TWELVE

RENZO TOOK A drink and looked out the door of his office, down the darkened hall. He was engaged to Esther now. For real.

And he had lied to her.

There were a great many occasions where he had employed creative truths in order to get his way. It was a necessity in business, and as everyone did it, it seemed as acceptable as anything else. He had done the same with Ashley. From marrying her in Canada to the way he had executed their prenuptial agreement.

He had never felt even the smallest bit of guilt for it. Perhaps because honesty had never gotten him much of anything. Whatever the reasoning, he felt guilty now. He felt guilty lying to Esther.

But would it matter if she never knew? It had cost him nothing to tell her that he loved her. It wouldn't matter one bit that he didn't. She needed to hear it, and that was what mattered.

Except she had told him about her father. About the way he'd controlled her.

He had to wonder how the hell he was any different.

He thought back to the hope shining in her dark eyes, and he crushed the surge of emotion with another slug of alcohol.

They had flown home from New York this morning, and he had done his best to keep his hands off her out of deference to her inexperience. And also, because even he had his limits. He had thought he might keep her mindless and loved up in order to keep her compliance, but that had seemed…distasteful even to him.

However, she seemed happy. She seemed settled in her decision.

And every time she had looked over at him with softness evident in her expression, he had forced himself to continue looking. Had prevented himself from looking away.

And so the guilt had taken even deeper root.

He had lied about a lot of things. But he had never lied about love. He had never once told Ashley that he had feelings for her he didn't have. Not ever.

It shouldn't matter. Because love meant nothing. It had been yanked from his heart by the roots sixteen years ago when his rights to his child had been signed away.

He had forfeited everything then. His right to love. His right to happiness. Even his right to anger. He took another drink.

He set his glass down on the bar with a clink, and then began to walk out of the room, his legs carrying him down the hall and toward Esther. He should stay away from her. He had no right to touch her again. And yet, he was going to.

Of all the things he could not regret that were part and parcel to this deception, it was the fact that he would have possession of her that stood out most. He wanted her. He wanted to keep her near him. Wanted her to live life under his protection, under his care.

And how are you different from the family she ran away from?

He was different. He would give her everything she needed. Everything she wanted. In return they would present a compelling picture of family unity to the world, and his children would have a sense of stability. He would inherit the Valenti family company, and as a result, so would the children. Doing anything less would rob them all of that.

There was nothing wrong with that. She would be happy with him.

Everyone would be happier for this decision having been made.

He curled his hand into a fist as he walked down the hall, trying to ignore the intense pressure in his chest.

He remembered her saying something earlier about letting it go. About how she'd had to let go of her past in order to move forward. He didn't know why it echoed in his mind now as he made his way into her bedroom. Perhaps it was because he was longing for her again. Perhaps it was because right now he could feel the weight of it all pressing down on him. All the things that he couldn't bring himself to release his hold on.

Because if he did, what was his life? If he forgot what had created him, then what would fuel him?

He pushed all of that aside, and he embraced the darkness. The darkness that was around him, the darkness that was in him. And he asked himself, not for the first time, what benefit it would be to his children to be raised in such a place, with such a man.

He put his hand to his forehead, pushing back against the tension that was overtaking him. He'd had too much to drink, maybe. That was the only explanation. For both the attack of conscience and the oppressive weight that seemed to assault him now.

"Renzo?"

Esther's voice cut through the darkness. He knew he must look like quite the looming villain, standing in the doorway dimly backlit by the hall. "Yes?"

"Come to bed with me."

That simple offer, so sweet and void of any underlying request, or motive, struck him even harder than it might have considering how deeply he was pondering his own ulterior motives. But he cast them aside now. As he began to cast aside his clothes. He had done the best he could. Keeping his hands off her as though that made him honorable, somehow, when he was manipulating her with his words already.

He had no honor here. He might as well embrace it. He had forgotten why he was even doing this.

He swallowed hard, pulling his shirt over his head then moving his hands to his belt.

"I love you," she said, shifting beneath the blankets and pushing herself into a sitting position. He clenched his teeth, shoving his pants and underwear down and leaving them on the floor. He felt…cold. His chest felt as though it had been wrapped in ice, his heart barely beating now.

He moved slowly to the bed, pressing his knee down on the mattress. Then he leaned forward, his palms flat on each side of her, caging her in. "I love you, too," he said, feeling nothing around his heart when he spoke the words.

He kissed her then, and everything seemed to come to life. All of the ice melting away beneath the heat of the fire that existed between them.

There were a few things that he was certain of in this moment. That she was an innocent. That she deserved better than him. That he was lying. And that he was going to have her anyway.

She moved her hands over his skin, the joy that she seemed to find in exploring his body stoking the flames of his libido and his guilt all at once. All of this was new for her. She'd never had a lover before. Had never even kissed a man before him, and he was going to be the only lover she ever had. Her sexuality would be completely owned by him, utterly shaped by him.

When it came to technique and skill, he supposed she could do worse. He knew that he satisfied her. He knew that he could give her what she wanted. Physically. Emotionally, the exchange would always be empty on his side.

He pushed the thought away. It didn't matter. She would never know. She pushed her fingertips through his hair, clutching his head as he deepened the kiss, as he flattened her against the mattress. She arched against him, a sound of desperation keening through her.

He despised himself then. He was all inside. Thinking all of these things, calculating his every move. And she was honest. Giving. Generous with her body, with her touch. She wiggled beneath him, managing to slip away and push him on to his back at the same time.

"Esther…"

She put her hand at the center of his chest, making a shushing sound as she leaned in and kissed him gently, right against his frozen heart. "Just let me."

She moved lower, blazing a trail down the center of his stomach, farther still until her soft lips brushed up against the head of his arousal.

"Esther," he said, his voice harder than he intended. But he didn't deserve this. Couldn't accept it from her. She was giving him her body this way because she believed there was an emotion that existed between them when it didn't. He was a relatively cold-blooded bastard, but even he had his limits.

Or maybe he didn't.

Because when she parted her lips and enveloped him

in the velvet heat of her mouth, he found he couldn't protest. Not again.

She tasted him as though he were a new delicacy for her to discover. Savored him. Lingered over him in a way that no other woman ever had. She seemed to draw pleasure from his, and that was a new experience. It was strange, to feel this intense, profound attempt at connection coming from someone when he was so accustomed to keeping his walls up at all times.

They were still up. Firmly. But she was testing them.

He wanted to pull away, but he couldn't. Not just because he had to continue on with this pretense, but because he was incapable. Because she held him in thrall, and he could do nothing but submit to the soft, beautiful torture she was lavishing him with.

Fire gathered low in his stomach, and he felt himself nearing the brink of completion. "No," he said, his breath coming out in hard gasps. "Not like that."

He was breathing hard, scarcely in control of his actions, scarcely in control of anything. Trying desperately hard to keep everything together. He was playing a dangerous game with her. And the worst thing he could possibly do was find himself in a position where he began forgetting exactly what he was doing. Exactly what he was trying to accomplish. This wasn't about them. It never had been.

Of course, he wanted her to be happy. But that was incidental. As was she. The only thing that mattered was keeping his children with him. Keeping their family together, keeping Ashley away. The only thing that mattered was building a solid foundation for the rest of his life.

It could be her, it could be any woman. Any woman whom Ashley had chosen, and he would be doing the same thing. He had to remember that. He had to.

On a growl, he pressed her back against the mattress,

claiming her mouth as he tested the entrance to her body with his hard length. She squirmed beneath him, arching into the invasion. And then he thrust deep inside her, all the way home.

His mind went blank then, of everything. Everything but this. This need for release. This need to be as close to her as possible. Everything he had just been telling himself burned away in the white-hot conflagration of need. He gripped her hips as he moved more deeply within her, as he changed the angle and made them both gasp with pleasure.

And then he lost his control completely, and he could only give his thanks when she cried out her release, her internal muscles pulsing around him, because he had lost any and all ability to hold his own at bay. And when it overtook him, it was like a hurricane, pounding over him, consuming him completely, leaving him spent and breathless in the aftermath.

And as he lay there, turmoil and the aftereffects of pleasure chasing each other through his veins, he knew that he was simply in the eye of the storm. It wasn't over.

He moved away from her, shame lashing at him. He hadn't felt quite so remorseful of his actions in a little over sixteen years. Everything was jumbling together. The past, the present, his future. And the reasons for his behavior.

"I'm so happy," Esther said, the bone-deep satisfaction in her voice scraping him raw. So now, she was peaceful, satisfied, and he was… Well, he was nothing of the kind. He felt utterly destroyed. And he couldn't quite figure out why. He had accomplished everything he had set out to accomplish. He had secured a future just like he had set out to do.

Had ensured that he would retain custody of his children, and that they would grow up with the family that they deserved. With the inheritance they deserved, because he was not going to allow his father to divide up Valenti to spite Renzo.

He was confident in these things. Confident that they were right. And she was happy. So nothing else mattered.

"Good," he said.

"But something's bothering me."

"Something is still bothering you? After that orgasm, if anything is still bothering you then I'm going to have to revise my opinion of you. You're a very greedy woman, Esther Abbott."

"I am," she said, nodding slowly, the gesture visible in the darkly lit room. "I want to experience the whole world. And I want to have you while I do it. That's pretty greedy, you have to admit."

"I have offered you both things. So there's no reason you shouldn't want and expect them."

"I want more now."

A surge of anger rocked him. "What exactly would you like, *cara*? The crown jewels, perhaps? What is it that I have denied you exactly that you feel you should have?"

"You," she said simply.

"You just had me. In fact, I find I am spent due to the fact that you had me so well."

"That isn't what I mean. I have a feeling you could share your body endlessly. It's the rest of you that you find difficult."

His chest, frozen before, burned now. "I told you that I loved you," he said, confident those words would end the discussion. "What more could you possibly need?"

"It's really great to hear those words. And I wish that they could be all that I needed. I wish that this could be everything that I needed. But unless I know what's behind it, unless I know what love means to you, how am I supposed to feel? How am I supposed to feel secure in this?

And what we have? We've only known each other for a few weeks. And I feel... I feel so much for you. It's real. But you know where I come from. I feel like I don't know half as much about you."

"You have had dinner with my family. Met my niece. Met my sister. What else do you need to know?"

"Something. Something about you. You said that you married Ashley because you were punishing yourself. To prove something... To prove that you were...bad in some way. I want to understand that. You're angry, Renzo. And I've done my best to ignore that because you've never been angry with me. But I want to know. I want to know what you're angry at. I want to know why you married her. Why marrying me will be different. Why you feel differently about me. I have to. I have to or..."

"You want to know whom I'm angry at?" He pushed himself off the bed, forking his fingers through his hair. "Well, *cara*, there is a very simple answer to that question."

"Give it to me. Give me something."

"Me. I'm angry at me."

CHAPTER THIRTEEN

ESTHER'S HEART RATE was still normalizing, and hearing those words come out of Renzo's mouth made it tumble over into a strange gear again. She wasn't sure what she had expected when she had demanded that he share something of himself.

Denial, she supposed. Because he was such a closed door she imagined she would have to kick at it more than once in order to get it open.

And so, she was suspicious. She had been growing more and more suspicious ever since their time together in New York. That there was more than he was saying. But he wasn't being as honest or as open as he appeared to be.

She was naive. She knew that. She didn't have experience with men or with romantic relationships, and she knew that it was entirely possible some of her feelings were heightened because of the fact that they were sleeping together.

Except, he hadn't touched her between that first night and tonight. He had been much more careful than she would have liked him to be. Giving her more space than she ever would have asked for.

And in that time all of the tender feelings around her heart hadn't eased. In fact, they had only grown more intense. She knew that there were all kinds of reasons that she might feel something for him that wasn't strictly real.

But with just as much certainty, she knew it was real.

She just wanted it to be real for him, too. She needed to be sure. She had to know. And in order to know, she had to know him.

"Why?" she asked. "Why are you angry at yourself?"

"I wasn't born a debauched playboy. I think that's the place to begin. I was once very sincere, and I believed deeply in love. Though, I perhaps did so in a misguided fashion. But I want to say that so you know I didn't toy with another man's wife as a matter of my own amusement."

Her heart squeezed tight. Another man's wife. If there was a more serious offense she'd heard of in all her growing-up years, she could hardly remember it. Marriage was meant to be sacred. And a man's wife was his. Logically, she knew now that women weren't property, even if they were married. But still, marriage vows were sacred.

"Oh, Renzo... You..."

"It isn't a good story. But then, most origin stories aren't. The man you know isn't one of honor, so you must know that my beginnings were never going to be honorable."

"Don't say things like that. You have honor. Of course you do. Look at everything you're doing to make a life for your children."

"Yes," he said, his tone going utterly flat. "But you have to understand that that need doesn't come from a void. It was born of something. Everything is created. Everyone is created by a defining event. Something that changes you just enough, twists you in your own particular way. You know something about that."

"Yes," she said, thinking of her family.

"My parents care about me. I grew up in privilege. But I made a mistake. I fell in love with the wrong woman. A married woman. She was…my first. My first lover. My first love." He paused, swallowing hard, a muscle in his jaw jumping. "The mother of my child."

Esther felt as though the bottom had fallen away from the bed. She felt as though the bottom had fallen away from the world. She couldn't fathom what he was saying. What he meant. "Your child? But you don't have…"

"Not legally. No. I signed away my parental rights. I have no child. Not as far as the court systems are concerned. Genetically, however, is another matter."

She put her hand to her chest, as if that might do something to still her shattering heartbeat. "Tell me," she said, "tell me everything. How old were you?"

"I was sixteen. And it was agreed there was absolutely no point in a man like me—a boy like me—breaking up a family so that I could… Raise a child? How could I do such a thing? I was nothing more than a child myself. It would be laughable to even think it."

Slowly, realization dawned on her. "That's what you meant. Proving that you were bad. That's why."

"A bit melodramatic, perhaps. But since self-destruction is so much fun, how can I pass up the chance to prove I had no other option? And really, if you look at all of my exploits, how could you possibly believe that I would make a good father?"

"But you will," she said, her tone fierce. "Look at everything you're doing for these children."

He laughed, a bitter sound. "Yes. I'm willing to do anything for these children. Because it is a wound…" His voice broke. "I did what I had to do. I did what I had to do," he said again, as though he were reinforcing it even to himself. "You do not heal from this. You can't. Especially not when…I see her."

"Your ex?"

"No," he said, "I have no lingering feelings for that woman. No attachment to her. I could see her every day and it would make absolutely no difference. But Samantha… My daughter. To watch her grow up across ball-rooms, knowing that I can never make contact with her… It is like being stabbed in the same place repeatedly. With no end in sight. The pain never goes away, the wound never heals. There is no chance."

Pain lanced her, for him, for all that he'd been through. For what he still continued to go through, this man who would so obviously sacrifice everything for the love of the children she carried. This man who was already a father, and unable to be with his daughter.

"How old is she?"

"Sixteen," he said. "The same age I was when she was born."

"So," she said, "she's nearly an adult. If you wanted to…"

"And destroy her life? Her view of herself? Her father, her mother, everything? Revealing that she's my child would decimate her entire existence. She has siblings."

"Does her… Does the man who raised her know that she isn't his?"

"I would be surprised if he didn't. I doubt very much he and his wife were ever faithful to each other."

"How did she know it was yours?"

"Jillian had a test done. Mostly because she wanted to make sure it was something I wouldn't contest later. She wanted to know everything. Wanted to make sure that she could protect her marriage. Protect her existing children."

It all made a horrible kind of sense. That it was a situation bound to create casualties. And the solution they had come up with perhaps left the least amount of destruction in its wake. Except when it came to Renzo. As he spoke about it she could see that he had been destroyed entirely over it. That he continued to be destroyed daily.

"You're her father," she said.

He began to pace the length of the room, all restless muscle in the dim light, leashed strength. And she realized it was him all over. Power that he could not wield to its fullest degree. Strength that was impotent in the face of the situation that had been created.

He was a powerful man. He was a wealthy man. But agreements aside, he couldn't go bursting into his daughter's life without destroying the balance. And it was more loving, more gracious, more everything for him to simply stand back and allow himself to bleed so that she never would.

If she hadn't been absolutely certain that she loved him before, this confirmed it. All of her earlier bad feelings about him being with a married woman sort of evaporated. Because he'd made a mistake, but it wasn't who he was.

Except, it had come to define him. Because the consequence was so permanent.

She couldn't continue to punish him by holding it against him. She couldn't hold any of this against him. She looked at him and she saw the man she was determined to make a life with. A man who was angry, injured, broken beyond anything she could possibly understand.

What could she offer him?

"I am not her father in any way that counts," he responded.

"But you are," she said. "You love her. Maybe more than anyone else involved in this, because the only reason that you've never crossed that ballroom and put yourself in her life is that you love her too much to rattle her."

"No," he said, his tone fierce. "It's not love. I can't feel that way anymore. I don't."

Those words hit her like a hammer fall. "But you said… You said you loved me."

"And if it makes you happy I will say it a thousand more times."

"If it makes me *happy*. But… What about if it's not true?"

"I am who I am. What has been done to me… It is done. There is no going back. I cannot go back in time and make a different decision. I can't change what happened. Not me, not her. I can't remake that decision. Don't you understand that? And just like I can't remake that decision, I can't feel things with parts of myself that I burned away. It doesn't work that way. It can't."

"Then why did you tell me that?"

"Have you been listening?" he asked, roaring now, when she had only ever heard him speak in calm command before. There was no sense of calm about him now. It was like watching him unravel in front of her, thread by thread. "I will do anything to keep my children with me. Anything."

"I never threatened to take them. Ever. I wouldn't. I wouldn't do that to you."

"It's more than that. Samantha… She has a family. She has a mother and she has a father. How could I provide less to my children now? What is my excuse? Look what I did. I ruined my life by marrying Ashley. I will not ruin my children's lives. I was making a statement, about my unsuitability, and I nearly swept two innocent children up in that. My own children. Again. Ruined by the selfishness of the adults around them."

She could see it so clearly. The way that he did. That he was somehow building the family that he owed his chil-

dren so he didn't give them less than what his first child
had been given.

He had tried so hard to prove that he wasn't able. To
prove that the right decision had been made, and then he
had been thrust into a situation where he had to prove
himself worthy.

But she had been caught in the crossfire. And understanding it didn't make her any less confused when it came
to her own feelings. It didn't make it hurt less.

"You didn't have to lie to me," she said.

"I did. You made that very clear."

"Renzo…I…I gave myself to you. In a way that I don't
know if I could have if…" She stopped then, because she
knew it wasn't true. It had nothing to do with the way he
felt, the way that she had been with him earlier. It had everything to do with the way that she felt. With how much
she felt for him. But still, she was hurt, she was confused,
and she wanted him to feel even a fraction of that, which
wasn't really fair considering she had a feeling he had been
awash in both from the moment he had found out she was
carrying his children.

And she could see fear in his eyes. Stark, naked. The
fear that somehow, another woman would contrive to take
away what he wanted most in the world. And he might say
he couldn't love, but his actions were not those of a man
who couldn't love.

She knew this was all about love. Deep, unending love
that hurt him every time his heart beat.

If he thought he was doing this out of a lack of love, it
was only because he couldn't see another way to deal with
it. And strangely, she understood that. It was easy to tell
herself that she was staying with him because he said he
loved her. Because she was having these babies.

Far scarier was to admit to herself that it was something

she wanted. To be with him because she cared. Because she was choosing it.

It was one thing to make a distinction between her father and Renzo in theory. And to make a case for signing herself up for something completely different from what she had imagined she would do with her life. To sign on for binding herself to a man who certainly had his own agenda and his own idea about things.

Because he had lied to her. And what if she was just walking into the same kind of thing again? To living a life dictated by somebody else. That scared her. But maybe… Maybe love was always scary.

Maybe it was a risk, and it was one that came with sacrifice, with cost.

That thought made her feel panic. She had sacrificed so much. To stay with her family as long as she had, she had ignored so much of herself that she wanted to explore. She had tried so hard to be everything her mother and father had wanted her to be.

And leaving… If leaving her siblings had been painful, just thinking about what might happen if she was forced to leave these children made her insides ache.

Renzo was a rock wall. And she was just so very soft and breakable, no matter how much she might want to fling herself against him and see if she could force a crack. Force a change.

To see if she could get to what she suspected was behind it.

But how could she do that if not even he would admit that it was there? If not even he seemed to know?

"I didn't mean to hurt you," he said. "But I'm never going to love you the way that you seem to want me to. But that doesn't mean I won't be a faithful husband. I was a faithful husband to Ashley in spite of the fact that she wasn't faithful to me. If you need a demonstration, I will even marry you here. In Italy. Where divorce will be difficult to achieve."

All of these promises, all of these things, she recognized as things that benefited him more than they did her. At the end of the day, if there was ever any genetic testing done, a judge would find that the children didn't belong to her. And then what?

Everything had changed so much in the past few weeks. Her life looked like an entirely different one from what she had imagined she would make for herself.

Had it been only four months since she had imagined that she would do the surrogacy and then walk away? That she would go on to go to school and visit exotic places, and do all of these things she had dreamed about without ever once thinking about the children she had given birth to again? Without ever once thinking of Renzo again. She knew now that none of that was possible.

She had trapped herself. Utterly and completely.

Out of the frying pan and into the fire. She couldn't even decide if she wanted out of the fire.

"You did hurt me," she said, choosing to ignore what he'd said about marriage and divorce, forcing him to discuss the lie. The lie that was, by seconds, growing bigger and bigger inside her.

Because it had been the difference. The difference between captivity and a relationship. The difference between a controlling, autocratic man and a caring, invested man.

Yes, in all of those scenarios he had done the same things, but if he did them from a position of love, if he did them out of caring for her, caring for the babies, it was different from simply wanting to make his life easier.

"That wasn't my intention. It doesn't have to change

things between us. You want me." He moved nearer to her, his fingertips brushing over her cheekbone, and much to her eternal humiliation, a shiver of need worked its way through her.

"It's not enough." She jerked away from him, shrinking back toward the headboard.

"Why not?" he asked, his tone fraying.

"I want you to be with me," she said, speaking slowly, trying to figure out a way to articulate what she was feeling, not just to him but to herself. "I want you to be with me because it makes me feel stronger. It makes me feel weaker. Because you make me want things I didn't even know a person could want. Because you make my body hum and my heart beat faster." She closed her eyes. "I thought I knew what I wanted. I thought I knew what I needed. Then I met you and I had to question all of it. I met you and looked at your eyes and found I couldn't move. Found that I didn't even want to. It's not convenient for me, Renzo. Nothing about this is. I don't want you because it makes my life easier. I don't want you because of everything you can give me, but because of all the little ways you have changed me. Because you hollowed me out and created a need that I didn't know existed before. And none of it's convenient. Not in the least. But it's that lack of convenience that makes me so sure it's real."

"But why does it matter?" he asked again. "We can be happy here. You can feel all of those things. We will be together, this whole family will be together."

"What do you feel when you touch me?"

"I want to have you."

Her throat tightened. "And when you think of me leaving you?"

He closed the space between them then, grabbing hold

of her arms and holding on to her tightly. "You won't. I want to keep you."

She reached up, brushing her fingertips over his cheek lightly. "And that's the difference. You want to keep me because it makes your life more the picture that you want. Because it's good for a man to have a wife, for his children to have a mother. But don't you understand, that's the exact reason my father wanted me to stay. The reason that he treated his children the way he did. Because he needed that picture. That perfect picture. Because it was about the way it made everyone look at him. About wanting to possess a perfect image." She swallowed hard. "I can't be someone else's trophy. I can't be the evidence of their perfect life lived. Not again. Not when it took so much strength to leave it the first time. Because if you're only telling me you love me to make me happy, then it's just more control."

"That isn't fair," he ground out. "I'm not talking about denying you anything. I'm not hiding the world from you. I have promised you an education. I have promised to show you all of life. All that the world has to offer."

"I know. I do…"

"Am I a selfish lover?"

Her cheeks heated. "No. Of course you aren't."

"How dare you compare me to the man who spent your life controlling you. It is different. It is different to come to an understanding based on mutual convenience, mutual attraction."

She lay down, letting misery overtake her, drawing her knees up to her chest and turning away from Renzo. "I need space," she said, feeling like her head was teeming with noise. She wasn't sure she'd ever be able to cut through it.

"I will see you at breakfast," he said, his tone hard.

She listened for him to leave the room. Didn't move again until she heard the door to his room close down the hall. And then she let the first sob rack her body.

She felt raw. Deceived. She felt foolish, because she had done exactly what inexperienced women did. She had believed him when he'd said he loved her, and she had used it as a shield. That lie had made her feel impenetrable. Had made her feel as though she could do anything, be anything.

And now, she just felt like a fool.

There was also something gnawing at the back of her mind. About the comparison she had made between Renzo and her father. About her life spent in the commune, and the month she had spent here.

She had known she wanted to escape that life. She had always felt like her home was a prison. She didn't feel that now, and she didn't know what that said about her. She wasn't even sure she cared.

She made a low, miserable sound and buried her face in her pillow. She didn't want to leave him. It didn't matter that he said he didn't love her. She wanted to be here. Wanted to be with him.

It had nothing to do with what he felt, and everything to do with what she felt. Her love wasn't a lie. Even his admission hadn't shaken it.

But it still confused her. Still made her feel like she had to do something, had to change something. To avoid becoming the sad, controlled creature she had once been.

"I don't want to," she said into the stillness of the room, a tear sliding down her cheek. She wanted to stay here with him. She wanted to make a life with him, and their children. She wanted him to have what he craved.

But for how long? How long would it take for her to start to feel smothered again?

What had felt like absolute freedom before felt like prison now. And regardless of her confused feelings on whether or not she wanted to leave, she felt trapped now when before she had felt liberated.

It was so easy to see the difference. Love. Love was the difference.

Knowing Renzo didn't love her, knowing that he never could, made all the difference to her.

CHAPTER FOURTEEN

RENZO SLEPT LIKE absolute hell. He felt every inch like the ass that he was. The things he had said to Esther. The way that he had hurt her. He had lied to her, it was true. Everything he had been through surrounding the loss of Samantha had done something to him. Changed him. If he had emerged from it with an edge of ruthlessness, no one could blame him.

Because he had been involved in a situation where he had allowed others to dictate things for him. But he resisted that now, more than anything. Resisted allowing anyone or anything to have the upper hand when he needed it at all times.

Still, Esther had not deserved his lies. If there was anyone truly good and sweet in the world, it was her. Anyone who had already been badly used by controlling men.

He slammed his cup of coffee down on the table and turned, seeing her standing at the bottom of the stairs. "Good morning," he said.

"Good morning," she said, shifting. And that was when he noticed her backpack.

She was back in her old clothes, too. Wearing a tight black tank top and the long flowing skirt, her stomach so much rounder than it had been when he'd first met her.

And he knew. Just what she was doing.

"You cannot leave," he said, his voice like shattered glass in the still surroundings.

"I have to," she said. "I'm not leaving town. I promise. But I can't stay here with you. Not while I'm so confused. I don't know what's going to happen between us, and I don't know…I don't know how I feel. I can't sit here where I'm comfortable, where I'm close to you, and think straight. And I owe myself the chance to think straight."

He was dimly aware of crossing the space between them, of taking her in his arms, much more roughly than he might have done if he were thinking straight. "You cannot leave me."

"I can. And I need to. Please, you have to understand."

He took hold of her wrists, backing her against the wall and pinning her there, looking deep into her eyes because she had said once that his looking at her had changed something. He needed to change it now. Needed to immobilize her now. Needed to stop her from leaving him.

"You can't go," he said again, more forcefully this time.

"Renzo," she said, "you can't keep me here. You don't want a prisoner. Mostly because you know that I've been one. You wouldn't do that to me, not again."

Desperation clawed him like an animal. In this moment, he was unsure if there was a limit to what he would do. Because he was about to watch his entire life, his future, walk out the door and away from him. "How can you do this to me?" he asked. "You know my past. You know what I have lost. I entrusted that secret to you. No one knows. My sister doesn't even know. And I told you."

"I will never take your children from you. I told you that already. I'm not going to take your chance to be a father. But…I don't believe that the two of us living together without love is going to give them a better childhood. I just don't. I grew up in a house that didn't have love. Where all of the relationships were so…unhealthy. And filled with control. It isn't going to help your children to live that way."

"Is the real issue that you want to leave? That you want to walk away? That you don't want to deal with this thing between us?"

"No."

"You feel your life will be hampered by raising children. You don't actually want the babies." That would almost make it easier. Because he would not expose children to her indifference. Though, he could not imagine Esther expressing indifference toward a puppy, much less a baby.

"This is about you and me," she said, pressing her hand to his face. She didn't struggle against his hold. She simply touched him, gently, with a kind of deep emotion he could not recall anyone ever pouring out over his skin. "About what we're supposed to be. That's all. I can't marry you. Not like this. I can't sign on to a life of being unloved."

She began to move away from him then, and he tightened his hold on her, desperation like a feral creature inside him.

"I love you," he ground out, the words coming from deep within his soul.

Suddenly, he was overcome by a sensation that all of the blood had drained from his head. That he couldn't breathe. That he might fall to the ground, black out, lose consciousness. And he was forced to come to the conclusion that it was because it was true.

That for the first time in his memory he loved a person standing in front of him more than the breath in his own body. That he loved her, in spite of his best efforts not to.

"I love you," he said again, desperation making it sharp.

"Renzo," she said, taking a step back. And he let her. "Don't do this to me. Don't lie to me. Don't use my feelings against me."

"I'm not," he said. "This is the truth."

"You already told me that you would tell me you loved me a thousand times if it would make me happy. I imagine you would say it a thousand more if you thought it would help you get your way. But I can't live that way. I won't."

"I won't live without you," he said, those words making her pause.

She turned back to face him. "When you can tell me what has changed because you love me, when you can prove to me that this isn't just another lie. When you can prove to me this isn't just you trying to keep ownership... Then you come find me. I'm going back to the bar. I'm going back to the hostel."

Then suddenly he was driven by the impulse to hurt. The wound as bad as if he was being injured. To make her bleed, because he damn sure was. "Run away, then. And tell yourself whatever story you need to tell yourself. About your bid for freedom. But this is just more of the same selfishness you showed when you left your family," he spat. "If somebody doesn't love you in exactly the way you wish them to, you don't recognize it. And you say it isn't real. Isn't that the same as your father? You accuse me of being selfish, Esther, but at least I took you at face value. You will not do the same for me."

She flinched, and he could tell that the words had hit their mark. That they had struck her in a place where her fear lived. Fear that what he said might be true.

"Maybe you're right. Except, I never lied to you. So maybe this is the one thing you'll never be able to get over, maybe this is my betrayal to you that you won't be able to let go. But yours was the first lie. How will I ever know if the words that come out of your mouth are real? How? You told me you loved me without flinching the first time. And then you told me it was all a lie, and now you ask me to believe that this is true. You ask impossible things of me, Renzo. I just wanted to see the world." She wiped at a tear that had fallen down her cheek. "I just wanted to go to a university and find myself. I didn't want to be broken. Not again. And that's what you've done. So now I have to go put myself back together again, and if you can come to me and show me, then please do. But if not… Leave me alone. I'll keep you informed about the doctor's appointments."

She moved to the door, holding on to her backpack tightly. "Goodbye, Renzo."

And then she was gone. And for the second time in his life Renzo felt like he was watching his entire future slip through his fingers. For the second time, he felt powerless to do anything about it.

When Renzo went to visit his father later that day, he was full of violent rage. Ever since Esther had walked out of his home, he had been angry, growing angrier. Ever since she had left him, the fire of rage had been burning hotter and hotter in the pit of his stomach.

It had fueled him, spurred him with a kind of restless energy that he couldn't control. And it had brought him here. His parents' home.

He walked into his father's office without knocking.

"Renzo," his father said, without looking up. "What brings you here?"

"I have something to tell you," Renzo said.

"I do hope that you've already married that woman. Because I would hate to hear that things had gone awry."

"Oh, it's gone awry. The entire thing is damn well sideways."

"Do you need me to intervene? Is that it? God knows it's what I did when your last youthful indiscretion—"

"My youthful indiscretion? You mean my daughter? My

daughter I'm not allowed to see, because you, mother and Jillian decided that it would be better that way?"

"As if you didn't believe the same. You were sixteen years old. You couldn't have raised the child. Your behavior over the last several years has proved as much."

His father said that as though it were accidental. As though it never occurred to him that Renzo had perhaps engineered his behavior around proving that very thing. But then, he supposed he couldn't blame his father for that. Not even Renzo had fully realized that until recently. Until he'd been forced to change what he was, what he wanted, so that he could seize the opportunity to be a father this time around.

"There is nothing youthful about this indiscretion," Renzo said. "I am not a child. I'm a man in his thirties. And beyond that, the situation is not as it appears."

"What is going on?"

"It's Ashley. Ashley struck up an agreement with Esther. Esther agreed to carry my children as a surrogate. Of course, I was not consulted about any of this. And then when Ashley decided that the pregnancy was not going to preserve our marriage, she contacted Esther and asked that Esther have the pregnancy terminated. She didn't want to do that. Instead, she came to me." He rubbed his hand over his face. "I lost one child, and I was bound and determined to hold on to this one. To these two," he amended, an arrow hitting him in the heart as he thought of his twins. "I was also determined to do as you said. To prevent any other scandal. Anything that might come back and hurt them. I was not going to allow my brother-in-law to get control of the company, not when it's the rightful inheritance of my children. As much as you might have hoped you were appealing to my selfishness, believe me when I say you were simply appealing to my desire to give my children everything they deserve this time around."

"I cannot believe this. It isn't true. Such a thing isn't even legal in this country."

"There are ways to circumvent legality, as I'm sure you know. But now I have ruined everything with Esther. And I have done so in part because I was letting you control things again."

"You say all of this as though you're angry about what I did back then."

"I am. I damn well am. I was sixteen, I didn't know. I didn't know what I would feel. Every time I look across the room I see her. Every time. It is like being stabbed straight through the heart. I cannot forgive myself for the decision that I made then. I cannot forgive you for the part that you played in it."

His father pounded his fist down on his desk. "That feeling that you have I have for you. Magnified with an intensity that you cannot possibly imagine. Because I raised you. Because you are the heir to everything that I have worked so hard to build. My hope is placed in you, Renzo. You are everything to me in more ways than you can know. I did what I had to do to protect you, and if I have earned your anger then I accept that. But I would not change what I did."

His father's words struck him hard. Along with the realization that while he could understand why the decision had been made, he still wished he could change it.

"Do you not think it hurts me?" his father asked, his voice rough. "Because I see her, too. She is my granddaughter. And especially since your sister had Sophia, I feel that loss. The loss of my first grandchild that I cannot acknowledge."

"But it was not as important to you as protecting the family reputation."

"The greater good," he said. "And it so happened that it also protected her mother's marriage. That entire family. You cannot claim that I am so selfish, Renzo."

"Still, you wanted me to marry Esther to preserve your reputation. I imagine you want to keep the circumstances around the conception of the babies a secret, as well."

"Do you suggest that putting all of it out in the open is for the best? What about the reputation of the Valenti family?"

"I don't know," he said, tapping the back of the chair that was placed in front of his father's desk. "I don't know. But I cannot protect the reputation of the Valentis. Not at the expense of my own life. Not at the expense of the people I love."

"And the love of your parents? Does that not figure into this at all?"

"You can protect yourself, Father. I think you're more than able. My children cannot. They are helpless. They are depending on me to make the right choice."

"And you think bringing them into the world under a cloud of scandal is the right thing to do?"

"I am tired of lies. I am tired of living a life built on a monument to the one thing I can never acknowledge. The one person I will always love that I can never acknowledge. I am tired of living in an existence that is an unholy altar to my failures. Confirmation that I had no other choice. No other choice but to give up Samantha when I did. And perhaps then it was true. But I have choices now. And perhaps I will humiliate myself. Perhaps I will humiliate our family. But if I have to do that to win back the woman I love, if I have to stop protecting myself in every way in order to prove my vulnerability, then I will do it. If the perfect reputation of our family is a casualty, then I accept it. But I will not be a slave to it." He let out a harsh breath, Esther, her lie, her story on his mind. "I can't control everything. I'll only end up breaking everything I care about."

"I did what I had to do," his father said. "I counseled you the way that I had to. I am the patriarch of this family, Renzo. Protecting it is my highest calling."

"Perhaps that is the problem. And where we have reached an impasse. Because I am the patriarch of my family. My family, which is Esther and the children she's carrying. I lost her. I lied to her, and I told her I could never love her. I was afraid, afraid because I could not subject myself to the kind of pain that I went through, the kind of pain I continually go through, where Samantha is concerned. But all I've done is made it worse. And I'm going to fix it. No matter what."

He turned, getting ready to walk out of the office. He stopped when his father spoke.

"Renzo. I might not agree with the decision you're making, but I do want you to know that I understand I can't protect you now. Moreover, that you don't need me to. You're a man now, a man who has understandable anger directed at me. I only hope that someday you will forgive me."

Renzo let out a hard breath, and he thought of something else Esther had said. About how she'd had to let go of the past to truly move forward.

He had one foot firmly in the past, and it had nearly ruined everything. He had to start walking forward. Forward to Esther.

"I imagine," he said, "that will all depend on what happens next."

CHAPTER FIFTEEN

ESTHER FELT DRAINED. Emotionally, physically. Going back to work at the bar was difficult now. Her stomach was bigger, her ankles were bigger, her fatigue was bigger. Plus, all she wanted to do was crawl underneath the bar and cry for the entire shift, because something inside her felt fundamentally broken since she'd walked away from Renzo.

It was oppressively humid tonight. And hot. Clouds had rolled in, and she had a feeling there was going to be a late-evening thunderstorm, the impending rain adding to the heaviness in the atmosphere. Adding to the heaviness in her heart.

She looked outside and saw drops begin to pound the cobbled sidewalk. Great. Walking home was going to be fun. All of her clothes would be stuck to her skin. Then she would spend the rest of the evening shivering, because the showers in the hostel never had enough hot water to get rid of a chill like this once it soaked into her bones.

A flash of lightning split the sky, and she jumped a little bit. "Esther?"

She turned and saw her boss, who was gesturing madly at the tables outside. She knew that he wanted her to bring in the seat covers. "Okay," she said.

She hurried outside, not bothering to put on a sweater or anything. The air was still warm, but the drops falling from the sky were big and aggressively cold. She hunched over, taking hold of the cushions, collecting them beneath her arm.

Suddenly, the back of her neck prickled and she straightened slowly. Another flash of lightning washed out the scene around her, and that was when she saw him. Renzo, standing there in a suit just as he had done that first night he had come to the bar.

He was standing in a suit, in the rain, water pouring down over him, his hands in his pockets, his dark eyes trained on her.

"What are you doing here?" she asked, the cushions suddenly tumbling from her arms. She hadn't even realized she had released her hold on them.

It was the same as it had always been. From the beginning. Those dark eyes rooting her to the spot, her entire world shifting around her, shifting around him.

Everything changed, even the air. If he had brought the thunderstorm with him, she wouldn't be surprised.

"I came to see you. You told me to come and find you when I was ready. When I was ready to prove this to you. To prove my love. And I am. Trust me, I was tempted to hold a press conference before I came to see you, but I did feel like I should talk to you first. Not for me. But for you."

"A press conference? What kind of press conference?"

"To explain. Everything. The surrogacy… Everything. Because, I thought maybe if I didn't have a reputation to protect anymore you wouldn't be able to accuse me of being motivated by it."

"I…I suppose it's easy for me to say when nobody is interested in me or my life. At least, not apart from you."

"Don't excuse yourself," he said, "not now. You were right about me. It was all about doing something that suited me, and I want to make sure that this no longer does. I want to make sure that I'm no longer doing everything with a view of creating a smooth facade over my life. All of that… It is the reason that I am the way I am now. And my dedication to it was to justify my earlier actions. But no more. I am prepared to go public with our story. To let everyone know that you are a surrogate, and that I was fooled by my ex-wife."

"But what about all the legality?"

He took a deep breath. "That's why I didn't have the press conference. I was afraid that you would be concerned I was using it to lessen your claim on the babies. That I was using it to try to make sure you didn't have a place in their life. So you see, even with the desire to enact a grand gesture, I'm somewhat hampered by the fact that I have an unequal amount of power here." He shook his head. "But only on the outside. Inside… Inside I'm trembling. Because I don't know how to make you believe me. Because I haven't earned the right to have you do it."

He moved closer to her, and she watched him come. The rain pelted her skin, her clothes completely plastered to her body. She didn't care. "My father told me that I had to make sure everything went right this time. That I had to keep the family together or he was going to take my inheritance from me. I understand that only puts another nail in the coffin of my sincerity, but please understand that in part I was motivated by the desire to keep all of the inheritance for my children."

"So, your father told you to marry me."

He nodded. "Yes, and it was the thing that pushed me to make it real. And then that first night we were together, I saw Samantha. And I knew… Whatever I had to do I would do it. Including lie to you. And that's the hardest thing, Esther. It is the hardest thing to come back from, because you know me. You know that I would do anything for my children. And I have proved to you that I'm willing to lie. But I thought for certain that I had already experienced the lowest moments life had to offer. How could I not? I watched my child grow up a stranger to me. But I was wrong. There is lower."

She hurt for him. Physically hurt. But she found that she needed to hear it. Needed to hear about the pain he'd been through, because he had hurt her so profoundly. "What was it?"

"Telling you that I loved you, knowing that it was true this time, and knowing there was nothing I could do to convince you. Knowing that I had destroyed that chance already. That I had taken something beautiful, wonderful—love and the ability to feel it—and turned it into a farce. That I had finally found that feeling and myself again, and that I wanted it, and that I had destroyed any chance of getting it in return."

She couldn't take it anymore. She couldn't hold back. She moved to him, wrapping her arms around him, letting the rain pelt them both, washing away all of the hurt that was between them. "I believe you," she said. "I do. And you haven't squandered anything. I love you. And I knew that you could love me. I did. Because the way that you rearranged your life so that you could be a father to these children, the way that you spoke about the pain you felt over Samantha, the way you continue to feel pain because you won't do anything to disturb her, that's love, Renzo. That's real love. Sacrificial love, not controlling love."

"I wanted to pretend that it wasn't there, because it was easier. Admitting that you love someone when you know you can never be with them in the way that you want to be is a terrible fate. I experienced that with Samantha. And then with you."

"I love you. I'm here. You don't have to prove anything

to me. I'm so touched that you were willing to do that, but I think it's probably for the best if we don't make our children a headline."

"Probably so," he said, sliding his hand down her back. "I love you, Esther. And what love has always meant to me has been something distant. From my father it was control. And with my daughter it was a required separation. You asked me what love was, and when it comes to loving someone and being with them, I'm not sure I know. But I want to learn. That is what I can offer you. My willingness to change. To be changed by this thing between us, in more ways than I already have been."

"I suppose that's fair," she said, sniffling. "I don't really know what it is either. All of my life it meant control, too. And I left home looking for something. Freedom. I thought that it would come with travel, with education, with no one to hold me back or tie me down. And that is a kind of freedom. But it's incomplete. I met you, I started to have feelings for you, and it made me ache. It made me want. It wasn't easy. Deciding to be a mother to twins when I had been planning on something else entirely isn't easy. But what I've learned spending these last couple of years alone is that things are easier when you don't care. The more you care the more it costs. We both know that. I would rather care. And I would rather have all of the painful things that go with that so that I can have the real, joyous things that go along with it, too. I would rather do that than drift along easily. And I would rather do it with you."

He cupped her chin, tilting her face up and kissing her, water drops rolling over their skin as he continued to taste her, as he sipped the moisture from her mouth.

"I'm going to get fired," she said.

"Well, it's a good thing you're going to marry a billionaire."

"Arrogant. I didn't say I would marry you. I just said that I loved you."

"I am arrogant. That is part of loving me, you will find."

"Well, I'll probably still eat cereal on the floor. That is part of loving me."

A smile curved his lips. "I want all the parts of loving you. From the flat shoes to the cereal, to the pain in my chest when I think of what it would mean to lose you. I want to teach you about the world, and I want you to teach me how to be a better man. How to be the man you need."

Thunder rolled through the air, through her chest, the bass note that seemed to match the intensity of the love inside her. "Renzo, don't be silly. You're already the man I need. You were, from that first moment I saw you. You're not the man I would have chosen, but you are the one I love. You are the one I needed. I wanted freedom, I wanted to see everything of the world, but believe me when I tell you I have never felt so free than when you're holding me. The world that we create between us is the most beautiful one I could have ever imagined."

"Even when I am overbearing? And impossible?"

She nodded, unable to hold back the smile that stretched her lips wide. "Even then. Because, you see, Mr. Valenti, the thing is I love you. And if you love me then everything else is just window dressing."

"I do love you, Esther. We may have had a strange beginning, but I think we're going to have the happiest ending."

"So do I, Renzo. So do I."

EPILOGUE

IT WAS AN interesting thing, to go from a family where love had been oppressive, to one where it was the very air Esther breathed.

But after five years with Renzo, their twins and two other children, plus nieces and nephews and her in-laws, Esther felt freer than she ever had. Surrounded, and yet liberated.

Renzo's parents were not the easiest people, but they loved him and their grandchildren with a very real ferocity that was irresistible to Esther.

She had become very good friends with her sister-in-law, Allegra, and her husband, Cristian. They had spent many long dinners laughing together while the children played.

The only thing that ever bothered Esther was the fact that she couldn't heal Renzo's every wound. He loved her, he loved their children. And he did it with absolutely no reservation. But still, Esther knew that he wondered about his oldest child, the one he had never gotten to know.

Until, one day a letter came in the mail. From Samantha. Somehow, she had found out about her origins and had decided to contact Renzo. Because she wanted to know her father, the man who had given her up quietly so that her family wouldn't be disturbed.

For Esther, it hadn't been a difficult thing to allow Samantha into their family. It had never even occurred to her to close the door on the daughter who meant so much to her husband. Still, one night after a visit from Samantha, Renzo pulled her into his arms and kissed her.

"Thank you," he said, "thank you so much for accepting her like you have. What we have here is so complete, and I know that adding more to it can be difficult…"

"No," she said, pressing her fingers to his lips. "It isn't difficult. Nothing about loving you has ever been difficult, and seeing you with all the pieces of your heart back in place is the most beautiful gift I could have ever been given."

Her husband's eyes were suspiciously bright when he went to kiss her again. And then he said in a husky voice, "The most beautiful gift I have ever been given was you. Without you, I would have none of this. Without you I would still be a debauched playboy who had absolutely everything except the one thing he needed."

"What's that?"

"Love, Esther. Without you, I would have no love. And with you my life is full of it."

Then he carried her upstairs and proceeded to show her just how little control he had where she was concerned, and just how much he loved her. And Esther never doubted—not once—that Renzo's love was the absolute truth.

* * * * *

A PROPOSAL
FROM THE
ITALIAN COUNT

LUCY GORDON

I dedicate this book to my Italian husband,
Roberto, who taught me so much about Italy,
and whose love inspired me to set
so many books there.

PROLOGUE

'I DID WRONG. I didn't mean to, but I couldn't help it. All in a moment I found that I could be wicked.'

The old man lying on his deathbed spoke weakly, for his strength was fading fast. Vittorio, the young man sitting beside him, grasped his hand and spoke urgently. 'Don't say such things, Papà. You're not wicked. You never could be.'

'Try saying that to George Benton. He was the man I robbed of a million, whose life I ruined, although he never knew it.'

Vittorio rubbed a frantic hand over his eyes and said fiercely, 'But that's impossible. How could he not have known?'

His father's eyes closed and he turned his head, as though too full of despair to say any more. Vittorio rose and went to the window, looking out onto the grounds. They were lavish, extensive, perfectly suited to the Counts of Martelli, their owners for five hundred years.

Franco, the present Count, lay still as his life slipped away. Vittorio knew that his father's mind had often been confused recently. And surely this was merely another example. Yet there was a desperation in the dying man's manner that warned him of something different; something fearful.

'Don't worry about it. Papà,' Vittorio urged, sitting by the bed again. 'It's all in the past.'

'It will never be in the past until it's put right,' the Count murmured. 'We were friends. We'd met here, in Italy, when he came on holiday. We became friends, and when I went to England a few weeks later I visited him. He was younger than me, and that made him fun to be with. We enjoyed a good time, going out for the evening, having a drink, charming women. And we placed a bet. It was just innocent fun—until his gamble paid off! He didn't know. He was too woozy with drink by then. So I cashed in his winnings, then supported him home and put him to bed.'

'What did you do then?' Vittorio asked quietly.

'I'd had the bank draft made out in my name. I did intend to cash it, and pass the money over to George once he was sober, but I fled before he could wake up.'

'And he never suspected?'

'How could he? I never told him about winning. The next day I cashed the draft and returned home to Italy. I never meant to do wrong. I'd just succeeded to the title, but my pleasure was tempered by the discovery of the debt hanging on the estate. Now suddenly I could clear the debt. The world was bright again. It was wonderful to have people showing me respect, calling me Count Martelli.' He managed a wry smile. 'Vittorio—my son—you'll soon know that feeling.'

'Don't, Papà,' Vittorio said with soft violence. 'I don't want you to die.'

The elderly Count squeezed his hand. 'You're a good son. But my time has come.'

'No,' Vittorio said fervently. 'You must stay with me a little longer.'

The thought of losing the father he loved was intolerable. His mother had died giving birth years ago. His father had raised him since then, and together they had been a team, each meaning more to the other than anyone else ever could. Now the man who was the centre of his life was to be snatched from him, and the pain was agonising.

'Fight it, Papà,' he pleaded. 'Another day, another month, another year. I'm not ready to do without you.'

'You won't have to. I'll always be there with you—in your mind, your heart, wherever you choose.'

'I choose to keep you with me in *every* way,' Vittorio whispered.

'My son—my son—there's just one thing I would ask of you.'

'Whatever it is, I'll do it.'

'All these years I've got away with what I did, and now that the end is near—' he shuddered '—I must seize my last chance to make amends—with your help. Promise me—swear.'

'I'll do anything I can. My word.'

'Find Benton. Ask his forgiveness. If he needs money—'

'I'll give him whatever he needs. He'll forgive you and you can rest in peace.'

'Peace? I can no longer remember how that feels.'

'But you will have it, Papà. Wherever you are. I promise.'

'Thank you—thank you.' Franco whispered the words over and over.

Vittorio rose quickly to pull the curtains across the window.

'Don't do that,' his father begged. 'You'll shut out the light.'

'I was afraid the sun was too dazzling for you.'

'It won't be for long.' He gave a sigh. 'Sunlight never lasts. You think it will. You think the light has come into your life for ever. But suddenly it's gone and there's only darkness.'

Vittorio sat down again, taking his father's hands in his. 'Darkness can be fought,' he said. 'I'm going to fight this for you.'

'One day you'll have your own darkness to fight. You

can never tell when it will come, or what will cause it. You must always be ready for what you've never expected. Take care of yourself, my son. Take care—when I'm no longer with you...'

His voice faded.

'But you will always be with me. You must be. Can you hear me? Can you hear me Papà? *Papà!*'

But there was no response. Franco's eyes had finally closed and he lay still.

Vittorio dropped his head against his. 'I promise,' he whispered. 'I gave my word and I'll keep it. Wherever you are—hear me, believe me, and rest in peace.'

CHAPTER ONE

THE WORLD WAS full of light and glamour. Excitedly Jackie danced this way and that, rejoicing in the vision of her beautiful self that appeared in the mirror. Music played in the distance, inviting her into a universe in which she was the heroine.

But abruptly the dream ended. As she opened her eyes the real world fell back into place. The mirror's reflection showed not the luscious beauty of her fantasy but Jackie Benton, a slender young woman with a face that was intelligent, but not beautiful.

She sighed, easing herself out of bed.

Surrounding her was the austere bedroom where she spent every night. By now she had hoped to leave it behind, move to a new home and a more exciting life. But fate had arranged things differently, confining her to Benton's Market—the little shop where she lived and worked.

She'd spent most of her life in the tiny apartment over the shop that her father, George Benton, had started twenty years earlier. He had fought to make it a success, always struggling with money worries, and raising his daughter alone when his wife had left him.

In his last years Jackie had been forced to run the shop alone—something that had given her an unexpected satisfaction.

She was clever and hardworking, able to retain information about all the stock, and produce it at a moment's notice. Something which had at first impressed her father.

'You really remembered all that?' he would exclaim. 'Well done! You're in the right business.'

'I get it from you,' she had reminded him. 'I remember when I was a child there were lots of times you made people gulp at what you could remember without having to look it up.'

It had been a happy moment, uniting father and daughter. He had been proud—not only of her memory but her ability to choose the best stock. Knowing this, she had felt her confidence grow, and she had begun to see herself as a serious businesswoman.

Just occasionally her father had given her a little warning advice. Once, when a temporary employee had flounced out in a temper, he'd said, 'Did you have to be so hard on him?'

'I wasn't hard on him,' she'd protested. 'I just pointed out that he'd got something wrong. And he had.'

'You might have been a bit more tactful.'

'Oh, come on, Daddy,' she had said, in a teasing voice. 'What you mean is that a woman mustn't tell a man that he's wrong in case he's offended. But we're not living in the nineteenth century.'

He'd patted her hand. '*You* may not be, darling, but a lot of men are. You're a bit too fond of giving orders.'

'Too fond for a woman, you mean? You think I should just go along with him? Even when I know he's an idiot?'

They had laughed fondly together, but she'd come to understand that he had been making a fair point. She had learned to speak with more care, but it was still exasperating to have to do so when she knew she was an expert.

She had gradually come to enjoy the feeling of being in command—not merely of their employees but of the whole running of the place. She had chosen stock and it sold well. She'd had the instincts of a talented businesswoman, and they had given her hope for the future.

But her hard work had come too late. Matters had started

getting worse, owing to the mountain of her father's debts that had piled so high that even her commercial success could not completely deal with it. Finally her father had been forced to sell the shop.

By then his life had been drawing to a close. Rik, the new owner, had reluctantly allowed them to stay in the little apartment upstairs, and Jackie had continued to work in the shop—but only part-time, so that she could always hurry upstairs to check that her father was all right. She nursed him gladly, giving him everything in her power in return for the loving care he had always shown her.

'It's so hard for you…to be caring for me and working downstairs as well,' he had said once. 'Such a burden.'

'Stop it, Dad. You could never be a burden to me. *Never.*'

'Bless you, darling. I wanted to leave the shop to you. I'd have been proud to give you a legacy. I hoped once— But there. It just didn't work out.'

She would have loved to own the shop. So much of its success was due to *her* work, and it still held the atmosphere created by her beloved father. But she had known she must abandon that dream.

Her father had died a few days later. And then Rik had offered her a lifeline.

'You're welcome to stay if you become full-time. You can go on living here.'

She'd thought carefully before agreeing. She disliked Rik— an ill-tempered man in his forties—But she had accepted the job because it would give her a little time to work out her plan to escape into a new life—one in which she would have her own business, organising everything, using the talents she'd so gladly discovered.

Her dislike of Rik was well-founded. He had a high opinion of his own knowledge and skills, but Jackie felt that he actually knew very little. He made silly mistakes for which he blamed *her.*

She had tried to save money, hoping that soon she would be able to afford to leave and explore new possibilities. But it had been a hopeless task. Following George's death had come the discovery of more debts that he hadn't managed to pay, even with the money he'd made from selling the shop. Her savings had soon been swallowed up by them. And she had no hope of saving much more, given the meanly low pay Rik allowed her.

'I give you a fair wage,' he would say. 'You live here for nothing. If you worked somewhere else you'd have to pay for accommodation.'

It was true. Frantically she had hunted for another job, but hadn't been able to find one that paid enough to solve the problem. Now she felt trapped, and with no obvious way out she just had to hope for a miracle!

She showered and dressed carefully. She presented a picture of efficiency—ideal for the work that consumed her life—but her looks didn't please her. She considered herself far too plain.

She opened her laptop and logged on to her bank to check the state of her account. The result made her groan with despair. She had very little money, despite her attempts to live frugally.

Dispirited, she opened an astrology website, and read her prediction.

The fates are planning a startling new beginning for you. The sun in Jupiter will bring things you never anticipated, and decisions that will change your life.

In her dreams, she thought wryly. Last week it had said she was going to be a millionaire. And look how *that* had turned out.

She read the prediction again, trying to see it as the approach of the miracle she longed for, and then hurried downstairs and opened up the shop. She served a couple of customers, then spent some time looking around.

The shop had a variety of stock, including home wares and groceries. She often wished she could persuade Rik to show a little more imagination about the stock. But he had no sympathy for her ideas.

'This is a practical place, full of practical items,' he'd once told her sternly. 'You're too fanciful, Jackie. That's your trouble. You want life to be fun, and it isn't designed that way.'

'Not always fun,' she'd protested. 'Just a little bit of excitement now and then. I remember Daddy felt the same.'

'You father spent too much time looking for fun. It was his ruin.'

'*Something* ruined him…' She'd sighed. 'But I don't think it was that.'

'Get on with your work and stop wasting time.'

On the flight from Rome to London, Vittorio sat sunk in thought, wondering where the search for George Benton would finally lead him. Common sense told him he need not search at all. If he simply refused, who would ever know?

But his conscience would know. His promise had brought his father peace in his final moments. If he broke his word the knowledge would be with him for ever. And somewhere in his heart he sensed that his father's reproaches would always haunt him.

Everything had changed with Franco's death. He'd spoken of the pleasures of being Count Martelli, and Vittorio had soon discovered that it was true. The first time someone addressed him as 'Signor Conte' he had hardly been able to believe he'd heard correctly. His employees now treated him with deference, almost awe.

But his father had also spoken of other things—of the

hidden problems behind the glamour, that the rest of the world knew nothing about. And here, too, he had been right.

Vittorio had gone through Franco's things, seeking clues about his father's past life and George Benton. He'd found a photograph of the two men together, which must have been taken during their meeting in England many years before.

How old would Benton be now? Middle-aged? At the height of his powers? Ready to take revenge on the family that had cheated him out of a fortune? He wasn't looking forward to their meeting, but there was no choice.

Franco's papers had also included a newspaper cutting, mentioning a shop called Benton's Market. There was a picture of a small, shabby-looking shop, and one of George Benton, looking older than in the other picture.

That was Vittorio's clue. He had a lead.

At the airport he hired a taxi and spent the journey studying a map of London. The area he sought was just north of the River Thames in the east of the city. As they approached the area Vittorio asked the driver, 'Is there a hotel near here?'

'There's one just around the corner. Mind you, it costs a lot.'

'Fine. Take me there.'

The hotel was pleasantly luxurious. He booked a room for the night, then went out to explore.

Almost at once he saw a corner shop with its sign proclaiming 'Benton's Market'. He took a deep breath, clenching his fists, vowing not to lose his nerve now.

Nearby was a small café, with tables outside. He found a seat, ordered some coffee and took out the photograph of Benton. From this angle he could see through the shop windows clearly enough to know if the man was there.

But time passed and there was no sign of him—only a young woman arranging stock in the main window. Much of it was already in place, but she was intent on reorganis-ing it, giving it all her concentration.

He admired the woman's dedication and artistic flair. He would value such an employee himself, to work in the department store he owned and managed in Rome.

Suddenly he tensed as a man appeared from the rear of the shop. Could this be Benton? But he looked nothing like the picture. His face was thin and severe. His manner to the woman suggested ill temper. When he spoke Vit-torio could just make out the words through the open door.

'*Must* you waste time faffing about over this? There's a pile of stuff at the back needs unpacking.'

'But I thought we agreed—' she began to say.

'Don't argue. Just do as I tell you. Get going.'

Looking exasperated, she retreated to the back of the shop.

Vittorio approached the shop, entering with the air of an eager customer.

'I'd like to buy some apples,' he said.

'We've got some here,' the man said. 'No—wait. They *were* over there. What has that stupid woman done with them?'

'I'd also like to talk to Mr Benton, please.'

The man glanced up, scowling. 'What do you want with him?' His tone became suspicious. 'You're not another debt collector, are you?'

'No, it's a personal matter.'

'Well, you can't see him. He's dead.'

'Dead?' Vittorio froze, feeling as though he'd heard a thunderclap. 'When?'

'A year ago. But his daughter still works here.'

'Was that her I saw? Can I talk to her?'

'You can, but not just yet. She's got work to do. You'll have to wait until she's finished for the day.'

Feeling depressed, Vittorio departed. Returning to the

café he settled again to watch the shop, trying to get his thoughts in order. Everything he'd planned was in a shambles. He must talk to Benton's daughter and just hope that she was a sensible woman who would accept financial compensation and let the matter end.

Throughout the afternoon he saw many customers go into the shop. The young woman dealt with them efficiently, always smiling and friendly. Every one of them bought something from her.

Benton's daughter was a natural saleswoman, it seemed.

He stayed there for four hours. He read the paper and then busied himself sending and receiving emails from his smartphone. The frustration of waiting was hard to endure but he forced himself. So much depended on this.

Inside the shop Jackie was working hard. Often she glanced out of the window, puzzled to see that the strange man was still there, sitting outside the café. She concluded that he must be a tourist, albeit a very well dressed one!

At last it was closing time. As she was preparing to leave, Rik arrived.

'Don't go yet,' he said, scowling. 'We need to have a talk about making new orders.'

'But I can't stay,' she protested. She gave him a wry smile, saying, 'And, let's face it, you don't pay me enough to make me want to do overtime.'

'Don't be impertinent. I pay you a fair wage. If you did better I might pay you more.'

'It's not *my* fault profits are low,' she said indignantly. 'I don't think you're buying enough of the right stock.'

'And *I* don't think you're making a big enough effort,' he said coldly.

In his anger he spoke with a raised voice.

Vittorio, a few feet away, heard him through the open

door. He rose and headed for the shop, from where Rik's grouchy voice could still be heard.

'I'm not asking. I'm telling you to stay where you are so we can discuss these orders.'

'*No!*' Jackie said furiously.

Once before she'd agreed to this demand and it had stretched to two hours, without so much as a penny being added to her wages.

'Now, look, Jackie—'

'We can talk tomorrow,' she said desperately.

Unable to bear any more, she fled blindly—and collided with a man entering through the front door. She began to fall, nearly taking him down with her.

'I'm sorry—' she gasped.

'No, *I'm* sorry,' Vittorio said, holding her firmly.

'Come back here,' Rik snapped, reaching out to take her arm in a fierce grip.

'Let me go!' she cried.

'I'll let you go when you do what you're paid to do.'

The last word ended on a yelp that burst from him at the feel of Vittorio's hand gripping his wrist.

'Let her go,' ordered Vittorio.

'Who the hell do you think you are?' Rik wailed.

'I said let her go, and you'd better do so if you know what's good for you.' Vittorio's voice was harsh and unrelenting.

Jackie felt Rik's painful grip on her arm loosen, until she was able to free herself.

A glance back at Rik showed he was scowling. She hurried away, following Vittorio, who put his arm protectively around her.

'Sorry about that,' he said. 'I didn't mean to get you in trouble with your boss.'

'Don't blame yourself.' She sighed. 'He's always like that.'

'I'm afraid I tripped you.'

'No, I tripped *you*. I wasn't looking where I was going.'

'But you stumbled. Are you sure you aren't hurt? I thought you might have twisted your ankle.'

'Just a little.'

'You should sit down. Let's go into the café.'

Once inside, he took her to a table in the corner, summoned the waiter and ordered coffee. When it was served he took a deep breath.

'*Signorina*—'

'My name's Jacqueline Benton. People call me Jackie.'

'Thank you—Jackie.'

'You called me *signorina*. Are you Italian?' She sounded hopeful.

'Yes, my name is Vittorio.'

She seemed pleased at the discovery. Smiling, she offered her hand. '*Buon giorno*, Vittorio.'

'*Buon giorno*, Jackie.'

'I really thank you for what you did—rescuing me from Rik.'

'He must be a nightmare to work for. But I guess you're out of a job now.'

'Probably not. You're right—he *is* a nightmare. But things like that have happened before. He always apologises afterwards.'

'He *what*? I find that hard to believe.'

'So do I, in a way. But if I left it would be hard for him to find someone who'd put up with his horrible behaviour while knowing the place as well as I do.'

'So he knows how to act for his own benefit?' Vittorio said wryly.

'Oh, yes. Mind you, I suppose you could say that of everyone. We all do what suits us, and we don't really think about anyone else's feelings.'

He knew an uneasy moment. Was it possible that she suspected the truth about his arrival?

But she was smiling pleasantly, and he told himself not to panic.

'I find it hard to believe that of you,' he said gently.

'Oh, I can be selfish when it suits me.' She gave him a cheeky smile. 'You wouldn't *believe* the lengths I go to just to get my own way.'

He smiled back, charmed by her impish humour.

'I'll believe whatever you care to tell me,' he said. 'But you don't need to go to any great lengths. Just say what you want and I'll take care of it.'

That could be quite a temptation, she thought, remembering what she had read on the astrology site.

The fates are planning a startling new beginning for you. The sun in Jupiter will bring things you never anticipated...

Certainly she hadn't anticipated a charming, handsome man declaring himself at her service.

Watching her face, Vittorio managed to read her expression fairly well. He guessed she was trying decide how much fun they might have teasing each other.

And it might be *really* good fun, he thought. As well as humour there was a warmth in her eyes that tempted him to move closer.

'Rik said a man was asking after my father,' she said. 'Was that you?'

'Yes. I was sorry to hear that he was dead.'

'Why are you looking for him?'

Vittorio hesitated, sensing the approach of danger. Suddenly he was reluctant to disturb the delightful atmosphere between them.

'My own father knew him several years ago,' he said carefully.

'How did they meet? Did your father try to sell him some Italian goods for the shop?'

'No, he wasn't a salesman. He was Count Martelli.'

He waited for her to react with delight to hearing his status, as he was used to, but she only said ironically, 'A count? You're the son of a *count*? Are you kidding?'

'No, I'm not. And, since my father has died, I *am* the Count.'

She burst into a delicious chuckle. 'You must think I'm so gullible.'

'Why don't you believe me?'

'Because my father never once mentioned knowing a *count*—or even admitted meeting one. I just can't imagine that my father was ever friends with an aristocrat, not when we were so poor.'

'Was he really poor? He managed to start his own business.'

'He borrowed a lot of money to buy the shop. And it was a big mistake. He never really made the profit he needed, and we always lived on the edge of poverty.'

'That must have been a very sad life for you,' Vittorio said uneasily.

'Not for me as much as for him. It destroyed his marriage to my mother. She left him for another man. For years Daddy and I had only each other. I adored him. He was a lovely man…sweet-natured, generous. I went to work in the shop, to help him. It wasn't the life I'd planned—I'd dreamed of going to university. But I couldn't abandon him. And in the end he was forced to sell. Rik beat him down on the price, but he offered me a job and let us go on living there. I did all I could for Daddy, but it wasn't enough. A couple of years ago he had a heart attack.'

Vittorio dropped his head, staring at the floor. In his

worst nightmares he'd never imagined anything as bad as this. If George Benton had received the money that should have been his everything would have been different for him. He might even be alive now.

What would she say when he told her?

He clenched his fists, trying to find the courage to do the right thing.

But his courage failed him, and to his relief the waiter appeared.

'We're about to close, sir.'

'Then I guess we have to go,' he said hurriedly, trying not to sound too relieved.

It was dark outside. He walked Jackie to the shop door and waited, wondering if she would invite him in. But she only said, 'I'm glad we met. It was nice to have coffee.'

'Yes, it was. Jackie…' He hesitated, uncertain how to go on.

'Yes?'

'Nothing. Perhaps we can—see each other again. I'd like to talk.'

'So would I. Tomorrow?'

'I'll look in.'

She went inside, locking the door behind her. For some moments Vittorio stood in silence, trying to come to a troubling decision.

He should have told her everything, but he knew the truth would hurt her greatly. He felt that in his heart, and flinched from striking that blow.

He'd planned every step of the way how he would confront George Benton, explain, apologise, and draw a line under it. Instead he found himself confronted with a woman whose sweetness and vulnerability touched his heart. And the truth was he didn't know how to respond.

After standing there hopelessly for several minutes he turned and hurried away into the darkness.

CHAPTER TWO

NEXT MORNING VITTORIO awoke early. The clock said half past five and suddenly there seemed no point in staying in bed. Showering and dressing quickly, he headed straight out.

It felt good to enjoy the fresh air and the fast-growing light. But then he saw something that alarmed him. A young woman walking away in the distance. It was hard to be certain of details, but she looked strangely like...

Jackie.

Wanting to be sure, he hurried after her, but she turned a corner out of sight.

Cursing, he ran desperately through the streets. He didn't know London at all. It was hopeless, he thought frantically when he found himself by the River Thames. She must be walking along the embankment—but in which direction?

Then luck was with him. After a hundred yards he could see her, sitting on a bench, staring out over the water. He moved closer, struck by the way she seemed sunk in another world. It reminded him of himself the night before.

He stayed silent, unsure whether it was right for him to disturb her, but after a moment she glanced up.

'Vittorio? What are you doing up this early?' she asked.

'I couldn't sleep so I thought I'd stretch my legs. How are you this morning, Jackie? Are you worried about facing Rik today?'

'I'm fine—honestly.'

'Forgive me, but I don't think you are.' He lifted her chin with his fingers, looking at her face. 'You've been crying.'

'Just a little.'

He put his arms round her, overtaken by a desire to care for her. Protectiveness was a feeling he'd seldom, if ever, known before, and now it was almost alarming. He had to tell her something that would break her heart, and suddenly he wasn't sure that he could do it.

'Hold on to me,' he whispered. 'It'll be all right.'

'Sometimes I think things will *never* be all right,' she said. 'I'm sorry to dump all this on you, but I can't talk about Daddy without—'

'Without remembering all the bad things that happened to him?'

'I don't know why, Vittorio, but I feel I could tell you anything.'

She looked up again and the sight of her vulnerable face swept him with a desire to kiss her. He yielded—but only to lay his lips on her forehead.

'Do you want to tell me any more?' he murmured.

'You can't want to hear such a terrible story,' she said.

She was more right than she could imagine, he thought wretchedly. But he owed it to her to listen.

'You can tell me *anything*, Jackie.'

She brushed the tears aside from her face. 'I don't really know what to say… It isn't my tragedy.'

'In a way it is. You lost too. You wanted to go to university. What did you want to study?'

'I wanted to study languages. They just seem to come easily to me.'

He regarded her wryly.

'Buon per te, signorina. La maggior parte delle persone non possono far fronte con le lingue.'

He spoke in Italian. His words meant, 'Good for you *signorina*. Most people can't cope with languages.'

'Italian is the language I manage best,' she said. 'I took a few classes at night school, because we were planning to take a holiday there together. My father longed to travel to Italy. He'd been there once as a young man.'

'Did he tell you a lot about his visit?'

'Yes, he said it was such fun.'

'Did he never mention meeting my father?' he asked.

'He mentioned an Italian friend, but said nothing at all about him being a *count*! They met in Italy and then again in England a few weeks later. From what Daddy said I gather they got on really well and enjoyed each other's company.'

Vittorio nodded. 'Yes I remember Papà saying something like that—I gather they had quite a few adventures together whilst he was there.'

'Daddy said things like that too. He had such a lovely time with his Italian friend. Only then—' She checked herself.

'Then?' Vittorio said tensely. He had an uneasy feeling that he knew what was coming.

'Then suddenly it was all over. One day they were close buddies—the next day his friend disappeared. He left a note but it didn't say much. Just *Goodbye my friend. Franco*'. No address, nothing. Daddy couldn't contact him and he never heard from him again. It left him very unhappy after what they'd been to each other.'

'He told you that? Didn't he tell you any more about who the man was?'

'No, just that his name was Franco. If he'd known more he'd have told me, I'm sure. Maybe your father never let him know that he was a count?'

'Maybe…' he murmured.

Their eyes met, and what Jackie saw took her breath away. There was an intensity in his gaze as though nothing but herself existed in the world. It was something she'd never seen in any man's eyes before, and she became suddenly conscious of the soft thump of her own heartbeat.

'Jackie—' Vittorio checked himself, unsure how to continue. This was taking more courage than he had anticipated.

'What's the matter?' she asked. 'Are you all right?'

'I'm fine—but there's something I must—'

She felt a sudden sense of brilliant illumination—as though the clouds had parted on a rainy day. She'd hardly dared to hope that the vibrant attraction that possessed her possessed him too, but now she let herself wonder if perhaps it did.

A memory returned to her. That astrology prediction had said, *The fates are planning a startling new beginning for you. The sun in Jupiter will bring things you never anticipated, and decisions that will change your life.*

It was happening. This was the great moment that fate had planned for her. Now surely he would tell her how their meeting had affected his heart, and that was something her own heart longed to know.

She clasped his hand between hers.

'Whatever you have to say, I know I'll like it,' she breathed. 'We've understood each other from the first moment, and—'

'Yes…' he murmured. 'Yes—*yes*—'

He knew the next few minutes would be tense, but something in her seemed to reach out to him, drawing him into a circle of warmth such as he'd never known before. It was what he needed most in all the world, and he knew a moment of fear lest his revelation ruin things between them.

He raised her hands and brushed his lips against them. 'I hope so much that you're right,' he said. 'But you can't imagine—'

'I think I can. Daddy always said you had to be ready for the unexpected.' She met his eyes, her own full of happiness and hope. 'And I'm ready for anything. Say it, Vittorio, and you might like my answer.'

He drew a sharp breath. Now the moment had come when he must find the courage to tell her everything.

But the sight of her eyes shining up at him caused his courage to fail. Suddenly he could see how that light would fade when she knew the terrible truth behind her father's suffering. The thought of her pain made him shudder, and he knew he could not force himself to speak.

'I have to go,' he said uneasily.

'What? But—'

'I'm expecting an important phone call. I have to get back to the hotel.'

He rose to his feet and she followed him reluctantly. Suddenly a moment filled with magic had dissolved into nothing, leaving her desolate.

As they walked back beside the river it began to drizzle.

'Better get back quickly, before it really starts to rain,' he said.

They hurried the rest of the way, until they reached the shop.

'I'll see you again soon,' he said. 'We'll talk then. Take care of yourself.'

Then he fled, devoured by thoughts whose bitterness was aimed accusingly at himself. He was no better than a coward!

His own words came back to him.

You can never tell what fate has in store for you.

It was more true than he could have dreamed. His plan for this meeting had never included the desire to hold her, comfort her, protect her—do anything rather than hurt her. It had overtaken him without warning, reducing him to helplessness. And there was no turning back.

Inside the shop, Jackie hurried up the stairs and looked

out of the window in time to see Vittorio vanish around the corner.

She sighed sadly. It was obvious what had happened. He'd been about to kiss her but had changed his mind at the last moment.

Did he want her or not? He had seemed to be trying to tell her something without words. Had she misunderstood him? But he *had* seemed on the verge of telling her something.

What could it possibly be?

She busied herself opening up the shop. Saturdays were always busy. But somehow she couldn't get stop thinking about him. He was there in her mind, his eyes glowing with a look that made her heart beat faster.

Next day was Sunday, which meant the shop was closed. Fearful of missing her, Vittorio hurried there early. He'd lost his nerve the day before, but he couldn't risk losing it again.

A window opened above him and a voice said coolly, 'Good morning, Vittorio.'

Jackie was looking down at him.

'Morning!' he cried, smiling brightly. 'Can you come down?'

'I'm not sure—'

'Please, Jackie, it's important. We really have to talk.'

'We could have talked yesterday.'

'Please.'

'All right. I'll just be a moment.'

She hurried down, full of hope that her tense wait would be over. He seemed to have come close and then retreated, and now she couldn't bear any more. It *must* be the dream she'd longed for. They had known each other such a little time, but what did time matter when their hearts reached out to each other?

Perhaps his feelings were stronger than he'd known before, which was why he feared expressing them. But she would open her arms and her heart to him and they would both know happiness.

As soon as she appeared downstairs he put his arm about her shoulders.

'Let's have some breakfast in the café. It's nice and comfortable in there.'

'And we can talk,' she said eagerly.

When they were settled she waited for him to speak, but again he felt silent, as though attacked by doubt at the last moment. Her heart sank. Her hopes had risen so high. She couldn't bear to lose them again.

'Vittorio, please tell me,' she said. 'Whatever is on your mind I can tell it's important.'

'Yes, it is…' he said hesitantly.

'Then please be brave and say it. Are you afraid of what I'll say?'

'I might be,' he said. 'I don't think you can imagine—'

She touched his face. 'Tell me, Vittorio. Let's get it out between us and then tell each other how we feel.'

'Yes,' he murmured. 'You're right. Do you remember—?'

'Remember?'

'How we talked about our fathers yesterday.'

'Yes, I remember, but—'

'I should have told you then. It's a terrible story, Jackie, but I have to tell you. Your father once placed a bet that won a million pounds.'

'But that can't be true! He'd have told me—we'd never have been in the situation we found ourselves in if that had been the case.'

'He didn't know. My father and yours were out together one night. Your father got tipsy, and he was dozing when the results were announced. When he awoke my *papà* had taken the winnings and kept them.'

Jackie had a terrible feeling of having crash-landed. The words reeled in her head. Only one thing was clear.

This wasn't what she'd expected to hear.

'What on earth are you saying?' she demanded. 'You *can't* mean that he didn't tell Daddy he'd won? That would be dishonest, and surely—'

'It was the only dishonest thing he ever did, and it tormented him. He told me about it just before he died.'

'Is this—this what you've been trying to say?' she stammered.

'Yes, it took me this long to pluck up the courage to tell you that my family has damaged yours. I'm sure you'll find it hard to forgive. Right at this minute you probably hate me.'

That was closer to the truth than he could possibly know. As her dreams collapsed, leaving her in the middle of a desert, she felt a terrifying rage begin to take her over.

'There's something else I have to tell you,' Vittorio said. 'I'm not sure how it will make you feel.'

'Try me,' she whispered, with a faint flicker of renewed hope.

'Papà made me promise to find your father and sort things out.'

'Sort things out? What do you mean by that?'

'I planned to give him the money Papà took from him. A million pounds. I hoped it would make everything all right.'

She stared at him, barely able to believe what she was hearing.

'You hoped *what*?' she said furiously. 'You really hoped things could be made *"all right"* after so many years? After Daddy suffered so much from poverty and it made his wife abandon him? After the way he died in despair? You can't give him your money *now*.'

'But I can give it to you.'

'You think that will make his suffering *all right*?'

'I didn't mean it that way,' Vittorio said tensely.

'Oh, yes, you did. You think money can solve everything—but when a man's dead it can't solve anything at all. You don't understand that, do you? Hand over a cheque and everything's settled! Maybe that's true in business, but not in real life. But you don't know anything about real life.'

'Jackie, please—let me explain. I only want to—'

'You only want to make yourself feel good.'

'I don't think money solves everything, but I'd like to pay the debt my family owes.'

'This is a con. Do you *really* expect me to believe that you can hand over a million pounds, just like that?'

'You think I don't have that much? You're wrong. My father didn't waste the million he gained.'

'You mean the million he *stole*,' she raged.

'Very well—he stole it. But he wanted to pay it back. He invested it successfully, so that it made several more millions. I can give you back every penny—plus a few thousand for interest.'

'Oh, you think it's so easy, don't you? I wouldn't take money from you if I was starving. This conversation is at an end.' She stood up. 'And don't you dare follow me.'

He'd reached out a hand to stop her, but something fierce in her manner made him draw back.

'Please—' he began.

'No. Don't you understand? *No!*'

She fled, fearful lest her true feelings become too plain. Instead of the loving emotion she'd hoped for he'd offered her *money*. If she'd stayed a moment longer she was afraid she might have done something violent.

Her departure left Vittorio in a state of total confusion and misery. Nothing had worked out as he'd intended. He'd failed to fulfil his father's dying wish. Guilt tore at him.

He paid his bill and went out into the street, walking back in the direction of the shop. There was no sign of her.

There was nothing to do but return to the hotel and do some serious thinking about what he was going to do next.

But he found that serious thinking was very little help in a situation he didn't understand.

The rest of Jackie's day and night was tormented. The incredible events of the morning whirled through her brain, and at the end of the day—even though she was exhausted and wrung out when she finally got to bed—she couldn't sleep. Instead she sat up in bed and opened the laptop she always kept with her.

She did a search on 'Count Martelli'. She was half ready to learn that he didn't exist, that the whole thing had been a con, and for a moment it seemed that her suspicions were correct. The picture that appeared on the screen was of a man in his sixties.

He's lying, she thought furiously. *That's the real Count.*

But then she saw the text.

Count Franco Martelli, taken just before his death four weeks ago. His heir is his son, Vittorio Martelli, latest in a line stretching back five hundred years.

She clicked the link marked 'Count Vittorio Martelli' and and at once saw a photograph of the man she recognised. There was no doubt.

Her temper surged once more at the memory of Vittorio trying to pay her off to assuage his family's guilt. But had she been too hasty? Had she let her temper get the better of her once again?

Vivid in her mind was the memory of her father's suffering. He'd tried to put on a brave face for her sake, but he hadn't always been able to manage it. Often she had found him in tears. He'd smiled and reassured her, but over time she had come to understand the problems. Her heart had broken for him. She had become his comforter, intent on giving him some kind of happiness.

But the last year of her father's life had been the saddest she had ever known. She still wept when she remembered his suffering.

Vittorio thought money was the answer to everything!

And yet she knew there was another reason for her rage. When she remembered how her hopes of winning Vittorio's feelings had risen, and then been smashed to the ground, she felt capable of murder.

He had just been playing a game until he had what suited him. He hadn't spared a thought as to what it was doing to *her*.

So accept the money, said a voice in her head. *He offered you a million—more than a million with interest.*

Because he thought it would put right what his father had done. If he wasn't such a heartless monster he'd know that nothing could *ever* make it right.

What would her father have done? If he were still alive it would be so different. Then of course they would have accepted the money. It would have been his due. But now he was gone would it be right for her to accept it on his behalf?

She closed the laptop and went back to bed. At last she managed to nod off, sinking into a deep and dreamless sleep.

Vittorio's night had also been troubled. He'd fallen asleep easily, but found his dreams haunted by Jackie's contempt until they were practically nightmares that woke him in a cold sweat.

He rose out of bed. He had no desire to go back to sleep lest the alarming female return to torment him. Day was breaking and he felt the need of a fresh air. Dressing hastily, he went downstairs and out into the street.

His thoughts were full of the promise he'd made to

his beloved father. Come what might he *had* to make this right—for everyone's sake.

Almost at once the shop came in sight. It was time for it to be open, so he went closer and looked through the glass door, but he could see no sign of anyone. Moving quietly, he opened the door and slipped inside. At once he heard the sound of voices coming from deep within. One was Jackie's, and the other he recognised as the weasely boss who had appeared during his first visit. His voice was raised in annoyance.

'Jackie, you're *mad*. You should have got all you could out of the Count and then invested in this place. I could do with some money to cover the debts. You could have helped me out and you just turned it down? How could you be so *stupid*?'

She replied in a voice filled with rage that reminded Vittorio of the way she'd spoken to him with equal fury during last night.

'You think I should have taken his money and used it for *your* convenience?' she raged at Rik. 'I'm not *that* stupid.'

Vittorio stepped a little closer, careful to keep out of sight but wanting to hear everything.

'You just can't recognise reality when it's under your nose,' came Rik's reply. 'You had the chance of a fortune. You could have taken it. But perhaps your fantasies are fixed on something else.'

'What does that mean?'

'It's *him*, isn't it? You refused his money because you're hoping for a better offer! You think you can lure him into marriage, but you're wasting your time. A man like that wouldn't marry *you* in a million years.'

'And I wouldn't marry *him* in a million years. He's cold—and arrogant enough to think that money can solve anything.'

Vittorio made a wry face. A wise man would have slipped

away at this moment, but he didn't feel wise. He felt as though Jackie had seized him and was holding him at her mercy in whirls of confusion.

'It can solve a great deal,' he heard Rik say. 'It could pay a lot of my debts—many of which are *your* fault.'

'How can you say that?'

'If you did a better job this shop would be doing well, instead of sinking into debt.'

'The shop was in a bad way when my father sold it to you. That's how you got it so cheap. I heard you—beating him down on the price when he was too weak to fight you.'

'Don't try to blame me for your father's failings. Luckily it's not too late. You've still got time to find this Italian Count and tell him you'll take the money.'

'You think I'd—? You're mad.'

'I'm *telling* you to do it.'

'And I'm telling *you* to go to hell.'

'I warn you, Jackie, you're walking a very fine line. Perhaps I'd better see him myself—'

'Perhaps you should,' Vittorio said, stepping out so that they could see him.

Rik noticed him first, and the shock on his face alerted Jackie, so that she looked behind her, also appalled at the discovery.

Rik assumed a severe manner. 'We have business to discuss,' he said.

'The only business we have is for you to listen to what I have to say,' Vittorio said bluntly. 'For you—not a penny.'

'But you have a debt to pay,' Rik squealed.

'Not to *you*.'

'Jackie, tell him,' Rik whined. 'Tell him he's got to pay you what he owes you.'

Jackie looked intently at Vittorio, but did not speak.

'Do it now,' Rik snapped. 'Let me hear you say it.'

'I have nothing to say,' she replied coldly. 'The Count's

debt is impossible to repay.' She met Vittorio's gaze and said emphatically, *'Ever!'*

Rik looked from one to the other, scowling.

'So *that's* it,' he raged. 'You two are in this together. As soon as I'm out of earshot you'll take the money and cut me out.'

'You can't be cut out because you were never *in*,' Jackie said fiercely. 'You bought this business fair and square, and any debts are now your responsibility. Besides, I will never take a penny of his money.'

'You're insane!' Rik seethed. 'What kind of fool turns down that sort of money? Well, if money's of no importance to you then you won't be needing this job. *Or* the accommodation I've provided for you. You're fired. I'll give you one hour to clear out your stuff from upstairs.'

Rik stormed out, pausing at the front door.

'One hour!' he yelled. 'I mean it.'

Then he was gone, slamming the door behind him.

Vittorio turned swiftly to Jackie. 'Good riddance.' he said. 'Forget him. He isn't worth bothering with.'

Jackie was shaken, but determined to maintain her dignity. 'How long were you there, listening?'

'I came to see you and arrived just as you were telling him what had happened.'

'I never meant to tell him, but he made me so angry that I said it to knock the smile off his face. I could have strangled him.' She gave a bitter laugh. 'I'd have enjoyed that.'

'Don't worry. He's bound to give you another excuse. He's a pig, Jackie, and you're better off without him.'

'But this isn't just my *job*. I've lived here all my life and now I've lost my home, too.'

'Then we must find you another one. Get packing and we'll be out of here—fast.'

'I've nowhere to go.'

'Trust me to arrange that.'

She knew an instinct to rebel against him. This catastrophe had happened only because he'd come to England and caused trouble. Now she'd lost her job and her home, and he was to blame.

But was he really? If she hadn't been silly enough to tell Rik about the money this wouldn't have happened. When was she going to learn to control her temper?

Never, she thought fiercely.

'Let's get you out of here,' Vittorio said. He took her arm and ran up the stairs with her and began opening drawers and cupboards, working hard to help her.

'Is that your only suitcase?' he asked, regarding the one she had produced.

'Yes, but I've got some plastic bags.'

Luckily the bags proved enough to take her few possessions.

'Anything else?' he asked at last.

'No, that's all.'

'You have nothing else?' he asked, looking astonished.

'This is all I need,' she said defiantly.

He gave her an odd look, as though wondering what madness had made her refuse his money when she seemed to own so little, but all he said was, 'Then let's go.'

She looked around nervously as they went downstairs, but there was no sign of Rik.

'Where are we going?' she asked as they went out into the street.

'I'm staying in the Davien Hotel, a couple of streets away. We'll get you a room there for tonight, then make our plans.'

She knew the hotel. It had a reputation as being costly.

'I don't think it's quite the right place for me,' she said uneasily.

'If you're worried about the money, don't be. I'm paying. I landed you in this mess and it's my responsibility to get you out.'

Suddenly she recalled Rik's warning to her. He'd suggested that Vittorio was hoping to lure Jackie into bed with the empty promise of a great fortune.

Suddenly she was uneasy. Was that why Vittorio was taking her to his hotel at his own expense? Did he mean her to share his bed?

Only recently that thought would have excited her. Vittorio attracted her powerfully. The thought of lying with him in bed would have been a pleasure. But now everything was different. Was he trustworthy? Could she be sure?

A short walk brought them to the hotel. Vittorio went to Reception and chatted with the woman there as she typed something onto the keyboard. Nodding to her, he headed back to Jackie.

'I've managed to secure you a room on the second floor.'

He escorted her upstairs, leading her to a door for which he had the key. She held her breath.

But when the door opened she knew she'd done him an injustice. There was only one single bed.

'Th-thank you,' she stammered.

'If you need me I'm three doors along the corridor.'

He departed at once, leaving her standing alone, trying to take in everything that had happened. Only yesterday she had quarrelled with this man, and today he had come to her rescue and she had accepted his help gladly.

It doesn't make any sense, she mused.

But nothing had made sense since she'd met him. Perhaps nothing ever would again.

He returned just as she finished putting her things away.

'They do a good lunch here,' he said. 'I'll have some sent up.'

'Couldn't we eat downstairs in the restaurant?'

'Do I make you feel nervous, Jackie? Are you afraid to be alone with me?'

'Of course not,' she said uneasily. 'I have no feelings about you one way or the other, actually,' she lied bravely.

'So you didn't mean it when you said you wouldn't marry me in a million years? Or the bit about me being cold and arrogant and a person who thinks money can solve anything?'

For a moment it was as though her worst nightmares were coming true. But then she saw he was grinning, and that his eyes were full of friendly humour.

'Forget it,' he said. 'People say things in the heat of the moment. And it's not far different from what you said to me yesterday. But it's time we drew a line under that. We have to work matters out between us and be friends—if that's possible.'

It was still embarrassing to know that he'd heard her, but his unexpected humour made it bearable.

'So—can I have some food sent up?' he asked.

'Are you asking my permission?'

Again he gave her a cheeky grin. 'Isn't that what you prefer a man to do?'

'Stop trying to make me sound like a bully.'

'Not a bully. Just a woman who knows her own mind— as Rik would tell us after the way you stood up to him. He's a nasty bully, but you really dealt with him.'

'Yes—and that was so successful that now I've got to start looking for another job and a home.'

'But where? You'll never get another job around here. He'll make sure of that.'

She groaned, recognising that Vittorio was right. Rik would spread the word that she was unreliable, destroying her prospects.

'I still feel that I owe you any help I can persuade you to accept,' Vittorio said.

'You have a job to offer me?'

'Not here, but in Italy. I could find many opportunities for you there. Why not come back with me?'

CHAPTER THREE

JACKIE STARED AT him in disbelief. 'Italy? Did I hear right?'

'Dead right. I want you to work for me in my family's department store in Rome. Your talents will be valuable.'

'But I've only ever worked in a little shop. I'd be useless in a department store.'

'Not in our glass and china section. It's a new department, and it isn't doing brilliantly because nobody really understands it. But you could bring it to life and make it profitable.'

'According to Rik, I was lousy at making profits.'

'Were you? Or did *he* make a lot of stupid decisions?'

'Yes, he buys all the wrong stuff.'

'So I can rely on you to buy all the *right* stuff?'

'Mightn't the language be a problem? I never got to finish my Italian course at night school. I had to stop when Daddy became ill.'

'A lot of people there speak English. Some of our customers are tourists, and your English would be a blessing to them. Your Italian seems already pretty good, and you can work to improve it.'

'It's very kind of you—' she began uneasily.

'No, it isn't. I'm not being kind. I'm a businessman and I'm doing what any sensible businessman does—turning the situation to my own advantage. I could make a lot of money out of you, and I'm not passing up the chance to do that.'

'But how—?'

'You won't just have that one department. I want you to cast your expert eye over the whole store and tell me how it looks to you—because that will tell me how it looks to our customers. Tourists are profitable, and you can help me attract plenty of them. And it could open some new doors for you, Jackie. I'll pay you a decent wage—far more than Rik paid you—and you'll have a position of authority.'

Authority. The word seemed to sing in her ears. This would truly be a new, more satisfying life—exactly what she had longed for. Again she had the mysterious feeling that Vittorio could read her mind.

'Authority?' she echoed. 'Do you really mean that?'

'You'd be in charge of your department. You'd have a team that would take your orders. Or don't you feel up to giving orders?'

'Oh, yes, I do. That was always my problem with Rik. And with my father too sometimes. He complained that I argued with him too much.' She gave a brief laugh.

'Don't worry. When you're working for me you can give all the orders you want. I'll make it clear to the team that *you're* the boss. You need never fear another bully like Rik.'

It sounded too good to be true, she thought, trying to suppress a flicker of confusion. Knowing the terrible truth about how her father had been treated had made hostility flare between them, but there were other feelings too— some warmer, some interested, all confusing.

But what else could she do? Where else was there for her to go? What other life was possible for her? It was as if all other doors had slammed shut and fate was driving her irresistibly into this man's power.

Surely she could take advantage of the situation, just as *he* planned to do?

Here was a chance to learn new skills and gain new experiences that might open up a world of fresh opportunities for her.

'All right,' she said in a daze. 'I'll go to Italy with you.'

'Good thinking. I knew I could rely on you.'

She ventured to say, 'You mean because I've agreed with you?'

'What else? That's my definition of good thinking. So, now there's nothing to hold you back we can go tomorrow. I'll book two tickets.'

After booking the tickets Vittorio ordered a meal and a bottle of wine from room service.

'After this I must attend to some business matters. I suggest you relax for the rest of the afternoon, and then I think we should both get an early night,' he said, adding in a teasing voice, 'In our separate rooms, I promise.'

'Stop teasing,' she said cheerfully. 'I wasn't thinking that.'

'Good. Then we can both relax.'

'Of course. We agree to be friends. That's all.'

'Friends…' he mused. 'What kind of friends? Best friends?'

'We'll have to wait and see.'

She was right. Friendship was their only hope. Had she really feared lest he come to her door? After their argument the day before he could well believe that she didn't want him. His own feelings for her were less clear.

Officially they were enemies, and his instinct to protect her was troublesome.

She was becoming important to him in ways that confused him. Perhaps soon he would understand them. For the moment he preferred to wait and see what fate had in store.

He lifted his glass of wine in her direction.

'Here's to you,' he said. 'You don't know how much I'm going to rely on you.'

And it was true, he thought. She didn't.

It was a quiet meal, with very little talk. Instinctively

they both knew that for the moment enough had been said. Perhaps too much.

At the earliest moment they finished eating.

'And now I really must get on with some work. I'll head back to my room, but if you think of anything else you need today please call through.'

He bade her a polite good day, and left.

Returning to his room, he recalled something he'd meant to say to her, and hurried back to see her.

A surprise awaited him. He looked out into the corridor just in time to see her getting into the elevator and the doors closing.

Where on earth could she be going? he thought frantically. Surely not to talk to Rik?

There was no hope of catching up with the elevator. He went to his window and looked down. There she was, walking away along the road, and then turning through a large gate that he knew led to a church.

Every cautious instinct told him to stay where he was—not to follow her. But something about Jackie always overcame caution.

In a moment he was out of the door, hurrying until he reached the church gate.

Inside was a cemetery. As he watched she approached a tombstone and knelt before it. He was too far away to make out the name, but he could hear Jackie saying urgently, 'I'm sorry, Daddy. I really am.'

So this was Benton's grave, and she had come here to talk to him. Vittorio backed away, unwilling to invade her privacy, but he couldn't help hearing her next words.

'I don't really trust him. I'd like to, but he doesn't understand what a terrible thing was done to you, and that makes him almost as much of an enemy as his father. But I must go to Italy. I'll come back, I promise. Only forgive me. Please, *please* forgive me.'

As watched she pressed her lips to the stone, then leaned against it, sobbing.

Torn by the instinct to comfort her, he took a step closer—but stopped just in time. Whatever happened, she mustn't know he was there. He had an unnerving feeling… as though he'd been suddenly stranded on a desert island. He hadn't expected this, and the sensation of being caught unprepared was alarming.

He backed off and hurried away, haunted by her words—

I don't trust him… Almost as much of an enemy as his father…

If that was how she thought of him he supposed he couldn't blame her. But it hurt more than he would have expected.

Back at the hotel, he returned to his room and went to the window, hoping to see her return. But hours passed with no sign of her and his heart sank. Where had she vanished to *now*? What trouble might she have fallen into? Had she changed her mind about accompanying him to Italy?

Then a noise from the corridor made him hurry outside. She was there, turning the key in her lock.

'There you are,' he said with relief.

'Were you looking for me? I'm sorry I vanished. I just had to— Well, never mind.'

He hesitated. All his cautious instincts warned him to keep the secret, but the need to be honest with her was greater.

At last he said, 'You just had to say goodbye to your father.'

She stared at him. 'How do you know?'

'I saw you.'

'But how?'

'I followed you to the cemetery.'

She gasped with outrage. 'You *followed* me? How *dare* you?'

She stormed into her room and tried to close the door, but he reached out to keep it open.

'Let me come in,' he said.

'I'd rather you didn't. In fact I'd rather you vanished off the face of the earth.'

'Well, I'm sure you'll eventually think of a way of making that happen. But for the moment we need to talk. Let me in, Jackie. *Please.*'

Furiously, she turned away. He followed her in, closing the door behind him.

'Don't judge me, Jackie—please. I'm not stalking you. I followed you because I'm concerned about you. You seemed so lonely, walking, and when you reached the grave...' He paused, feeling desperate. 'You cried so terribly. I wanted to take you in my arms and comfort you. I didn't because I knew you'd be angry that I was there. I went away. I wasn't sure that was the right thing to do, but I don't seem to get anything right these days. The more I try, the more wrong I get it. But I'm glad I was with you for a few minutes. I think I understand you better now.'

He saw a strange, slightly puzzled look come into her face.

'Yes, that surprises you, doesn't it?' he said. 'I'm the last person you'd expect to understand you.'

'People don't easily understand other people,' she murmured.

'But I think we manage it. We must talk about that another time. For now, please just tell me that you believe I meant no harm and you forgive me.'

'All right,' she said reluctantly. 'I realise you didn't mean it badly.'

'And I'm forgiven? Please Jackie. Let me hear you say it. *Please.*'

She drew a sharp breath, stunned by the desperation in

his voice and the intensity in his eyes. There was no way she could refuse this man anything he asked for.

'I forgive you,' she said.

'And you mean it?'

'Yes—*yes*—'

'As long as you *do* mean it. Things could so easily go wrong between us—but we won't let that happen. Best if you go to bed now and have a good night's sleep. Tomorrow will be a busy day. Goodnight.'

'Goodnight.'

Before leaving he turned to look back at her once more. Jackie tried to understand his expression, but there was something about it that confused her.

Nor was that the only thing about him so unexpected that she could hardly believe it. The way he'd almost begged her for forgiveness had startled her, revealing a side of him she'd never suspected.

She was glad to lie down. She needed sleep, but for some reason it didn't come. It was alarming that he'd been there while she spoke to her father. Had he heard her say that she didn't trust him?

She lay still, listening for the sound of his footsteps outside, wondering if they would return to her door. But nothing happened.

At last the silence seemed to overwhelm her and she fell asleep.

As Vittorio had said, they rose early next day and were soon ready to leave.

'You won't be insulted if I pay your bill, will you?' he asked as they went downstairs.

'Would it make any difference if I was?'

He grinned. 'Not the slightest.'

'Then I'd better give in—until I find a way to make you sorry.'

'I'll look forward to that,' he said ironically.

She watched as he went to the reception desk and paid. Then all was ready and they headed for the front door.

But as soon as it was open she saw something that made her stop, frozen with dismay.

'Oh, no!' she groaned.

'What is it?' Vittorio asked. 'Ah, I see. *Him!*'

Rik was standing there, barring their way, his face full of spiteful hilarity.

'So there you are!' he jeered. 'Just as I thought—you stupid woman!'

'You told me to leave so I went,' she said coldly.

'Yes, you went running to *him*. Think you're going to be a countess, do you? Don't kid yourself! He's playing a clever game to stop you suing him for the money his family stole. He'll use you, then throw you out.'

'The only one who's being thrown out is you,' Vittorio said coldly.

Rik gave contemptuous laugh. 'Don't tell me you're taken in by her—? *Argh!*'

The scream was dragged from him by the feel of Vittorio's hand about his neck.

'I know all I need to know about this lady,' Vittorio said harshly. 'But let me tell you something about myself. I'm a man who won't tolerate an insult to a friend, and who'll do anything necessary to make someone sorry they caused trouble. Do you understand me?'

'Yes…' Rik choked.

'Then get out of here while you still can. Otherwise I might do something we'd both regret.'

He released Rik, who staggered away, looking terrified. He gave one last appalled glance at Jackie. Then he fled.

'Are you all right?' Vittorio asked her.

'Yes—fine—thank you.'

In truth she was far from all right. She'd seen yet another

side of Vittorio—one that shocked her. The look in his eyes had been that of a man who would go to any lengths to punish someone who had defied him. She knew it had been in her defence, but that couldn't ease her horror.

'Would you really have hurt him?' she whispered.

'No, of course not. But I had to make him believe that I would. Scare someone enough and you don't need to do anything else to them. Being frank. Isn't that something you've tried yourself.'

'Now and then,' she admitted. 'Not violently, but—'

'But making him believe you know something he doesn't want you to know? I'd give a lot to know how often you've used *that* one.'

'You'll just have to wonder,' she said lightly.

'Congratulations. You're as bad as I am. Shake.'

He held out his hand.

Laughing, she took it. 'I'll never be as bad as you are,' she said. 'But I'm working on it.'

'Perhaps he was right about one thing. *Should* I be afraid of you suing me?'

'Of course not. How can I?'

'I've admitted the theft.'

'It was your father's theft, not yours. And there were no witnesses when you told me. You could just deny it and there'd be nothing I could do.'

'Maybe Rik overheard me?'

'Don't believe anything Rik says—especially that nonsense about me wanting to be a countess.'

'Of course. I know you wouldn't marry me in a million years. I heard you say so yourself, remember?'

'Look, about that… I really am sorry—'

'Don't be sorry. You're not the first woman who's said that about me.' He grinned wryly. 'As you can probably imagine.'

'I'm not going to be tricked into answering that!'

'Very shrewd. I can see you're a real discovery.'

'Because I'm not trying to trap you into marriage? Never fear. You're quite safe from me.'

Was he safe? he wondered. Despite the circumstances, and the fact that she wasn't beautiful, he found her fascinating. She was intriguingly clever and her sharp humour appealed to him.

But more than that was the intense emotion that seemed to reach out from her in a way he couldn't understand. They never spoke of it. There was just a feeling that their mysterious closeness was inevitable, and that it was bound to grow.

The thought made him cautious. Developing warmer feelings for her would put him in her power, and that was something he always strove to avoid.

As the son of a count, he was used to young women pursuing him for the sake of his title. He'd thought himself well protected until the girl who'd once won his heart had betrayed him with the son of a duke. He would never forget the moment he'd discovered them in bed together—or the look she'd bestowed upon him, as though she despised him for daring to hope for her.

That had been several years ago, but the memory stayed with him. Love was unsafe. It caused danger and pain, and a wise man kept his distance.

But life without love did not mean life without marriage. One day he would have to take wife for the sake of producing an heir. His father had spoken of it in the last moments of his life.

'Marisa,' he'd murmured. 'She's perfect for you.'

Marisa was the daughter of a *barone* and an ideal choice for Vittorio's wife—at least according to his father. For a year he'd made his wishes plain. But Vittorio had resisted. He was on good terms with Marisa, but only in a brotherly way. Despite her youth and beauty, she did not attract him. Nor did he want a wife he hadn't chosen for himself.

When he returned to Rome he knew that Marisa and various similar problems would be waiting. But with Jackie's friendship to support him he felt more at ease.

The taxi was waiting to take them to the airport.

'You'll like Rome. Your Italian is good enough to help you feel at home.'

'Do you spend a lot of time in the city?'

'Yes—plenty.'

'But isn't your time taken up with managing your estates?'

'I have to do that as well, of course, but I have an estate manager who handles the difficult stuff. Mostly my time is taken up with the department store.'

'You actually *work* there?'

'Does that surprise you? You think I'm useless for anything except lying around enjoying my title while others do the work?'

'After the way you've rescued me I'm not likely to think you useless.'

He gave her a teasing glance. 'Very tactfully said.'

'Yes, I've got to stay on your right side, haven't I? Why don't you tell me some more about the store so that I can flatter you further?'

'It sells a wide range of goods which I buy from all over the world. You're going to be very valuable to the business. But I've already told you that.'

'Yes, you grabbed me because I could be useful. Sheer cynical self-interest. Just what a businessman needs. Well done.'

They shared a laugh.

'Glad to see you're a realist,' he said. 'Would it be insulting to suggest that you too have some cynical self-interest?'

'No, I'd take it as a compliment.'

'Good for you.'

'Working for you is going to teach me a whole lot of

things that I can use in my future career.' She gave him a thumbs-up sign. 'Here's to cynical self-interest.'

'The most useful motive in the world,' he agreed, making the same gesture.

'Cheers!'

They shook hands.

At last the airport came into view. Soon they were queuing for their flight and boarding the plane.

Jackie was taken aback to discover that Vittorio had booked the most expensive first class seats. But then, why wouldn't he? He was a count and a successful businessman, wasn't he?

'Take the window seat,' he said. 'It's more interesting that way.'

'Is it a long flight?' she asked as the plane began to move slowly down the runway.

'Only two and a half hours.'

Never having flown before, she was nervous. But she managed to stay at ease until take-off, and then gazed out of the window as the ground fell away.

'What will happen when we get there?' she asked.

'We'll be met at the airport by my Aunt Tania. She lives with me and looks after the house. I called her this morning and asked her to prepare a room for you.'

Before she could reply, the plane quivered. She took a sharp, nervous breath and clenched her hands.

'It's all right,' Vittorio said. 'Planes always shake when they go through clouds. We're not going to crash.'

'No—I realise—it's just that—'

'It's just that you're afraid of flying.'

'I've never flown before.'

'Is there anything else bothering you?' he asked, regarding her with concern.

'Just a little headache. It's not too bad.'

He took her hand in his. 'Probably caused by nerves. Don't worry. We'll soon be there.'

CHAPTER FOUR

AT LAST THEY landed at Leonardo da Vinci Airport. They spent a few minutes collecting their bags and then they were able to make their way out. Jackie looked around, trying to come to terms with what was happening.

'Ah, there she is,' Vittorio said suddenly.

He began waving into the distance at a middle-aged woman who was waving back to him. The woman began to run forward and he hastened towards her until they were in each other's arms. Jackie reckoned this must be the Aunt Tania he had mentioned.

She moved a little closer, waiting for him to introduce them. But then his aunt turned aside, revealing a young woman who ran forward and threw herself into Vittorio's arms.

Jackie could see that he was tense. He embraced the girl formally, before standing back and turning to indicate Jackie. She couldn't make out exactly what he was saying, but she gathered it wasn't revealing.

'This is my Aunt Tania,' he told Jackie. 'And my friend Marisa. I've told them that we are planning a business arrangement that has made it necessary for you to see Rome.'

'Welcome to our city,' Aunt Tania said politely. 'Vittorio says you will be staying with us. That will be lovely.'

'Did you give her the best guest room?' Vittorio asked.

'Yes, just as you said. Now, let's go home.'

'Have you got a taxi waiting?'.

'No, Marisa drove me here.'

'And I can drive you home,' Marisa said quickly. 'This way.'

When they reached her car she pulled open the door next to the front passenger seat, indicating for Vittorio to get in beside her. He did so, leaving Jackie and Tania to sit together in the back.

It was a lengthy journey out of the city and through the countryside to the Martelli estate. Jackie studied the scenery, occasionally looking round to find Vittorio's aunt regarding her with curiosity.

'So you're here on business,' Tania said. 'What kind of business are you in?'

She took a sharp breath, caught off-guard, and felt troubled about how to answer.

Vittorio came to her rescue.

'Jackie's a specialist in merchandising,' he said, glancing back over his shoulder. 'What she doesn't know about display and point of sale isn't worth knowing.'

Jackie suppressed an ironic smile at his way of describing her work behind the counter in a little shop.

'So you're going to help my nephew run his business?' Tania queried.

'If I can. And I hope he can teach me something that will be useful,' she said.

To her relief, the subject was allowed to drop. Soon they reached the estate and the car swept through extensive grounds up to a great house.

'We're nearly there,' Vittorio said, pointing out of the car window. 'A little further and you'll see my home.'

As he spoke a large building came into view. Jackie gasped at its elegance and beauty.

'My goodness, it's like a palace!' she gasped.

'My ancestors had rather grandiose ideas. It was a matter of pride for them to live in a splendid home.'

And I bet it took a lot of money to maintain, she thought, forcing some of them into acts of dishonesty.

Perhaps the same thought had occurred to Vittorio, for he fell silent then.

'We only live in small part of it now,' Tania said. 'But we still relish the rest, which has a marvellous history.'

A woman whom Jackie took to be the housekeeper was waiting for them as they left the car and climbed the steps to the front door. Vittorio took the bags.

'I'll take these up to Jackie's room,' he said. 'Come along, Jackie.'

Inside, the building was just as luxurious. In a daze she followed him up the stairs and along a corridor until they reached her room. Like the rest of the house it was luxuriously appointed. A large bed took up most of the space, and the walls were lined with elegant wardrobes.

'The maid will be here to help you unpack,' he said. 'Are you all right? You look as though something's the matter.'

'I'm just confused. I can't get my head around everything that's happening. I've never been anywhere like this before.'

'Don't worry—you'll soon feel at home. I'll see to that.'

The words were kindly spoken, but it flashed across her mind that she could never feel at home in this place, surrounded by a luxury that haunted her with memories of her father's impoverished home.

Marisa appeared in the doorway, followed by a maid.

'This is Gina,' she said. 'She speaks English and she will help you.'

Vittorio patted her shoulder. 'I'll leave you to unpack now and I'll see you at supper.'

He followed Marisa out of the room.

Gina immediately got to work, unpacking the bags and putting things away.

Jackie watched her, trying to believe what was happening.

'Here you have a little bathroom,' Gina said. 'And through these windows you have a wonderful view.'

It was true. She was only one floor up, but looking out onto lawns that soon vanished into trees. The sun was setting, casting a glow ever everything.

'No, no, no!'

The cry from a female voice streamed upwards from below. Leaning out, Jackie was unable to see anyone, but she could tell the sound had come from behind a wall.

'Marisa—'

That was Vittorio. But after that one word he got no further for Marisa exploded again.

'Perche, Vittorio? Perche?'

Marisa was talking too fast for Jackie to understand much, but she knew that *perche* meant *why*. It was clear that Marisa was demanding an explanation and Vittorio was trying to make her be quiet.

Jackie recalled the suspicious glances Marisa had given her. Plainly her arrival was unwelcome.

The sound died and she turned back to the room. Gina was a skilled maid with a shrewd eye. She studied Jackie's appearance before casting her glance over several of the clothes.

'You are lucky, *signorina,*' she said. 'You have a slim figure. That is a blessing.'

'Slim?' Jackie brooded. 'That's one way of putting it. In England I've been called skinny—even scrawny.'

'*Scusami, signorina*. Scrawny?'

'In English it's a way of telling someone they're too thin.'

'No, no,' Gina protested passionately. 'You cannot be too thin for fashion. Rome is a city of great fashion. Everything will be fine for you here—especially when you've bought some new clothes.'

'Oh—well—I don't think I'll be buying new clothes,' Jackie said uneasily.

The maid's words were like a blow, reminding her how little cash she had.

'But you *must*. Everyone will want to meet you.'

'That's true,' said Vittorio from the doorway.

How long had he been standing there? Jackie wondered. How much had he seen and heard?

'My new business associate will make quite an entrance,' he said.

With a slight gesture of his head he dismissed Gina, who left the room.

'New clothes,' he said. 'You do need them. We can make arrangements tomorrow.'

'But I can't. I haven't got any money to buy clothes.'

'You crazy woman! I offered you a million pounds and you chucked it back in my face. Now you're complaining about poverty.'

'I'm not complaining,' she said defiantly. 'I'm being practical.'

'So be practical and accept my offer.'

'*No!* Not that. You don't understand, do you?'

'No—and I don't think you understand your own actions.'

He was wrong, she thought. She completely understood the reasons for her stubborn refusal to yield.

If she accepted the money he would consider the debt settled. And that idea was agony to her. For the sake of her father's memory she would never allow him to do that—however much she might need the money.

'Oh, you really *are* contrary, woman,' he growled.

'What's that supposed to mean?'

'You've hardly got a penny to your name but you turn down the best financial offer you'll ever have and treat me as a villain for making it. That's carrying illogicality to new heights.'

'Not illogicality. Pride. Memory of my father's suffering.'

'You think your father would want you to refuse?'

'Yes, because accepting would be like saying what happened to him doesn't matter.'

'I think he loved you too much for that. I think he'd have been glad to see things get better for you.'

'You— How dare you speak of him like that?'

'I only said he loved you. Didn't he?'

'Yes—with all his heart. But you have no right to make use of him like that.'

'All right, I'll say no more. But think about it, Jackie. What sort of future would he have wanted for you? Prosperous? Or living on the edge of poverty? If he was here now, listening to us, what do you think he'd say to you? *Take every penny and live well.* Or, *Tell him to keep his money and get stuffed. Give yourself the pleasure of kicking him in the teeth. Then live on the edge of poverty.*'

'Stop it!' she cried, backing away from him, hands over her ears. *'Stop it!'*

He reached out and for a moment she thought he would take hold of her. But then he dropped his hand, moving quickly away.

'I'll see you at supper,' he said, and left without another word.

As he closed the door she struggled with the desire to hurl something at it. It was shocking for him to put words into her father's mouth just to suit himself. But there was no doubt that he *was* baffled by her refusal to take his money, and she reckoned the reason was plain. A man so wealthy was used to being able to buy whatever he wanted.

Not just wealthy, she mused. He was handsome also. *Too*

handsome. He must be used to women collapsing at his feet and promising to do anything he wanted.

But not me, Vittorio. You've met the one woman who'll gladly tell you exactly where to go.

She wondered if she'd been wise to come here when their hostility was still acute. But he'd saved her from Rik. She would just have to cope as best she could.

To distract herself, she began going through her possessions.

She soon realised that Gina had put her finger on an unexpected problem when she'd spoken of Rome as being a city of great fashion. None of her clothes were fashionable. At best they might be described as serviceable, with several pairs of jeans and dresses that were plain.

Hurriedly she went through the clothes and found something that might do for the evening meal. It was pale grey, neat and slightly elegant. A few moments in front of the mirror gave her a chance to work on her hair, but she wasn't pleased with the result. Drawn back tightly it merely looked dreary. Left to fall around her face it seemed neglected.

There was a knock at the door and Gina appeared.

'Ah, *signorina*, I know what I can do for you. It will soon be time for supper, so I will take care of your hair.'

She had come prepared with hair tongs, and Jackie watched in awe as Gina turned her severe locks into a bundle of delightful curls.

'Thank you,' she said with feeling. 'It's so nice of you to take so much trouble for me.'

'Signor Vittorio said I was to do everything you needed to help you be at your best. He wants you to be happy.'

'How kind of him.'

Was he being kind, or did he just want to keep her quiet and uncomplaining? she wondered.

A moment later there came a knock on her door, and Vittorio entered.

'Excellent,' he said, regarding her. 'Our guests will be impressed.'

'Guests? Are there many coming?'

'Yes, we've had a few phone calls from friends who want to drop in. It's going to be quite a busy party. Shall we go?'

He held out his arm to her and she took it. Together they left the room and headed along the corridor to the top of the stairs. As they arrived she saw a little crowd gathered in the hall below. There were three middle-aged men and several young women. Most notable among them was Marisa, who stood looking up as they descended.

'Our guests are here already,' Vittorio observed.

When he began the introductions Jackie could hardly believe her ears. Every man seemed to have a title. She managed to pick up the words *duca*, *visconte*, *barone*… They exchanged greetings with them, their wives and their elegant young daughters.

Wow, she thought. Cinderella certainly had come to the ball tonight.

She wondered why they were all here. But when she saw how she was being regarded by the younger women a suspicion came over her. It was no accident that they were here. Marisa had clearly spread the word of her arrival, alarming all those who aimed to be the next Contessa.

'Let's go and have something to eat,' Tania said, leading the way into the dining room.

A long table dominated the centre of the room, with twenty places laid out. Vittorio escorted Jackie to a chair and sat beside her. She had the impression there was a faint disagreement on his other side, as two young women sought the chair beside him. But it was over in a moment.

The other seat beside Jackie was occupied by Aunt Tania, who was clearly still regarding her with interest. She had a thin, sharp face, which had a disconcerting habit of flashing into a brilliant smile.

'You must tell me all about yourself,' she said now. 'I'd never heard of you until Vittorio called me this morning to say he was bringing you. You're obviously a very significant business associate.'

'I'm afraid he makes me sound too important.'

'Jackie is too modest about her abilities,' Vittorio said. 'When I expand my English business in Rome I'll be doing everything she says.'

Tania raised her coffee cup in salute.

'Congratulations, *signorina*. If you knew how rarely he follows anyone else's advice—or even listens to it—you'd realise what a unique position you hold. Believe me, I'll do all I can to make you feel welcome here.' She smiled. 'My nephew would be very annoyed with me if I didn't.'

'Of course. I'm here to help him make a profit. That's what really matters.'

The two women shared a laugh. Vittorio noticed and nodded with pleasure.

Servants appeared with the supper. Between the excellent food and the friendly talk Jackie had an enjoyable evening.

At last the younger women began to leave the table and settle on sofas. Two of them seized Vittorio and playfully forced him to join them. He was immediately surrounded by admirers.

'I look forward to showing you our house,' Tania said. 'There has been much history here—many notable people. Sometimes we have even opened it to tourists.'

'That sound fascinating,' Jackie said. 'I love history. In England I used to like visiting great historical buildings where dramatic things had happened in the past.'

'Then you'll enjoy Castello Martelli. We've had our fair share of excitement there.'

'Lovely. I even—'

She was checked by a shriek of laughter that came from a nearby sofa.

Glancing over, she saw that Vittorio was deep in conversation with Marisa and the other young women who crowded round him. All of them were rocking with laughter.

'Some more wine?' Tania asked.

'No, thank you,' Jackie said. 'Would you mind if I went to bed? It's been a long day. It was my first flight and it's left me a bit shaken.'

'Yes. It can take it out of you, can't it? Especially if you're nervous.'

'That's very true.'

'You look as if you've got a headache. Go to bed now. I'll send Gina up with something to drink.'

'Thank you.'

At the door Jackie looked back to wave goodnight to Vittorio, but he was still enjoying himself with his female companions, managing to be enfolded in three pairs of arms at once. He seemed to have forgotten that she existed.

As she watched Marisa intervened, pulling the others away but doing it with laughter, as though claiming Vittorio as her property was no more than a joke to her.

Vittorio looked up, noticed Jackie in the doorway and waved. She gave him a slight wave back and departed.

As promised, Gina brought something up to her room.

'English tea,' she said. 'My mistress said you were to have the best.'

'She's being very kind to me.'

'She likes you. She doesn't like that other one, but if the Count marries her—well, what can we do? Goodnight, *signorina*.'

Gina slipped away, leaving Jackie to brood. And there was a great deal to brood about. However she had thought this visit would work out, it was happening very differently, and somehow she would need to find a way to deal with it.

She tensed suddenly, alerted by a noise from the corridor outside. There was the sound of a door being opened, and then Marisa's voice.

'Perché non si può solo ascoltare me?'

Jackie just managed to make out the meaning. 'Why can't you just listen to me?'

Vittorio's reply was also in Italian, but his meaning was blindingly clear. 'Because there's no point. We talk too much and it gets us nowhere. *You* won't listen to what *I* say.'

'Because I don't believe you really mean it. Listen to your *heart*, Vittorio—'

'I *am* listening to it, and it's saying no. There's nothing there. Goodbye, Marisa.'

Quietly Jackie looked out, just in time to see Marisa storming away down the corridor as the door opposite was closed.

So that was his room, she thought.

Glancing around to make sure Marisa was no longer there, she went and knocked at his door.

He opened it at once. 'Marisa, *per favore*— Oh, it's you.'

Looking shocked, he checked himself and drew back to let her in.

'Yes, it's only me,' she said, following him. 'I reckon it's time for you to come clean, Vittorio. You've concealed the truth for long enough.'

'What truth? What are you talking about?'

'I mean the reason you brought me here. You played the gallant knight, rescuing me from Rik, but it was actually about Marisa, wasn't it? You wanted to stop her troubling you and I'm a handy excuse.'

Vittorio closed his eyes like a man wondering how to cope with another disaster.

'It's a bit more than that...' He groaned. 'It's not just Marisa.'

'So it's all the others who hunted you down today?'

'I don't think it's an accident that so many people—women—turned up. They came to see *you*.'

'You think they're all competing for *you*? I've heard of conceit, but that takes the biscuit.'

'You're wrong. I'm not vain enough to think girls are after me for myself. It's the title they want, and they're not the only ones. My father tried to arrange a marriage between myself and Marisa. I told him I wasn't keen, but he wouldn't listen. He was so certain he could persuade me that he let her think it was all arranged. She reckons I'm her property, and if I so much as look at another woman she acts like a betrayed wife. It's getting more than I can stand. Why do you think they came today? Marisa spread the word that I'd arrived with you and they all descended on us to get a look at you. So, yes, I thought your presence here might help me, and I seized the chance because I'm going crazy with this situation.'

'But you didn't think to tell me?'

'I was going to but—well—I just lost my nerve. Suppose I *had* told you? What would you have done? Agreed to help me? I don't think so.'

'You're wrong. After the way you helped me deal with Rik I'll do anything I can for you.'

His eyes gleamed. 'Anything?'

'Anything at all.'

'You'll help save me from Marisa?'

She smiled. 'I'll go into battle against her and you'll be quite safe.'

'That would be wonderful. Just keeping her thinking we're an item. It may just work.'

'But why does it have to be me? Why couldn't you pick someone else?'

'Because you have one great advantage that makes you a better choice than anyone else.'

'What could that possibly be?'

'You've made it plain you don't like me or trust me. Another woman might take my attentions seriously, think I meant them, and then be hurt when she learned the truth. But *you* see me as a cold and arrogant—mercenary, even. That's fine. There's no danger that you'll ever fall in love with me. I know we've decided to be friends, but it's a cautious friendship with suspicion on both sides, and that makes us both safe.'

She regarded him ironically.

'So you chose me because you knew I'd never embarrass you by indulging in romantic thoughts about you? Oh, were you right about that!'

'That's what I reckoned. You'd sooner swoon over a slimy octopus than me.'

'I wouldn't go so far as to say *that*.'

'But you were thinking it?'

She regarded him with her head on one side. 'Maybe. Sometimes it's best to keep your thoughts to yourself. I'm sure you know all about that.'

'It's been useful. Let's shake on it.'

They clasped hands.

'Your aunt doesn't like Marisa, does she?' she observed.

'No, but she's my father's sister, and as such she feels bound by his wishes.'

'Nonsense. The only wishes that matter are yours.'

His face brightened. '*That's* what I like to hear a woman say.'

'Aha! You think it shows I have a submissive nature?' She rubbed her hands. 'I could have a nasty shock waiting for you.'

'I'm sure you will. And I'm equally sure it will be interesting.'

From outside the building came the sound of voices. Vittorio opened the window and looked down.

'They're leaving,' he said. 'Come here.'

She went to stand beside him and he put his arm around her. Down below, Marisa was approaching her car while the other guests streamed out around her. Suddenly Marisa turned her head, gazing up at them.

'Shall we try to convince her now?' Vittorio murmured.

'Yes—what shall we do?'

'Rest your head on my shoulder.'

She did so, and he tightened his arm about her.

'Look up at me,' he murmured.

As soon as she did he leaned down and kissed her forehead.

Jackie drew a slow breath, waiting for him to drift lower until his lips touched hers. But he stayed as he was.

'She's there…watching us,' he said. Let's make this look good.'

His arms tightened, drawing her closer. His free hand caressed her cheek before drifting down, briefly touching her breasts. Jackie trembled, longing fiercely to take things further.

'You said you wanted me to help you…' she whispered.

'Yes—what are you going to do?'

'This,' she said, and reached up so that her arms went around his neck, drawing his head down so that she could caress his mouth with her own.

She could sense the surprise that shook him, then felt his grip on her tighten as he took control, moving his mouth against hers with growing urgency.

Caution told her that she shouldn't do this, but she couldn't make herself be cautious. Desire stormed through her, destroying everything but the need to be his and make him hers.

At last he spoke, his voice shaking. 'I think—I think we've done almost enough to convince her.'

'Yes—yes—'

'Just a few moments more…' His mouth brushed hers again.

Down below, Marisa got into her car. At the last moment she glanced up at them, made a sneering face, then started the car and drove away.

CHAPTER FIVE

'SHE'S GONE,' VITTORIO WHISPERED.

He could almost hear his own voice shaking. The last few minutes had affected him intensely, making him yearn to go further. But he struggled for control, fearful of driving Jackie away.

Reluctantly he released her. 'You did it. Marisa saw enough to get the message. Perhaps I should be grateful to you for taking command.'

'I didn't take command—'

'Didn't you?'

She thought she could guess his meaning. When she had reached up to draw his head down closer to hers, he'd known that her desire was as strong as his, and there was no way she could deny it. He had probably read the message in her eyes.

'You found the right way for both of us,' he said. 'You could say I followed your lead.'

'It was necessary for the performance,' she reminded him. 'Anything's worth doing for an effective performance.'

'Well said! A woman with efficient instincts.'

'And efficiency is everything,' she said lightly.

She met his gaze, both of them knowing that the real message was something quite different.

'Sometimes efficiency really *is* everything,' he said softly. 'But then—things change.'

'Well, they've changed for Marisa. I can't think why

she's worried about me. I'm no beauty. And don't bother to give me a polite answer or I'll thump you.'

'Right. You're no beauty. I heartily agree,' he said, trying to sound casual. He met her eyes. 'But you do have something else that's more than looks. You've got wit, and an intelligence that I find most appealing. In fact, since the day we met you've caught me out and tripped me up more than anyone's ever done before.'

'Then I'm surprised you brought me here.'

'Yes, I wonder what I was thinking of. I guess I don't mind being caught at a disadvantage—every now and then.'

'I'll remember that. I could have fun tripping you up.'

'I bet you will. There are women who conquer a man by their beauty, and those who conquer him by keeping him nervous, even scared.'

'And there's no doubt which one *I* am!' She laughed. 'But maybe I don't *want* to conquer you.'

'You won't make the effort? Then I'd feel insulted. Besides, you do it without meaning to.'

'You don't know that. I might have a fiendish plan going on.'

'I live in hope. But for the moment I'll say goodnight. We have a busy day tomorrow. You should beware. When we get to Rome I'm going to work you to death.'

'That's what I hoped. Anything else would be dull.'

'And let's not be *dull*, whatever we do.'

'No. Not that you could ever be dull here,' she murmured, glancing around at his bedroom. Like the rest of the house, it was lavishly decorated in a medieval style.

'This was my father's room,' he said.

'And now it's yours because you're the Count? Do you think you can be grandiose enough?'

'I'll try to be. I've never thought of myself as grandiose, but I suppose everything is going to be different now.'

'Yes,' she murmured. 'That's true. You won your battle

tonight. Marisa saw us, which is exactly what you wanted. From now on you'll be a free man.'

'A free man?' He looked into her eyes. 'I wonder just what that means?'

She met his gaze, suddenly confused. 'You'll find out gradually. I'm here to help you.' A sudden impulse made her say. 'It's getting late and I'm tired. I think I'll go to bed now. Goodnight.'

'Goodnight. And, Jackie—thank you for everything.'

She smiled and fled. It had suddenly become vital to escape him quickly and take refuge in her room.

Once there, she paced the floor, trying to understand the conflicting thoughts and feelings that struggled for supremacy inside her head.

It was madness to be upset, she told herself. Vittorio was a man of good looks and charm. Any woman would be thrilled to be taken into his arms. And for a brief moment she had known that delicious excitement. To feel his lips caressing hers, sense the tremors in his body—those pleasures had consumed her. He had wanted her, and the blissful knowledge had driven her to a response that had been almost beyond her control.

But then, like a warning blast, a voice in her mind had warned her to take care. To guard her feelings. He'd embraced her in order to deceive Marisa, then released her when Marisa had no longer been able to see them.

He was only pretending, she thought. He'd pretend for just long enough to get what he wanted and then she'd have outlived her usefulness to him. Just as if she fell in love with him he'd find it useful. And that was all he wanted of her—to be useful. Useful in the department store, useful about the money problem, useful about Marisa.

She'd do well to remember that falling for Vittorio would be extremely hazardous to her health. Mind you, he'd be as a big a fool to fall for *her*!

* * *

With Jackie gone Vittorio stood without moving for some moments, trying to cope with conflicting feelings. This had been his father's bedroom, and it still contained many memories.

Here they had spent their last few moments together, and Franco had revealed the secret that had set Vittorio on a new path. Putting right his father's wrongs had seemed like the right thing to do—and a simple thing.

But before that there had been other talks. Some of them about Vittorio's mother. He knew that both his parents had been unfaithful in their brief marriage. Adele, his mother, had married for the title—something which Franco, deeply in love, had not suspected until it was too late.

Looking at the surroundings where his father had made his last confession, he found that another scene came back to him. Then, too, Franco had lain there, dizzy with suffering, driving himself to tell the painful truth to his son, who had knelt beside the bed.

'I lost track of all the men she had...' He'd sighed.

Filled with fear, Vittorio had asked quickly, 'Do you mean that I'm not your son?'

'No, you're mine. When you were born I had a DNA test done to check, and the result was all I had hoped. But the fact that such a test was needed—' He had given a deep groan before adding wretchedly, 'And the other child...'

'What other child?'

'Do you remember how we lost your mother when you were twelve? She died giving birth. The baby also died. It wasn't mine. We hadn't made love for a long time, so I knew. She had never loved me as I loved her. I would have forgiven her, because I so much wanted her to stay with me, but then she was gone.'

'But how could you have kept her with you, knowing what you knew?' Vittorio had asked desperately.

'Yes, it's madness, isn't it? But love *is* a kind of madness. When you love a woman so much that you'll forgive her anything as long as she doesn't leave you, it's as though you cease to be yourself. I should have divorced her years before. I'd have been safer without her there to torment me. But I couldn't do it. I told myself I stayed with her for your sake, because you needed a mother. But the truth was I couldn't bear to let her go. So we stayed together…she kept living her riotous life. And then she died.'

Vittorio hadn't been able to reply. He'd dropped his head down into the bed, close to his father's, feeling only despair.

Franco had touched him. 'I pray that your life may be filled with more hope,' he'd said. 'Don't give your love to a woman who deceives you. Be cautious, my son. Don't trust too easily. Keep your love to yourself as long as you can.'

The advice had touched Vittorio's heart. Only recently he'd quarrelled with a young woman who'd briefly inspired his trust and affection before turning to another man. Everything in him had accepted that his father had been right, and that he must be cautious.

But then he'd met Jackie—frank, honest, different from any other women he'd met. Or so he'd thought until his growing attraction to her had begun to alarm him. Holding her in his arms, he'd felt a surge of feeling that was not merely desire, but also tenderness. And the awareness of her trembling in his arms, the fervour with which she'd kissed him, had left him feeling stunned.

She'd called it efficiency, claiming to have done no more than follow his lead. But the memory of her response lingered…delightful, alarming, warning him that the road ahead led into mystery.

It was unbearable not to know the answer. He went out into the corridor, looking to see if there was a light under her door. But there was none. Had she really gone to sleep?

Or was she lying in the darkness, facing a confusion as great as his own?

He stood outside her door, listening to the silence inside, trying to decide whether to call her or knock. But after hesitating a long time he backed away, sensing that this was not the right moment.

Next morning Jackie awoke early and took a shower. Standing under the water, she wondered what she would see in Vittorio's eyes this morning. She'd felt sure he would call on her the previous night, but nothing had happened.

She'd heard a faint sound, as though his footsteps had approached her room, but then there had been only silence. Unable to bear the tension, she'd leapt out of bed and pulled open her door. But the corridor outside had been dark and empty, with no sign of him. She had gone back to bed and lain there fretting until she'd managed to fall asleep.

This morning her thoughts were still troubled—even more so because her attraction towards Vittorio made her feel that she was failing her father again.

Somehow, somewhere, there must be a way to do the right thing. If only she could find it.

She dressed and went downstairs into the hall. Through an open door she could see Vittorio sitting at a desk.

He glanced up and waved to her. 'We'll be going in to breakfast in a moment,' he said. 'And then we can—'

The sound of the phone interrupted him, making him curse slightly and then answer it. Jackie went to stand by the window, gazing out at the grass and trees, entranced by their beauty. Clearly it was a magnificent estate, and she was curious to see more of it.

Glancing around, she saw that he had his back to her, absorbed in the call. Yielding to temptation, she slipped out of the door into the garden. For a few moments it was delightful to run across the lawn to where she could see a seat under one of the trees. She sat down on it and leaned back, closing her eyes and breathing in the cool air.

When at last she opened her eyes she found herself gazing at the building that reared up so magnificently, beautiful and luxurious. But the sight caused sorrow to fall over her heart, as it had done so often since she'd arrived here. This had been the home of the man who had cheated her beloved father, reducing him to poverty and despair.

In her mind's eye she saw her father again, his head sunk in misery when his wife had left him.

He had nothing, she thought. *And the man who lives here has everything.*

She could feel tears pouring down her cheeks and ducked her head, seizing a handkerchief to wipe them away. But there were more tears, followed by sobs. She sat there shaking, trying vainly to control her grief.

'Jackie— *Jackie?*'

The voice from overhead made her look up to see Vittorio standing there. At once he sat down beside her, reaching out to her.

'Come here,' he said.

'No!' She pulled sharply away. 'Go away. Leave me alone.'

'But I—'

'I said leave me alone. I don't want to talk to you.'

She jumped up, fleeing away from him until she plunged into the trees. When she felt safely out of sight she leaned against a tree trunk and abandoned the effort to control her tears.

Suddenly she felt a pair of strong arms go around her, pulling her against him.

'I'm sorry,' he said. 'I don't mean to crowd you, but stay with me a while. Let me help you.'

She couldn't answer. The feel of his chest was warm

and comforting, giving her a pleasure she hadn't thought to know. She trembled and felt him draw her even closer.

'Cry,' he said. 'You need to. Don't fight it.'

It felt incredible that she was letting this man, of all men, comfort her. But the feel of his arms about her was unlike anything that had ever happened to her before.

'Let's go inside,' he said. 'We'll have breakfast and then go into the city. We've got a lot to do.'

'Oh, yes,' she said wryly. 'I'm going to give you all that expert opinion—if I can think of anything. I really felt very awkward when you were telling your aunt how good I am.'

'You played your part beautifully.'

'But I don't even know what I'm supposed to be expert *about*.'

'That's why we're going into town. By the time we've finished you'll be able to give me your orders.'

She rubbed her hands. 'Roll on the day!'

'Well, I've been meaning to tell you—' He stopped, realising that he no longer had her attention. She was looking about her at the medieval beauty of her surroundings as though something had suddenly struck her, 'What's the matter?' he asked.

'Nothing. It's this place,' she said. 'I just have to keep looking at it. It's wonderful how history seems to live here all around us, as though your ancestors were still alive.'

'I know the feeling. I've felt them with me all my life, and if I want to meet them I go to the gallery, where their portraits hang. Would you like to see it?'

'I'd love to.'

He led her into a great room at the back of the house. Portraits hung all along the walls, of people dressed in clothes that spoke of past centuries.

'And *all* these are your ancestors?' Jackie mused in wonder.

'Not all. Have a look at this one.'

He drew her to a full-length picture showing a young woman in a horse-drawn chariot. With one hand she controlled the horses, in the other she held a sword. On her head she wore a military helmet.

'That's Bellona,' Vittorio told her. 'The Roman goddess of war.'

'You have a *female* deity of war? Surely—?'

'Surely it should be a man?' he said, grinning. 'In any other society it probably would be. But in Rome we like strong, powerful women.'

'Unless they happen to disagree with you?' she teased, her eyes challenging him.

'Ah, well, let's not go into that.'

'Very wise,' she said with mock solemnity. 'Just think of all the awkward things I could remind you of.'

'And how you'd enjoy doing it.'

Tania had slipped into the room behind them and was listening to them with pleasure.

'You'll have a chance to meet Bellona,' she said. 'We celebrate her festival every year. You'll probably enjoy that.'

'Yes, you two have a lot in common…' Vittorio observed.

'Vittorio!' Tania protested. 'I hope you're not being rude to our guest.'

'Don't worry, Aunt. Jackie's not offended. And here's someone else you should meet,' Vittorio said, turning her towards a picture of a man in a suit of armour. 'He was the very first Count Martelli. And the two men in the next picture are his sons. The elder one died and the younger one inherited the title.'

Along the walls they went, with Vittorio describing his ancestors one by one, introducing them as though they still lived with him.

One portrait especially seized Jackie's attention. It showed a man in the luscious garb of the seventeenth century, with long curling hair falling over his shoulders. But it was his face that claimed her attention. It was Vittorio's face that had come down the centuries.

'He was my great-great-great-great-grandfather,' Vittorio said.

'Yes, I can see. It's incredible. You're really one of them. Hey—what's that?'

Her attention had been seized by another picture, a few feet along. It showed two men dressed in the attire of ancient Rome. One of them also had a face similar to Vittorio's.

'He must be another ancestor of yours,' she said. 'Who's the man with him?'

'Julius Caesar—the Roman Emperor.'

'One of your family was a friend of *Julius Caesar*? They even had their portraits painted together?'

'Not at all. There's a common belief that one of my ancestors was part of Caesar's court, but that picture was painted hundreds of years later. It's just a fantasy. There are several fantasies like that in this gallery. Over here is Napoleon. When he was Emperor of France he annexed Rome, but when he was defeated we regained our freedom.'

The picture had been carefully designed to show Napoleon regarding his companion with admiration and respect. The companion's face also bore a notable resemblance to Vittorio's.

'It's marvellous, isn't it?' said Tania.

'That face—it's *him*!' Jackie exclaimed in wonder.

'Yes, you can't get away from me even a few hundred years later.' Vittorio laughed.

'Have you shown Jackie the picture of Lady Nanetta?' Tania asked.

'Not yet, but I'm looking forward to doing it.' He guided her across the room. 'Nanetta is a family legend,' he explained. 'She was a magnificent woman, but also an alarming one.'

He paused before a full-length picture of a tall, slender woman.

'She had dozens of suitors,' he said, 'but she rejected them all. Legend says that she was a witch. It's never been proved or disproved, but she inspired a lot of fear.'

'Why did she reject them all?' Jackie asked. 'Didn't she ever fall in love?'

'Never. She had a great fortune and she believed that was all men wanted of her. She said no man could be trusted, nor was ever worthy of love.'

'How sad to believe that,' Jackie murmured. 'How could anyone endure life with nothing to believe in?'

'Is love the *only* thing to believe in?' he asked wryly.

'Of course there's always money.'

'But you don't believe in that, having turned down so much.'

'If you mean your million pounds, I turned it down for love—of my father.' She saw tension come into his face and added, 'There's more than one kind of love.'

He hesitated before saying, 'You're right, of course.'

She went to stand before the woman's picture, trying to see if her face revealed anything. But Lady Nanetta stared into the distance, concealing her secrets.

'I wonder what taught her so much distrust?' Jackie said.

'She saw a lot of evidence to distrust in her life. She was hugely rich.'

'Which was why so many men wanted to marry her?'

'Probably. Of course they may have been attracted to her as well.'

'I doubt that,' Jackie said, studying the picture. 'She was no beauty.'

Vittorio considered the picture before glancing back at her. 'That matters little,' he said. 'A woman doesn't have to be a great beauty to intrigue men. Her moods, her wit, the hint of mystery she can carry—those can lure men as keenly as mere good looks.' After a thoughtful moment he added, 'Sometimes more so.'

He was giving her a look that might have been significant. She tried to be cautious about understanding it, but there was a glint in his eye she couldn't ignore.

She called common sense to her rescue. 'If you say so,' she said cheerfully.

'I *do* say so.'

'Then I'll have to believe it—however unconvincing.'

He chuckled and put his arm around her. 'Let's get going—we have a busy day ahead of us,' said Vittorio. 'But first we'll have breakfast.'

They ate quickly, and when breakfast was over he led Jackie out of the palace to a garage around the side. He regarded her curiously as she took out her purse and examined its contents.

'Need some money?' he asked.

'No. Thank you, but I'm quite independent. I can use my bank card to draw money from my English account, can't I?'

'If you've got the pin number, yes.'

In a few moments they were on their way to Rome.

'What are we going to see first?' she asked.

'My department store. I need to see how it's managing. And I'll be interested in your opinion. After that, I'd like to show you some of the city.'

At first the road wound through the estate, and Jackie watched from the window, charmed by the green fields and forests, until finally the estate was behind them and they were heading along the motorway that led to the city.

Once in Rome, Vittorio drove straight to an area where there were shops, restaurants and commercial buildings. He parked the car and led her through the streets, letting her absorb the atmosphere until it was time to visit his department store.

It was a huge place, selling goods from many different countries and a vast range of sources. There were departments for furniture, glass, hardware and jewellery.

Jackie walked through it in a daze of delight. Everywhere Vittorio introduced her to the staff as 'my expert from England'. In the glass and china department he explained that she was to be in charge, and she was treated with great respect.

When he was called away for a moment the staff crowded round her, full of eager questions. Their English was efficient, as was her Italian.

'There are some products I'd like to show you,' she said. 'I'll need a computer.'

One was immediately made available, and she went online to show them the many sites where she found products that made them exclaim with admiration. It was clear that her visit was a success.

At last she looked up to find Vittorio regarding her with amused satisfaction.

'Found me any new stock?' he asked.

'One or two things I think might go well.'

She indicated several choices. He nodded in agreement to all of them, and a staff member began making purchases.

'We'll leave him to it while we look around some more,' Vittorio said. When they were outside he said, 'I wish you could have seen your face while you were giving everyone instructions. I think that's your idea of heaven.'

'If you mean that I'm a bully—'

'Only the kind of bully that I need working for me,' he said with a grin. 'You promised to make profit for me, and I can see that you will. Well done!'

'Thank you. After all, you did promise me authority.'

'I must have known by instinct that authority is your default position.'

'You might have a point there,' she said with a brief laugh. 'I must admit I *do* enjoy being the one to give the orders.'

'After the way you had to put up with Rik, I'm not surprised.'

'Not just Rik. I used to annoy my father a lot by arguing.' She regarded him cheekily. 'I'm a very difficult character.'

'Well, I already knew *that*.' He took her hand in his and gave it a comforting squeeze. 'I can put up with you if you can put up with me.'

She squeezed back. 'I'll do my best—however hard it is.'

'I've got a feeling we're going to be a big success.'

Coming to Italy was proving to be everything she had dared to hope, thought Jackie. Here there were opportunities and a chance for the kind of new, more adventurous life that had once seemed impossible.

Suddenly she stopped.

'I didn't realise that your store stocked clothes.'

'Of course—it's our most popular department. Come and look.'

Jackie was soon in heaven! Vittorio introduced her to the staff and she watched, entranced, as boxes were opened to reveal costly gowns. She examined them, trying to imagine her dull self in any of the exquisite dresses.

'Perhaps—' she began, turning to Vittorio. 'Oh, where's he gone?'

'He was summoned to his office,' said Donna, the head assistant. 'Do you like our stock?

'Oh, yes, it's all so beautiful. Especially this one.' She gazed admiringly at a black satin evening gown.

'Yes, it's one of our new range. Would you like to try it on?'

'I'm not sure... It looks very sophisticated, and I'm not really like that.'

'But you might be if you saw yourself in it.'

'Oh, go on, then—let's try.'

Donna's advice was good. The dress was tight-fitting, and clung perfectly to Jackie's slender figure, giving it a drama and mystery she'd never been aware of before.

She turned back and forth, enjoying the sight of her new self in the mirror. Totally absorbed, she failed to notice the middle-aged woman who had arrived, and was watching her with pleasure.

'Is that dress for sale?' the woman asked Donna.

'Yes, Contessa. It's part of the stock that's just arrived.'

'It would suit my daughter perfectly. I'll buy it.' The shopper turned to the man who had just appeared beside her. 'You're really extending your talents in this store. Doesn't your model look lovely?'

'Yes,' Vittorio murmured, 'she does.'

He backed away quickly before Jackie could notice him. After a moment the Countess joined him. She was beaming.

'Now you have a satisfied customer,' she said. 'That dress looked so good on your model that I just *had* to buy it. Donna says it can be delivered tomorrow.'

He replied politely and escorted her away, before returning to the dress department. Jackie was still there, once more in her own clothes. For a moment Vittorio had a dizzying sensation that briefly she had become a different Jackie.

'It's time to move on, Jackie. We have a lot to fit in today.'

'Oh, that's a shame. I've had an amazing morning, and your store is magnificent.'

'No, no,' he said quickly. 'You mustn't say that. You're going to tell me how to bring it up to standard.'

'Suppose I think I can't?'

'Hush, don't say such a thing. Never admit failure.' He gave her a cheeky grin. 'You're here as an expert, giving me your lofty advice.'

'And you'll *take* my advice? I don't think so.'

'Then you can call me some suitable names. *Stupido, idiota, buffone.* You understand Italian well enough to take your pick.'

'I'll try to remember. Where to next, then?'

'I'd like to take you to my other shop. This one is much smaller. It could do with expansion, and I'd value your opinion.'

CHAPTER SIX

A SHORT STROLL brought them to the 'other shop', which she examined with interest, making notes. She was enjoying herself.

After a couple of hours they left.

Wherever they went Vittorio was instantly recognised. Even in the street people addressed him respectfully as 'Signor Conte', and regarded her with curiosity.

She could guess why she fascinated them. Word of her arrival had obviously spread fast, and she was clearly being regarded as the latest candidate for the position of Countess.

Me, she thought hilariously. *Plain, dreary me. Whatever next?*

'What's so funny?' Vittorio asked.

'Sorry—what?'

'You suddenly started laughing. People don't usually find Rome funny.'

'It's not Rome that's funny. It's me. Haven't you seen the way everybody is staring at me?'

'Sure—you've really got their attention.'

'And why? For the same reason Marisa is troubled by me. I'm seen as the latest candidate for your hand.'

'And that's funny, is it?'

'It is from the proper angle. Look.'

She pointed him towards the window of a shop they were passing. Turning, they looked at their reflections: Vittorio splendidly handsome, herself ordinary.

'Ever since the moment I came here,' she said, 'I've felt like Cinderella arriving at the ball.'

'Really? Does that make me Prince Charming?'

'Prince Charming or Prince Charm*less*. It depends on your mood.'

'You don't pull your punches, do you? Are you trying to lure me in or put me off?'

'What do *you* think?'

'I think you're trying to scare the life out of me. And succeeding.'

'That's all right, then. As long as you don't think I'm trying to lure you into marriage.'

'I promise never to think that.'

Vittorio wondered what he should have understood from her words. If she ever did set her sights on him he doubted he'd guess. She was too clever to be obvious. But the conversation had amused him too much to be troublesome.

'I'd better go into the bank while I'm here,' he said. 'The one across the road is the one I use.'

Inside the bank, she saw him treated with the same intense respect she had noticed before—which she guessed told her everything about the size of his bank balance.

'It would be easier if you banked here also, since you'll be living and working in Italy from now on,' he said. 'Tell them you want to transfer your London account.' He added lightly, 'Unless, of course, you're planning to dash back to the joys of working for Rik.'

'No chance!'

'Wise woman.'

He came to the counter with her and spoke in rapid Italian.

'There'll be bank cards for you in a couple of days,' he said at last. 'And now it's time for some lunch at last. This way.'

He led her to a little restaurant on the next corner.

As she looked through the menu he said, 'What would you like?'

'I don't know; I can't decide. I'll let you order for me.'

He regarded her with amused suspicion. 'You trust me to order for you? That's not like the Jackie I've come to know. Are you trying to catch me off-guard?'

'Well, I've got to do *something* to worry you, haven't I?'

'Don't bother. You worry me quite enough as it is.'

'In that case, please do your duty and order for me.'

He instructed the waitress, and in a few minutes a dish was set before her. It was a bowl filled with tiny lumps of meat and a few vegetables.

'It's called lamb *tagliata*,' he said. 'I remembered that you like lamb.'

'But that was the lunch we had in the hotel in London,' she said, astonished. 'You remembered from then?'

'Of course. I'm a businessman. I make efficient notes about my business associates and use them to my advantage.'

But he winked as he said it, and gave her a grin which she returned.

The food tasted magnificent. She devoured it with pleasure, aware that he was watching her closely.

'Mmm…lovely,' she said. 'You choose food well. I must put that in my own notes about *you*—along with a few other things.'

He nodded, implying that he understood her perfectly. 'Of course,' he said, 'my observations will have to include how careless you are about doing your job.'

'What?'

'You were supposed to be giving me an expert opinion of my store. So far all you've done is eat. I want to lodge a complaint.'

'I said it was magnificent!'

'But you were just being polite.'

'I'm *never* polite. Haven't you learned that yet? Hmm…
I'll have to give you a few lessons.'

'I'll look forward to it. But, in the meantime, you didn't
really *mean* magnificent, did you?'

'Suppose I say yes? Would that make me disappointing?'

'Come on, Jackie. Criticise. It's what you're here for.'

'Well, I *did* notice one thing missing. You have a huge
range of things from all over the world, but I saw nothing
from England.'

'That's because we've never had any real English ex-
pertise—until now. I did the right thing, kidnapping you.'

'You didn't exactly *kidnap* me,' she insisted. 'I wanted
to come.'

'Suppose you hadn't? Do you think that would have
made any difference?'

'No, I guess not.'

'You did a great job in the shop—especially when you
modelled that dress.'

'Modelled—? You saw me?'

'Yes, I keep turning up when I'm not wanted, don't I?
I was there with Contessa Valierse. She liked the sight of
you so much she bought the dress for her daughter. I seem
to gain from everything you do. As soon as I realised that,
I decided that you must belong to me.'

'And if I resist?' she teased.

'It won't make any difference. When an efficient businessman finds something that suits him he takes possession of it, ignoring all distractions.'

'And you think nobody can successfully fight you?'

'That's right. I always get my own way. Make a special
note of that.'

'Yes, I think I will.' She took out a scrap of paper, then
discovered a problem.

'Damn! I haven't got a pen.'

'Here.' He handed her a pen.

'I wonder if I should accept that…' she mused.

'You mean because you're about to write something critical about me? Go on. Be brave.'

'Thanks.' She took it and scribbled, *He always gets his own way,* adding a little swirl afterwards.

'What's that squiggle at the end?' Vittorio asked.

'It's code. It means, *That's what he thinks.*' Jackie chuckled.

'Hmm… At least you're honest.'

'Well, I'm not sure you get your own way as much as you think you do.'

'You will be. In time.'

Despite the seemingly harsh words, the atmosphere was teasing and friendly.

'Of course it doesn't do for a guy to be too self-confident around you,' he said. 'He'd pay a heavy price.'

'Or *I* would,' she said wryly.

He considered her. 'Is that the voice of experience?'

'There was a man I was once fond off. Just fond. His name was Peter. I wasn't passionately in love, but when he mentioned marriage I was interested.'

'What went wrong?'

'My father became ill. I was looking after him and Peter didn't like that. It made him feel that he came second.'

'*Did* he come second?'

'Yes, I suppose he did. He wanted me to put Daddy in a care home, but I couldn't do that. It would have broken his heart.'

'And Peter was angry about that?'

'We had a quarrel. I told him that he couldn't give me orders and that was that. In my admittedly limited experience I've discovered that men like to be in charge.'

'Surely that isn't aimed at *me*? You have as much control as I do.'

'Not as much. Maybe a bit.'

'We'll agree to disagree. So you sent him away with a flea in his ear?'

'Yes. He couldn't believe I meant it, but I wasn't going to change my mind. How about you? Have you never been tempted to settle down with any of the beautiful women who seem to throw themselves at you at any given opportunity?'

He made a face, but said nothing.

'I'm sorry,' she said. 'I didn't mean to pry. Your love life is none of my business.' She added cheekily, 'But perhaps you don't *have* one. Perhaps you live on a pinnacle of lofty indifference.'

'If only I did. There was one woman who taught me to be careful, and it was a strong lesson that I've never forgotten.'

'Was she after your title?'

'She was. But at first she played her role so convincingly that I didn't realise the truth. I was completely taken in—until the day I found her in bed with another man.'

'What? How *could* she?'

'The man was heir to a dukedom. His social standing and personal fortune were therefore much greater than my own. That told me everything I needed to know. Her fine words and loving behaviour towards me had been because she wanted my title. When a better title came along I ceased to exist as far as she was concerned.'

'She pretended to love you—?'

'It was a good act. Fooled me.'

'And you loved her?'

He hesitated, and she could tell that he found this hard to answer.

'I thought I did. But it was a useful lesson. I've never been deceived again. I keep my suspicious side working.'

His words were cool, but she had a sense that they concealed feelings he didn't want to admit. This deceitful woman had caused him a lot of pain—some of which had never completely abated.

'What a dreadful thing to happen,' she said. 'Can you ever trust anyone again?'

'Probably not. But it's safer that way. What about you? After this guy you sent away—has there been anyone since?'

'No, I've had too much to think about. First my father died, and after that I set my heart on saving up enough money to escape my miserable existence, start a new life.'

'But you could be doing that now, by taking the money I offered you. Why did you turn it down?'

'For Daddy's sake. It would have felt like insulting him—saying that his suffering didn't matter as long as I gained the money.'

'But he wouldn't know.'

'Maybe—maybe not. But I still value his opinion. What he would've thought about things is of paramount importance to me. What about you and *your* father's wishes? Don't you take *his* views into account when you make decisions? Isn't that what you were doing in trying to give me that money?'

Jackie was exactly right, he realised. His father was still there in his mind and his heart. At times it was as if he could hear his voice in his ear. And clearly the same was true of her. It was almost alarming.

'And do you feel that *he* would know whether you've managed it or not?' she asked.

'I don't know, of course,' he said quietly. 'But *I* will know.'

'And so will I. That's why I can't give in and take your money. I feel that it would break his heart.'

'And I have to keep my word to *my* father. If I don't, that would break *his* heart.'

'If only they could have talked to each other while they

were still alive,' she said wistfully. 'They could've sorted it out without us.'

He took her hand between his. 'Instead we must honour their memories and do right by them both.'

'Yes. I'm glad of that.'

He squeezed her hand. 'So am I.'

A waiter approached, making him release her quickly.

When he'd ordered some coffee he said, 'Let's discuss the store. You said it needed more stuff from England. Tell me exactly what you mean…'

After lunch they were soon in the car, heading back through the country to the Castello Martelli. As darkness fell she saw the building's lights from a distance, and marvelled again at its magnificence and beauty.

Tania was waiting in the hall.

'Shall I get you some supper?' she asked.

'No need—we've enjoyed a late lunch,' Vittorio told her cheerfully. 'And now we have something to celebrate. This way, Jackie.'

His arm around her waist, he guided her into his office. Tania regarded them wryly. After a moment she went to the office door and stood watching while Jackie worked on the computer, accessing one English website after another while showing Vittorio her ideas for supplying his stores.

'Can you go back to the last one?' Vittorio said. 'I like those metal ornaments. Yes, that's it. Zoom in on that one. Great. Yes, I'll have that.'

He became aware of Tania stood in the doorway.

'Come and look, Aunt. Jackie's doing a wonderful job for us.'

'So I see,' Tania said, coming forward, smiling. 'You really seem very knowledgeable, *signorina*.'

'Please call me Jackie.'

'Jackie. Yes. Now, if my nephew is going to work you to death can I get you some coffee—or tea? A glass of wine?'

'I'm okay—thank you, Tania.'

'I will take a wine, please, Aunt Tania,' said Vittorio.

The other woman smiled at them both and headed to the kitchen. Jackie sensed that Tania was still undecided about her, but her manner was pleasant.

Once Tania was gone, Jackie's attention was brought back to the computer screen.

'I want to go back to town tomorrow,' announced Vittorio, 'but tonight I want to see some of those websites again.'

'I'll get started now,' Jackie said.

He sat with his attention fixed on what she was doing. Suddenly he said, 'Let me look at that.'

She enlarged the picture, which was of a metal vase with elaborate engraving.

He studied it for several minutes before saying, 'Fine. I'll buy some of those.'

He purchased the items online, studied more websites and purchased several more things. By the time they were finished he'd spent a thousand euros and was in good spirits.

'Fantastic job!' he said. I'd never have found that stuff without you. And tomorrow there'll be more. We must make an early start.'

'Then I'll have an early night,' Jackie said, rising.

He rose too, but she signalled for him to sit down. Tania had just returned to the office with Vittorio's drink, and Jackie got the sense that she wanted to talk with her nephew privately.

Vittorio nodded, gave her a gentle kiss on the cheek, and let her go.

When they were alone Tania poured him a glass of wine. 'It's been a good evening,' she said.

'Yes. I knew bringing Jackie here would be brilliant. She really knows her stuff.'

'And she makes sure you realise it,' Tania observed lightly.

'You sound suspicious. I thought you liked her?'

'In a way, I do. That's what makes it confusing. I want to believe in her but—' She sighed.

'But what?'

'What exactly is she *after*?'

'Nothing.'

'Oh, my dear boy, be realistic. Every young woman you meet is after something. Usually money.'

'No, that's one thing I can be sure of. She's not after my money. I offered her money and she refused it.'

'Obviously it wasn't enough.'

'I offered her in excess of a million English pounds.'

'A million—? Are you out of your mind?'

'In a way, yes. I've been partly out of my mind since Papà admitted on his deathbed that he'd cheated Jackie's father out of a million years ago.'

Tania gasped. 'No, that's not possible. You've imagined it.'

'It's true. He told me he and George Benton both placed a bet. Benton's paid off, but Papà stole the winnings before Benton knew. I've been desperate to put it right by paying back the money. I was going to give it to George Benton, but he's dead. So I offered it to Jackie and she turned me down.'

Tania gasped. 'She actually refused to take a sum like that? I don't believe it.'

'It's true. I'm not lying.'

'No, I mean I don't believe her refusal was genuine. She wants you to think her honest so that you'll be lured in further—perhaps even marry her.'

'I don't believe that.'

'No, because you've formed a high opinion of her—exactly as you were meant to.'

'So you don't really like her after all?'

Tania hesitated before saying carefully, 'I'm not sure. She makes me cautious. But she's so clever and sharp-witted I wonder if she might be the right woman for you, because *she* could be the one who could make you stop your nonsense.'

This seemed to strike him. He considered thoughtfully before saying, 'My *nonsense*? I think you two must be in cahoots.'

'Why? Has she called you out on your nonsense too?'

'Not outright, but she implies it every time she opens her mouth.'

'Good for her.'

'Today she called me Prince Charmless.'

'Indeed? She actually said that?'

'Without any hesitation.'

Tania chuckled. 'Now I'm *really* beginning to like her.'

'I like her too,' Vittorio admitted. 'In some ways. But not in others. It comes and goes, and the feelings get intertwined.'

'You mean you have opposite feelings at the same time?'

'Yes—it's hard to know what to think of a woman with several different aspects.'

'That can be the best kind of woman,' Tania observed.

'Certainly the most interesting,' Vittorio murmured. 'And now I think I'll have an early night myself.'

'I hope you're not going to go knocking on her door.'

'I wouldn't dream of it. She and I are just friends. We've both made that very plain.'

'As long as you're both realists.'

'Not a doubt of it. Goodnight, Aunt.' He gave her a friendly peck on the cheek and departed.

Despite retiring early, Vittorio found that his need for sleep deserted him as soon as he went to bed. After tossing and turning for a while he rose, pulled on some jeans and a T-shirt, and went downstairs, then out into the garden.

He couldn't be certain what had disturbed him. Although he knew his aunt's words had touched a nerve, he was unwilling to admit how that touch had agitated him.

We're just friends. We've both made that very plain.

Was that being realistic? Despite her lack of conventional beauty, Jackie held an attraction for him that was unsettling—all the more so because he doubted if she felt the same way.

He walked for a long time before returning to his room and going back to bed. But still sleep evaded him, and he lay there restlessly for several hours until he nodded off just before it was time to get up.

Bad news was waiting for him when he went down for breakfast. Leo, the permanent driver he employed, was feeling poorly.

'He can't drive you to Rome,' Tania told him. 'He isn't well enough.'

'No matter. I'll drive.' But he said it reluctantly. His disturbed night had left him feeling less than his best. But the trip was necessary, and he was sure he could be strong.

He reckoned it was the right decision as he observed Jackie on their journey. She had clearly done some research and knew where she wanted to visit.

'I'd like to see some more of the smaller shops,' she said after a few miles. 'The department stores are impressive, but a little shop can sometimes take you by surprise.'

'Yes, it can,' he said. 'I remember a little shop in London that took me *completely* by surprise. It was being run by a really prickly woman who trampled me underfoot, chucked me out and called me all kinds of names. And a few days later I was fool enough to bring her home with me. I can't think why…'

'I guess you just like being ill-treated,' she teased.

'That's right. And I'm sure she's got some more up her sleeve.'

'Never mind. If you fight back she'll probably make a run for it.'

'Don't you dare! Now I've got you here I'm going to keep you. You're my prisoner. Don't forget it.'

They laughed. And then they were in town, travelling the back streets where Vittorio discovered small businesses that impressed him in unfamiliar ways.

He watched as Jackie examined them, made notes, and drew his attention to things he hadn't noticed.

'You really *do* know your stuff,' he said at last as they got back into the car. 'I'm impressed.' He glanced around and said suddenly, 'Wait here, I'll be just a moment.'

On the far side of the road was a branch of the bank where he'd taken her the day before. He went in, stayed a few minutes, then returned to her.

'I've got something for you,' he said. 'Here.' He handed her a bundle of banknotes.

'But what—?'

'Now you're working for me, and that's your first commission.'

She flicked through the notes, astonished at the amount.

'It's more than I was expecting.'

'You're doing a good job. It's ten per cent of what I spent online under your advice.'

'We didn't actually agree my wages.'

'No, and if I was anything like the last man you worked for I'd cut the amount in half and defy you to challenge me. I wonder how far you'd get…'

'I never got anywhere arguing with Rik until you came and defended me,' she admitted.

'Right. But you're my employee now, and I don't expect you to work for nothing.'

'Well, if you put it like that—'

'You've *earned* that money, Jackie. Now, I'm starving,' Vittorio said. 'Just round that corner is a hotel with one of the best restaurants in Rome. Let's go. Unless you want to be difficult about that too?'

'No, I've had enough fun for today. Let's go.'

CHAPTER SEVEN

'You meant that about fun, didn't you? That's how you get your kicks—driving me mad.'

'Some people are more fun to drive mad than others.'

'You'd better watch out,' Vittorio said. 'It might be *my* turn to have fun.' He swung into a car park. 'Here we are.'

He escorted her inside the hotel and headed for the restaurant. When they were settled inside, Jackie's eyes widened at the sight of the menu.

'Best Roman cuisine,' Vittorio said. 'Does it tempt you?'

'Yes, it looks delicious.' He summoned the waiter and they ordered their food.

'Would you like wine?' he asked.

'Not really.'

'Me neither. I've got to drive us home. Let's have sparkling water.'

When the water arrived he filled both their glasses.

'To a successful business arrangement,' he said.

They clinked glasses.

'Here's the food,' he said with relief as the waiter approached them.

The dishes that were laid before her looked delicious, and tasted that way too.

'Lovely!' she said.

'Good.'

He paused, and she had a strange feeling that he was summoning up his courage. When he spoke again he sounded uneasy.

'The fact is I wanted us to spend a little time together. Because I feel we need to talk.'

Jackie stared at him, puzzled. 'Do we?' she asked softly. 'You might say that we're the last people to want to talk.'

'But that's wrong. We connect because I'm the only person who knows exactly how you feel.'

'I don't think you *do* know how I feel. You can't imagine how all your money and luxury depresses me.'

'Because of your father and what was done to him? I understand how that makes you feel, but I wasn't the man who did it.' He took a deep breath. 'Why do you hate me, Jackie?'

She gave a brief ironic laugh. 'I guess it's because you're the one who's available to me. I can't chastise your father, because he isn't here. But you are, so I can—' She gave a slight shrug.

'Well, that's honest, anyway. So when you kick me in the teeth you just pretend you're kicking him?'

'I guess you're right.' She sighed. 'I keep telling myself to be reasonable, but then I remember Daddy's face looking the way I saw it so often. His life was terrible at the end. He'd lost everything.'

'He hadn't lost you. He had a daughter who cared for him.'

'Yes, but I couldn't fill all the empty spaces in his life. Even now I'm still trying to do my best by him.'

Vittorio closed his eyes. 'I can't describe hearing how my father had cheated his friend, stolen from him—what that did to me. I'd always admired him, practically worshipped him as a man to be trusted and honoured. Suddenly to discover that there was another truth about him—that he was capable of such a terrible action—'

Jackie was dismayed to see that he was shaking. She reached out and took his hand. 'It's not your fault,' she said.

He opened his eyes, gazing straight at her. 'I never thought to hear you say something like that,' he said.

'Well, it's true. You didn't steal the money.'

'But I lived on it. I grew up in luxury that I had no right to. And when I started out in business my father supported me financially. He couldn't have done that if he hadn't had that stolen money. The knowledge tortured me, but I had to keep my feelings to myself. I couldn't let him know while he was dying. And there's been nobody else I could talk to. Until now.'

'And talking helps, doesn't it?' she murmured. 'I never thought to say this, but in a strange way your loss has been greater than mine. My father remains in my heart just as he always was—loving, gentle, sweet-natured. That will never change. But you've lost the father you loved and admired. He's vanished and been replaced by another father who horrifies you. I do understand how that must be a miserable loss to you.'

From the way he stared at her she could tell she'd taken him completely by surprise.

'How did you…?' he murmured. 'However did you…?'

How did she know? she wondered. Perhaps it was connected with the fierce sympathy for him that had risen in her so unexpectedly.

'You must have a gift for seeing into other people's hearts and minds,' he said.

She wasn't sure how to answer that. He was the last man in the world whose heart and mind she would have expected to see into.

'What is it?' he asked, looking at her face. 'Have I said something to disturb you?'

'No. I'm just thinking of the day we left England and Rik tried to stop me—the way you dealt with him. You said you'd do anything necessary to make him sorry he'd opened his big mouth, and that if he didn't get out you might do something you'd both regret. You were really scary.'

'And you thought that was the real me?'

'No—well, I did then. But now…'

He smiled. 'We all have different sides to our natures. I do have a side that's brutal, cruel, unforgiving, but I save it for creatures like him. Don't worry. You won't see it.'

'I'm not afraid,' she said, not entirely truthfully. 'As you say, we all have different sides. My own cruel, unforgiving side is lurking somewhere.'

'Hovering about *me* a lot recently, I guess?'

'I must admit I had it all geared up and ready for you. But now I know how different you are from what I expected…'

'You think perhaps I'm human and not an unfeeling robot?'

'I never thought you an unfeeling robot.'

'Liar.' But the word was said gently, and with a touch of humour.

'I guess I deserved that,' she said. 'If you were unfeeling you couldn't be suffering about your father as you do. You've really taken me by surprise.'

'I think we've taken each other by surprise.'

Vittorio rubbed a hand over his eyes, suddenly feeling wrung out by the emotions swirling in his head.

'Perhaps it's time we left,' he said.

His weariness was growing by the minute, and the tension of the evening was becoming more than he could cope with.

He signalled to the waiter, who approached with the bill.

Watching him, Jackie was struck by the heaviness in his manner, and the way he kept closing his eyes. Alarm began to grow in her.

At last the bill was paid.

'Time to go home,' he said.

'No.' She laid a hand on his arm. 'Vittorio, I don't think leaving is a good idea. You're in no fit state to drive.'

'But I haven't drunk any alcohol. You know that.'

'I know, but you're shattered. Your head's spinning.'

'You're right. I didn't sleep well last night.'

'You didn't sleep at *all*. You spent most of the night wandering in the grounds.'

'How the devil do you know that?'

'I saw you from my window—several times.'

'Yes, I suppose I was pretty obvious. I kept meaning to go inside and get some sleep, but somehow I couldn't make myself do it. I should have done. It's left me tired. But that's not the only thing. This evening—I've never talked about all this before.' He met her eyes. 'With you, it's different. You understand things that nobody else could, and I've said far more than I meant to say. It's hard to cope with what I… Things I said that I didn't mean to.'

She laid her hand over his. 'Can't I help you?'

'You've already helped by being you. At first the past seemed to make us enemies, but it's also—' Words seemed to fail him.

'It's also opened a door of fellow feeling that we never imagined,' she said softly.

'Yes. Suddenly everything in the world seems to be different—I'm confused, but I'm also glad.'

'Perhaps it means that we really have managed to become friends?' she suggested tentatively.

He gave a wry smile. 'My best friend. Who would ever have imagined that?'

'Friendship can come out of the strangest places.'

'They don't come much stranger than ours.'

'And now, because I'm your friend, I'm telling you not to try to drive home tonight. It wouldn't be safe.'

'Don't panic. It'll be all right.'

'I don't think so.'

'You think I can't be trusted to drive properly?'

'I think you're not well enough. I've seen how you keep closing your eyes the way people do when their head's aching. You're in a bad way, and you could collapse at the wheel.'

'I promise not to. Now, let's go.'

Jackie took a deep breath. What she was about to say was momentous. 'No. Vittorio, if you get into that car I'll call the police.'

He stared at her. 'Did I hear you right? That's the act of a *friend*, is it?'

'Yes. A friend who's trying to protect you from harm. I guess that's something you're not used to.'

'I'm certainly not used to people telling me what to do.'

'Don't worry. Now *I'm* here you'll get used to it.'

'So what's going to happen? Will *you* drive us home?

'No way. I'm not a confident driver, and I couldn't handle the Italian roads at night.'

'Then what are we going to do?'

'This is an hotel. We can stay the night and leave tomorrow. I'll go to Reception and book us two rooms.'

She tried to rise but his hand tightened on hers.

'I'll see to it,' he said.

He summoned the waiter and spoke in Italian. The waiter nodded and departed.

After a few moments he returned and addressed Vittorio, also in Italian.

'Oh, hell,' Vittorio groaned.

'What did he say?' Jackie asked. 'He spoke too fast for me to follow.'

'They don't have two rooms available. Just one. A double room.'

'Then take it,' she said. 'You need to go to bed. I can sleep in the car.'

'Why would you do that? Don't you trust me to behave decently?'

'Of course. It's just that— Well—'

'It's just that I'm on the point of collapse. I couldn't seduce you if I wanted to. You're quite safe.'

He rose to his feet.

Suddenly he staggered, reaching out to grasp at something. But there was nothing there. Jackie leapt to her feet, just managing to catch him in time to stop him falling.

She supported him to the reception desk, where he booked the double room. The receptionist cast curious glances back and forth between them, but said nothing.

'I wonder what he's thinking,' Jackie observed as they went up in the elevator.

'I imagine we can guess what he's thinking,' Vittorio growled. 'I planned to tell him you were my wife, but—'

'You're too well known around here to get away with that one,' she supplied. 'It wouldn't have worked. Much better for him to think I'm your latest lover.'

'That doesn't worry you?' he asked curiously.

'Why should it? Who cares about *my* reputation?' She gave a teasing chuckle. 'Yours is another matter. But I expect they're used to you appearing in this situation. All right—don't answer that.'

'You're enjoying this, aren't you?' he demanded.

'Well, I admit the sight of your face just now gave me a little cheeky pleasure.'

Cheeky, he thought wryly. If ever a word described someone that one described her. And she loved it.

Not for the first time he reminded himself to be on his guard. But his guard never really protected him against her.

At last the elevator reached their floor, stopping with a shudder that disturbed his balance again. Instinctively he seized hold of her. She clasped him in return, leading him out into the corridor.

'Room thirty-seven,' he gasped.

A notice on the wall gave her the direction of the room, which luckily wasn't far away. He reached into his pocket for the key and opened the door.

The room was large, dominated by a double bed. Slowly she led him across the floor so that he could slide onto it. He lay down with relief.

'Let me pull the duvet back so that you can lie underneath,' she said.

'No, I'm fine as I am. Thank you for getting me here.' He squeezed her hand. 'You're a life-saver. I'm sorry to do this to you.'

'No need to be sorry. Friends help each other.'

'I thought I'd be able to cope...'

'But what was there to cope with?'

Vittorio struggled to find the words to tell her about how his own thoughts and feelings had overcome him. But they were taking him over again.

'Forgive me...' was all he could say.

'There's nothing to forgive. We all have bad spells sometimes.'

'But I didn't handle it very well, did I?'

It was true, but she guessed he wasn't used to this kind of burden.

'Go to sleep,' she said. 'You need it.'

'I should call Tania first. She'll be expecting us home.'

'Yes, but tell her we can't come home because you've met a business associate and need to talk to him. We have to stay until your serious discussion is over. I'll be taking notes—like a secretary.'

'But where are we supposed to be sleeping?'

'You in here. Me in another room down the corridor.'

'But there isn't one.'

'Tania doesn't know that.'

He managed a smile. 'I guess you're right.'

She picked up the phone. 'Give me the number and I'll call her.'

Tania answered at once. Jackie immediately handed the phone to Vittorio, who managed to assume a vigorous, cheerful voice. Jackie couldn't follow every Italian word, but she could just about understand that he was doing as she'd advised.

'Thank you,' he said, hanging up at last. 'That's bought us a little time. You're a great organiser. Perhaps I really *should* go into business with you—not as an employee, but as a partner.'

'You never know. We might surprise each other.'

'I'm sure of it. Heavens, but my head is aching.' He closed his eyes and rubbed his hand over them.'

'Go to sleep,' she said. 'You'll feel better in the morning.'

'Where are you going to sleep?'

'There's a sofa over there.' She pointed to the sofa beneath the window.

Vittorio looked at it in concern. 'You'll never be comfortable there. It's too narrow and not long enough. Sleep here. This is a king-size bed. We can each take one side.'

'Not while you're lying diagonally on it,' she said. 'It doesn't leave me any room.'

He made some awkward movements to the side, but they seemed to tire him.

'It's no good,' she said. 'You need the whole bed. Stretch out and get comfortable.'

'But what about you? Who'll look after *you*?'

'I'm fine. You're the one who needs looking after. Shall I get something to cover you?'

'No, I'm warm enough. You go and lie down.'

He watched as she backed away and lay on the sofa. He felt as though he was sinking into a different world, overtaken by another self—one who was reaching out to her for safety. He frowned, trying to understand the mystery, but suddenly all thoughts vanished and a warm darkness descended on him.

Watching him, Jackie saw the exact moment when Vittorio fell into sleep. At last, she thought with relief. Now he could find a little peace.

But almost at once he began muttering in his sleep, then tossing and turning as though driven by some inner torment. It troubled her to see him floundering towards the very edge of the bed. At last one agitated movement brought him so near that he started to slide off, and she hurried across to hold him just in time.

'Steady,' she said.

'Mmm…' he murmured.

She couldn't tell if he'd heard her, or even knew she was there. His eyes were still closed but his hands grasped her, as if clinging to safety.

'Move back,' she urged him.

'Mmm?'

'Move back before you fall right off.'

He edged backwards, still holding her. She followed, joining him on the bed but not getting too close.

Suddenly he turned, throwing an arm over her. His eyes were closed, and from his deep breathing she sensed that he was still asleep. She tried to nudge him away gently, but his arm tightened, drawing her close until his head rested on her shoulder.

Instinctively she wrapped her arms about him completely. She was amazed at the feeling that swept over her. This man, who always seemed so strong and determined, had aroused in her an instinct to protect. She knew that he needed the safety she could give him.

'Goodnight,' she whispered. 'Sleep well.'

His answer was a soft murmur. She couldn't make out the words, but she felt the movement of his lips against her neck and tightened her arms at the sensation that went through her. At once she felt his arms tighten in response.

He lay still for a while, but soon his lips began to move again. She leaned closer, trying to hear what he was saying, but the words were indistinguishable.

She could make out only one.

'Elena,' he murmured. 'Elena— Elena—'

Then he was silent again, leaving her wondering.

Who was Elena? Was she the woman he'd spoken of? The one he'd found in bed with another man? Or was she some other ghost that haunted him?

He spoke again. 'Jackie— Jackie—'

'It's all right,' she said. 'I'm here.'

She wondered if he'd heard, and perhaps understood. Now he lay still. She listened intently for anything else he might say, but there was no more mention of Elena.

Who *was* she? And why was she with him in his head at this moment?

At last she felt her own body relax.

Her last thought before she drifted into sleep was that somehow this was perfect.

Vittorio had the sensation of being in another world. As time passed thoughts and impulses disturbed him more, driving sleep away, so that at last he opened his eyes.

He had no idea where he was. He only knew that he was being held in an embrace so comforting that blissful feelings streamed through him. But gradually everything became real and he discovered that he was lying in Jackie's arms.

At first he couldn't believe it. It was a dream. It must be. But her warmth against him, the feel of her breasts beneath his head, were sensations of such sweetness that he was filled briefly with pleasure—and then with alarm.

How could he have let this happen? With what crazy

lack of caution had he yielded to the desire to enfold her in his arms?

But at least she was asleep. If he was very cautious she might never know.

Moving with great care, he edged away, holding his breath lest she awake and discover how vulnerable he could be where she was concerned. That was something that must never happen. Inch by inch he drew back his arm and then his head, retreating to the safety of the far side of the bed.

There he lay tense and still, watching her for any sign of wakefulness. To his relief there was none. After a while he turned over and lay facing away from her, trying to get his thoughts and feelings in order. It wasn't easy…

Submerged in peaceful silence and sleep, Jackie was unaware of passing time until she felt herself returning to the world and opened her eyes. Memories were there of holding Vittorio in her arms, feeling him cling to her. But now she lay alone, and his back was turned to her.

A faint sense of disappointment was followed by a stronger feeling of relief.

He'd claimed her as his friend, but they didn't yet fully trust each other—and if he knew how she'd embraced him while he was unaware he might feel suspicious.

And he would not be pleased, she was sure. She remembered that he'd told her he wouldn't seduce her even if he wanted to.

He didn't want to. There was no doubt about that. If he'd woken to find himself in her arms he would have been embarrassed. Luckily fate had saved her from that disaster.

But then she remembered how she had enjoyed the sensation of holding him, the feel of his body against hers. And she knew there was another disaster that threatened her.

He stirred and turned to her. 'Ah, you're awake,' he said. 'Did you sleep well?'

'Perfectly, thank you.'

'No disturbing dreams?'

'Not a thing.'

'That's all right, then.'

She thought she detected relief in his voice. He couldn't have said more plainly that there was nothing between them but practical matters.

CHAPTER EIGHT

THE BEDSIDE PHONE RANG. Vittorio answered it and found himself talking to Tania, who sounded agitated.

'Are you *mad* to have that woman in your room?' Tania demanded.

'I told you we were both staying here.'

'But not in the same room. I just called the hotel to speak to her and they told me where she is. Have you *no* common sense?'

Vittorio ground his teeth and spoke quietly, hoping Jackie would hear little and understand less. 'There was only one room available. We had no choice.'

'Can you assure me you haven't lost control?'

'I'm not even tempted. She doesn't like me, and our relationship is strictly business.'

'So she hasn't even tried to put her arms around you?'

Vittorio ground his teeth. 'No,' he said. 'She hasn't. Goodbye, Aunt.'

He slammed down the phone.

'What's she so upset about?' Jackie demanded. 'I could hear her yelling even over the phone.'

'She's shocked because we're in the same room. She's concerned for your virtue.'

'Concerned for *yours*, you mean. Does she think I lured you into a double room because I have a scheme in mind?'

'We both know that you didn't want to share my room, disliking me as you do. I've reassured her that you don't want me.'

'But can she believe that *any* woman wouldn't seize the chance to seduce you and perhaps become a countess?'

'I guess not.'

Jackie began to chuckle. 'I can't believe this is happening. The idea of me acting the role of *femme fatale* is ludicrous.'

'Don't put yourself down,' he told her. 'You've got your attractions.'

'Not the kind likely to appeal to a man who can have any woman he wants,' she said cheerfully. 'I'm a realist. How much did you tell your aunt about what happened?'

'Nothing. She asked if you'd put your arms around me. I told her you hadn't.'

'Well, that's true. It was you who put your arms around *me*.'

He stared. 'Did I?'

'Don't worry. You didn't know what you were doing. I came over to the bed because you were close to the edge and I was afraid you'd fall. You were flailing wildly about and suddenly you grabbed hold of me. I couldn't get away.'

'Didn't you thump me hard enough?'

'Damn! I never thought of thumping you. Stupid of me.'

'Want to try now?'

'No, I'll save it and get some practice first. When I finally thump you—oh, boy, will you know you've been thumped!'

He grinned, but it soon faded.

'So we just lay there all night? Did I do anything? Say anything?'

She was tempted to ask him about Elena, but she backed away from the thought. Some deep instinct told her that she would be better not knowing.

'You muttered a load of nonsense,' she told him cheerfully.

'In other words typical me?'

'I didn't say that.'

'You didn't have to. What about you? Did you talk to me?'

'A little. You seemed so agitated that I told you it was all right.'

Suddenly he could hear exactly what she had said then. *'It's all right. I'm here.'* Again he felt the peaceful sensation that had overcome him earlier, as he'd lain in her arms. Everything had been all right because *she* was there.

So she knew that they had clung to each other by chance, but not how they had lain together so gently. It was a relief that she didn't recall the moment and blame him for it, but also disappointing that she didn't share the memory of it with him.

He rose and went to the door. 'I'll go and sort the bill downstairs,' he said. 'Then we can leave.'

'Let's have some breakfast first,' she said. 'We don't want you falling asleep at the wheel.'

Turning to leave, he gave her a wry grin. 'I'll forget you said that.'

He closed the door softly behind him.

Somehow she must banish from her mind the sweet memory of lying in his arms. A shared memory would have been lovely, but he seemed not to know everything that had happened between them. So it would be dangerous for her to brood on it lest her feelings riot out of control.

After that it seemed best to be businesslike. Downstairs they ate breakfast, discussed sensible matters and left the hotel.

Vittorio's headache had gone and he was relieved to find himself driving at the height of his ability. That was what a restful night did. It was a reason to thank Jackie, but he mustn't tell her, he warned himself wryly . She would be sure to turn it against him in a cheeky challenge. There was just no way of coping with this infuriating woman.

But she was more than infuriating. Alarming, troublesome, teasing, tempting, alluring. And never more than one of them for five minutes at a time.

They were almost home before Vittorio broke the comfortable silence between them. 'I hope we haven't got another problem waiting for us.'

'What kind of problem?'

'Tania. How do we cope with her suspicions about last night?'

'That's easy,' Jackie said. 'We assume indifference.'

'You mean we don't speak to each other? As if we've quarrelled?'

'No, that would only convince her she's right. When we get there, just follow my lead.'

As he'd been doing for the last few days, he reflected ruefully.

At last the car drew up outside the castle—and there was Tania, standing by the door.

As they headed towards her Jackie said, loudly enough to be heard, 'You're quite wrong about this, Vittorio. It would be a very poor purchase and not worth the money.'

Catching on quickly, Vittorio enthusiastically joined the conversation. 'Of course I respect your opinion, Jackie, but I think that item would be a good buy.'

They continued this back and forth until they were at the front door, where Tania was still waiting to greet them.

'What are you two arguing about now?'

'Ask her—*she's* the expert,' Vittorio said. 'I don't even understand.'

'Do you *ever* understand?' Jackie demanded. 'That thing looked good, but you're too easily fooled.'

'What thing?' Tania asked.

'Let *her* tell you,' Vittorio said. 'I'm going to get a drink.'

He vanished, leaving the two women regarding each other.

'What thing are you arguing about?' Tania asked.

'I can't even remember. We've seen so many things that he might buy, but he's being awkward.'

'Has he been misbehaving?' Tania asked.

'Only in one sense. He thinks he knows everything about business, but he doesn't understand as much as he thinks he does. And if you dare tell him he's got it wrong he gets insulted.'

'Then perhaps you shouldn't tell him.'

'Oh, I think I should,' Jackie declared. 'It's not good to let a person think they're always right about everything. Of course, certain people are *always* going to be convinced of that, no matter what.'

'It's lucky he can't hear you saying that,' Tania observed.

'He's heard me say worse. He knows I'm not afraid to condemn him. Luckily he doesn't care about my opinion any more than I care about his.'

'I was rather worried about you two being in the same bedroom last night.'

'Don't be. Nothing happened.'

Tania still looked unconvinced.

'Look, Vittorio doesn't want anything from me except efficiency in business. And I don't want anything from him either. So don't worry. I'm not trying to drag him up the aisle.'

Tania gave her an amused look. 'Am I supposed to believe that?'

'Believe it. All the others may yearn to be a countess, but I don't. He's quite safe from me.'

'Has he told you about how lively things are going to get soon?'

'No. Why? What's going to happen?'

'Every June we give a ball. Everyone comes from miles around. It's a huge, exciting event. You'll have great fun choosing something to wear.'

'Do people wear fancy dress?

'Some of them. Some wear conventional ball gowns and some wear historical costumes. We even have a Lady Nanetta costume you could wear.'

'I'll really look forward to this ball.'

'And I want you to enjoy it. Ah, there's Gina. Please excuse me, Jackie, but I must get on.'

After Tania had left Jackie headed up to her room, intending to type up the notes she'd made in Rome. But after a few minutes there came a soft knock on the door. She found Vittorio standing there, and stood back to let him in.

'That was a brilliant idea of yours,' he said. 'If we're arguing about business there can't be anything else between us.'

'I promised her I wasn't trying to drag you up the aisle.'

'I know. I heard you.'

'You—? You were *listening*?'

'Of course. Just behind the door. You're more fun to eavesdrop on than anyone I know. Nobody else complains about me with as much imagination as you do. But I seem to have improved in your estimation. Saying I always think I'm right isn't as bad as saying I'm cold and arrogant.'

'All right—enjoy your laugh. I have to be tough on you in front of Aunt Tania so that she knows I'm not one of the crowd chasing you. That way you can use me as a defence.'

He nodded. 'And you're the perfect defence.' He hesitated before saying, 'Are you all right after what happened last night?'

'*Nothing* happened last night,' she said firmly.

'No—of course nothing did. I only meant— Well, it was nice to be in your arms.'

So he *did* know, she thought.

'Yes,' she agreed. 'It was nice and friendly.'

He regarded her for a moment before saying softly, 'Just friendly?'

'I don't know,' she murmured. 'It's hard to say.'

He didn't answer at first. Then he placed his fingers under her chin and raised it, before dropping his head to brush her lips with his own.

'I'm sorry,' he whispered. 'I shouldn't have done that. I just wanted to know—'

'Yes,' she said. 'But it's not possible. We *can't* know.'

'Can't we?'

'It's too soon.'

'Too soon can be the best time—when you're learning about each other and want to know more. Am I offending you? Do you want to push me away?'

'No—no—'

He lowered his head again, placing his mouth on hers more intensely than before, although not enough to alarm her. She responded with pleasure, moving her lips gently against his and relishing his instant reaction. She felt his arms tighten and a tremor go through his body.

Where was this leading? Control was slipping away from both of them.

And then— 'I'm sorry,' Vittorio said, releasing her. 'That was thoughtless and selfish of me.'

He stepped back, leaving a clear gap between them.

'Was it?' she asked, bewildered.

'You're vulnerable. I should have remembered—'

'But—'

'Forgive me, Jackie. I didn't mean to— Just forget it ever happened.'

'Forget what? How can I forget something that didn't happen?' she said in a freezing voice.

He backed further away. 'You're right—it didn't. It couldn't happen because we have to understand— I'd better go.'

He turned and abruptly left the room.

Jackie stood motionless, possessed by such a fury that

she was tempted to hurl something at the door. She restrained the impulse, lest he hear and realise how he had affected her.

She could hardly believe how intensely she had responded to him. The touch of his lips, the feel of his embrace had started an excitement that had spread swiftly through her, igniting a fierce response.

The best part of it had been her awareness of a response in *him*. In one blazing, beautiful moment she'd known that he wanted her as much as he'd managed to make her want him. But then, in an assertion of strength, he'd silenced his own desire, rejecting her with a pretence of chivalry that didn't fool her for a moment.

Did he *know* that he'd inflamed her passion before rejecting her? Or didn't he care about her feelings while he was protecting his own?

No, she thought bitterly. He didn't care. He didn't care about her at all. To yield to his own needs would have meant letting her know that she had a kind of power over him. And that was something that he wouldn't risk.

All the power had to be on *his* side. He'd left to protect himself, not her.

Well, two could play the power game!

The next morning Jackie went downstairs to find only Tania waiting for her in the breakfast room.

'Your argument must have been fiercer than it seemed,' she said. 'Vittorio's gone away on estate business.'

'Doesn't he often have to do that?'

'Sometimes. There's a tiny village on the far side of his land, and he needs to stay there for a couple of days.'

Before Jackie could reply her cell phone rang. Answering it, she found herself talking to Gary, a salesman who had frequently called in to the shop in London, usually with good products to offer. They were on friendly terms.

'Hello, Gary,' she said cheerfully.

'It was quite a shock to find you missing. Are you going to be over there long?'

'Hard to say.'

'Well if you return to England, don't forget me.'

'Not a chance. It'll be nice to see you again.'

She hung up.

Tania was arranging things on the breakfast table.

'That looks lovely,' Jackie said, regarding the food. 'When I've had breakfast it's time I started attending to some business.'

'What business?'

'Vittorio has left me in charge of a new department in his store. There's a lot to do, and I must go into Rome and get to work.'

'You don't have to if you don't want to,' Tania said.

'But I *do* want to. He's paying me well and I'm going to work hard and earn it. I'm really looking forward to it.'

It was true. Taking charge of the new department could be exactly the kind of pleasure she would most enjoy. But instinct warned her of another aspect.

After what had happened in the hotel Vittorio had gone away in order to avoid her. Well, if he thought she was going to play the rejected woman—watching for his return, wondering when he would find time for her—he was mistaken.

Tania called her a taxi and she was soon on her way to Rome. Entering the store, she wondered what reaction would greet her. Had Vittorio really declared her authority as definitely as she'd believed he had?

Her fears were eased at once. The staff in her department greeted her respectfully—especially Lisa, the chief assistant.

'We have some new stock just delivered,' she said eagerly. 'We were about to start unpacking it.'

'Splendid. Let's get going.'

The next few hours were delightful. The new arrivals were glass items, elegant and expensive, not just dishes but also small statues of animals.

'These are incredible,' Jackie said, lifting one up to study it. 'I think this is a lion...'

'Yes, and this one is a tiger,' Lisa said. 'Over here we have a horse and a bear.'

'All made of glass and *so* lovely. Where shall we put them?'

'I think we already have buyers,' Lisa said suddenly.

Jackie looked up to find a husband and wife descending on them. They were entranced by the statues and insisted on buying every one.

'I can't believe that really happened,' Jackie said in a daze. 'One minute we'd unpacked them—the next moment they were gone.'

'You must have bought the right thing,' Lisa said brightly. 'We'd better replace them quickly.'

In a moment Jackie was back on the computer, contacting the manufacturer and concluding another purchase.

'I've ordered three times as many,' she said. 'And they'll be delivered tomorrow.'

Her staff cheered. Jackie wondered if she had ever known a happier occasion in her life. To be in charge, to see everything work out so well, to know that she was more than capable of handling the situation—all this inspired a pleasure and a satisfaction that was almost beyond her understanding.

She plunged back into work, loving every moment. When the time came to leave she was almost reluctant.

'I know the store's closing, but I've got so much I want to do,' she said, indicating the computer.

'You could stay the night,' Lisa told her. 'Signor Vittorio has a place where he sleeps.'

'Then I'll use that.'

Jackie called Tania, wondering if Vittorio had arrived home yet. But she told her he wasn't expected for another day.

'I'm staying here at the store tonight,' she said.

'But are you sure?' Tania asked. 'I can arrange a taxi—'

'I must stay. There's so much work to do that I can't leave. Vittorio gave me this job so that I can make money for him, and I mustn't neglect it.'

'Very well. I'll explain to him when he returns.'

A tiny bedroom, almost as small as a cupboard, was attached to Vittorio's office. Clearly this was an emergency refuge, for use only when he was so submerged in work that nothing else mattered.

The bed was narrow, but comfortable. Jackie had worked late before retiring for the night. Now it felt good to brood over the success of the day. She looked forward to displaying everything to Vittorio.

She was up early next morning, greeting the staff, watching closely as their work got under way.

'The delivery is here,' Lisa said excitedly.

'Great. We'll get it displayed at once.'

'But there is so much!' Lisa protested. 'Where can we put it all?'

'Over there,' Jackie said, pointing to a large cabinet. 'Move the stuff out of that and we'll have room for everything.'

They got to work. Jackie watched, delighted at the way everything was changing for the better—not just in the store but in her life.

'It's going to look wonderful,' Lisa declared. 'We'll have to move some more things but—'

Lisa checked herself, clearly distracted by something she'd seen a few feet away.

Turning, Jackie saw Vittorio. After a glance at his grim face Lisa scuttled away.

'Tania told me I'd find you here,' he said. 'She says you stayed all night.'

He was scowling, and he sounded angry.

Jackie regarded him, puzzled. 'That's right,' she said. 'I got so involved in my work here that I wanted to concentrate on it, so I was here all night. I'm sure you're glad to know I've been working hard.'

'I'm not sure I'm *glad* about what I'm seeing. You've taken over and changed a great deal here. I don't remember us discussing it.'

'We didn't discuss it. There was a lucky chance—new stock that sold well. I've simply bought some more.'

'Which I can see is being delivered now. When did you order it?'

'Yesterday.'

'Surely not. It can hardly have been delivered so soon.'

'Let me show you.'

She accessed the computer, bringing up details of the order, which Vittorio regarded with growing shock.

'Look at the price of that stuff!' he breathed. 'You've bought so *much* of it, and paid all that extra money for a fast delivery. And you've done it without consulting me. Are you trying to make me bankrupt?'

'Are you saying you can't afford it? This from the man who tried to bribe me with a million pounds?'

'Don't dare say that. I didn't try to *bribe* you. I just want to pay you what you're entitled to. This is quite different. It isn't about money. It's about you trying to push me aside and take over.'

'I'm not *taking over*. I'm just exercising the authority you gave me.'

'I never meant it to be like *this*.'

Her temper rose. Everything had seemed so wonderful before, and now he was ruining it.

She faced him with blazing eyes. 'You said I'd be in

charge of my own department. That I'd have a team who would take my orders. I thought you meant it—but perhaps I should have understood you better.'

'What the devil do you mean by *that*?'

'I should have realised that you're a man who says what suits him but doesn't mean a word of it. When I ask you to live up to your promises, you object. When I stand up to you, you can't cope.'

His face tightened. 'We've made jokes about you being a bully,' he snapped, 'but it's *not* a joke. That's what you are.'

'I do *not* bully my staff.'

'No, but you're trying to bully *me*.'

'Then we're equal. We're both bullies. That's why we can never get things right between us.'

'Don't tempt me to fire you!' he snapped.

'You don't need to. I resign here and now. It's over. Finished.'

'No, wait— Jackie—'

'I mean it. I *won't* put up with you dictating to me. It's not what we agreed.'

'We didn't agree about you meeting men behind my back, but that didn't stop you.'

'What?'

'That's why you're here, isn't it? This guy named Gary called and you hurried here to meet him yesterday. And you stayed the night,'

'Did Tania—?'

'Yes, she heard you talking to him. Where is he?'

'In England.'

He paused to give her a bitter glance, before turning away and heading for his office, where he wrenched open the door to the tiny bedroom. He saw that it was empty.

'Where is he?'

'He's in England,' Jackie said furiously. 'He never came here and I haven't seen him. I came here to get on with some *work*. Vittorio, you're out of your mind. It was pure chance that he rang when he did.'

'And you said you looked forward to seeing him.'

'Only when I go back to England—which will now be soon. I'm finished here. I can't work for you any more. You're impossible.'

He took hold of her at once. 'I don't want you to go.'

'I didn't ask what you want. I'm going.'

'You're not.' His grip tightened. 'We made an agreement—'

'Which *you* have broken.'

'That's not true. I promised you status and authority—'

'And you didn't mean a word of it.'

'You think so? Let's see if I can change your mind.' He glanced out through the door, where Lisa could just be seen. *'Lisa!'*

Lisa entered the office, looking back and forth between them with a puzzled frown.

'I want to talk to the other staff,' Vittorio said. 'See how many of them you can get in here.'

'Some of them are busy serving.'

'Just get the ones who are free. I have an important announcement to make.'

When Lisa had gone Jackie asked, 'What are you going to tell them?'

'Wait and see.'

'But isn't it something I need to know?'

'You mean I need your *agreement*? No way. Listen to what I have to say, and then you'll know everything.'

'But you can't—'

'Don't tell me what I can and can't do. I'm your boss. Whatever I say, you'll have to accept it.'

She could have screamed with frustration. His meaning was all too clear.

Rather than let her embarrass him by resigning, he was

going to shame her by dismissing her in front of an audience. She'd thought him better, more generous than this.

The rest of the staff were coming into the room. Vittorio's grip on her arm remained firm as he greeted them.

'Gather round, everyone. I've got an announcement to make which will probably surprise you, but it's the inevitable result of Jackie's actions over the last two days.'

Jackie tensed in anguish. Could this *really* be happening?

'You've all seen how she's plunged herself into work,' Vittorio continued. 'Increasing the stock, changing the arrangements. I reckon there's only one response I can make to everything she's done…' He took a deep breath. 'So I've decided to promote her. From now on she'll have a place on the leadership team and a significant payrise.'

A friendly cheer broke out, backed up by the sound of applause.

Jackie barely heard. She was staring at Vittorio, trying to believe the words that were spinning in her head.

He met her eyes, his own gleaming with ironic humour and something else that she wasn't sure she could understand. He leaned down, murmuring, 'Now you know what I wanted to say. Do you have any objections?'

'I don't know.'

Everyone crowded round her, patting her, congratulating her.

'I don't *think* I have any objections,' she said.

He leaned down again and whispered in her ear. 'Think about it and tell me later.'

'Yes,' she agreed.

Like everything else between them, it would have to be decided on later.

CHAPTER NINE

'WE'LL SETTLE THE details later,' Vittorio told his employees. 'For the moment all you need to know is that Jackie is a great power.'

He took Jackie's hand so that she had no choice but to follow him out of the building to a small restaurant nearby. 'Now for something to eat,' he said. 'After that I need something to boost my strength,' he added when they were settled at the table.

'So do I. You really enjoyed catching me on the wrong foot, didn't you?'

He turned, regarding her with an indignation that amazed her.

'*What* did you say?' he demanded. 'You think I caught you on the wrong foot? No way. You threatened to leave and I responded by improving your position. Who won? I'd say *you* did.'

'Oh, come on—'

'*You* come on. You've transformed the department to suit your own ideas. When I ventured to protest you reduced me to silence. Let's be clear who's the strong one— and it's not me.'

His tone was almost light, yet she detected a hint of definite annoyance.

She smiled at him. 'For a moment I thought you were really angry,' she said.

'No, I know how to accept defeat.'

'I wasn't trying to defeat you—'

'We'll have to disagree about that. But the sight of your face when I said you were promoted is something I'll always remember.'

'Did you really mean it?' she asked. 'It sounds so incredible.'

'Then you'll have to prove I got it right, won't you?'

'I'll try. And, however it may seem, I really *am* grateful. I thought you were going to dismiss me—'

'No way. You're far too valuable for me to risk throwing you away. You're going to make me a big profit.'

'But think of the money you've risked by doubling my salary.'

'True. I shall have to work you twice as hard.' He grinned. 'Perhaps you should be afraid.'

'The one thing I *can't* imagine is being afraid of you.'

'Is that true?' he asked ironically.

It wasn't, but just now it seemed better to be tactful.

'True enough,' she said. 'Thank you for what you did today. I'm really grateful.'

'So we're friends again?' he asked.

'I guess we are.'

He smiled and began to lean towards her. For a moment she thought he meant to kiss her, but suddenly his face lit up.

'Stefano!' he cried. 'Fancy finding you here!'

Looking around, Jackie saw a good-looking man in his thirties standing a few feet away. The man approached the table and sat down in the chair that Vittorio had pulled out for him.

When they had clapped each other on the shoulder Vittorio said, 'Jackie, let me introduce you to my great friend—Barone Stefano Fedele.'

She shook his hand. 'Signor Barone.'

'Call me Stefano,' he said, kissing her hand theatrically. 'A friend of Vittorio's is a friend of mine.'

'Come and eat with us,' Vittorio said.

'I would love to, but I'm in a hurry. I'll see you at the ball.' He grinned cheekily. '*If* I'm invited.'

'You know you are. Always!'

'It'll be a great evening. As always. Now, I must go, but I look forward to seeing you.'

He hurried away.

'What a nice man,' Jackie said.

'Yes, he's got a lot of charm. Too much sometimes.'

'Too much?'

'A bit of a flirt. Did you notice how he kissed your hand?'

'Yes. Charming…'

'His name means "faithful". And never did a man have a less appropriate name. He's what is politely known as a playboy. The impolite version you can probably imagine.'

'Okay, you've warned me. I won't go falling for him.'

'Do you *ever* fall for any man?' he asked with a touch of humour.

'That depends on the man. Sometimes I have to be wary of a man because he's nice enough to tempt me. Others don't fit the bill.'

'How long does it take you to decide which category a guy fits into?'

'It varies. Sometimes ten seconds is enough, and sometimes I have to give him a chance.'

She sounded well experienced in dealing with unwanted men, Vittorio thought. He wondered in which of the two categories she would place himself, and was briefly tempted to ask her—in a jokey manner. But caution made him resist the temptation.

He was still troubled by the memory of the kiss he had ventured to give her two days ago, and how it had affected him so intensely that he'd backed off in fear—rejecting her and rejecting his own inner self that had started to make him aware of things that troubled him.

He longed to know if the memory haunted her too. But he had an uneasy feeling that perhaps it amused her.

They barely spoke on the journey home. Once there, he returned to work in his office and she joined Tania, who was deep in planning for the ball.

'Things are building up,' she said. 'We've started receiving replies to the invitations. All acceptances. Nobody ever refuses.'

She showed Jackie the guest list, on which some names had been marked with a tick to indicate acceptance.

'You can tick Baron Stefano Fedele,' Jackie said. 'We met him this afternoon and he's looking forward to it.'

'You met him? Tell me more.'

Beaming, Tania listened as Jackie described the meeting.

'He's a good friend,' Tania said. 'And we need some of those to counterbalance the crowd of women who'll turn up and flaunt themselves. I wish we could keep them out, but they come from notable families and we have to invite them all out of good manners. We can't tell them to leave their daughters behind!' Tania sighed. 'By far the worst woman we will be forced to endure is the woman who betrayed my nephew in the past.'

'She's actually *invited*?' Jackie gasped. 'After what she did?'

'Her husband is the Duke of Revendo. His family have always been part of high society, invited to all notable occasions. If they were left out everyone would know why. And the gossip would be terrible. Vittorio simply can't risk having people giggle about how he was rejected by the Duchess because he wasn't noble enough.'

Jackie was stunned. In her mind Vittorio was the stern, determined man who had rescued her from Rik and used his strength to defend her. They had shared occasional jokes, and the night he had collapsed in the Rome hotel had shown her a gentler side to him. But never for a moment had he seemed as vulnerable as Tania's words now suggested.

Had something changed for him that night? Had there been a moment when he'd dreamed the woman lying beside him was the beloved he'd lost? Had she, Jackie, looked different to him ever since?

She couldn't tell. But suddenly, with all her heart, she longed to know.

Tania hesitated before asking quietly, 'Is everything all right between you and Vittorio—about that other man?'

'There isn't another man. I know you heard me talk to Gary on the phone, but I didn't go into town to meet him. He's in England.'

'Oh, dear. I'm afraid I told Vittorio about his call and...' She sighed helplessly.

'And he thought the worst because he thinks no woman can be trusted. Why is he so sure of that? I know about this woman who deceived him with another man, but surely he's had time to grow out of that?'

'You're right. It's not just her. It was his mother too. He adored her. They were very close, and he felt he was the centre of her life until she deserted him.'

'She ran away with another man?'

'No, she died in childbirth—but the baby came from an affair with another man. The baby died too. They're buried together. I once saw Vittorio looking at that grave, and what I read in his face was heartbreaking. He loved her so much, and had always felt she loved him, and yet she lay there with another son in hers arms for ever.'

'But that's terrible,' Jackie said. 'How could he bear it?'

'It still causes him great pain. To be fair, I can't entirely blame his mother. His father was never faithful. He slept with dozens of other women and she took refuge in affairs of her own. They did it to get back at each other, but it was their child who suffered.'

'And it's still with him, even now?'

'Yes. If even his *mother* couldn't be trusted, then he believes no woman can be trusted.'

'And then there was this girl who betrayed him?'

'Worst of all is our being forced to receive her at the ball. But now I suggest an early night,' Tania said. 'From now on we will have a mountain of work to do.'

As they left the room Jackie and Tania continued to discuss the ball for a while longer before Vittorio joined them. Tania was talking enthusiastically about the costume she planned to wear before turning to Jackie.

'Jackie, I really think you should wear Lady Nanetta's gown. What about you Vittorio? Modern evening dress?'

'No, if Jackie agrees I will be taking my costume from the guy in the picture next to Lady Nanetta. Let's have a look at him now.'

Vittorio and Jackie went to the gallery to find the picture he was talking about. Jackie studied it with fascination. He was a tall man in Regency attire. The trousers were white, the jacket dark blue.

'You're going to wear *that*?' Jackie asked.

'If I can get into it. I think I probably can.'

'All the women who want to be in your harem will love it.'

'If I wanted a harem I'd be flattered by that remark. As it is, I'll remind you that you're here to protect me.'

Tania appeared in the doorway of the gallery then, beckoning Vittorio over. He went to talk to her and Jackie went up to her room. She wanted to be alone to get her thoughts together.

She had been troubled before by a guilty feeling that she was enjoying this luxury at the expense of her father's suffering.

She reached into her bag. After few moments she found what she was seeking and took it out to study it. It was a photograph that she had taken of her father ten years ago. There was George's face, gazing back at her, his eyes as gentle and warm as she remembered them.

'That's a nice picture,' said a deep voice.

Turning, she saw Vittorio standing close. He had slipped in through the half-open door and come over to her without her realising.

'It's my father,' she said.

'I know. I recognise him from the picture my father had of him.'

'You have a picture of my father? Oh, please, let me see it.'

'I'll get it.'

He left her room, heading across the corridor to his own.

Impulsively she followed him, and saw him going through a drawer, turning out papers. He handed a photograph to her, and she stared at it in astonishment.

'Yes, that's Daddy. And the other man is your father.'

'You say that as though you've seen him before.'

'The day after we met I went online to look up the Counts of Martelli. I was curious about you.'

'And you wanted to know if I was who I'd said I was, or whether I'd been telling you a pack of lies?'

He spoke cheerfully, without resentment, but she felt self-conscious enough to say, 'I didn't know you so well in those days.'

'And now you know me better you trust me even less?' he said, in the same light-hearted voice.

'It depends on the circumstances. Sometimes I think you're the biggest fraudster ever. At other times our minds seem to connect so well that…' She paused.

'That you don't believe me to be so bad after all?'

'You probably knew that already.'

'Well, whatever you think of me it's pretty obvious that our fathers got on well. This picture says a lot, don't you agree? It was taken in Italy. You can see that they were good friends.'

The two men faced the camera, grinning, arms raised exuberantly, clearly rejoicing in each other's company.

'They *do* look happy together,' she murmured.

'Yes, they do. There's no hint there of what was to happen later.'

'No. I don't think I ever saw Daddy enjoy himself so much.'

'Nor me. My father was a serious man, and an honourable one—or so I once thought. I don't recall ever seeing him bouncing with glee like this.'

In silence they met each other's eyes. Each knew what the other was thinking, but neither spoke. No words were necessary.

At last she said, 'Do you have any more pictures of your father?'

He rummaged in the drawer and produced a head shot. It depicted what Vittorio had described—a serious, honourable man, who looked incapable of any shameful action.

Jackie gazed at him, hoping her desperate emotion couldn't be seen on her face.

You did it, she thought. *You ruined my lovely father's life and got away with it. And your son thinks he can put it right with money because he can't understand that nothing can ever put it right.*

She handed the picture back.

Vittorio put it aside and clasped his hand over hers. 'I'm sorry,' he said.

'Don't be. He did it. Not you.'

'If only there was something you would let me do—'

'Stop it. *Stop it!*' she said quickly. 'Don't talk about it again.'

'Yes, it's dangerous ground, isn't it? Jackie, will we ever be able to risk treading that ground?'

'I don't know. Sometimes I think not—but how can we know?'

'We can't know,' he said. 'We can only hope.'

'Yes,' she murmured. 'But for the moment hope will take time.'

She hurried away, escaping to her own room and locking the door. She seized her father's picture again and looked at it for a long moment.

'Oh, Daddy,' she whispered, 'what shall I do? Please tell me?'

But if his loving eyes were sending her a message she could not understand it.

The next morning Tania departed to visit friends overnight. Jackie and Vittorio returned to Rome. She had noticed a small empty shop on a corner, and become fascinated by the idea of taking it over.

'It might be useful as a showcase for people who don't want to go to a huge store,' she said.

'That's an interesting idea,' Vittorio replied.

They spent some hours in the shop, which belonged to the man who lived above it. Vittorio made an offer that he accepted and the deal was quickly settled.

He finished the day by taking her into a nearby jeweller's shop and buying her a diamond necklace.

'That's—that's very generous of you,' she stammered.

'You've more than earned it. And if anyone asks you, tell them it was a gift from me.'

Thus supporting their pretence of being a couple, she thought. It was a severely calculated act, and there was nothing emotional about the gift, but she had to admit that it was beautiful and looked lovely about her neck.

'I need to call in to the bank,' he said. 'I won't be long.'

He was back in a moment, with an unusual, slightly mischievous look on his face that puzzled her.

'What's happened?' she asked.

'It'll tell you when we get home.'

'Why do you have to make a mystery of everything?'

'Because when a man knows he's doing the right thing he has to make sure nothing can get in the way.'

'Am I *likely* to get in the way of the right thing?'

'Let's say we don't always see eye to eye about what the right thing is.'

She longed to press him further, but felt it would be wise to wait until their journey was over.

At last they arrived home and he followed her to her room.

'Tell me,' she said, smiling with anticipation.

He produced a piece of paper from his pocket and handed it to her.

'You'll find the answer there,' he said.

Eyes wide, she opened it. In a moment she was overtaken by shock.

'What—what is this?'

'It's your bank statement.'

'But—how come—?'

The statement clearly indicated receipt of over a million British pounds converted to euros.

'How does that money come to be there?' she demanded.

'I put it there. You're entitled to it.'

'But I told you I wouldn't take it. You have no right to force it on me.'

'And you have no right to refuse it. It was something I *had* to do, Jackie.'

'Why? So that you can feel better about your thief of a father? I told you *no!* If you could have given it to Daddy that would have been right, but he's dead and it's too late. You can't ease his suffering now and you can't buy me off.' She looked at the statement again. 'When did you do this?'

'Yesterday. I called the bank and instructed them on the phone.'

'You dared to—?'

'I told them to take that money out of my account and transfer it to yours.'

'But I've told you a dozen times not to do anything like that,' she snapped.

'Don't *my* wishes count for anything?'

'Not when they make so little sense.

'No, it doesn't make any sense to you that I loved my father and can't forgive what was done to him. If he was alive and could accept the money himself, that would be fine. But he can't. And now it's your own feelings that matter to you. And your father's.'

'Jackie—'.

'Listen to me, Vittorio, and try to understand. The only thing that would ever make things right would be if you gave back the money not to me but directly to Daddy.'

'But that's impossible!'

'Yes. It's impossible. And that's why we'll never agree about this. When you put that money in my account you did something bad and arrogant.'

She came to stand before him, regarding him with a cynical face.

'What trick did you play to get a copy of my bank statement? Do people obey you in everything?'

He seemed uneasy. 'Not everything, but they do know me at the bank. I told them that you're my fiancée.'

'You told them what?'

'I said we were going to be married.'

'And what happens when they find out you were lying?'

'I wasn't lying. Marriage would be the best thing for us, and I count on your good sense to make you see it.'

'Are you out of your *mind*? We're the last people in the world who should think of marriage.'

'On the contrary. We're the first. From the moment we met we've understood each other—'

'*No*. It's seemed like that sometimes, but all you understand is wanting your own way. This isn't about *my* father's suffering—it's about *your* father. You want to restore your image of him as a decent and honourable man. And I can't let you do that because of how guilty it would make me feel to let you buy me off. You don't understand how I could actually turn down your money. Tell me, Vittorio, has anyone in your whole life actually refused to let you buy them?'

'No,' he said, white-faced. 'People are sensible about money.'

'But I'm not sensible and hard-hearted. I'm human. I've got feelings. What would you know about that?'

'And what would *you* know about feelings?' he raged. 'The only one you have is hatred.'

'Just for you.'

'All this because I asked you to marry me?'

'But you *didn't* ask me. You told me that the decision had been taken—after you'd informed the rest of the world. Well, now you'll have to tell them that you got it wrong, because I'd sooner die than marry you. I want nothing from you—not your money *or* this.'

She seized the box containing the diamond necklace.

'Take it,' she said.

But he backed away, holding up his hands to ward her off. 'Jackie, please don't do this.'

'*I said take it.*'

She wrenched open the box, tore out the necklace and hurled it at him. He managed to seize it in time to stop it hitting his face, and tossed it back into the box.

'We won't talk about this now,' he said. 'Not while you're in such a state. When you've calmed down you'll see matters more rationally.'

'Don't fool yourself. I know what you mean by "rationally". It means me seeing things from your point of view. Well, that will never happen. I can't stand the sight of you, I can't bear to be in the same room as you, and I never want to be with you again, you monstrous bully. Now, get out. I'm leaving.'

He left at once, anxious to get away from the hate-filled atmosphere.

Jackie watched him go and locked the door. At all costs he must not be allowed to return.

Oh, how she hated him. Once she might have loved him, but not any longer. Not now that he'd insulted her with an offer of marriage and money. It might seem crazily illogical, but this man had inflamed her feelings and then tried to take possession of her as a business venture.

Now there was only one thing left that she could do.

She had to get out of here. To get away from him and fast.

She threw her things into her suitcase and checked to be sure she had her passport and purse.

It would be a long walk to Rome, and briefly she considered asking Leo, the chauffeur, to drive her. But she abandoned the idea as risky. She must walk.

Before leaving, she wrote a note to Vittorio.

I'm sure you realise why I have to go. It wasn't working between us and it never would.

She slipped it under his bedroom door. Then she went to the back staircase, where she could descend unseen. At the bottom she found herself near the back door. She would be able to slip out unnoticed.

She began to walk. Her best hope lay in reaching the main road, where she might get a bus or a taxi the rest of the way. But her walk went on and on with no sign of hope.

The light was fading, and when a hut appeared in the

distance ahead of her she could only just make it out. It had started to rain. Just a soft drizzle at first, but it had swiftly become a downpour. She began to run, heading for the hut, hoping to reach it quickly, but she was already soaked when she got there.

Opening the door, she saw that it was shabby. In the poor light she could see little else, but there was at least a bed where she would be able to rest until light broke next morning.

She stripped off her clothes, seizing the small towel she'd brought with her, and drying herself as well as she could. She put on some basic items from her suitcase and lay down.

Gazing into the darkness, she wondered at herself for choosing this way out.

Might she not have stayed in the *castello* with the man who had once seemed to be winning her heart? Did she *really* have no chance of winning his?

Maybe she was being cowardly, running away, but what choice did she have? How could she stay with Vittorio knowing she could never win his love when he was so determined not to let her? No, she'd served her purpose. He'd paid the debt, assuaged his guilt, and now he'd surely be relieved to see her gone. Besides, she was glad to get away from him—wasn't she?

CHAPTER TEN

FOR WHAT FELT like hours Vittorio sat at his desk, trying to concentrate. At last he threw down his pen and faced facts. As so often before, the infuriating woman had wiped everything except herself from his mind.

If they were to have a future together she'd have to learn that he must sometimes think of other things. And the sooner they sorted it out the better.

He went to her bedroom and opened the door.

But she wasn't there.

Downstairs, he searched room after room without finding her. Tearing his hair, he went to the kitchen to find Gina.

'Do you know where Jackie is?' he asked.

'I saw her go out an hour ago.'

'Go out? Where?'

'For a walk, I think. She was carrying a case, but she couldn't have been going far or she'd have asked Leo to drive her.'

'Did she leave a message?'

'No, Signor Conte.'

So now Gina knew he'd been deserted, and suddenly it was unbearable that she should see him at such a moment.

In fury and despair he ran upstairs to his bedroom. There on the floor he found Jackie's note, and read it with mounting disbelief.

Downstairs he confronted Gina again. 'Which direction did she go?'

'In that direction.' She pointed through the window.

The path she indicated led to the main road and ultimately to Rome. Given the note Jackie had left him, the meaning was obvious.

'Poor Jackie,' Gina said. 'It's raining so hard now. How terrible for her. Shall I tell Leo to go after her?'

'No need,' Vittorio said through gritted teeth. 'I'll go myself.'

The rain seemed to get heavier as he headed for the car. What on earth had possessed her to do this?

The only possible answer appalled him.

She was heading for Rome—perhaps the railway station, perhaps the airport. Whichever it was, she was on her way back to England, leaving him with her cruel message and nothing to hope for.

Through the darkness the car's headlights flooded the road ahead, showing no sign of her. But she *must* be somewhere near here, he thought frantically. In the time she'd had to walk she couldn't have got much further than this.

Then he saw the hut, and pulled up quickly.

There were no lights on inside, but he had a torch in the car and took it with him.

He opened the door tentatively, unable to see much. 'Is anybody there?' he called.

The response was a choking sound. Turning his torch to the far wall, he saw Jackie lying on a bed.

'Jackie!'

He rushed forward and knelt beside the bed.

'What the hell are you doing, leaving like this?' he demanded. 'Are you mad?'

'Yes,' she murmured. 'I had to get away from you.'

'Because I'm a monstrous bully. That's what you called me, and you were right. I'm a bully and I'm about to prove it. I'm taking you home with me. Don't argue. You're coming with me whether you want to or not—because you're soaking wet and I'm not leaving you here to get pneumonia. If you refuse then I'll be forced to carry you.'

'You think I'm just going to give in to your bullying?'

'Why not? When we were in that hotel you bullied *me* to stop me driving home and I gave in, didn't I?'

She rubbed a hand over her eyes. 'Then I guess I can't say no…' She sighed.

'Wise woman.'

He helped her to her feet. At once she swayed, making him seize her urgently.

'I'd better carry you anyway,' he said.

'No, I can manage.'

'Jackie, please—'

'I said I can manage. Let me go. I don't need your help.'

He released her, but stayed close, keeping his hands only a few inches away, so that she could cling to him if necessary. She managed to get to the door without needing him, but then let him support her the last few yards.

She had insisted that she didn't need his help, but as he eased her into the car she had to admit that she wasn't sorry to be returning to warmth and comfort.

Ten minutes brought them back to the house, where Vittorio parked the car before helping Jackie out.

'Go up to bed,' Vittorio said. 'I'll send Gina to dry you off and make sure you're well.'

It was lovely to snuggle down in the comfortable bed, and even lovelier to reflect on what had just happened. True, Vittorio had shown his authoritative side, insisting that she return. But he'd also shown his kinder side, looking after her carefully as he'd driven home.

It was the same old confusion. Which man *was* he? The coldly authoritative one who would tolerate no disagreement? Or the gentle, concerned one who kept a kind eye on her needs?

He was both, she decided.

There was a tap at the door.

'Can I come in?' he asked.

'Yes, come in.'

'I had to see how you were.'

'I'm very sleepy, but I don't feel too bad.'

'Then you must have a nice long sleep.'

He reached out for the blanket and drew it up over her shoulders. She snuggled down blissfully.

'I'm sorry if I caused you a lot of trouble,' she said. 'It was just—'

'I think I know what it was.' He sat down on the bed. 'When you're better we must have a talk to see if we can sort out all the ways we misunderstand each other. It's strange when you remember how many times we've noticed how well our minds connect. Yet sometimes the connection fails.'

'It comes and goes,' she mused, 'but will we ever really understand each other? We're so different.'

'*Are* we different? Haven't we found a hundred ways in which we're the same?'

'Yes,' she murmured, 'I guess so...'

As she spoke her eyes closed. Vittorio watched as her breathing grew deeper, more peaceful. When he was sure she was asleep he took a gentle hold of her hand.

'It's been a lesson for both of us,' he said. 'And there's still some way to go. But we'll get there, won't we?'

When she didn't reply he leaned down and whispered in her ear.

'We will, because we must. We really must, Jackie.'

He laid his lips softly against her cheek and left the room quickly, before she could wake.

Jackie slept well that night, and the next morning went downstairs to find Vittorio already eating breakfast.

'How are you this morning?' he asked.

'Fine.'

'Good. We must get things sorted out.'

'What things?' she asked cautiously.

'We've got the ball to think about. It wasn't very kind to Tania, the way you dashed off. Hate *me*, if you want to, but don't take it out on her.'

'I don't hate you.'

'Really? You could have fooled me.'

'That was because you'd forced that money on me. You're so sure you can buy me off, aren't you? But you can't. I want you to take it back.'

'No way.'

'If you don't take it back I'll be out of here tomorrow.'

'You'll—? After all we—? Surely we agreed on that?'

'No, you *thought* I'd agreed because I shut up about it. But I still feel the same. If I accept that money I'll be saying that my father's suffering doesn't matter. But it *does* matter. It matters more than anything in my life. It would be an insult to him that I couldn't endure. Why do you want to make me suffer?'

'The last thing I want is for you to suffer,' he said, speaking the truth.

'Then what are you going to do?'

He picked up the phone, dialled a number and engaged in a sharp-sounding conversation in Italian.

When he'd put the phone down he said, 'I've told the bank that transferring that money to you was a mistake and they're to transfer it back.'

'Will it work? Won't they say that since it's in my account I have to tell them myself?'

'Perhaps they should—but they'll do what I tell them. Let me show you.'

In his office he switched on a computer, logged in to his bank and showed her that the money had immediately been transferred.

He stared at the screen, feeling blank despair at what it told him. He'd promised his father to return the money to Jackie, and felt glad when he'd managed to do so. But now he'd yielded, taken it back, and in his heart he'd betrayed his beloved father.

Jackie was also staring at the screen, trying to take in the incredible sight that she could see.

'They just obeyed you,' she murmured. 'However did you persuade them?'

'I've got a place on the board.'

'Of course. Why didn't I think of that? Is there anywhere you *don't* have power?'

Suddenly his temper rose. 'Are you out of your mind to say that? You just told me what to do and I did it. Who obeyed whom? And you dare to accuse *me* of having all the power.'

'I'm—I'm sorry,' she stammered. 'I didn't think—'

'Do you *ever* think? You've got it so firmly fixed in your mind that I'm a controlling bully that you never look at our relationship closely enough to see how often it's the other way around. You told me to get on to the bank and transfer the money, and I did it straight away!'

'Yes, I'm sorry. I didn't see it that way—'

'No, because it doesn't fit your convenient picture of me. Heaven help me if I do something that doesn't fit your expectations. You'll wipe it out of your mind the way you tried to wipe *me* out.'

'Stop it,' she cried, suddenly weeping. 'Please stop.'

Tears had come without warning. She turned her head but it was too late. He'd already seen them.

'Hey, come on, there's no need for that.' His rage vanished and he took her into his arms, resting her head on his shoulder. 'Don't cry,' he said kindly.

She pulled herself together and drew back.

'You're wrong,' she said huskily. 'I *do* know you can be nice.'

'However hard it is for you to admit it?' he said, smiling.

'I'm sorry.'

'Enough of that. It's good that we're talking. We can sort everything.'

'Can we? There's so much to be sorted.'

'I know. But we can do anything if we try. Come here.'

He drew her close and placed a kiss on her mouth. It was gentle rather than passionate, and it warmed her heart.

'Sit down and have some coffee with me. Then we can plan what we're going to tell Tania.'

'She doesn't know about what happened yesterday?'

'Nothing happened. As far as she's concerned you didn't dash off and banish me into the wilderness.'

'I certainly didn't banish you into the wilderness!'

He regarded her wryly. 'That depends on what you mean by "wilderness".'

He guessed she had no idea of the bleak desert in which he'd found himself when he had found her gone. It had felt like the worst kind of wilderness. And that had alarmed him because clearly there was no wilderness for her.

'We'll have to get to work on the ball,' he said. 'Tania's counting on our help.'

'Yes. You're right. I should have thought of that before I left. I was selfish.'

He touched her face. 'You're not selfish. You just panicked at the thought of being stuck with me for life. We all panic.'

'You? Surely not. I can't believe you *ever* panic.'

Briefly he recalled the wild churning of his stomach when he'd found her goodbye note.

'You're right,' he said quickly. 'Not me. Ever. Now, let's—'

He was interrupted by a beep from the computer.

'It's an email I've been waiting for,' he said.

He did a quick check and opened the new message.

'It's from the store,' he said. 'Some stuff we ordered has started to arrive. I need to be there.'

'I'm coming with you. We'll go to the store and then on to the railway station to meet Tania.'

They drove into town, straight to the store, where they found a mountain of new arrivals. Jackie was briefly nervous, lest they be more of the glass statues that had caused their row, but these were different items. They had come from England and they pleased Vittorio.

'Great,' he said, looking at them. 'Well done, Jackie. I did the right thing promoting you and doubling your salary. You're really benefitting the store.'

She smiled and thanked him, but at the back of her mind was a sense that his action was rooted in their disagreement over money that constantly haunted them. It was always there. When he couldn't give her money one way he found another way to lavish it upon her. Would this nightmare ever go away?

Another thought troubled her. She knew the need to fulfil his father's wishes was so vital to Vittorio that he would seek to keep her close to him until he'd achieved what he sought. Was it anything but that? When he had eased his pain would he feel able to dismiss her?

For another half-hour they worked in his office. Then a knock on the door made him look up to see Donna from the clothes department.

'I've brought what you ordered, Signor Conte.'

Carrying a large parcel, she advanced into the room, laid it on his desk, and departed.

'Have a look,' he said to Jackie. 'It's yours.'

Puzzled, she opened the parcel—and stared at what she found there.

'The dress!' she gasped. 'The one—'

It was the black satin dress she'd tried on when she'd first visited the store.

'It's a gift,' he said.

'You're *giving* this to me? You mean that?'

'You can wear it at the ball.'

'But Tania says I'm supposed to be Lady Nanetta.'

'That's up to you. You *can* be Lady Nanetta—severe, rigorous, terrifying every man she meets. Or you can be a different woman…the one I saw in this gown the other day.'

'And what is *she* like?'

'I'm not quite sure. I'm still waiting to find out.'

In truth, he felt he already knew. When he'd chanced upon her wearing the seductive gown, its satin clinging to her figure, he had discovered something startling about her and how she could affect him. The time had not yet come when he could speak of it, but the moment *would* come. He promised himself that.

'I'll wear it with the diamond necklace you gave me,' she murmured.

'And you'll be the belle of the ball.' He paused. 'You know, it would help me if we could seem like we're even more of an item. Maybe engaged? And it will help you look the part. I don't want Marisa and the others to think I'm in need of a wife!'

'Okay, I'll do my best,' she agreed simply, knowing if she said much more she would start grilling him about exactly what he was looking for.

And she didn't even know what she wanted as the answer. Did he want a bride—just not Marisa? Or did he not want a bride *ever*?

'Come now,' he said, interrupting her thoughts. 'Let's take this with us and go to meet Aunt Tania at the station.'

When the train drew in an hour later they were there, waiting for Tania.

'Lovely to see you both,' she declared when they had

all embraced. 'How are you getting on? Not strangled each other yet?'

'We're saving that until after the ball.' Jackie chuckled.

'Splendid. Nice to know that you can put important things first. We've got a mass of things to do…'

From the moment the next day dawned it was clear that Tania had been right. The castle was buzzing with preparations.

Over the next few days quantities of extra food were delivered and temporary staff were hired. A television company had even made contact.

At last the great day arrived. In her room, Jackie donned the black satin gown.

'Can I come in?' Vittorio called.

'Yes.'

He entered the room. 'How's this?' he said.

He was wearing the historical costume of the man in the portrait of Lady Nanetta. Jackie stood back to survey him, hardly able to believe her eyes. As had been fashionable at the time, the white trousers were tight-fitting, emphasising the fact that Vittorio's legs were long, slim and attractive.

And sexy, she thought, against her will.

'What do you think?' he asked, turning to give her a better view.

'I think that costume is very…efficient,' she said coolly.

'Yes. Luckily it fits me. And I think *you* chose the right dress. That one will lure every man in the room.'

'*Every* man?' she teased. 'Every single man?'

'Well, you can't ignore me tonight, can you? Not when everyone's expecting to hear that we're engaged.'

'No, I promise to do whatever you want.'

'Do you *know* what I want from you?'

She looked up at him with shining eyes. 'I'm sure you'll let me know.'

'You can count on it. Now, we must make everything perfect. Why aren't you wearing the necklace I gave you?'

'I've tried to put it on but I can't fasten it. It's too difficult.'

'Give it to me.'

He took the necklace and moved behind her, reaching around her neck to position the jewels. She tensed at the feeling of his fingers brushing her flesh.

At last he turned her so that he could look at her face. 'Are you all right?' he asked. 'Nervous?'

'I'm fine.'

From outside they heard the noise growing.

'People are beginning to arrive. Let's take a look.'

Going to her window, they looked out. They could see cars arriving, discharging their passengers. Wide-eyed, Jackie looked at the costumes that were appearing.

Some were obvious fancy dress—clowns, animals—others were historical costumes.

Tania appeared behind them.

'You look very fine,' she told Jackie. 'You'll be a big success. *Oh!*'

The exclamation was drawn from her by the sight of a splendidly attired couple whose arrival had caused others to stare in admiration.

'Whoever are *they*?' Jackie asked in astonishment.

'The Duke and Duchess of Revendo. I must go down and welcome them in.'

Tania vanished, leaving Jackie staring down at the couple.

So *that* was the woman who had broken Vittorio's heart by dumping him for a loftier man. She turned her head to look at Vittorio. He was looking down at the Revendos but his face revealed nothing at all.

It never does, she thought. *Whatever he's feeling, he*

doesn't want anyone to know. It's almost as though he's afraid of the world.

She gave a brief gasp of laughter.

Afraid of the world. He'd be so mad at me if he knew I was thinking that.

But it was true. Vittorio didn't trust anyone. Even her.

'What's funny?' Vittorio asked sharply.

'Nothing. Why?'

'You laughed. Why? Is the crowd below so funny?'

'Some of them.'

'Meaning Elena Revendo? I expect Tania's told you about her, hasn't she?'

'Yes,' she said reluctantly. 'But you told me about her first. How can you bear to invite her?'

'Why not? She did me a great favour. Because of her I know things about female deceit, ambition and greed I might not have learned soon enough to be useful. As it is—'

'As it is you learned that lesson in time to distrust every woman you ever meet. Good for you. What would life be like if you made the mistake of *trusting* a woman?'

He regarded her wryly. 'There *is* one woman I trust,' he said. 'One who isn't greedy for money or a title, who's intelligent, honest, and brave enough to express her opinion even when it annoys people.'

The gleam in his eyes made it obvious that he meant her. It might be unwise to feel flattered by such ironic praise, but she couldn't help it.

'You mean when she annoys *you*,' she said. 'Does she annoy anyone else as much as you?'

'I doubt it. Infuriating me is something she's brought to an art form.'

'She sounds like a nightmare,' she observed lightly. 'For safety's sake you should avoid her like the plague.'

'I try, but she has a habit of popping up in my mind when I'm not expecting her.'

'Then the answer's obvious. Expect her all the time. She's so awkward that it'll make her stay away just to confuse you.'

He grinned. 'Yes, she enjoys confusing me.'

From below, they could hear the orchestra start to play. 'It's time we went down,' he said.

Offering her his arm, he walked with her, out and along the corridor to the top of the stairs.

As soon as they appeared there was a squeal from below. Everyone looked up to enjoy the sight of their elegant entrance. Some of them laughed, some cheered, some applauded.

Jackie had no difficulty seeing Marisa's face. She was at the front, staring up at them with an expression that could not hide her dismay.

Wondering if Vittorio had noticed, she gave him a sideways glance. He returned it, smiling. She smiled back, happy to know they were in this together.

Marisa, watching them from below, scowled.

Most of the guests had heard about Jackie, and eagerly crowded forward to be introduced to her. It was clear she was the star of the evening, and every guest, male and female alike, seemed to be charmed by her.

Vittorio revelled in the attention Jackie was receiving, but soon enough was enough. He wanted her to himself for a while.

'Shall we dance?' he asked.

Together they proceeded to the ballroom, where the orchestra had just started a waltz.

'We've fooled them,' he said, turning her gently around and around. 'Let's give them a bit more.'

'By doing what?'

'Can't you smile at me as though I'm your heaven on earth?'

'But what would that prove?' she asked. 'Only that I'm

one of the crowd chasing you. Now, if *you* smiled at me that would be better. But don't worry. I understand why you don't want to.'

'Don't I?'

'Heaven on earth? *Me?* More like purgatory, driving you mad.'

'Which is just how you like it.'

'I can't deny that.'

They laughed together. Those dancing near them observed them and assumed that they were in perfect accord and exchanged significant glances.

'Now we've *really* given them something,' she teased.

'And if they were to hear me tell you that you look wonderful tonight they'd enjoy that even more.'

'No, don't say that. Some of them already want to murder me.'

'But I *want* to say it.' He raised his voice. 'You're lovelier than I've ever seen you.'

'Hush, don't overdo it.'

They laughed again. Then he whirled her around and around until the music came to an end.

'That was a great dance,' he said. 'I hope we can have another one before the night is over.'

'I'm sure we can. But now you have your duty to do with every hopeful woman here.'

'Yes, ma'am.'

Turning away, she found herself facing Vittorio's Baron friend—the one she had recently met in the city.

'Stefano,' she said happily. 'How lovely to see you.'

'And you, *signorina*. I remember our meeting with great pleasure. Since then I've hoped to meet you again. Shall we dance?'

'That would be lovely.'

He put his arm around her waist, drew her close, and began to spin her into the dance.

CHAPTER ELEVEN

STEFANO WAS AN expert dancer, and Jackie found her own moderate skills rising to meet his. It was an exhilarating experience. With his help she discovered her feet could move faster and in more complex movements than she had ever dreamed.

'That was great,' he said as the music ended. 'Now let's waltz together.'

'Yes, let's,' she said, moving into his open arms.

The gentle movements of the waltz made it easier for her to look around at the other dancers. One couple stood out. Vittorio was dancing with the Duchess of Revendo.

'Oh—' she gasped.

'What is it?' Stefano asked. 'Are you feeling unwell?'

'No, I'm fine. Everything's fine.'

'I'm not sure I believe you. When people say it like that things are never really fine.'

'Yes, they are,' she said quickly.

This was something she couldn't bear to talk about. She tried to catch a glimpse of Vittorio's face, to see if it revealed any emotion. But as he whirled around with the woman who had once meant everything to him there was only a blankness in his face that might have meant indifference, or an emotion too strong to reveal.

But then he smiled. And his partner smiled back at him. And suddenly they seemed magically connected.

It lasted only a moment before they turned away, out of

Jackie's sight. She took a deep, troubled breath, wondering what life was doing to her and what it would do next.

'You're not going to have any trouble finding partners,' Stefano said as the dance came to an end. 'Look at them all, watching you.'

He was right. There was another offer for her to dance, and then another. She accepted two partners, and then Stefano came forward and claimed her again.

'You're the belle of the ball,' he said as they twirled.

'Only because I'm dancing with the best dancer in the room!' she said. 'I gather you've got quite a reputation.'

'For dancing?'

'Only partly,' she teased.

She recalled what Vittorio had said about Stefano and his reputation as a playboy.

He was handsome, delightful, and he could make her laugh. Many women would have fallen for him, but these days Jackie was too wise. All sorts of new feelings had grown within her now, protecting her from a man as obvious as this.

But to spend a few minutes dancing with him was an innocent pleasure.

'How are you coping with Vittorio?' he said.

'He's not easy, but I don't manage too badly.'

'Everyone knows he's in love with you and heading for the altar.'

'Nonsense,' she said firmly, remembering Vittorio's face as he'd danced with the Duchess.

'Apparently he told someone at the bank that you were engaged.'

'Oh, that—oh, no. That was just a careless mistake.'

He chuckled. 'Who do you think you're kidding? If there's one man who would never make that kind of mistake it's Vittorio.'

'Yes, but—I'm not one of those women chasing him.'

'Of course you're not. That's why you've caught him.'

'Oh, nonsense. I haven't.' She thought for a moment. '*Have* I?'

'Don't you think you have? Or didn't you want to?'

'I haven't quite decided about that yet.'

A burst of laughter overcame him and Jackie joined in, unable to help herself.

Feeling her shake in his arms, Stefano grasped her more firmly. 'Steady,' he said. 'Don't lose your balance. Hold on to me.'

She did so, and felt herself once more whirled dramatically across the floor,'

Standing near the door with Vittorio, Tania was regarding them with her head on one side.

'The man Jackie's dancing with,' she said. 'Isn't that Stefano?'

'Yes.'

'I hope you warned her about him. Women lose their hearts to him so easily.'

'Not Jackie,' Vittorio observed. 'She never loses her heart to *anyone*.'

'Is that personal experience talking?' asked Tania curiously.

'It could be.'

'But you haven't decided yet? Perhaps you should take your own advice.'

'What advice is that?'

'You once told me that a shrewd businessman never lets a good deal escape him. Seize it while it's going, you said. Perhaps *there's* your deal.'

'A businessman?' he murmured. 'Is that all I am?'

'At one time you'd never have doubted it.'

'At one time I was a different man.'

As they watched the dance ended. At once another man appeared to claim Jackie, who went happily into his arms.

The two of them waltzed contentedly until the music ended, at which moment two more young men approached her, both trying to claim her. All around them the other dancers paused to enjoy the sight.

'Don't let a good deal escape,' Tania urged.

'You're right,' he said. 'Time I acted.'

He strode out onto the floor, arriving just as the two hopeful men were getting deep into argument.

'Sorry to break up the party,' he growled. As he spoke he put his arms around Jackie, drawing her close in a clasp too firm for her to resist. 'But the lady belongs to *me*.'

'Do I?' she asked lightly.

'You do. And if you don't know it now you soon will.'

Vittorio knew a strange feeling as he took her into his arms. Only a few minutes ago she'd been dancing with a well-known charmer, gazing up into his face, collapsing with delighted laughter, and then whirling away with him as though aiming for another world.

Now she was in his own arms, looking coolly up into his eyes and thinking—

Just what *was* she thinking? What lurked behind her gaze?

'I warned you not to fall for Stefano,' he said.

'I didn't. I was just being polite.'

'Polite to him *and* every other man in the room—thus making me look an idiot.'

'Why should it affect you?' she asked lightly.

'Because there's a rumour that we're engaged.'

'A rumour *you* started, for your own convenience. You just wanted to get the better of me about our disagreement.'

'And yet somehow you're the one who always finishes on top,' he observed. 'Isn't that strange?'

'Not strange at all, seeing that I've got right on my side,' she said.

'You *always* think that, don't you?'

'Sure—it's something I learned from you. Oh, boy, the things you've taught me! Get your own way at all costs. Never ask anyone else's opinion, and if they dare to offer one tell them to shut up.'

'I didn't ever tell you to shut up,' he protested.

'Not in words, but you don't need words. Why are you complaining? I had a few dances…enjoyed some innocent fun. It didn't do you any harm. We're not really a couple. We just made a bargain.'

He didn't answer. He had an uneasy feeling that the bargain was slipping away.

'Vittorio, listen to me. You claim that all women are deceitful liars, playing one man off against another. So what are you saying now—that I'm just one of them? Am I no better than the Duchess?'

'Leave her out of this.'

'How can I when you made such a point of dancing with her?'

'That was a courtesy. I danced with her to show that she doesn't trouble me. She did once, but now when we meet things are different.'

'Different? That could mean anything.'

'It means that my heart no longer belongs to her. It belongs to someone else—but I shouldn't have to tell you that. You should know without words.'

'Perhaps,' she whispered. 'But sometimes words can help.'

'Or they can make things worse—which they often do with us. Why are you so determined to quarrel with me, Jackie?'

'*I'm* determined to quarrel?'

'You know how badly I want to sort things out between us. Maybe I was clumsy about the money, but I was desperate to put things right between us, to make you stop hating me because of your father. You can see that, but you won't yield an inch.'

'Why *should* I? Stop this, Vittorio. You talk of putting it right, but nothing will *ever* put it right for my father because he isn't here any longer. If I took the money from you his tragedy would still be the same as it always was. The only difference would be my conscience, tormenting me because I'd benefitted from his suffering, knowing that after all his lovely treatment of me I'd just shrugged my shoulders and said it didn't matter.'

'Would he have blamed you for that?'

'No, he'd have told me to put myself first.'

'Then *listen* to him.'

'I can't take advantage of his sweet nature. I owe him better. But, Vittorio, this is no time to venture over such dangerous ground.'

'You could be wrong.' His arms tightened, drawing her closer. 'Perhaps the best way to tread on dangerous ground is in each other's arms.'

'Perhaps,' she agreed.

'Sometimes I think "perhaps" is the most troublesome word in the world. *Perhaps* I have feelings for you that frighten me. *Perhaps* you have the same, but you fight them off.'

'Perhaps…' she said, giving him a challenging look.

They were dancing slowly past a large open door. Suddenly he whirled her through it and into a dark corridor.

'What are you *doing*?' she demanded.

'Finding out what "perhaps" means.' His voice became intense. 'There's something I need to know. Jackie.'

'What?'

'This.'

He dropped his head so that his mouth covered hers. For an instant she tried to resist, remembering their last kiss which had ended in rejection. But the feel of his mouth was thrilling, devastating. Her mind sought to reject him, but her flesh warmed and trembled with pleasure.

Her arms seemed to go about him of their own accord, drawing him closer, seeking something that only he could give her. She moved her lips against his, revelling in the excitement of his response. She had the sudden devastating conviction that he was hers. He belonged to her because that was what he had chosen.

And with shattering conviction she knew that if she weakened she would belong to him. But how weak did she dare to be?

He raised his head a little. Her mouth was free but she could still feel the whisper of his breath against it.

'Well?' she murmured. 'Did you find the answer you wanted?'

'Perhaps…perhaps…' he said softly. 'There was just a hint. But you're not going to let me guess too soon, are you?'

Her smile teased and challenged him. 'If it's true you shouldn't need to guess. You should *know*.'

'Only if you'll *let* me know. You like to keep me wondering, don't you?'

'It can be fun,' she said.

'There's more in this for us than fun, Jackie. Can't you feel that?'

'I'm not sure *what* I feel. I'm still waiting for you to teach me.'

'Devil! Witch! Stop playing games with me.'

'All right,' she whispered, and drew his head down again until his lips touched hers.

She knew at once that she'd taken him by surprise, and a sudden determined impulse made her embrace him with greater fervour, enveloping him with her desire and rejoicing in his responding passion.

'Vittorio—'

'Jackie— Jackie—'

There was something in his voice that made her heart soar. But suddenly it was all over. He released himself from her and stepped back.

'Why do you torment me, Jackie?'

'I don't—'

'Don't deny it. You knew what you were doing tonight would drive me mad. That's how you get your pleasure, isn't it?'

'I've told you—'

'Did you enjoy dancing with them knowing what the sight of you was doing to me?'

'But I *didn't* know. How was I supposed to know you cared either way? You don't care about me. You pretend to for the sake of our audience, but it's all an act—'

'And *that's* why you hate me? Oh, yes, you've made yourself very plain about that. You hate me because I gained from what my father did to yours. You say all those polite things about how *he* did it, not me. But I see the truth in your eyes every time you look around this place. You see him, don't you? You see your father standing there. And he tells you to hate everything—including me.'

'Yes, he's here for me, but he doesn't tell me to hate. Hatred was never his way. All I feel is his love, which will always be with me.'

Before he could answer there was a shriek of laughter from further along the corridor. Instinctively they both backed off.

'Do you want to go back to the ball?' he asked.

'Not yet—I'm not quite ready.'

'Nor I. Let's stay away together for a while.'

'I'd like to go and have a cup of tea.'

'Tea? Not coffee? Ah, yes, you're English aren't you? Come along.'

Smiling, he offered his arm and they went along the corridor to the kitchen together.

But a surprise was waiting for them. There were already several young women in the kitchen, and as they neared she heard one of them say, 'What a shock Jackie must have given you all!'

The reply came in Italian, causing the first woman to say, 'I don't understand Italian. You know I don't.'

'Scusami. In English you would say Signorina Jackie is fooling herself. She thinks she can win Vittorio, but she doesn't know him. Jackie hasn't got a chance, but she's too stupid to realise that. Vittorio will take her to his bed, have what he wants, then throw her out. And *we'll* all have a good laugh.'

Jackie began to shake. To hear all this with Vittorio standing there, hearing it as well, was a nightmare.

'Are you sure he'd do that?' someone asked. 'He might really be in love with her.'

'Get real. Vittorio's *never* really in love with anyone. I've seen the way he looks at her,'

'So have I,' said a voice that sounded like Marisa's.

Jackie tensed as the voice continued.

'And *I've* seen the way he looks at any woman he's trying to seduce. That special expression he can put in his eyes— he's brilliant at that. Fools them every time.'

'I shouldn't think Jackie's easily fooled. I reckon she's tougher than that.'

'That just makes her more of a challenge. It'll make it all the funnier when she realises what a fool he's made of her.'

'But there's a rumour that they're engaged. Apparently he told someone at the bank.'

'I'll bet *he* didn't tell anyone. *She* told someone, trying to back him into a corner.'

'Wasn't he supposed to be engaged to *you*, Marisa? I remember when everyone was talking about it.'

'People talk about everything,' came Marisa's voice. 'What does it matter?'

'Perhaps you should think about Dino Norese,' said someone else. 'He's mad about you.'

'Dino's all right. Nothing special.' Marisa's reply was cool and lofty.

'Let's get out of here fast,' Vittorio murmured in Jackie's ear. 'We don't want them to see us.'

He drew her along the corridor until they were out of danger.

Her head was whirling with what she had heard. The world saw her as a woman foolishly trying to enjoy an impossible conquest and making herself absurd. And Marisa was trying to gain from this too, seeking to reclaim Vittorio.

Some of her words came back to her.

'I've seen the way he looks at any woman he's trying to seduce. That special expression he can put in his eyes...'

That special expression. She had seen that expression in his eyes, and it had pleased her more than she cared to admit.

He wanted her. She wanted him to want her. And there lay danger.

Suddenly Vittorio stopped, taking hold of her shoulders and looking determinedly into her face.

'You're not taking any notice of that nonsense, are you?' he demanded. 'Do you *really* believe I'm trying to lure you into bed for the pleasure of dumping you afterwards? Is that what you think? *Is it?*'

'No,' she protested. 'But obviously it's what everyone else thinks. It makes me look like the biggest fool on earth. I've got to get out of this place—and this time I'm going to leave for good.'

'Jackie, please think straight. If you leave again you'll make *me* look like the biggest fool on earth.'

'Can't you understand? They think I'm so desperate to marry you that *I* spread the rumour we're engaged.'

'And if I know one thing about you it's that you're *not* desperate to marry me. This is my fault, for what I said at the bank. And I have to put it right.'

'Fine. Go back there and tell them the truth.'

'What truth?' he demanded. 'We have so many truths, and some of them contradict each other.'

'The truth that we fight all the time—that we don't trust each other and can't talk without hurling accusations.'

'That won't convince them that we're not going to marry. Quite the reverse. Some of the most successful couples I know keep up their battle from morning till night. I'm beginning to think we're perfectly suited to each other.'

'Very funny.'

'True—it *is* funny. I like a laugh. The thought of laughing with you for the rest of my life has a certain appeal.'

'But laughter fades after a while,' she said. 'We've got to be sensible.'

'Sensible? Us?'

'Yes, it doesn't sound likely, does it? But I think it's time to put things right.'

'How do you want to do that?'

'We return to the ball separately. We're very polite to each other—'

'You mean with the kind of frigid politeness people use when they actually want to murder each other?'

'Yes. But I've had that temptation often enough to know how to overcome it.'

'Okay, I'll obey your orders. We act indifferent, but I think we should have a polite dance with each other.'

'To confirm the indifference,' she said.

'Right. Let's make a start.'

'You go first.'

He went in ahead of her. Jackie waited several minutes

and then she too returned to the ballroom, going at once to where coffee was being served, and talking politely to the guests she found there.

On the far side of the room she could see Vittorio dancing again, talking cheerfully to his partner. He seemed oblivious to her presence—but that was the polite distance they had promised each other.

'Will you dance with me, *signorina*?'

The man standing before her was a duke. Extending his hand, he led her onto the floor, silently announcing to the world that he had heard the rumour of their engagement and she was accepted in Vittorio's high society.

After him she was claimed again and again. There was no doubt that she was a success.

Across the floor she could just make out Marisa, approaching Vittorio, speaking to him intensely. From her expression she seemed displeased, and clearly his reply did not improve her mood.

So he'd made her understand that she had no hope, Jackie thought. But what had he told her about their imaginary engagement?

Her mind was spinning with everything that had happened that evening. Between herself and Vittorio things seemed to change from moment to moment, leaving her permanently confused.

And now came the moment for which she had been waiting. Vittorio advanced towards her, hand outstretched, and asked theatrically, 'Will you do me the honour, *signorina*?'

She went into his arms, feeling them close around her as they went spinning across the floor. Even as they whirled she was acutely aware of the curious faces following their every movement.

'They've heard the rumours of our engagement,' he said. 'They're trying to decide how true it is. Time to tell them.'

As the music ended he raised his voice.

'Can I have your attention?'

All around them couples slowed to a halt, staring at him curiously.

'I think you know Jackie,' he said. 'Ever since we came here as a couple everyone has wondered about her. Are we lovers? Are we going to announce our engagement soon? Guess what. We've wondered that ourselves. We have our disagreements—sometimes too often. And we've told ourselves—and each other—that these troubles made it impossible for us to be together.'

Jackie turned wild eyes on him. What was he thinking of, to let strangers into their private lives? This way he would make her look more foolish than ever.

'But there's something more important than troubles,' Vittorio declared, still speaking loudly to the crowd. 'And this is it.'

Before Jackie realised what he was doing he pulled her into his arms and laid his mouth passionately over hers. At first she was too stunned to react, but the feel of his lips caressing hers soon took possession of her mind, her heart and her flesh.

From all about them came cheers and applause. Everyone was delighted.

'It's time we gave them the message finally,' he whispered.

'How do you mean?'

Suddenly his arms released her and he dropped down to one knee.

'Jackie, will you marry me?' he called, loud enough for everyone to hear. 'Will you make me the luckiest man on earth? Will you make me unbelievably happy?'

He looked up at her.

'Do I get an answer?' he said.

'Do you really want one? Aren't you just fooling?'

'No, I'm not fooling. Will you marry me?'

'Then my answer…' she took a deep breath '…is yes.'

The cheers were riotous.

She had the dizzying sensation of having won a triumphant victory for the first time in her life. Plain, dull Cinderella had won Prince Charming.

Well, perhaps Prince Charmless, she thought. But she wasn't complaining.

Tania came forward, arms outstretched to embrace her.

'What a lovely thing to happen!' she declared, loud enough for everyone to hear. 'I'm so glad.'

Everyone got the message that despite her low birth Jackie was being welcomed into the Count's family. It was all settled happily and the ball could continue to the end of the evening.

Together Jackie, Vittorio and Tania bade the guests farewell, and at last the castle was empty.

Tania kissed them both.

'He has made the right choice,' she told Jackie. 'It's so lovely to see that just for once he's got it right.'

'Just for once?' Jackie queried comically. 'Surely he gets things right more often than not?'

'You'll find out about that—but hopefully not too soon. Wait until after the wedding before you discover what a clown he can be. Then it'll be too late for you to escape.'

'Thanks a lot, Aunt.' Vittorio said wryly. 'What would I do without you?'

'You'd have married one of those stupid debutantes. As it is, you've got a woman who'll keep your feet on the ground and make you act sensibly.'

'Hush,' said Jackie urgently. 'He doesn't *want* to act sensibly.'

'That's what I like to hear,' Vittorio said, slipping his arm around Jackie's waist. 'A woman who understands me.' He laughed. 'And now I think I'll go to bed. It's been a heavy day. Jackie—we'll celebrate tomorrow. I'll buy you a ring.'

'Lovely,' she said, smiling.

She doubted if he was really tired. He simply wanted to get away from her to sort out his thoughts. She understood, because it was the same with her.

They left the ballroom together. As they went upstairs she waited for him to say something about that devastating scene, but he was silent.

At her door he said, 'We'll talk tomorrow. We have much to say.'

In her room she stripped off the black satin dress, hanging it up with great care. From now on she would treasure it as a sign of the new Jackie.

But who *was* Jackie now? she wondered.

Suddenly she no longer knew.

Was Jackie the woman whose heart reached out to Vittorio despite her sensible resolutions?

Tonight should have been a delight. He had declared his longing for her before the world.

Yet deep within her there was still the suspicion that he wanted to marry her not for love but to silence the troubles that still disturbed him. He longed to make things right with his father's memory. Other people would have found that strange and incredible, but to Jackie, also intent on keeping her father's memory alive, it made sense.

Suddenly there was a slight sound from outside, followed by a click as the door was opened.

'Can I come in?' Vittorio asked.

'Yes.'

'I thought I should come and apologise,' he said. 'It must have been a shock when I sprang that proposal on you. I just got a bit carried away.'

'It's all right. Don't worry. I'm not actually expecting you to marry me.'

'Everyone else is.'

'Meaning Marisa and the other women? Soon she'll grab herself a husband and we can pretend until then.'

Vittorio gazed at her incredulously. 'I said you were a woman who understands me, and I was more right than even *I* knew.'

'I understand you well enough to know you don't want to get married—so don't worry.'

He gave a brief, wry laugh. 'You're only half right about that. Sometimes I'm not keen on marriage, but sometimes I feel that you're the one person who could tempt me.'

She regarded him with her head on one side. 'Temptation is there to be resisted,' she said. 'Be sensible.'

'According to you, I always resist being sensible. Maybe I'm right. Perhaps it's something we should think of.'

'Think of *marriage*?'

'Unless this is your way of rejecting me. Is your answer no, Jackie?'

'I don't know,' she said slowly. 'Everything is so confused between us. We're often friends, but we hover on the verge of being enemies.'

'I know. But somehow enmity just doesn't work. We always return to being—well—'

'Friends?'

'That too, but friendship is too simple.'

'Don't you feel friendship for me?'

'I feel all sorts of things for you that I don't want to feel. I try to fight them, but they fight me back.'

She nodded. 'I know what you mean.'

'Do you remember that night we spent together in Rome?'

She considered. 'I'm not sure we actually spent it *together*. We were on the same bed, but in different worlds.'

'There were some very close moments. I can remember lying in your arms. I wasn't sure how I got there, but it

felt wonderful—warm and safe, and as though the whole
world had changed and become kinder.'

His gentle tone revived her memory of waking with
him, looking into his face and seeing it vulnerable as it
had never seemed before. The sight had touched her heart,
arousing a feeling of protectiveness towards him that had
never entirely faded.

'Yes,' she murmured. 'The world was different.'

'We can make it different, if that's what we want.'

'If we want it badly enough.'

He stroked her face with tender fingers. 'I know what
I want, and how badly I want it. But is it what *you* want?'

'Perhaps,' she whispered.

'Ah, yes—perhaps. The word that we said could decide
everything. Perhaps we need to know more.'

He drew her closer, placing his mouth over hers.

He was right. They needed to know more. They needed
this.

She moved her mouth against his, telling herself that she
was merely seeking information, and what she learned sent
shivers of delight through her.

But then she was invaded by a thought that made her
draw back.

'What is it?' he asked. 'Am I doing something wrong?
Don't you want me?'

'Perhaps…' she said, echoing their significant word.

'Is that your way of keeping me doubtful?'

'No, it's my way of saying I want to be sure if you really
want me. Have you forgotten that time when you began to
kiss me and then backed off, saying I was too vulnerable?
You might be going to do that again.'

He groaned, and dropped his head so that she could no
longer see his face.

'Why did you do that, Vittorio? Why did you reject me?'

'I didn't reject you. Believe me, Jackie, I didn't. I *forced* myself to let you go. I wanted you so much that I didn't dare go on any more.'

'But why? What would have happened if you'd gone on?'

'We would have made love, and then you would have known—everything.'

'Would I? Do we ever know what "everything" is?'

'Not really. We think we do, but there's always something—' He gave a sigh. 'I meant everything about *me*—how I feel, the power you have—'

'What power? I don't have *any* power. You could turn your back on me and leave at any minute.'

'Could I?'

'Go on—prove it. Reject me.'

He regarded her for a moment with a curious expression, as though he was trying to be quite certain of how she was manipulating him. At last a knowing smile took over his face.

'You know I can't reject you. You're just demonstrating your control and my weakness.'

'Then prove me wrong. Go on. Toss me aside.'

'If I could, I would. But I can't. You have me. I'm yours. Now you can crow with triumph.'

'I don't think I'll do that,' she said, sliding her hands around his face. 'I think I'd rather enjoy exercising my control.' She smiled. 'Kiss me. That's an order.'

He obeyed at once, touching his lips to hers. She waited for the kiss to grow more forceful, but that didn't happen. The soft touch continued, filling her with a sensation of sweetness that made her want to weep with pleasure.

Then he increased the pressure, and suddenly the kiss was as forceful as she could possibly have desired. She responded joyfully, urging him on further, and felt his embrace grow more intense as he moved towards the bed and drew her down beside him.

His hands began to explore her body, pulling away her

clothes. Her heart beat more strongly as things progressed to their inevitable conclusion.

When it was over peace descended on her as they lay together.

'Are you all right?' he asked, gazing anxiously down into her face. 'Did I do wrong?'

'Do you *think* you did?'

He shook his head. 'Having you in my arms feels more right than anything has ever felt before. Do you mind if I stay?'

'For as long as you like.'

He gave a sigh of pleasure and eased down so that his head lay on her breast.

She enfolded him with an instinctive protectiveness that overcame her to her own surprise.

Who would ever have thought this man would need her protection? Yet instinct told her that he did, for reasons that he himself had never suspected.

'Go to sleep, my love,' she whispered. 'I'm here. I'll always be here for you, as long as you need me.'

He didn't move, but she felt his breathing grow deeper.

'And you *do* need me,' she murmured.

He slept almost motionless for the rest of the night, and awoke looking lively.

'That was a great night's sleep.' he said. 'No bad dreams. What about you? Did I keep you awake, lying on you in that position?'

'Not at all,' she said cheerfully.

In truth she was feeling slightly stiff, but the pleasure of giving him a peaceful night was stronger than anything else.

'I'd better go before anyone sees me here,' he said, rising quickly.

At the door he turned to look at her anxiously.

'Jackie, things *are* all right between us, aren't they?'

'Perhaps,' she said.

'Perhaps?' He laughed. 'You know, that's a perfect answer. Bye, now. See you later.'

He vanished, closing the door behind him. Jackie lay back, closing her eyes, relishing memories of the night before, wondering where they would lead.

CHAPTER TWELVE

SHE WENT BACK to sleep and overslept, and was late going downstairs. Vittorio wasn't there, and only arrived half an hour later. From the frown on his face it was clear that he was displeased.

'I need a word with you,' he said.

'Has something happened?'

'Yes. I've been in touch with the bank. I wanted to return your money, but I can't. It seems you've put a block on your account so that nothing can be put in it. Did you do that?'

'Yes.'

'Why?'

'Why did *you* try to put the money in again, against my will? You *know* how I feel about it, yet you've tried to force it on me again.'

'So you fought back by blocking your account against me?' he snapped.

'I didn't fight—'

'Didn't you? Isn't that we do?'

'Only when there's no choice!' she cried. 'Why did you try to make me accept that money again?'

'Because it's the right thing to do.'

'The right thing? To ignore my feelings and make me accept something that hurts me? That's the *right thing* to do?'

'I didn't mean to hurt you—'

'No, you just don't care whether you hurt me or not.'

'I'd hoped to help you understand that you're making a fuss about something that doesn't matter.'

'My feelings don't *matter*? Thanks. I was beginning to understand that anyway.'

'Jackie, please talk sense. Why has this issue of money become so important to us?'

'It's not the money itself. It's what it *means*. You want me to take it for your father's sake, and to comfort you, but it wouldn't comfort *me*. The pain would stay with me. And if you had any feeling for me you would understand that. But you don't, and if we stayed together this would be with us all our lives, spoiling everything we might have had. I love you, but I'm beginning to think I could never be happy with you, and I could never make you happy.'

'How can you *say* that? How would you know what makes me happy?'

'Look ahead down the years, Vittorio. Can you really see happiness when we feel so differently about the things that matter?'

'We can make it happen. We don't have to give in just because we have a disagreement.'

'This isn't just a disagreement. It's more important than that. It's a difference that could last all our lives, poisoning everything. It was only because of a disaster that we met in the first place. Perhaps we were never meant to.'

'Stop it!' he said savagely. 'Don't talk like that. *Stop it.*'

'Yes. There's no point in talking, is there?' she said.

She fled the room, desperate to get away from a conversation that was breaking her heart. Against all likelihood Vittorio had claimed her love. Now, before her loomed a vision of a future without him.

He still didn't understand. He thought it was about money, but it wasn't. How could they ever be united as one when they saw life so differently?

In her own room she switched on her laptop, seeking

the distraction it could sometimes give. She forced herself to concentrate on the emotionless screen, hoping to control all feeling before she yielded helplessly.

An email had arrived. Opening it, she read it.

Things are chaos at the shop without you. Rik has managed to sell it and the new owner is desperate for staff who understands the place. Gary.

This was it. The sign she'd been waiting for—her chance to put the past behind her. Vittorio, Rome—everything she wanted to forget.

It had to happen. They weren't right together. She'd thought she could make it work because she loved him, but maybe sometimes love wasn't enough.

Going downstairs, she found Vittorio, as she'd expected, in his office, buried in paperwork.

'I have something to tell you,' she said. 'I'm going back to England.'

'Will you be away long?'

'I'll be away for ever. I'm saying goodbye, Vittorio.'

'Goodbye? So you really think we no longer have a chance?'

'Did we ever have a chance? We thought we'd got things right at last, but it was an illusion. Let's be honest. We need to forget that we met—and especially forget *how* we met. That has always been a kind of poison between us. Now it's time for us to face the truth and part. And you need never worry that I'll start any legal action. I promise I never will.'

'Is that what you imagine has been troubling me all this time?' he demanded angrily.

'I don't know *what's* been troubling you. I don't think I'll ever understand you any more than you will understand me. It's best that we say goodbye now.'

He gave a bitter laugh. 'Perhaps I should have expected this. You've meant more to me than any other woman because the others were after my title and my money. I valued you because I thought you wanted only me. But you don't want me. So you're right. Let's call it a day.'

His words were like a blow to her heart. If he had said he loved her everything would have changed. But he wanted her only for reasons of pride.

'Yes, let's,' she said. 'I'll call the airport now.'

'Let me do it for you.'

He immediately got on the phone.

After making a few notes he said, 'There's a flight at midday tomorrow. I'll book you on it.'

A few minutes were enough to do the job. Then all was settled.

'I'll print your ticket off for you,' Vittorio said. 'And I'll arrange a taxi to get you there in good time.'

'Will you see me off?'

'Yes, I'll come to the airport and make sure you get on the right plane. We don't want you to get lost, do we? Don't worry. Everything will go well.'

But nothing was going well, she thought sadly. They were parting, and all he cared about was arranging things properly. His insistence that she'd meant more to him than any other woman had been just empty words. She meant nothing to him.

But as she lay in bed that night she managed to find a little hope. There had been times when he'd treated her with something that might have been affection. Perhaps when they were at the airport tomorrow he might show some feeling. Perhaps he'd ask her to change her mind and come back. She would kiss him goodbye and then— *oh, please*—let him kiss her back. Let him discover that they really loved each other. Surely she could make him want her?

Still clinging to hope, she finally fell asleep.

She awoke early, dressed quickly and hurried downstairs, full of hope and determination. She would not give in. Today she would open her heart to Vittorio and persuade him to open his heart to her. It would be a day of victory.

She was smiling as she went into the kitchen.

But there a shock awaited her. There was no sign of Vittorio.

Tania was sitting alone at the table. She looked up and smiled at Jackie.

'Have a good breakfast,' she said. 'Vittorio said you'd be leaving early for the airport. He asked me to tell you goodbye for him.'

'He—what?'

'He got called away to an important meeting. He says he's sorry, but he couldn't help it.'

Jackie drew a sharp breath, fighting back the desire to cry out.

It was over.

He had abandoned her without a word of goodbye, and in doing so he'd made plain his indifference to her.

'I'll leave at once,' she said. 'Goodbye.'

'Must you go?' Tania asked. 'I've so liked having you here.'

'Thank you, but the sooner I go the better. I've turned into a different person here—one I'd better get rid of.'

'But why? It's true you've become another person, but she's very attractive. She's bright and witty, always ready to join in the fun.' Tania smiled fondly, adding, 'She's a true Roman.'

'That's very kind, but my *other* self is actually rather stupid. She's easily taken in because she believes what she wants to believe. Now it's time for her to face facts.'

'But does she know which are the right facts to face?'

Tania asked, regarding her curiously. 'Sometimes one makes mistakes about these things.'

'Not this time,' Jackie said with a sigh. 'I got it wrong at first, but now I've seen the light and—well, that's all that matters.'

'But there might still be things you should know.'

Jackie managed a smile. 'If there are, I think I'll discover them at the right moment. Now, I must go and finish my packing.'

She made a quick escape. Tania's unease told its own story. Vittorio's aunt knew that he was up to something that would hurt Jackie badly, and she was unsure what to reveal.

But Tania didn't need to tell her, Jackie thought. Vittorio was angry with her for daring to leave him.

Jackie hurried upstairs. The sooner she was out of here the better.

Tania waited until she was out of earshot, then picked up the phone and dialled a number.

'Vittorio? Is that you? Oh, good. Listen—she's just been down here. I told her that you'd been called away early— no, I didn't tell here where you've really gone. I kept quiet about that, as we agreed. My dear boy, are you sure you're going about this the right way? I know she's an attractive young woman, but she can also be very difficult— All right, I suppose you're right to take the chance, but you might have to duck for safety when she finds out what you've actually been up to today.'

The flight to London seemed to take for ever. Jackie tried to tell herself that one stage in her life was finished and she must prepare for the next. But no common sense thoughts could heal the pain in her heart.

Her love was over—which meant that her life was effectively over. And she didn't know how she would endure it.

Arriving in London, she headed straight for the shop. It seemed strange when she arrived—more restricted, less interesting.

Perhaps she could find a job here. The place apparently needed her.

Going inside, she saw nobody—until a man appeared from the back.

'Can I help you?'

'I'm looking for a job,' she said. 'Are you short-staffed? Do you need anyone?'

He shook his head.

'I'm afraid I can't give you a job. Only the owner can do that.'

'Then can I talk to the owner?'

'I'll fetch him.'

He went deep into the back of the shop and she heard him call, 'Can you come here, sir?'

After a moment a man appeared, the sight of whom made Jackie gasp.

'Vittorio!'

Smiling, he came towards her and laid his hands gently on her shoulders.

'But what are you—?' she gasped. 'How did you get here?'

'I booked you on the midday flight, but I booked myself on the flight at six in the morning. That's why I'd already gone when you woke up. I needed to get here well ahead of you.'

'So *you're* the new owner?' she said, stunned.

'No. You'll find the owner's name here.'

He drew out a piece of paper bearing the owner's name, and showed it to her.

'But that—it's *my* name there.'

'That's because you're the owner,' he said simply. 'Just as your father would have wanted.'

'But Rik—'

'I contacted Rik from Italy and persuaded him to sell to me. A lawyer here finished the formalities, and when I arrived I went straight to the lawyer and transferred the property to you. That's why I needed to get here well ahead of you.'

'But—how am I going to run this place? Are you telling me that it's all right for me to move back to London?'

'No, I'm telling you that you're coming home with me, because I'm not letting you go—now or ever. I hope you agree to that, or I'll be forced to bring my bullying side to the surface.'

There was a gleam of humour in his eyes, but also something else that might have been an anxious plea.

She gave him a warm smile, saying, 'Perhaps you should beware. I might have to bring my bullying side to the surface.'

'And we both know I don't cope with that very well. But it's lucky you're a great businesswoman, because you can organise this place while living with me in Rome. Please, Jackie. *Please.*'

She touched his face. 'I guess it would be heartless of me to refuse. We'll do it your way.'

He smiled and kissed her hand.

'I've taken over the apartment upstairs, where you used to live. Come up with me. I've got something to show you.'

It felt strange to be climbing the stairs to her old home—like moving back in time. Inside she found it much the same as she remembered: plain and basic.

While he made her a cup of tea she studied the papers that made her the owner of the shop.

'However did you do this? And how can I accept it?'

'You can because I've got something else for you—something that will solve the great problem that has always come between us. I mean the money. We will never be at peace over that until we find a final decision that feels good to us both.'

'But is there such a thing? How could there be?'

'I think I've found it. Look at this.'

He handed her a letter that she read with mounting astonishment. It came from a charity and was addressed to her father.

'It says he's donated a quarter of a million pounds,' she gasped. 'But how could he?'

'Easily—with a little help.' Vittorio handed her several more letters. 'Look at these.'

The letters were from three more of her father's favourite charities, each one thanking him for the gift of a quarter of a million pounds.

'*You* did this?' she breathed.

'Let's say I was your father's messenger boy. I told you I'd find a way of handing over the money in a manner that you couldn't resist, and I've done it. It's really just a way of forcing you to do what I want, selfish bully that I am. You said I couldn't understand why this was so important to you, and at first you were right. But then I started to fall for you and the more I came to love you the more I saw it through your eyes.'

'You can *do* that?' she cried joyfully. 'You really understand now?'

'I knew you didn't want the money yourself, but it was painful to you to know that I had it. You told me that we needed a way to return it to him without involving you, but that didn't seem possible.'

'You found one,' she breathed. 'You found it. Look what it says about him.'

She read from one of the letters. '"After his magnificent gift George Benton will be celebrated as one of our greatest benefactors—a man whose generosity knew no bounds and for whom no admiration and respect would be enough."' She looked quickly through the other letters. 'All four of them say something like that. Look!'

He took the papers from her, gazing with a pleasure that matched her own.

'They do him justice,' he said. 'That's the best we could hope for.'

We. The joyful word echoed through her brain. They were together in this.

'We,' she breathed. 'You said "we".'

'It's "we" because now everything matters the same to both of us. We're a team, and we always will be. Forgive me, my darling, for taking so long to see the light, but now I have seen it. I was desperate for a way to reach out to you and prove that my heart understood yours. I knew nothing else would ever make you love me.'

'And you're right,' she breathed. 'I thought you'd never understand the truth about what was keeping us apart, but you do. And now you've actually found a way—' She seized the letters. 'This is brilliant. I've never been so happy in my life.'

'Then why are you crying?' he asked anxiously, for tears had begun to pour down her cheeks.

'I can't help it,' she wept. 'Suddenly—'

Suddenly she was invaded by an emotion more powerful than any she had ever known.

Vittorio put his arms around her. 'Hold on to me,' he said. 'You're safe now. I'll never let you go.'

'Never? Promise me?'

'I promise. What greater tribute could I pay to your late father than by promising to love, protect and care for his daughter for the rest of her life?'

He kissed her. She returned the kiss joyfully, then rested against him, feeling the warmth and sweetness of knowing he was hers for ever.

'Did you always mean to give me the shop?'

'Of course. A man should give his bride a wedding gift. And this is mine to you.'

'A wedding gift?'

'We're getting married. You promised to marry me ages ago and I'm holding you to that promise. I won't take no for an answer. Say yes. Say you'll marry me and accept the shop.'

The words sounded forceful, but he said them with a gentle smile that ended all her fears. Now she could only do what her heart urged.

'All right,' she said softly. 'I'll marry you. *And* I'll accept the shop.'

Now that they understood each other perfectly she could sense that everything was different. They had reached their destination at last and there was no more to fear.

They spent the night together—not making love, but lying peacefully in each other's arms.

In the darkness of the night Jackie awoke to find Vittorio standing at the open window, looking up into the sky.

She went to stand beside him. 'I think our fathers would be overjoyed that we've found each other. They'd be even more delighted that we've finally begun to love and understand each other in the way they always wanted.'

He put an arm around her. With the other he reached up to the heavens. She followed his gaze to where the stars glittered and the moon glowed.

'They're up there too,' he said. 'Can't you tell?'

'Yes,' she breathed. 'And I think—I think they're shaking hands to congratulate each other.'

'That's what I think too,' Vittorio said.

Then he drew her closer, enfolding her in an embrace that would protect them all their lives.

* * * * *

A RING FOR VINCENZO'S HEIR

JENNIE LUCAS

To Pippa Roscoe,
editor extraordinaire

CHAPTER ONE

"YOU HAVE TWO CHOICES, Scarlett." Her ex-boss's greedy eyes slowly traveled from her pregnant belly to the full breasts straining the fabric of her black maternity dress. "Either you sign this paperwork to give your baby away when it's born, and become my wife immediately, or…"

"Or what?" Scarlett Ravenwood tried to move away from the papers he was pushing toward her. But the man's overmuscled bulk took up most of the backseat of the limousine.

"Or…I'll have Dr. Marston declare you insane. And have you committed." His fleshy lips curved into a pleasant smile. "For your own safety, of course. Because any sane woman would obviously wish to marry me. And then you'll lose your baby anyway, won't you?"

Scarlett stared at him, barely seeing the gleaming buildings of Manhattan passing behind him as they drove down Fifth Avenue. Blaise Falkner was handsome, rich. And a monster.

"You're joking, right?" She gave an awkward laugh. "Come on, Blaise. What century do you think we're living in?"

"The century a rich man can do whatever he wants. To whomever he wants." Reaching out, he twisted a tendril of her long red hair around a thick finger. "Who's going to stop me? You?"

Scarlett's mouth went dry. For the last two years, she'd lived in his Upper East Side mansion as nursing assistant for his dying mother, and over that time Blaise had made increasingly forceful advances. Only his imperious mother, horrified at the thought of her precious heir lowering himself to the household help, had kept him at bay.

But now Mrs. Falkner was dead, and Blaise was rich beyond imagination. While Scarlett was nothing more than an orphan who'd come to New York desperate for a job. Ever since she'd arrived, she'd been isolated in the sickroom, obeying the sharp orders of nurses and doing the worst tasks caring for a fretful, mean-spirited invalid. She had no friends in New York. No one to take her side against him.

Except…

No, she told herself desperately. *Not him.*

She couldn't. Wouldn't.

But what if Blaise was right? What if she escaped him and went to the police, and they didn't believe her? Could he and his pet psychiatrist find a way to carry through with his threat?

When he'd crassly propositioned her at the funeral that morning—literally over his mother's grave!—she'd tried to laugh it off, telling him she was leaving New York. To her surprise, he'd courteously offered a ride to the bus station. Ignoring her intuition's buzz of warning, she'd accepted.

She should have known he wouldn't give up so easily. But she'd never imagined he'd go this far. Threatening her into marriage? Trying to force her to give her baby away?

She'd made a mistake thinking of Blaise as a selfish, petulant playboy who wanted her like a spoiled child demanded a toy he couldn't have. He was actually insane.

"Well?" Blaise demanded. "What is your answer?"

"Why would you want to marry me?" Scarlett said weakly. With a deep breath, she tried to appeal to his vanity. "You're good-looking, charming, rich. Any woman would be happy to marry you." *Any woman who didn't know you*, she added silently.

"But I want you." He gripped her wrist tightly enough to make her flinch. "All this time, you've refused me. Then you get yourself knocked up by some other man and won't tell me who." He ground his teeth. "Once we're wed, I'll be the only man who can touch you. As soon as that brat is born and sent away, you'll be mine. Forever."

Scarlett tried to squelch her rising panic. As the limo moved down Fifth Avenue, she saw a famous cathedral at the end of the block. A desperate idea formed in her mind. Could she...?

Yes. She could and she would.

It hadn't been her plan. She'd intended to buy a bus ticket south, use her small savings to start a new life somewhere sunny where flowers grew year-round and raise her baby alone. But as her own father often said when she was growing up, new challenges called for new plans.

Her new plan scared her, though. Because if Blaise Falkner was a frying pan, Vincenzo Borgia was the fire.

Vin Borgia. She pictured the dark eyes of her unborn baby's father, so hot one moment, so cold the next. Pictured the ruthless edge of his jaw. The strength of his body. The force of his will.

A shiver went through her. What if he...

Don't think about it, she told herself firmly. One impossible thing at a time. Another maxim she'd learned from her father.

As the chauffeur slowed down at a red light, she knew it was now or never. She took a deep breath, then opened her eyes with a brittle smile.

"Blaise." Scarlett leaned forward as she tightened her hidden right hand into a fist. "You know what I've always wanted to do...?"

"What?" he breathed, licking his lips as he looked down at her breasts.

"This!" She gave him a hard uppercut to the jaw. His teeth snapped together as his head knocked backward, shocking him into releasing her.

Without waiting for the limo to completely stop, she yanked on her door handle and stumbled out onto the sidewalk. Kicking off her two-inch heels, she put her hand protectively over her belly and ran with all her might, feet bare against the concrete, toward the enormous cathedral.

It was a perfect day for a wedding. The first of October, and every tree in the city was decorated in yellow, orange and red. St. Swithun's Cathedral was the most famous in New York, the place where the wealthy and powerful held their christenings, weddings and funerals. Two hundred years old, it was a towering midtown edifice of gray marble, big as a city block, with soaring spires reaching boldly into the bright blue sky.

Panting as she ran, Scarlett glanced down at the peeling gold-tone watch that had once belonged to her mother. She prayed she wasn't too late.

A vintage white Rolls-Royce Corniche was parked at the curb, bedecked with ribbons and flowers. Next to it, a uniformed driver waited. Bodyguards with dark sunglasses, scowls and earpieces stood guard on the cathedral steps and around the perimeter.

The wedding had started, then. Scarlett had been trying not to think about it for the last four months, since she'd seen the announcement in the *New York Times*. But the details had been blazed in her memory, and now she was glad, because only Vin Borgia could help her.

A bodyguard blocked her with a glare. "Miss, stand back..."

Clutching her belly theatrically, Scarlett stumbled forward on the sidewalk. "Help! There's a man chasing me! He's trying to kidnap my baby!"

The bodyguard's eyes widened behind his sunglasses. "What?"

She ran past him, calling back, "Call the police!"

"Hey! You can't just—"

Scarlett ran up the cathedral's steps, gasping for air.

"Stop right there!" A second bodyguard came toward her with a thunderous expression. Then he turned when he heard the shout of his colleague as two of Blaise's bodyguards started throwing punches at him on the sidewalk below. "What the…"

Taking advantage of his distraction, she pushed open the cathedral doors and went inside.

For a moment, she blinked in the shadows.

Then her eyes adjusted, and she saw a wedding straight out of a fairy tale. Two thousand guests sat in the pews, and at the altar, beneath a profusion of white roses and lilies and orchids, was the most beautiful bride, standing next to the most devastatingly handsome man in the world.

Just seeing Vin now, for the first time since that magical night they'd created a baby, Scarlett caught her breath.

"If anyone here today has reason," the officiant intoned at the front, "why these two may not lawfully be joined…"

She heard a metallic wrenching sound behind her, then Blaise's harsh triumphant gasp as he burst through the cathedral doors.

"…speak now, or forever hold your peace."

Desperate, Scarlett stumbled to the center of the aisle. Holding up her hand, she cried, "Please! Stop!"

There was a collective gasp as two thousand people turned to stare at her. Including the bride and groom.

Scarlett put her hands to her head, feeling dizzy. It was hard to speak when she could barely catch her breath. She focused on the only person who mattered.

"Please, Vin, you have to help me—" Her voice choked off, then strengthened as she thought of the unborn child depending on her. "My boss is trying to steal our baby!"

Unlike many grooms the night before they wed, Vincenzo Borgia, Vin to his friends, had slept very well last night.

He knew what he was doing today. He was marrying the perfect woman. His courtship of Anne Dumaine had been easy, and so had their engagement. No discord. No messy emotion. No sex, even, at least not yet.

But today, their lives would be joined, as would their families—and more to the point, their companies. When Vin's SkyWorld Airways merged with her father's Air Transatlantique, Vin would gain thirty new transatlantic routes at a stroke, including the lucrative routes of New York–London and Boston–Paris. Vin's company would nearly double in size, at very advantageous terms. Why would Jacques Dumaine be anything but generous to his future son-in-law?

After today, there would be no more surprises in Vin's life. No more uncertainty or questions about the future. He liked that thought.

Yes, Vin had slept well last night, and tonight, after he finally made love to his very traditional bride, who'd insisted on remaining a virgin until they married, he expected to sleep even better. And for every other night for the rest of his well-ordered, enjoyably controllable life.

If he wasn't overwhelmingly attracted to his bride, what of it? Passion died soon after marriage, he'd been told, so perhaps it was a good thing. You couldn't miss what you'd never had.

And if he and Anne seemed to have little in common other than the wedding and the merger, well, what difference did that make? Men and women had different interests. They weren't supposed to be the same. He would cover her weaknesses. She would cover his.

Because whatever his enemies and former lovers might accuse, Vin knew he had a few. A lack of patience. A lack of empathy. In the business world, those were strengths, but once he had children, he knew greater sources of patience and empathy would be required.

He was ready to settle down. He wanted a family. Other than building his empire it was his primary reason for getting married, but not his only. After his last sexual encounter, an explosive night with a gorgeous redhead who'd given him the most amazing sex of his life, then disappeared, he decided he was fed up with unpredictable love affairs.

So, a few months later, he'd sensibly proposed to Anne Dumaine.

Born in Montreal, Anne was beautiful, with an impeccable pedigree, certain to be a good mother and corporate wife. She spoke several languages, including French and Italian, and held a degree in international business. Best of all she came with an irresistible dowry—Air Transatlantique.

Vin smiled at Anne now, standing across from him as they waited to speak their vows. She looked like Princess Grace, he thought, blonde and grave, with a modest white gown and a long lace veil that had been handmade by Belgian nuns. Flawless. A picture-perfect bride.

"If anyone here today has reason," the archbishop presiding over their marriage said solemnly, "why these two may not lawfully be joined…"

There was a scuffle, a loud bang. Footsteps. From the corner of his eye he saw heads in the audience turn. He refused to look—that would be undisciplined—but his smile grew a little strained.

"...speak now," the minister finished, "or forever hold your peace."

"Please! Stop!"

A woman's voice. Vin's jaw tightened. Who would dare interrupt their wedding? One of his despondent ex-lovers? How had she gotten past the bodyguards? Furious, he turned.

Vin froze when he saw green eyes fringed with black lashes in a lovely heart-shaped face, and vivid red hair cascading down her shoulders, bright as heart's blood. She stood in the gray stone cathedral, his dream come to life.

Scarlett. The woman who had haunted his dreams for the last eight months. The flame-haired virgin who'd shared a single night with him he could not forget, then fled the next morning before he could get her number— or even her last name! No woman had ever treated him so badly. She'd inflamed his blood, then disappeared like Cinderella, without so much as a damned glass slipper.

She was dressed completely in black. And barefoot? Her breasts overflowed the neckline of her dress. His gaze returned sharply to her belly. She couldn't be...

"Please, Vin, you have to help me," she choked out, her voice echoing against the cool gray stone. "My boss is trying to steal our baby!"

For a moment, Vin stared at her in shock, unable to comprehend her words.

Our baby?

Our?

There was a collective gasp as two thousand people turned to stare at him, waiting for his reaction.

Vin's body flashed hot, then cold as he felt all control— over the wedding, over his privacy, over his life—ripped from his grasp. Nearby, he saw the glower of Anne's red-faced father, saw her mother's shocked eyes. Fortunately he had no family of his own to disappoint.

He turned to his bride, expecting to see tears or at least agonized hurt, expecting to have to explain that he hadn't cheated on her, of course not, that this had all happened months before they'd met. But Anne's beautiful face was carefully blank.

"Excuse me," he said. "I need a moment."

"Take all the time you want."

Vin went slowly down the aisle toward Scarlett. The people watching from the pews seemed to fall away, their faces smearing into mere smudges of color.

His heart was pounding as he stopped in front of the woman he'd almost convinced himself didn't exist. Looking at her belly, he said in a low voice, "You're pregnant?"

She met his eyes. "Yes."

"The baby's mine?"

Her chin lifted. "You think I would lie?"

Vin remembered her soft gasp of pain when he'd first taken her, holding her virgin body so hot and hard and tight against his own in the darkness of his bedroom. Remembered how he'd kissed her tears away until her pain melted away to something very different...

"You couldn't have told me before now?" he bit out.

"I'm sorry," she whispered. "I didn't..." Then she glanced behind her, and her expression changed to fear.

Three men were striding up the aisle, the leader's face a mask of cold fury.

"There you are, you little..." He roughly grabbed Scarlett's wrist. "This is a private matter," he snarled at Vin, barely looking at him. "Return to your ceremony."

Vin almost did. It would have been easy to let them go. He felt the pressure of his waiting bride, of the pending merger, of her family, of the cathedral and the archbishop and the many guests, some of whom had flown around the world to be here. He could have told himself that Scarlett was lying and turned his back on her. He could have walked back to calmly speak the vows that would bind his life to Anne.

But something stopped him.

Maybe it was the man's iron-like grip on Scarlett's slender wrist. Or the way he and his two goons were dragging her back down the aisle, in spite of her helpless struggles. Maybe it was the panicked, stricken expression on her lovely face as all those wealthy, powerful guests silently watched, doing nothing to intervene.

Or maybe it was the ghost of his own memory, long repressed, of how it had once felt to be powerless and unloved, dragged from his only home against his will.

Whatever it was, Vin found himself doing something he hadn't done in a long, long time.

Getting involved.

"Stop right there," he ordered.

The other man's face snapped toward him. "Stay out of this."

Vin stalked toward him. "The lady doesn't want to leave with you."

"She's distraught. Not to mention crazy." The man, sleek and overfed as a Persian cat, yanked on her wrist. "I'm taking her to my psychiatrist. She's going to be locked away for a long, *long* time."

"No!" Scarlett whimpered. She looked up at Vin, her eyes shining with tears. "I'm not crazy. He used to be my boss. He's trying to force me to marry him and give our baby away."

Give our baby away.

The four words cut through Vin's heart like a knife. His whole body became still.

And he knew there was no way he was going to let this man take her.

His voice was ice-cold. "Let her go."

"You think you can make me?"

"Do you know my name?" Vin said quietly.

The man looked at him contemptuously. "I have no…" His voice trailed off, then he sucked in his breath. "Borgia." He exhaled the two syllables through his teeth. Vin saw the fear in the man's eyes. It was a reaction he'd grown accustomed to. "I…I didn't realize…"

Vin glanced at his own bodyguards, who'd entered the cathedral and surrounded the other men with surgical precision, ready to strike. He gave his chief of security a slight shake of his head, telling them to keep their distance. Then he looked at the man holding Scarlett. "Get. Out. Now."

He obeyed, abruptly releasing her. He turned and fled, his two bodyguards swiftly following him out of the cathedral.

Noise suddenly rose on all sides. Scarlett fell with a sob into Vin's arms, against the front of his tuxedo.

And a young man leaped up from a middle pew.

"Anne, I told you! Don't marry him! Who cares if you're disinherited?" Looking around the nave, the stranger proclaimed fiercely and loudly, "I've been sleeping with the bride for the last six months!"

Total chaos broke out then. The father of the bride started yelling, the mother of the bride wept noisily and, faced with such turmoil, the bride quietly and carefully fainted into a puffy heap of white tulle.

But Vin barely noticed. His world had shrunk to two things. Scarlett's tears as she wept in relief against his chest. And the tremble of her pregnant body, cradled beneath the protection of his arms.

CHAPTER TWO

OUT OF THE frying pan, into the fire.

Scarlett had escaped Blaise, but at what price?

For the last hour, she'd tried to calm the fearful beat of her heart as she sat in a faded floral chair next to a window overlooking a private garden. Vin had brought her to the private sitting room in the rectory behind the cathedral and told her to wait while he sorted things out. A kindly old lady—a housekeeper of some sort?—had pushed a hot cup of tea into her trembling hand.

But the tea had grown cold. She set the china cup into the saucer with a clatter.

Scarlett didn't know which scared her more. The memory of Blaise's snarling face. Or the fear of what Vin Borgia might do now to take over her future—and her baby's.

She should run.

She should run now.

Running was the only way to ensure their freedom.

Growing up, Scarlett had lived in over twenty different places, tiny towns hidden in forests and mountains, sometimes in shacks without electricity or running water. She'd rarely been able to go to school, and when she did, she'd had to dye her red hair brown and use a different name. Things that normal kids took for granted, such as having a real home, friends, going to the same school for a whole year, were luxuries Scarlett had only dreamed of. She'd never played sports, or sung in the school choir, or gone to prom. She'd never even gone on a real date.

Until she was twenty-four. The day she'd met Vin Borgia, she'd been weak, emotional, vulnerable. And he'd caught her up like a butterfly in a net.

She looked out the window with its view of the back garden, full of roses and ivy. A secret garden, surrounded by New York skyscrapers. A strangely calm, verdant place that seemed miles from the noisy traffic and honking cabs of Fifth Avenue. Rising to her feet, she started to pace.

A frosty gray afternoon last February, she'd been picking up a medicine prescription for Mrs. Falkner when she received a text from an old Boston friend of her father's with news that had staggered her.

Alan Berry had just died in an inconsequential knife fight in a Southie bar. The man who'd betrayed her father seventeen years before, who'd cut a deal for his own freedom and forced Harry Ravenwood to go on the run with his sick wife and young daughter, had died a meaningless death after a meaningless life. All for nothing.

Standing in the drugstore, Scarlett's knees had gone weak. She'd felt sick.

Five minutes later, she'd found herself at a dive bar across the street, ordering her first drink. The sharp pungent taste had made her cough.

"Let me guess." A low, amused voice had spoken from the red leather banquette in the corner. "It's your first time."

She'd turned. The man came out of the shadows slowly. Black eyes. Dark hair. Powerful broad shoulders. A black suit. Hard edges everywhere. Five-o'clock shadow. He was like a hero—or a handsome villain—from a movie, so masculine and powerful and handsome that he'd affected her even more than the vodka shot.

"I had a…bad day." Her voice trembled.

An ironic smile lifted the corners of his cruel, sensual mouth. "Why else would you be drinking in the afternoon?"

She wiped her eyes with a laugh. "For fun?"

"Fun. That's an idea." The man had come close enough to see her red-rimmed eyes and tear-streaked cheeks in the shadowy dive bar. She'd braced herself for questions, but he just slid onto the bar stool beside her and raised his hand to the bartender. "Let's see if the second shot goes down easier."

In spite of what she knew about him now, Vin Borgia still affected her like that. When Scarlett had seen him standing at the altar with his beautiful bride, all the memories had come back of their night together in February, when he'd taken her back to his elegant, Spartan, wildly expensive penthouse. He'd seduced her easily, claiming her virginity as if he owned it. He'd made her life explode with color and joy.

She'd known Vin's name, since his doorman had greeted him with the utmost respect as "Mr. Borgia." But she'd never told Vin her last name. Some habits were hard to break.

A phone call from Mrs. Falkner's nurse had woken Scarlett when Vin still slept. Only her sense of duty had forced her to wrench herself from the warmth of his bed. She'd returned to the Falkner mansion and handed over the prescription, then dreamily looked up her one and only lover online.

That had woken her up fast. She'd been horrified by what she found.

Vincenzo Borgia was a ruthless airline billionaire who'd risen from nothing and didn't give a damn who got hurt in his pursuit of world domination. She couldn't imagine why a man like that had seduced her, when he usually had liaisons with socialites and supermodels. But she was grateful she hadn't given him her last name. She wouldn't give him the chance to hurt her.

Later, when she'd discovered she was pregnant, she'd

wondered whether she'd made the right decision. But seeing Vin's engagement announcement in the paper had clinched it.

Scarlett had never expected to see Vin again. She'd planned to raise her baby alone.

She wasn't scared to be alone. She'd grown up on the run, and her fugitive father had secretly taught her skills after her mother got too sick to notice. How to pick pockets. How to pick locks. And most of all, how to be invisible and survive on almost nothing.

Compared to what she'd already lived through, raising a child as a single parent would be easy. She wasn't a fugitive. She'd never committed any crimes. She had a marketable skill as a nurse's aide. She'd even saved some money. She no longer had to hide.

Or did she?

Scarlett stopped pacing the thick rug of the cathedral rectory, staring blankly at the faded floral furniture. Did she really want to take the chance that Vin Borgia, the man she'd read such horrible things about, could be a good father? Did she dare take that risk, just because she'd loved her own father so much?

She could see the soft shimmer of dust motes through a beam of fading golden sunlight from the window. She put her hands gently on her belly.

Vin had saved her from Blaise, but rich, powerful men all had one thing in common: they wanted to be in control. And Vin Borgia was richer and more powerful than most.

She should just leave before he returned.

Right now.

Scarlett took a step, then stopped when she remembered her suitcase and handbag were still in Blaise's limo, with her money, ID, credit card, phone. When she'd fled him in terror, those had been the last thing on her mind. But now... How could she run with no money and no passport?

She looked down glumly at her bare toes snuggled into the plush rug. She didn't even have shoes!

"What's your name?"

She whirled to face the door. Vin had entered the room, his jaw like granite as he loosened his tie. Just looking at his hard-muscled body caused a physical reaction in her, made her tremble from the inside out, with a mixture of fear and desire. Even the sleekly tailored tuxedo couldn't give him the look of a man who was entirely civilized. Especially with that hard, almost savage look in his black eyes.

She swallowed. "You know my name. Scarlett."

He glowered at her. "Your *last* name."

"Smith," she tried.

Vin's jaw tightened. Turning away, he picked up a carafe of water sitting on a tray on a nearby table. He poured water into one of the glasses. "Your last name is Ravenwood."

Her lips parted in shock. "How did you—"

Reaching into his jacket pocket, he held up her wallet, his handsome face impassive.

"How did you get that?"

"Falkner sent your purse to me. And your suitcase."

"*Sent?* You mean he dumped them in the street?"

"I mean his bodyguards personally brought them to me, neatly stacked, with his compliments."

Oh, this was so much worse than she'd feared. Scarlett breathed, "The worst man I know is afraid of you?"

He smiled grimly. "It's not unusual." He held her wallet out toward her. "Here. Seventeen dollars cash and a single credit card. With an eight-hundred-dollar limit."

"Hey!" She snatched at it. Her cheeks burned. "How do you know my credit limit?"

Picking up his glass, Vin swirled the clear water thoughtfully. "I wanted to know what I was dealing with.

An orphan who never lived anywhere for long, who came to New York for a thankless live-in job, who saved every penny for two years, who made no new friends, who worked all the time and never went out." He tilted his head, looking at her with heavily lidded black eyes as he murmured, "With one memorable exception."

A flash of heat went through her, then cold. She couldn't think about that night. Not now. "You have some nerve to—"

"The Falkners barely paid minimum wage, but you saved every penny you could. Impressive work ethic, considering your jailbird father—"

"Don't you dare call him that!" she shouted. "My dad was the kindest, best man who ever lived!"

"Are you serious?" Vin's lips curved. "He was a bank robber who became a fugitive and dragged you and your mother into a life on the run. You had no money, barely went to school, and your mother died of an illness that she might perhaps have survived with proper care. What am I missing?"

"Stop judging him," she raged. "My father gave up that life when I was a baby. But a friend of his convinced him to try for one last score. After my mother found out, she gave him an ultimatum. He gave the money back to the bank!"

"Just gave it back, hmm?"

"He left the bags of money outside the police station, then tipped them off with an anonymous call."

"Why didn't he turn himself in?"

"Because he didn't want to leave my mom. Or me." Scarlett took a deep breath. "We would have been fine, except Alan Berry was caught spending his own share of the money six months later and threw my father under the bus as the supposed mastermind of the crime! After he'd tried to do the right thing—"

"The right thing would have been for your father to turn himself in at the start," Vin said mercilessly, "instead of waiting ten years to find the courage, and dragging you and your mother through such a miserable life on the run." He calmly took a sip of water. "The only truly decent thing your father ever did was die in that plane crash after he got out of prison. Giving you that tidy multimillion-dollar settlement offered by the airline."

Scarlett nearly staggered to her knees at his easy reference to the greatest loss of her life, one that still left her grief-stricken every day—her father's sudden death, along with thirty other people, in a plane crash a year and a half before, as he was coming to New York to see her, finally free after five years in a medium-security prison.

Vin looked at her curiously. "You gave all that money away." He tilted his head. "Why?"

She was so shocked, it took her a moment to find her voice. In mere minutes, Vin Borgia had casually ripped through her privacy and exposed all the secrets of her life.

"I didn't want their blood money," she whispered. "I gave it to charity."

"Yes, I know. Cancer research, legal defense for the poor and help for children of incarcerated parents. All fine causes. But I don't understand why you'd choose to be penniless."

"Like you said, maybe I'm used to it. Anyway." She clutched her wallet. "Some things matter more than money."

"Like a baby?" Vin said coldly. He put the glass down with a *thunk* on the wooden table. "You let me seduce you and take your virginity, then snuck out while I slept. You never bothered to contact me. You waited until my wedding to spring the news on me that you were pregnant."

"I had no choice—"

"There were plenty of choices." His jaw tightened. "Tell

me the truth. If Falkner hadn't threatened you today, you never would have told me about the baby, would you?"

She stared at him for a long moment, then shook her head.

"Why?" he demanded.

The warmth from the cathedral garden was failing. Scarlett glanced at the fading afternoon light, now turning gray. She didn't answer.

"You refused to even tell me your last name that night. Why?" he pressed, coming closer. "Was it because you were also encouraging Falkner's attentions?"

"I never did!" She gaped at him. "I knew he wanted me, but I never thought he'd attack me while giving me a ride from his mother's funeral!"

"Ah. That explains the black dress." He looked down at her pale pink toenails. "But why are you barefoot?"

"I kicked off my shoes running on Fifth Avenue. I knew your wedding was here today." She looked down. "I'm sorry I ruined it."

"Yes. Well." His jaw tightened as he said grudgingly, "I suppose I should thank you."

"You didn't know your bride was cheating on you?"

"She convinced me she was a virgin and wanted to wait for marriage."

A laugh rose to her lips. "You thought she was a virgin? In this day and age?"

"Why not?" he said coldly. "You were."

Their eyes met, and Scarlett's body flooded with heat. Against her will, memories filled her of that night, of being in his arms, in his bed, his body hard and hot and slick against hers. She tried to smile. "Yeah, but I'm not normal."

"Agreed." His dark gaze seared hers. "Am I really the father of your baby, Scarlett? Or were you lying just because you needed my help?"

"Of course the baby's yours!"

He bared his teeth into a smile. "I will find out if it's not true."

"You're the only man I've ever slept with, so I'm pretty sure!"

"The only man? Ever?" For a moment, something stretched between them. Then it snapped. "So what do you want from me now? Money?"

She glared at him. "Just point me in the direction of my suitcase and I'll be on my way!"

"You're not going anywhere until this is sorted."

"Look, I'm deeply grateful for your help with Blaise, and sorry if I ruined your big wedding day, but I don't appreciate you digging into my life, then assuming that I'm either a con artist or a gold digger. I'm neither. I just want to raise my baby in peace."

"There will be a DNA test," he warned. "Lawyers."

She looked at him in horror. "Lawyers? What for?"

"So we both know where we stand."

Scarlett felt a *whoosh* of panic that made her unsteady on her feet. Her voice trembled. "You mean you intend to sue me for custody?"

"That will not be necessary." She exhaled in relief, before he finished, "Because once I have proof the baby's mine, Scarlett, you will marry me."

With those words, Vin took control over the spinning chaos of the day.

He'd been wrong about Anne Dumaine. He'd convinced himself she was modest and demure when all the while she'd been cheating on him and lying to his face. To say she'd turned out to be a disappointment was an understatement.

"Sorry," she'd whispered the last time he'd seen her, when she'd pressed the ten-carat engagement ring into his palm. But she hadn't looked sorry as she'd joyfully turned to her lover—a boy of maybe twenty-three, ridiculously shabby in a sweater, and they'd fled the cathedral hand in hand, Anne's wedding veil flying behind her like a white flag.

Leaving Vin to face the annoyed glower of her father.

"If you'd bothered to show my daughter the slightest attention, she wouldn't have fallen for that nobody!"

The merger with Transatlantique was clearly off.

Vin's mistake. He'd never bothered to look beyond Anne's cool blonde exterior into her soul. Truthfully, her soul hadn't interested him. But he should have had his investigators check her more thoroughly. *Trust no one* had been his motto since he was young. Trust no one; control everything.

Scarlett Ravenwood was different. She didn't have the education or pedigree of Anne, her manners were lamentable and she had no dress sense. Her only dowry would be the child she carried inside her.

A baby. His baby. After his own awful childhood, he'd decided long ago that any child of his would always know his father, would have a stable home and feel safe and loved. Vin would never abandon his child. He'd die first.

Standing in the shabby room of the rectory, surrounded by chintzy overstuffed furniture, Vin looked at Scarlett, so vivid with her pale skin and red hair.

The dark sweeping lashes over her green eyes, the color of every spring and summer of his Italian childhood, seemed to tremble. When he'd first seen her in that bar nearly eight months ago, right before Valentine's Day, coughing over her first taste of vodka, it had been like a burst of sun after a long cold night, a sunrise as bright and red as her hair, filling him with warmth—and fire.

His mind moved rapidly. She had no fortune, but perhaps that was an advantage. No father-in-law to scream in his ear. No family to become a burden. She had nothing to offer him but their baby. And her sexy body. And the best lovemaking of his life.

He shivered just remembering that night…

It was, he reflected, not the worst way to begin a marriage. He could make of her what he wanted. She could be the perfect wife, made to his order. She had no money. She was grateful to him for saving her from that imbecile Falkner. He already had complete control.

Now she just had to realize that, as well.

"You want to marry me?" Scarlett repeated, staring at him in shock. "Seriously?"

"Yes." He waited for her to be suitably thrilled. Instead, she burst into laughter.

"Are you crazy? I'm not marrying you!"

"If the baby is mine, it is our only reasonable course of action," he said stiffly.

As if he'd told her the best joke in the world, she shook her head merrily. "You really don't want to lose your wedding deposit, do you?"

"What are you talking about?"

"Am I expected to just put on your last bride's wedding gown, and you'll let the guests know there's been a slight change in the lineup? You'll just change the color of the bride's hair on the cake topper from blond to red, and proceed as planned?"

"You think I'd marry you to avoid losing a little money?" he said incredulously.

"No?" She tilted her head, on a roll now, clearly enjoying herself. "Then what is it? Is marriage just on your schedule, and you need to check it off your to-do list before you pick up your dry cleaning and pay your electric bill?"

"Scarlett, I get the feeling you're not taking this seriously."

"I'm not!" she exploded. "Why on earth would I marry you? I barely know you!"

Vin felt irritated at her irrational response, but he reminded himself that she was pregnant, and therefore to be treated gently. "You've had a trying day," he said in the most soothing voice he could muster. "We should go to my doctor."

"Why?"

"Just to check you're doing fine. And we'll get the paternity test."

"You can't just take my word the baby's yours?"

"You could obviously be lying."

For some reason, she seemed upset by this. She glared at him. "I'm not doing some stupid paternity test, not if it causes risk to the baby—"

"The doctor just draws a little blood from your arm and mine. There's no risk to the baby whatsoever."

"How do you know that?"

Vin didn't care to explain the sordid story of the one-night stand who last February had tried to claim her baby was his, even though he'd used a condom and she'd claimed to be on the pill. It had turned out the DNA test was unnecessary as she wasn't pregnant at all. She'd just hoped he would marry her and she'd get quickly pregnant—and he'd be too stupid to do the math. That experience had left him cold.

It was ironic that after confronting that one-night stand over her lies, he'd stopped for a drink in a new bar—and, meeting Scarlett, they'd ended up conceiving a child.

Looking at Scarlett now, he felt his body tighten. She had no right to look so lovely, her riotous red curls tumbling over her shoulders, her eyes so wistful and luminous, her lips so naturally full and pink. Her breasts strained the modest neckline of the simple black dress, and her large baby bump made her even more voluptuous, more sexy.

Pregnant. With his baby.

If it was true, he would devote his life to giving this baby a very different childhood than he'd had. His child would always be safe, and loved. Unlike Vin, his child would always know who his father was.

If her child was even his, he reminded himself. She could be lying. He needed proof. He held out his hand. "Let's go."

With visible reluctance, she put her hand in his. "If I go with you to the doctor, and you get proof you're the father, then what?"

"I'll have my lawyers draw up a prenuptial agreement."

"A pre-nup?" Her voice sounded surprised. "Why?"

He gave a grim smile. "I can hardly marry you without control."

"Control of what?"

"Everything," he said honestly.

He led her through the now empty cathedral, with only rapidly wilting wedding flowers and a few despondent janitors sweeping up. Her voice trembled as she asked, "What specifically would be in the pre-nup?"

"Standard things." He shrugged. "Giving me final say on schooling and religion and where we will live. Things like that. I am based in New York but have homes all over. I am often required to travel while running SkyWorld Airways, sometimes for months at a time. I would not want to be away from my children."

"*Children?* I'm not carrying twins."

"Obviously, our child will need siblings." She made a sound like a squeak, but he ignored her, continuing, "I expect you to travel with me whenever and wherever I wish."

Her forehead furrowed. "But how would I hold down a job?"

"Money will no longer be an issue. As my wife, your only requirement will be to support me. You will be in society. You will learn to properly entertain powerful people to promote my company's best interests. You may need comportment lessons."

"What?"

"And, of course," he added casually, "in the event we ever divorce, the pre-nup will simplify that process. It will clearly spell out what happens if you cheat on me, or either of us decides to separate. You'll know what amount of money you'll be entitled to based on years—"

"Of service?"

He smiled blandly. "Of marriage, I was going to say. Naturally, I would automatically gain full custody of our children."

"What?!"

"Don't worry. You would still be allowed to visit them."

"Big of you," she murmured. As they walked down the cathedral steps to his waiting car, his bodyguards waiting beside the large SUV behind it, Scarlett abruptly stopped.

"Before we go to your doctor and have the paternity test, could you do me a favor?" She smiled prettily, showing a dimple in her left cheek, then waved helplessly at her bare feet on the sidewalk. "Could we stop at a shoe store?"

Like Cinderella, Vin thought. He was surprised how well she was taking everything. The way she was looking at him so helplessly, so prettily. She would be easy to mold and shape into the perfect wife.

"Of course," he said almost tenderly. "I'm sorry. I should have thought of that before." Picking her up in his arms, he carried her. In spite of being heavily pregnant, she seemed to weigh nothing at all. He gently set her into the waiting car, still bedecked with flowers.

The driver's eyes were popping out of his head to see Vin had left the church carrying a redhead, when he'd gone in to marry a blonde. But he wisely said nothing and just started the car.

Vin climbed into the backseat beside her. "Any preference about the shoe store?"

He expected her to name a designer store, the sorts of luxury brands that Anne had constantly yammered about, but here again Scarlett surprised him.

"Any shoes good to run in," she said demurely, her black eyelashes fluttering against her pale cheeks.

"You heard her," he told his driver.

Ten minutes later, Scarlett was trying on running shoes at an enormous athletic store on Fifty-Seventh Street. She chose her favorite pair of running shoes, along with a pair of socks, exclaiming at Vin's generosity all the while.

"Thank you," she whispered, suddenly giving him a hug. For a moment, he closed his eyes. He could smell the peppermint of her breath and breathed in the cherry blossom scent of her hair. Then she abruptly pulled back. Staring up at him wide-eyed, she bit her lip. Vin could imagine the sensual caress of those full, plump lips.

Then she smiled, and her eyes crinkled. "I'll wear the shoes starting now. Excuse me."

Vin watched her walk toward the ladies' restroom, past the displays of expensive athletic shoes and equipment. His eyes lingered appreciatively over the curve of her backside, the sway of her hips. Scarlett made even a plain black funeral dress look good.

What a wife she would make. And as for the honeymoon…he shuddered.

Determined to hurry them into the car, he turned toward the cashier. Normally his assistant would have dealt with such mundane details, but he'd left Ernest at the cathedral to handle the logistical problems of the ruined wedding—returning mailed gifts, organizing early rides to the airport for disgruntled guests, donating the expensively catered reception dinner to a local homeless shelter. So Vin himself went to pay for the shoes.

There would soon be lots of other purchases, he thought. Baby booties. A crib. A nursery. He'd have his houses baby-proofed. He'd hire a larger staff. He would buy a few more family-sized SUVs to add to his personal fleet of expensive cars. Small tasks that would distract him from building his empire, but it would be worth it to finally have a family of his own.

He'd be the parent he himself had never had. His child would never know what it felt like to be abandoned. To be used. To be neglected and alone.

Reaching into his tuxedo jacket, Vin felt for his wallet. Frowning, he looked in his pockets. Empty. Had he left it in the car, or back at the cathedral? Scowling, he motioned for one of his bodyguards to pay and told the other one to track down the wallet. Sitting down at a nearby bench, Vin called his doctor to arrange for an immediate appointment. Then he tapped his feet.

Scarlett was taking a long time.

"Go check on her," he ordered his bodyguard impatiently.

Vin paced. Checked his phone again. Stopped.

Suspicion dawned.

She couldn't. She wouldn't.

She had.

"Miss Ravenwood is nowhere to be found, boss," Larson said when he returned. "I had the bathroom checked. Empty." He hesitated. "There is a door beside it that leads to a storeroom, then out to the alley."

With a low curse, Vin strode through the sporting goods store, his two bodyguards behind him. In the back, near the ladies' restroom, he found the storeroom. Store employees shrank back at his glare as he threw open the back door with an angry bang.

Outside was an alley with graffiti-littered brick walls. Vin walked slowly past the Dumpsters to the end: busy

Madison Avenue, crowded with people and cars packed bumper to bumper. He stared around him in shock.

Scarlett Ravenwood had not only walked out on him, she'd most likely stolen his wallet. Not only that, she'd warned him first! "Shoes good to run in" indeed!

Clawing his hand back through his dark hair, he gave a single, incredulous laugh. He'd been ditched twice in one day. Lied to by two different women.

Anne's loss he could accept. That had involved only money.

Scarlett was different. He'd never stopped desiring her. And now she was carrying his baby.

Or was she? Perhaps she'd lied. He rubbed his forehead. Why would any woman run away when he'd asked her to marry him and live in luxury for the rest of her life? Unless she was afraid of the paternity test. That was the only rational explanation: the baby wasn't his. The thought caused a sick twist in his gut.

Then he remembered the angry gleam in Scarlett's green eyes.

I don't appreciate you digging into my life, then assuming that I'm either a con artist or a gold digger. I'm neither. I just want to raise my baby in peace.

Standing motionless as pedestrians rushed by him on Madison Avenue, Vin narrowed his eyes.

Either way, he had to know.

Either way, he'd find her.

And this time, she wouldn't trick him so easily. Nothing would stop him from getting what he wanted. He wouldn't listen to her excuses. Next time, he'd bend her to his will.

Barefoot, if necessary.

CHAPTER THREE

THERE WAS ONLY one thing that mattered in life, Scarlett's father had always told her as a child. Freedom.

Freedom. It was Harry Ravenwood's rallying cry every time their family had to flee in the night, tossing their belongings into black trash bags and heading blindly to a new city. At seven years old, when Scarlett accidentally left her teddy bear—her only friend—behind, she'd cried until her father comforted her with stories of Mr. Teddy backpacking around the world, climbing the Pyramids and the Pyrenees. His funny stories of her bear's adventures finally made her smile through her tears. On cold winter nights in Upstate New York, as their family shivered in unheated rooms and icy wind rattled the windows, Harry sang jaunty songs about freedom.

Freedom. Even on the bleak night when Scarlett was twelve, when her mother died in the emergency room of a hospital in a faded factory town in Pennsylvania, her father kissed Scarlett as tears streamed down his weathered face. "At least now your beautiful mother is free of pain."

Scarlett had her freedom now. From Blaise Falkner. From Vin Borgia. She and her unborn baby were free.

But it had come at a cost.

To start with, her flight two weeks ago, from Boston to London, had had a little trouble over the Atlantic.

A small fire in the cargo hold caused the plane to divert to a small airport on the west coast of Ireland. As the plane descended, she saw dark clusters of birds through her porthole window, flying rapidly past the plane. "Bird strike!" a passenger cried out, and as one flight attendant rushed toward the cockpit, another tried to murmur reassuring, unconvincing words to the passengers. Wide-eyed, Scarlett gripped her armrests as she felt the plane ominously vibrate and groan in midair.

All she'd been able to think was, she shouldn't be on this plane. Pregnant women weren't supposed to fly after their seventh month. She was nearly at eight. She'd fled from New York, with a quick stop in Boston, because she thought it was her only way to escape Vin. But now that danger seemed small when she and her child were both going to die. Just like her own father had died in that wintry plane crash a year and a half ago. *She never should have gotten on a plane.*

"Prepare for crash landing," came the pilot's terse voice over the intercom. "Brace for impact." The flight attendants repeated the words as the nose of the plane started to plummet and they rushed to buckle themselves in. "Heads down! Brace for impact! Stay down!"

Scarlett had braced herself, hugging her belly, thinking, *please don't let my baby die.*

Like a miracle, the plane had finally steadied on one engine and limped hard, landing with a heavy bang on the edge of the runway. No one was hurt, and passengers and crew alike cheered and cried and hugged each other.

Sliding off the plane on the inflatable yellow slide, Scarlett had fallen to her knees on the tarmac and burst into noisy, ugly sobs.

She never should have gotten on a plane. Any plane. After her father's death, she should have known better.

But just like when she'd accepted that limo ride from Blaise Falkner, she'd ignored her intuition and convinced herself that her fears were silly. And both she and her baby had nearly died as a result.

She'd never ignore her intuition again. From now on,

she'd listen seriously to her fears, even when they didn't make rational sense.

And above all: she would never, ever get on any plane again.

But why would Scarlett need to? She had no family in New York. No reason to ever go back. Vin Borgia had done her a huge favor, warning her in advance that he intended to rule her life and their child's with an iron fist and separate her from her baby if she ever objected or tried to leave him. She didn't feel guilty about leaving him, not at all.

She did feel guilty about stealing his wallet. Stealing was never all right, and her mother must be turning over in her grave. Scarlett told herself she'd had no choice. She'd had to cover her tracks. Vin was not only a ruthless billionaire, he owned an airline and had ridiculous connections. If she'd stepped one toe on a flight under her own name, he would have known about it.

So she'd contacted one of her father's old acquaintances in Boston to buy a fake passport. That cost money.

So she'd taken—borrowed—the money from Vin. She hadn't touched anything else in his wallet. Not his driver's license, or his credit cards, most of them in special strange colors that no doubt had eye-popping credit limits. And after she'd arrived safely in Switzerland via ferry and train from Ireland, and gotten her first paycheck at her new job, she'd mailed back Vin's wallet, returning everything as he'd left it. She'd even tossed in some extra euros as interest on the money she'd borrowed.

She'd gotten the euros from northern Italy, where she'd gone to mail back the package. She could hardly have sent Vin money in Swiss francs, letting him know where she was!

But that was all behind her now. She'd paid everything back. She and her baby were free.

Scarlett took a deep breath of the clear Alpine air. She'd been in Gstaad for over two weeks now, and finally, *finally* she was starting to relax. She just had to hope when Vin couldn't easily find her, he would forget about her and the baby, and she'd never have to worry about him again.

Scarlett passed out of the gates of the chalet, if the place could be called a chalet when it was the size of a palace, and turned her face up toward the sun.

It was mid-October, and the morning air was already frosty in the mountains around the elegant Swiss ski resort of Gstaad. The first snowfall was expected daily.

She had her own event to expect soon, too. Her hand moved over her belly, grown so large she could no longer button up her oversize jacket. Only two and a half weeks from her due date. Her body felt heavier, slower. But luckily her new job allowed plenty of opportunity for gentle morning walks.

She'd been lucky to get this job. When she'd fled the shoe store in New York, racing down the alley to hail a cab on Madison Avenue, she'd already decided exactly where to go. Her mother's best friend, Wilhelmina Stone, worked as housekeeper to a wealthy European tycoon in Switzerland. Though Scarlett hadn't seen her since her mother's funeral, she'd never forgotten the woman's hug and fierce words, "Your mother was my best friend. If you ever need anything, you come straight to me, you hear?"

Since then, she'd gotten only an occasional Christmas card. But when Scarlett had shown up uninvited and shivering at the gate of the enormous villa outside Gstaad, the plump, kindly woman had proved good as her word.

"My boss just asked me to hire a good cook for ski season. The best Southern cook in the US, he said. Can you make grits and fried chicken? Jambalaya? Dirty rice?"

Eyes wide, Scarlett shook her head. Wilhelmina sighed. "All right, he usually starts coming here in early December, after the season starts. So you've got six weeks, maybe more, to learn how to make amazing fried chicken and all the rest. I'll put you on staff payroll now. Just make sure you learn to cook for groups of ten or more, because Mr. Black always brings friends!"

For the last two weeks, Scarlett had been trying to teach herself to cook, using cookbooks and internet videos. She was still pretty bad. The security guard routinely teased her that even his dog wouldn't eat what she cooked. It was sadly true.

But she would learn. Being a specialty chef for a hard-traveling, hard-partying tycoon who was rarely around was the perfect job for any single mother with a newborn. She would be able to take a week or two off to heal after the birth, then work with her baby nearby, almost as if this were her own home.

Plus, Switzerland was the perfect place to raise a baby. Scarlett tucked her hands in her jacket pockets as she walked along the slender road. Gravel crunched beneath her soft boots as she took a deep breath of crisp mountain air smelling of sunlight and pine trees. For a brief moment, she closed her eyes, turning her face to the sun. Her heart was full of gratitude.

Then she heard a snap in the forest ahead of her.

She opened her eyes, and the smile dropped from her face.

"Scarlett," Vin greeted her coldly.

He stood ahead of her, wearing a long black coat, a sleek dark suit and a glower. She saw a sleek sports car and a black SUV parked on the road behind him. Three bodyguards lined the vehicle, an impenetrable wall of money and power.

She stumbled back from him. He was on her in seconds, grabbing her wrist.

"Don't touch me!" she cried.

His grip tightened, his eyes like black fire. "You stole from me."

"I paid all your money back—with interest!" She glanced back desperately toward the guarded gate, but it was too far. Johan would never see her. And how could one security guard take on Vin Borgia and at least three of his men?

"I wasn't just talking about the money."

She put her free hand protectively over her belly. "You're not my baby's father. I—I lied!"

"I think you're lying now."

Scarlett tried to pull her wrist from his grip. "Leave me alone!"

"I do not understand your behavior." He wrenched her closer. "Most women would find it fortunate to be pregnant by a billionaire."

"A billionaire who destroys people?" She shook her head. "You don't just take companies—you ruthlessly crush and annihilate your rivals. Their marriages, their families, their very lives!"

Silence fell in the Swiss forest. The only sound was the call of birds.

Then he spoke, his voice low and flat. "So you did some digging on the internet, did you?"

"Why do you think I never tried to contact you after our night together?" She took a deep breath. "I had a good reason to leave you that first morning. A nurse called and I was needed at the Falkner mansion. I hoped to see you again. Until I looked you up online." She glared at him. "If you think I'm going to let my precious baby be raised by a man who takes pleasure in other people's pain—"

His lip twisted contemptuously. "If you think I'm such a bastard, why did you ask for my help?"

"I was terrified of Blaise."

"And now you're terrified of me?"

"After I interrupted your wedding, I thought maybe I should give you a chance. My own father wasn't perfect, but I loved him." She narrowed her eyes. "Then you made your intentions clear."

"What are you talking about? My intention to take responsibility, marry you and be a good father?"

"If I honestly believed we could be a family, and love and trust each other, I'd marry you in a second. But I'd rather raise my baby alone than with a man who might hurt me!"

"Hurt you?" he said incredulously. "I've never hurt a woman in my life!"

"With your cold heart? I bet you've hurt plenty."

He relaxed. "Oh. You mean *emotionally*."

"Yes, emotionally," she retorted. "You don't think that counts?"

"Not really, no."

"And that's why I don't want to marry you."

He abruptly released her wrist, his eyes strangely alight. "I've never killed anyone, no matter what the rumors say. I never poisoned someone or sabotaged an engine. Nor did I hire someone else to do it. A reporter just happened to notice that during some points in my business career, some men have coincidentally had problems."

"You expect me to believe that? It was pure coincidence?"

"It's the truth. A man was discovered in an affair while doing business with me. It was hardly my fault his wife took offense and dumped poison in his morning whiskey. Another man had a heart attack from stress during my hostile takeover. He could have walked away at any time but chose to fight and take the risk. Another man chose to start a feud with his sister when she sold her shares to me. Their family was ripped apart, yes—but again, not my fault."

"Then why was Blaise so afraid of you? And you expected him to be!"

"I know the rumors about me. They're not true, but people believe them. I'd be a fool not to take advantage of it."

"And you're no fool."

"No." His jaw tightened. "So I don't appreciate that
you've made me look like one. Twice."

She turned her head back again toward the distant gate
of the chalet. She wished she could run. But she'd become
so heavily pregnant and slow—

"I want a paternity test," Vin said coldly. "You have an
appointment today with a doctor in Geneva."

"I've got my own doctor in the village, thank you."

"Dr. Schauss has a world-renowned clinic. She was ob-
stetrician to a princess of Sweden and has delivered half
the babies of the royal houses of the Persian Gulf. She's
well qualified."

"I'm not gallivanting off to Geneva just because you
want some extra-fancy doctor."

"The choice isn't yours to make."

"And if I refuse?"

Vin's eyes flickered. "I am acquainted with Kassius
Black, the owner of this chalet." He looked up at the im-
posing roofline over the trees. "What would he say if I
told him that your friend, his trusted housekeeper, had
knowingly hired a fugitive and thief to live here, and you
were both conspiring to steal from his houseguests this
coming ski season?"

"You wouldn't," she gasped. "It's not true!"

He shrugged. "You are a proven thief and liar. It *could*
be true. But the point is, are you willing to repay your
friend's kindness in giving you a job by causing her to
lose hers?"

"You are despicable."

His face hardened. "No, *cara*. You are despicable. I

have done nothing but seek to fulfill my responsibility. I am trying to do the right thing, the honorable thing. It is you who are the thief."

"I repaid every penny!"

"Yes, with interest. At an annualized interest rate of thirty percent. The money you repaid yielded a better return than many of my other investments. So it was profitable." He gave a slight, ironic bow. "Thank you for stealing my wallet."

"Oh?" she said hopefully. "So you're not—"

"Stealing my child is something else."

Scarlett's brief hope faded. What could she do? She couldn't let Wilhelmina be hurt for her loyalty and kindness.

The clinic in Geneva. That could be her escape route. Clinics had back doors. She could sneak out before her blood was even drawn.

Scarlett let her shoulders sag, scuffling her feet in the gravel, hoping she looked suitably downhearted. Her heart was beating fast. "You win."

"I always do." He gave a quick motion to the bodyguards waiting outside the black SUV with dark tinted windows, then turned back, his voice brisk. "The trip to Geneva will take two hours by car, and in your state of advanced pregnancy I am concerned this will be uncomfortable for you. I can have a helicopter here in ten minutes—"

"No!" she said a little too quickly. At his frown, she said in a calmer voice, trying to smile, "The drive will give us a chance to talk. It's so beautiful around Lake Geneva this time of year."

He stared at her for a long moment, then shrugged. "As you wish."

Five minutes later, as a bodyguard went upstairs to pack up her meager possessions, she went to the kitchen to say farewell to Wilhelmina. The older woman seemed bewildered by the sudden turn in events.

"You're quitting your job, Scarlett? Just like that?"

"I'm sorry, Wilhelmina. You came through for me, and I'm leaving you in the lurch. I'm so sorry—"

"For me it's fine. Honestly, your fried chicken still is something awful. Mr. Black would have thought I lost my mind, hiring you. You're the one I'm worried about." She looked doubtfully at Vin. "So this man is the father of your baby, but do you really want to go with him?" Her eyes narrowed in her plump face. "Or is he forcing you?"

The suspicion in the older woman's face was less than flattering to Vin, but as she was a housekeeper to Kassius Black, a man whose reputation for ferocity was even worse than his own, he could understand her lack of automatic admiration for the average billionaire. The housekeeper, like Scarlett, had obviously had enough experience with the wealthy to know the ugliness that could lie behind the glamorous lifestyle.

"I will take good care of Scarlett and her baby," he told her gravely. "I promise you."

The housekeeper stared at him, then her scowl slowly disappeared. "I believe you."

"Good." Vin gave her his most charming smile. "We intend to marry soon."

She looked accusingly at Scarlett. "You're engaged?"

Scarlett looked a little dazed. "We haven't decided anything for sure…"

"Mrs. Stone," Vin interrupted, "I appreciate your loyalty and kindness to Scarlett. Should you ever want to switch jobs, please let us know."

Handing her a card, he took Scarlett by the hand and led her out of the chalet as the bodyguards followed with her shockingly small amount of luggage: a purse and a single duffel bag. He watched as they packed it into the back of the glossy SUV. An unwelcome image floated through Vin's mind of his own meager belongings when he'd left Italy at fifteen, after his mother's devastating revelation and death, to go live in New York with an uncle he barely knew. He'd felt so alone. So hollow.

He pushed the memory away angrily. He wasn't that boy anymore. He would never feel so vulnerable again— and neither would any child of his.

Vin opened the passenger door of the red sports car, then turned to Scarlett coldly. "Get in."

"You're driving us? Yourself?"

"The bodyguards will follow in the SUV. Like you said—" he gave a hard smile "—it's a beautiful day for a drive."

Once they were buckled in, he stepped on the gas, driving swiftly out of the gate and down the mountain, to the paved road that led through the expensive village of Gstaad, with its charming Alpine architecture, exclusive designer boutiques and chalets with shutters and flower boxes. The midmorning sun glowed in the blue sky above craggy forested mountains as they looped onto the Gstaadstrasse, heading west.

Vin glanced at Scarlett out of the corner of his eye. She was dressed very casually, an unbuttoned jacket over an oversize shirt, loose khaki pants and fur-lined booties. But for all that, his eyes hungrily drank in the sight of her. Her flame-red hair fell in thick curls down her shoulders. Her lustrous eyes were green as an Alpine forest. He could remember how it had felt to have those full, pink lips move against his skin, gasping in ecstasy…

He shuddered.

Why did Scarlett have such power over him?

For the last two weeks, since she'd left him standing on Madison Avenue with a stunned look on his face, he'd thought of nothing else. All of his considerable resources had been dedicated to one task: finding her.

She was in his blood. He hadn't been able to forget her. Not from the first moment he'd seen her in that bar. From the moment he'd first taken her in his arms. From the moment she'd disappeared from his bed after the best sex of his life.

From the moment she'd violently crashed his wedding and told him she was pregnant with his baby.

Scarlett Ravenwood was half angel, half demon. There was a reason he hadn't seduced any other woman for over eight months—an eternity for a man like Vin. He'd been haunted by Scarlett, haunted body and soul, driven half mad by memories of her naked in his arms.

Scarlett was the woman for him. The one he wanted. And he intended to have her.

"How did you find me in Switzerland?" she asked him quietly now.

Lifting his eyebrow, Vin focused on the road ahead. "It was a mistake for you to mail my wallet from a small Italian village. I still have connections in that country. It was easy to track down the *postino* who'd helped you. He remembered seeing your car with Swiss plates."

"He noticed my car?"

He smiled grimly. "There are surprisingly few Swiss registrations of a 1970 Plymouth Hemi Cuda convertible in pale green. The *postino* kissed his lips when he described it. *'Bella macchina.'* He remembered you, too, a pregnant redheaded woman, very beautiful but a tragic driver. He thought the car deserved better."

"I chose that car from the chalet's garage because I thought it was the oldest," she said, sounding dazed, "so figured it was the cheapest."

"They're rare and often sell for two or three million dollars."

"Oh," she said faintly. "So if I'd taken the brand-new sedan…"

"I wouldn't have found you." Gripping the steering wheel, he looked at her. "You keep wondering if I'm trustworthy. I could wonder the same about you, except I've seen the answer. You've lied to my face, stolen my wallet. Kidnapped my child—"

"Kidnapped!"

"What else would you call it?" He looked at her. "How do I know our baby will be safe with you? The criminally minded daughter of a felon?"

"Felon!" Fury filled her green eyes. "My father never should have gone to prison. If his accomplice hadn't betrayed him—"

"Spare me the excuses," Vin said, sounding bored. "He was a bank robber."

"He returned all the money. Can you say the same?"

"What are you talking about?"

"I'm talking about you and Blaise Falkner and every other billionaire—you are the real ones who should be…"

She abruptly cut herself off.

"Go on," Vin said evenly. "You were about to accuse me of something?"

Scarlett looked him straight in the eye. "Every rich man I've ever known was heartless. My dad in his worst year was less a thief than all the corporate embezzlers and Wall Street gamblers with their Ponzi schemes, wiping out people's pension funds, their savings, their hope!"

"You're comparing me to them?"

"You wouldn't sacrifice one of your platinum cuff links—" she glanced contemptuously at his wrist "—let alone risk your life or happiness, to save someone else."

"You don't know that."

"Don't I?" She lifted her chin. Through the car window he could see the gray-and-blue shimmer of Lake Geneva behind her. "You told me yourself. You don't think twice about causing emotional pain. I bet you've never loved anyone in your life. And you asked me to marry you!"

"Love isn't necessary."

"That's a screwed-up way of looking at things. That's like saying there's no point in eating things that taste good. Marriage without love, isn't that like eating gruel for the rest of your life? Why eat gruel when you can eat cake?"

"Cake is an illusion. It all turns out to be gruel in the end."

"That's the saddest thing I ever heard." She shook her head. "I feel bad for you. A billionaire who's content to eat gruel for the rest of his life."

Vin could hardly believe this penniless girl who had nothing and had once stolen his wallet actually felt sorry for him. "Better a hard truth than the sweet comfort of lies."

"No, it's worse than that. You're a cynic who claims not to believe in the existence of love." She looked up at him through dark eyelashes. "Some woman must have hurt you pretty badly."

Yes. One woman had. But it wasn't what Scarlett thought. "Then she did me a favor. Taught me the truth about life."

"Taught you wrong." She rubbed her belly, looking out the window as they drove closer to Geneva.

"Right or wrong, once the paternity test proves I'm your baby's father, we will be celebrating our marriage."

She tossed him a glance. "No, thanks. I'm no fan of gruel."

Vin ground his teeth. "Are you trying to tell me your childish, foolish dreams of love are more important than our child's welfare? A baby deserves two parents. A stable home."

Her expression changed. "Don't you think I know that?

All I ever wanted my whole childhood was to have a real home. I don't even know what it feels like to make roots, have friends, be part of a community." Her voice cracked. "But you know what? We were still happy, even on the run. Because my parents loved each other. And they loved me."

He didn't know what that felt like, Vin thought unwillingly. He'd grown up in a derelict villa in Rome, neglected and ignored by a mother who was only interested in her love affairs. Her son was valuable for one reason only: to extort money from his father.

His *so-called* father.

Vin's shoulders tightened.

Anyone he loved, he lost. His mother had coldly used him as a bargaining chip to finance her lifestyle, before she violently died. Paid nannies left or were fired. His kindly grandfather had had a stroke when Vin was eight. He'd become estranged from his loving father and stepmother at fifteen. Sometimes he felt like he'd been alone his whole life. As alone as that Christmas Eve, when he was only eight and was left utterly alone in the villa, forgotten in the dark—

He shook the memory away. His own child's life would be very different. And he'd make sure his child's mother was either a loving, stable, nurturing influence—or no influence at all.

"Why did you run away from New York?" he demanded. "Because you decided to believe everything you'd read about me?"

"Are you kidding?" Scarlett looked at him in amazement. "That pre-nup."

Gripping the steering wheel, he glanced at her in surprise. "You wanted to avoid the pre-nup?"

"Did you really think I would sign papers to give you total power over not just me, but our child? Did you think

I'd be so happy to become your trophy wife, I'd trade away my freedom for the rest of my life?"

"The pre-nup has been vetted by my lawyers to be completely fair…"

"Completely fair." For the first time since he'd known her, he heard a cynical note in her voice. "When you would get to make every decision about our lives? And if we ever decided to divorce for any reason, you would automatically get full custody of our baby?"

"Divorce is not my plan," he said sharply. "But I know I could not prevent you from leaving, if you wished it. Whatever you might think, there are no dungeons in my penthouse. The prenuptial agreement is merely a tool to minimize the impact of all your potentially bad decisions on our innocent children."

"*My* bad decisions?" She shook her head almost sadly. "And that's just the stuff in the pre-nup you told me about. Who knows what would have been buried in the fine print, a requirement that I give you five blow jobs a week?"

It was a crude comment, said matter-of-factly. There was nothing sensual or suggestive about her tone. If anything, she meant to insult him, to drive him away.

But his body's reaction was instantaneous. He turned from coldly furious to burning hot in a second, blood rushing to his groin as images went through his mind of that full rose-red mouth, hot and wet, around his hardened length… He tried to clear his head of the erotic image as he shifted uncomfortably in the leather seat of the car.

"That was not my intention." Although it sure as hell was now. Vin wondered what his lawyer's expression would be if he told him to add a blow job requirement.

Scarlett continued stubbornly, "You accuse me of being childish and foolish. But in refusing to marry you, I'm protecting our baby."

"How can you say that?" As they drove through the

outskirts of Geneva, he stopped at a red light. "I can offer both you and the baby a lifestyle you could never dream of. Six houses around the world, private schools, jewels, cars. Private jets…"

She shuddered at his mention of the jets. It seemed strange to him.

"I'm protecting our baby from a man who would only want to control us," she said softly. "Not love us."

That brought Vin up short.

As they arrived at the clinic, a modern building with clean lines on the edge of the lake, he pushed his thoughts aside. Parking the car, with the dark SUV parking nearby, he got out and opened Scarlett's door. He extended his hand to assist his very pregnant future bride.

With visible reluctance, she placed her hand in his.

Vin felt an electric jolt from the contact. As they walked together toward the front door of the clinic, he wouldn't—couldn't—let her hand go. He stopped, lifting it to his lips, and gently kissed the back of her hand. Her skin was soft. He felt her tremble.

"You could never love anyone." Her voice trembled. "Because you'll never trust anyone. Just the fact you're making me take this test…"

"I believe you, Scarlett," he said softly. "I'm only insisting on a paternity test because I've been lied to about it before."

"What?"

"A woman once claimed I was the father of her nonexistent baby, trying to get me to marry her. But this time, in my heart, I already know the truth. You're carrying my baby."

"Vin…"

Reaching out, he tucked a tendril of her red hair behind her ear. Her green eyes were wide.

"I like it when you look at me like that," he murmured.

"You are so beautiful, *cara*. Your eyes are such a deep emerald. Like a forest." He gently stroked the side of her face. "Your lips," he whispered, "are red and plump and ripe as fruit. I'll never forget—" he ran the tip of his finger along the full length of her bottom lip "—how it felt to taste them…"

Her tremble became violent. She looked so vulnerable, so stricken, so caught—she, who could have had any man she wanted with her beauty! Vin realized that he, too, was shaking.

His blood was pounding with the need to take her.

Then he remembered the bodyguards watching from the parking lot, the appointment at the clinic looming overhead.

Soon, he vowed to himself. Soon, he would satiate himself with her completely.

"You're right about one thing." He cupped her cheek. "I don't believe in love. At least not the romantic kind. But I do believe," he whispered, "in desire. I never stopped wanting you. From the moment we first met."

"But you were going to marry another…"

"Because I thought you were lost to me. I thought I couldn't have you. Now… I know I will." Vin ran the pads of his fingertips lightly along the edge of her jawline, to her earlobes, to the tumbling red waves of her hair. "I will have you, Scarlett," he growled. "At any price."

CHAPTER FOUR

"THERE CAN BE no doubt, Mr. Borgia. The baby is yours."

The Swiss doctor beamed at them. She was obviously pleased to be giving them good news.

Scarlett saw a flash of emotions cross Vin's hard, handsome features—pride, relief, joy and then, as he looked at her, anger. He hadn't forgiven her for running away.

Just you wait, Scarlett thought, giving him a bland smile.

But she'd thought she'd escape before this. Certainly before they drew the blood that they'd already tested in their in-house, state-of-the-art medical lab. She'd never intended for Vin to have the actual proof he was the father of her baby, proof he could use against her in courts of law.

But he'd never given her the opportunity. From the moment they'd arrived at the medical clinic, to the hour they'd spent waiting for the results, having lunch at a nearby elegant restaurant on the lake, Vin had never let Scarlett out of his sight. Even when she'd excused herself to use the restroom, he'd waited outside in the hallway, in an apparently courteous gesture. When she needed to get her handbag from the car, he'd insisted on sending a bodyguard to collect it.

Over lunch at the Michelin-starred restaurant, as he'd enjoyed lamb and asparagus in a delicate truffle sauce and a glass of wine, he'd expounded on what he would expect of her as his wife, each detail more outrageous than the last. He expected to dictate everything in her life, from the friends she kept to the clothes she wore!

She'd tried her best to lull his suspicions, listening meekly as she ate her lunch and sipped sparkling water. But inside, she was fuming.

Vin was so sure he'd won. He thought he could bully her into giving all her rights away—being nothing more than his indentured servant, the wife he could dominate, holding power over her future and their child's! He was as bad as Blaise!

What century do you think we're living in?

The century a rich man can do whatever he wants. To whomever he wants.

Actually, Vin was more dangerous. Because from the moment she'd met him, when he'd taken her in his arms and made her feel things she'd never felt before, pleasure and joy beyond imagining, he'd made her want to surrender to his demands. And he could do it again, if she let him.

I will have you, Scarlett. At any price.

She shivered as she remembered the hunger in his black eyes. The same hunger she felt for him.

But the price was too high. She couldn't allow herself to surrender, not when it would cost her everything!

"Do you want to know the baby's sex?" Dr. Schauss asked now in slightly accented English.

Vin's eyes were wide as he looked at Scarlett. He cleared his throat and said in an unsteady voice, "Sure."

The doctor smiled. "You're having a boy!"

A boy? Scarlett's eyes filled with tears. In just a few weeks, a sweet baby boy would be in her arms!

"A boy?" Vin's face lit up, and he looked at Scarlett. His usual hard, cynical expression fell away and he looked suddenly young and joyful. Then he turned back to the doctor. "And the pregnancy? Is Scarlett well?"

If she'd loved him, or even trusted him, she might have been touched by the anxiety in his deep voice.

The doctor nodded. "Mademoiselle Ravenwood is doing well. Her blood pressure is fine and in spite of being so close to her due date, she shows no signs of imminent labor. Though that can quickly change, of course…"

"Then we have time to be married." His expression hardened as he turned to Scarlett. "My lawyer in New York has sent the prenuptial agreement. As soon as we leave here, you will sign it, and we will marry."

Scarlett's heart fell all the way to her fur-lined boots. "I…"

Holding up his hand, he pressed his phone to his ear. "Ernest, find out where we can be married quickly. Yes, I know it's more complicated in Europe. Tonight if possible, tomorrow at the latest."

Staring at him, Scarlett instantly saw her mistake.

My God, she was stupid. She never should have let him get the legal proof that he was the father of her child. She should have screamed bloody murder rather than willingly give blood for the paternity test. Running away would be ten times harder now. He'd never give up looking for her. And he'd have the law on his side.

She rose unsteadily to her feet. "Thank you for the news, Doctor." Her teeth were chattering as she glanced at Vin, who had turned away to bark questions to his assistant, about places like Gibraltar and Denmark and even, heaven help her, Las Vegas. In another moment, he'd be arranging the plane, then he'd be back to giving her his full attention. She had only seconds.

Adrenaline pumped her heart. It was now or never.

"Mademoiselle Ravenwood—" the Swiss doctor looked at her with concern in her kindly bespectacled eyes "—are you quite all right?"

"Fine, I'm great." She forced a smile. "I just need to go to the ladies' room. If you'll excuse me."

"Of course—"

Scarlett swiftly exited the brightly lit exam room. She saw Vin's eyes look up piercingly as she closed the door.

She fled down the hall, past other beaming couples holding ultrasound photos and smiling nurses and doctors in white coats. She ran down multiple hallways, looking desperately for the back exit, since she knew that Vin's bodyguards were waiting at the front entrance of the clinic.

She found the back staircase and raced down it, one hand over her heavy belly as she scrambled to think of a coherent escape plan. She'd go back to Gstaad and beg Wilhelmina to use her influence with her boss—Kassius Black—to hide her. If that failed, she'd borrow money and hop a train for somewhere Vin had no connections at all. She scrambled to think how far she'd have to go. Samarkand? Ulaanbaatar? Vladivostok?

Scarlett burst out of the steel-framed door to the sunlight and fresh air of the wide lawn behind the clinic. She saw the shining gleam of the lake, saw a local bus approaching on a distant road. She started to run across the grass—

Then came to a screeching halt.

Vin was on the grassy hill beside the clinic, his arms folded. "Going somewhere?"

Out of earshot but watching the exchange with interest, she saw his bodyguards. Her lips parted, but she couldn't find her voice. Couldn't find a single word of explanation or excuse as he came forward, his handsome, implacable face set in stone.

She stammered, "How did you—"

"I expected you to run."

"But I didn't argue with you at all!" she gasped. "I didn't even criticize the obnoxious things you said at lunch!"

"That's how I knew." His voice was almost amused.

"The fiery woman I know would never let such a thing pass."

"It was a test?" Her voice squeaked in outrage.

He shrugged. "You seemed like you were willing to come quietly for the paternity test. I was glad to let it ride. But of course I knew." He put his hands in his pockets, looking more devastatingly handsome than ever in his tailored dark suit and long black coat. He tilted his head curiously. "Actually, I'm a little disappointed in you, trying the same trick twice. I'd like to think you had a little more respect for my intelligence."

She sucked in her breath as he came closer. His dark eyes were almost feral above the hard hungry slant of his cheekbones and rough edges of his jaw, shaded with five-o'clock shadow.

"Why are you so afraid of me?" he asked softly. "You seem to think I'm a murderous villain, merely because I seek to take responsibility for my child and marry you."

She lifted her chin furiously. "You don't *wish* to marry me. You're insisting on it! You're no better than Blaise Falkner!"

He grew dangerously still. "And now you insult me?"

"He wanted me to sign papers forcing me to give the baby away, too!"

"That's not what I—"

"At least with Blaise," she interrupted, "I knew from the start he was a monster. But I liked you. I slept with you." She hated the tears that rose in her eyes. She wiped them away furiously. "But beneath your charm, you're just the same as Blaise. Selfish to the core. You're determined to force this prenuptial agreement on me. Well, guess what, I'm not going to sign it! You can't make me marry you. We're in modern-day Europe, not the Dark Ages!"

"Oh, for…" A low mutter of hard words that she guessed to be Italian curses escaped his sensual lips. He set his jaw. "I don't have time for this. I'm due in Rome in five days. The prenuptial agreement is waiting in the car. You can read it thoroughly while we're driving to the airport."

Her stomach fell. "Airport?"

"En route to our wedding in Las Vegas."

"I'm not getting on a plane!"

"Why," he jeered, "because you're afraid I will kidnap you to some shadowy place not so civilized as Switzerland? You think so little of me. Why did you let me seduce you, let me fill you with my child, if the idea of taking my name and being under my protection and letting me provide for you is so unpalatable? If you truly believe me to be such a villain, why did you give me your body?" he said softly. "Why did you grip my shoulders and cry with joy as I made love to you again and again?"

Scarlett looked up at him, hardly able to breathe. He was so close to her. "I didn't…"

"It took a week for the nail marks to disappear from my back."

She flinched, then glared at him, folding her arms. "So you're good in bed. Big deal. I didn't have the experience to fight my desire for you then, but I do now. I won't sell myself to you and I definitely won't sell my baby."

His dark eyes narrowed. "So you prefer that our son has no father? That he is raised without my name or my protection or my love, all of which I freely offer you now?"

"Your…love?"

"Of course, you think I would not love my own child?"

Oh. Of course that was what he meant. Biting back her disappointment, angry with herself for feeling it, she said, "You're not offering me anything for free. If you were, you wouldn't make me sign those horrible documents."

"You expect me to marry you without a pre-nup? Leaving you free to take half my fortune?"

Scarlett shook her head stubbornly. "Of course not. You wouldn't want to take the risk. But neither do I. So, the answer is simple. We will not marry."

Vin stared at her in the Geneva sunlight. A soft wind rustled the autumn leaves above the grassy slope, between the modern two-story clinic and the sparkling water of the lake. She heard the soft call of a bird, the distant sound of honking and noise from the city.

"Because you're hoping to marry for love." He glared at her. "You are just like my mother was, before she died. Ignoring your responsibilities to run toward some romantic fantasy."

"I'm not! I'm running *away* from a nightmare. You!"

His lips pressed together. "Perhaps once our child is born, you will run away from him, too."

"Never!" she gasped.

"How do I know?"

"I love my baby more than anything!"

"So all you want from me is child support—is that it?"

"I don't want your money."

"You'd be the first."

"Money comes with strings, as you know perfectly well. Or you wouldn't offer it."

"So how do you expect to support our baby alone?"

"Well…" She tilted her head, thinking. "If you weren't pursuing me, and I didn't have to hide from you, I might go back to Gstaad and learn to cook fried chicken."

Vin looked at her incredulously. "You mean, instead of living in the lap of luxury as my wife, you'd pursue a career as a common cook?"

"You're such a snob! Fried chicken makes the world a better place. Can you say that about what you do?"

"Owning a billion-dollar airline?"

"Yeah, stuffing passengers like cattle into economy class, in seats the size of a postage stamp!"

He ground his teeth, letting her insult slide. "I have great appreciation for fine meals and for the talented chefs who prepare them. But according to Wilhelmina Stone, that's definitely not you."

"So I'll learn." Scarlett folded her arms. "I worked my way through a year of community college to become a nursing assistant, studying at night after working all day. I can handle it. All it takes is hard work and a willingness to do without sleep, and fortunately I've had experience with both."

Vin's dark eyes glinted so dangerously, she was almost surprised she didn't burst into flames beneath the force of his glare. "So you don't want my name, you don't want my money and you won't marry me. You prefer for our child to have no father at all while you aspire to low-paying jobs and try to survive."

Scarlett looked at him uneasily. When he put it like that, he made her sound like an idiot.

Vin looked into her beautiful eyes and a realization chilled him to the bone.

He had no leverage.

No way to force Scarlett's compliance, at least not one he felt comfortable with. This wasn't the business world, where he could offer a higher price or blackmail shareholders over their secrets in order to make them comply with his requests. The standard rules of mergers and acquisitions didn't apply.

Or did they?

He'd learned enough from his investigator to realize how little Scarlett had going for her. No family. No savings. Her savings account held the same amount one might spend for a business dinner with a few bottles of wine. She had no bachelor's degree, and worst of all, thanks to Blaise Falkner, she'd have no job recommendation.

But Falkner would suffer for that. Vin's lips lifted. He'd regret treating Scarlett so badly. He'd regret threatening Vin's future wife and child.

If Scarlett ever actually became his wife.

He didn't understand why this was so hard. Why shouldn't he be able to just buy her? He'd be willing to pay quite a bit, as long as it didn't cost something he actually cared about. Like his time. Or control. Or any requirement for him to be vulnerable.

But money? He had more than he could spend. Money was confetti to him. A way to keep score. A way to buy toys. And he wanted Scarlett Ravenwood more than any toy.

Shifting his strategy, he lifted an eyebrow. "What if I sweetened the pre-nup with a million-dollar payout for every year of our marriage?"

"No."

He frowned. "Two million?"

"Vin, you can't buy me."

"Everyone says that. But everyone has a price. Ten," he said. "My final offer. Ten million dollars for every year we stay married. Think about that."

Her eyes widened. For a moment he thought he had her. Then her chin lifted. "I told you. Not for any price." Her green eyes glittered furiously. "I'm not giving you the right to order me around like a slave—and permanent custody of our baby if I ever try to fight back. Freedom is worth more than some stupid money."

Vin stared at her, then regretfully decided he believed her. Damn it. Everything about her body language spoke of stubborn sincerity. He was dealing with an idealist, with a heart as stubborn as his own.

He had mixed feelings about it. That made her different from his own mother, which would be good for his son's happiness.

But it made Scarlett a more challenging adversary for Vin. How could he gain his objective, if money wasn't enough to sway her?

Standing on the grassy hillside behind the clinic, Vin looked at the sunlight flickering across Lake Geneva.

He wanted Scarlett as his wife, as his lover. In his bed, at his beck and call.

He also wanted his son to be safe and secure and loved, raised in the same home, with the same name. He wanted his son to have siblings. Vin wanted to know exactly where his family was and that everyone was protected, and provided for, at all times.

He looked at Scarlett. "How can I change your mind?"

"You can't," she said firmly. "The only reason to marry someone is for love. And I don't love you."

"You wanted a home. I can give you six." Or more. He couldn't quite remember which ones he'd sold or bought lately.

She looked wistful, then squared her shoulders. "A home without love isn't a home at all."

"That's the most ridiculous thing I've ever heard."

But he suddenly knew his answer. He'd use her romantic heart against her.

Scarlett cared about two things: love and freedom. All he had to do was give her both.

Or at least make her *think* he was giving them to her.

Vin had never tried to pretend to be in love before, but how hard could it be? He'd been raised by a woman who was a master at it, who'd used the pretense of emotion as a means of manipulating others.

But could he pull it off? Scarlett was no fool. Would she buy it?

He'd have to move slowly…

Vin tilted his head as if in thought, then took a deep breath and looked up almost pleadingly.

"Maybe you can show me I'm wrong. Prove to me that love isn't an illusion for fools."

Her eyes widened in surprise, then faded. "Please. You'll never give your heart to anyone. You've made it clear that to you marriage is a business deal."

"Maybe I'm wrong. Because you're different from any woman I've met." That was certainly true. "I want you as I've never wanted anyone." Also true. "You're carrying my child. I respect your intelligence, your warm heart. I need you. Want you." Clawing his hand back through his dark hair, he gave her a crooked smile. "Maybe that's how it starts."

He held his breath, waiting for her response.

"You expect me to believe that... That you could someday love me?" She gave a harsh laugh. "Nice try. What kind of idiot do you think I am?"

"Just give me a chance," he said quietly. "To see where this could lead."

"How?"

He thought furiously. Then he knew.

His eyes pierced hers. "I'll marry you without a prenup."

"What?" she breathed. She shook her head in disbelief. "Like you said—you'd risk half your fortune! From the moment we spoke our vows!"

Vin watched her carefully, watched the play of conflicting emotions cross her pale, lovely face. The way her white teeth nibbled furiously at her full, pink bottom lip. "Maybe it's worth the risk."

Yes. He was taking a risk, gambling that he'd quickly make her fall in love with him, placing her securely under his thumb and willing to sign a postnuptial agreement before the ink on their marriage license was dry. Which, he thought arrogantly, was almost no risk at all.

He'd never tried to make a woman fall in love with him

before. Usually it was the opposite—getting women into bed and leaving them before any emotional attachment was formed. This would be interesting. He felt strangely excited by the challenge.

Or maybe it was just standing so close to Scarlett, beneath the golden sun, feeling the cool October breeze against his overheated skin, knowing that he would soon possess her. In this moment, he would have been almost willing to pay half his fortune just to get her in his bed.

"Will you?" he said softly, coming closer. "Will you take a chance on me, if I take one with you?"

She seemed to shudder, looking up into his eyes. Her expression was bewildered, vulnerable, as if she were fighting hope itself. "But why?" she whispered. "Why does marriage matter so much to you?"

He didn't want to answer, but the new role he was playing, that of a secretly vulnerable man who could possibly be open to love, forced him to at least partial honesty. "I know what it's like to grow up without a father. My son must have a better childhood. He must always know who his parents are."

She looked confused. "How could he not know that?"

Vin changed the subject. "Family starts with a name. With a home. Our baby must feel safe and loved. He must know where he belongs." He looked at her. "Marry me, Scarlett. Right now."

She bit her lip, visibly wavering.

He pressed his advantage. "My private plane is fueled up and waiting. We can be in Las Vegas in…"

"No!" He was surprised at the sudden vehemence of her tone. She licked her lips. "Um, Dr. Schauss said I could go into labor at any time—"

"She also said she saw no imminent signs." He looked at her pale face and added soothingly, "We can bring a doctor on board with us, just in case."

"Forget it." She swallowed. "I'm not getting on any plane."

"Why?"

She took a shuddering breath. "If I do, I'll die! We'll both die!"

"What are you talking about?"

Tears spilled over her lashes. "My father died in a plane crash…"

"Yes," he said, his voice gentle, "but that doesn't mean—"

"Two weeks ago, my own flight almost crashed." He vaguely recalled reading something about an emergency landing in Ireland for her London-bound flight. She continued, "After what happened to Dad, I should have known better than to get on a plane for any reason! I told myself I was being silly. I ignored my intuition, and it almost killed us!" Hugging her belly, she shook her head fiercely. "I'll never get on another plane—ever!"

"But, Scarlett," he said quietly, "there are, on average, a hundred thousand flights every single day. Almost every one takes off and lands safely, without incident. Statistically—"

"Shut up! Don't you quote statistics to me!"

Her voice sounded almost hysterical. He had the feeling if he pushed her, he'd lose even the small bridge of trust he'd created. So he changed tactics. "I own an airline and also have two private jets for my own use. I even have a pilot's license, should I ever need to fly a plane myself. So I can supervise the equipment check, Scarlett. I can personally guarantee you'll be safe."

Scarlett choked out a tearful laugh. "And I can personally guarantee that I'm never getting on another plane!"

He tried to think of a way to reason with her. But as he looked into her beautiful, anguished eyes, as he saw the tears streak down her cheeks, he suddenly didn't want to argue. He just wanted to make it better.

Without a word, he pulled her into his arms. She fell against him, and he wrapped her in his coat, stroking her hair and back, murmuring gentle words until her sobs quieted and she was no longer shaking.

"All right," Vin said softly. "We don't have to fly. I'll never make you do anything you don't want to do. I'll always look out for you, Scarlett. Always."

Nestled against his white button-up shirt, wrapped beneath the lapels of his long black coat, Scarlett lifted her head with a ragged breath. She looked so beautiful in the sunlight, he thought. Her tearful eyes shone like emeralds.

She was vulnerable. It was the moment Vin should have pressed his advantage, gotten her to acquiesce to his proposal, boxed her in.

Instead, he felt something twist in his heart. And instead of pouncing on her weakness, forcing her to agree to his demands, he did what he'd wanted to do since he'd first seen her standing in the New York cathedral, her red hair tumbling over her shoulders, her green eyes luminous and pleading beneath a beam of golden light.

Cupping her face in his hands, Vin lowered his head and kissed her.

CHAPTER FIVE

SHE HADN'T EXPECTED him to kiss her.

The world seemed to whirl around Scarlett, making her dizzy as Vin's lips moved against hers. The kiss deepened, his mouth becoming hard and demanding, as if she belonged to him, and he owned the right of possession. He held her tight, her rounded belly and overflowing breasts pressing against his taut stomach and the hard muscles of his chest. He wrapped her in his warmth, protecting her from the wind, and she shook as she felt a hot rough pulse of electricity course through her.

She'd forgotten what it was like to kiss him. She'd forced herself to forget. But now, as she felt the tip of his tongue flick inside her mouth, as she felt his hot mouth silky against hers, she clutched him closer, never wanting to let him go. She couldn't. Not when every night for eight and a half months, she'd ached for him, dreaming of the hot night he'd ruthlessly taken her virginity, given her mind-blowing pleasure and filled her with his child.

He'd made her feel wanted. Adored. Even…loved.

"I've wanted you so long," he whispered against her skin. Her heartbeat tripled in her chest. "Say you'll marry me, Scarlett. Say it…"

"I'll marry you."

His handsome face lit up with joy and hope, and she realized what she'd just said. With an intake of breath, she met his eyes.

"Do you mean it?"

She saw in his dark eyes that he wanted her to marry him. Desperately. And she...

She wanted to be in his arms. She wanted her baby to have a father. She wanted her child to be safe and loved and live in a comfortable home. Was she a fool? Of course she wanted those things!

But only if their marriage could be real. If she and Vin actually cared for each other, they might have a chance at happiness...

Will you take a chance on me, if I take one with you?

Vin was willing to marry her without a prenuptial agreement. He was taking the biggest risk. Was she willing to take a smaller one?

For the potential happiness—for all of them?

Yes.

"I'll marry you," she choked out and realized she was crying. She had no idea why, until he pulled her into his arms and held her tight, and she knew.

Vincenzo Borgia, so handsome and powerful, could have chosen any woman for his wife.

But he'd chosen her. Not only that, he was giving her incredible power over his life. If he could be brave enough to do that, so would she.

She'd be brave enough to make the choice based on her hopes, not her fears...

"I'd never take advantage of your trust," she whispered.

"I know," he said with a private smile, then kissed her tenderly. "You've made me so happy."

"Me, too," she said, smiling through her tears.

"Let's marry as quickly as possible." He caressed her cheek. "But the marriage laws are much stricter in Europe. My assistant says the quickest options include Gibraltar and Denmark, but at your state of pregnancy, I'm not sure you'd find a long car ride comfortable. I also have to be in Rome in five days to close a business deal."

"What deal?"

"A controlling interest in Mediterranean Airlines. After I lost the deal with Air Transatlantique so spectacularly a couple of weeks ago—" he gave a wry smile "—I'm determined to get it. It's a closely held company and the founder insisted on meeting with me before he'd sell his shares."

"So let's get married in Rome."

He hesitated, then nodded. "It'll take a little longer to get married there, with the required paperwork, but if we drive straight through, we could be in Rome by late tonight. I think I even own a house there."

She gave an incredulous laugh. "You *think* you own a house? You're not sure?"

A ghost of a smile traced the edges of his sensual lips. "I haven't been back to my birth country for twenty years. I grew up in Rome, but—" his lips twisted bitterly "—my memories aren't terribly happy there."

His voice was strained, and his jaw tightened in a way that suggested she shouldn't ask any more questions. But Scarlett was dying to ask them. It occurred to her that she knew very little about his past, or what had driven him to become a self-made billionaire who was cynical at the thought of love.

But before she could try to think of a way to formulate the question that he might actually answer, Vin took her hand and led her across the grass, back to the clinic's parking lot, where the bodyguards waited with the cars.

As they walked, Scarlett glanced down at Vin's hand holding her smaller one. Feeling the warmth of his rough palm against hers, skin on skin, his fingers wrapped so possessively around hers, made her tremble as she walked. Her lips still tingled from his kiss.

"Congratulate us." Vin brought her to the three hulking, scowling bodyguards. "Scarlett has agreed to be my bride. We'll be married in a few days."

The three bodyguards lifted up their mirrored sunglasses, and their scowls gave way to bright smiles. They looked almost human as Vin introduced each of them by name. Each man shook her hand, murmuring congratulations. It was amazing how much less scary they suddenly seemed. Scarlett couldn't help smiling back.

"You're on her protection detail now," Vin told them, "as much as mine."

The men snapped to attention. "We're on it, boss."

"Welcome to the family, Miss Ravenwood," the first bodyguard told her with a big smile. Then the sunglasses snapped back, along with the scowl. "We'll keep you safe."

"Thank you." She hid a smile. As if she needed protecting! What was she, some politician or celebrity or something? But she was willing to play along.

Vin opened the door of the red sports car for her, then spoke quietly to the bodyguards before he climbed into the driver's seat beside her. He started the engine with a low smooth roar.

To her surprise, he didn't drive back immediately to the expressway but went the other direction, with the bodyguards following them in the SUV, deeper into downtown Geneva. "Where are we going?"

Vin turned onto the exclusive Rue du Rhône. "You agreed to marry me."

"So?"

His eyes slanted sideways to her hand. "You need a ring."

An hour later, they'd left the elegant jewelry store and were crossing into the French Alps, near Chamonix and Mont Blanc, en route to Italy. The mountain scenery was breathtaking, but Scarlett couldn't take her eyes off the biggest rock she'd ever seen: the ten-carat, emerald-cut, platinum-set diamond now on her left hand.

As she moved her finger, the enormous diamond reflected sparkling prisms of sunlight against her body, against her face, against the luxurious interior of the car. Against the handsome, powerful man driving beside her.

"I didn't need such a big diamond," she said for the tenth time.

He changed gears. "Of course you need it. You're going to be my wife. You must always have the best."

The ring was spectacular, but she felt briefly troubled. She would have been fine with a plain gold band, but his desires had overridden hers. What if her original fears were proven true—that he would attempt to rule her life?

Calm down, it's just a ring, she told herself. And if she were truly honest with herself, part of her was dazzled by the huge diamond, over-the-top and impractical as it was. She tried not to think about how much it had cost. More than she'd ever earn in a lifetime, that was for sure.

The highway wound through mountains and tunnels as they headed south. As they traveled, Vin kept asking if she was comfortable, if she'd like to stop for a meal, for a break or just to stretch her legs and admire the view.

Anxious to arrive in Rome so she could be done traveling and settle in, she mostly refused, stopping only briefly at a truck stop near the Italian border.

As they crossed through Tuscany, the orange sun was lowering into the west horizon of lush autumn fields like a ball of fire, and Scarlett's stomach started to growl. "Could we stop for dinner?"

"Of course, *cara*." Vin glanced at the countryside around the highway. "There is an excellent restaurant not too far from here, in Borgierra. I often visited the town when I was young."

"Borgierra? Sounds like your last name."

"My family founded the village five hundred years ago." He paused, then mumbled, "My father still lives there."

Her jaw dropped. "Your *father*?"

"So?"

"You never mentioned him. I assumed he was...well..."

"He's not dead. I just...haven't seen him for a while. Since I left Italy."

"Wait—twenty years ago?"

"Contrary to popular opinion," he said irritably, "creating a billion-dollar airline doesn't just magically happen. I've had to work all day, every day, from the time I was fifteen and set foot in New York. Gambling every penny I had. Working until I bled."

"Don't try to distract me from the main point."

"Which is?"

"You haven't seen your father for twenty years. Why? Was he horrible? Abusive?"

Vin's hands tightened on the steering wheel. "No."

Then she didn't understand at all. "I want to meet him."

He stared stonily ahead. "We don't have time."

"We have time to stop for dinner."

"I'm not talking about this."

"Too bad, because I am." The interior of the sports car suddenly seemed very small. "Weren't you the one who insisted it would be morally wrong of me not to allow our child to be raised by a father, as well as a mother? Now you expect me to ignore his chance to have a grandfather?"

His jaw tightened.

She tried again. "You say your father is a good person, but after two decades, you seriously intend to drive right by his house without stopping?" She glared at him. "It makes me wonder..."

He glared back at her. "Wonder what?"

She looked down, twisting the enormous diamond engagement ring. "When you said family was so important, I actually believed you."

"You are my family now, Scarlett. You and our son."

"The more family, the better." She took a deep breath. "I never had any siblings or cousins. Since my parents died, I've been totally alone. Do you know how that feels?"

He didn't answer.

Their eyes locked, and Scarlett's heart twisted at something she saw hidden deep in his dark eyes. Some pain. She took a deep breath. "You should want our baby to have as much family—as much love—as he possibly can," she said quietly. "Two parents are great, but what if something happens to us? Your father is our baby's only grandparent. Why haven't you seen him in twenty years?"

"It's complicated." He stared grimly forward at the road. "My mother never married Giuseppe. She preferred more exciting men who treated her badly." He smiled grimly. "But she enjoyed keeping my father on a string, not letting him fall out of love with her, making him suffer. Most of all, she enjoyed him as a source of income to her jet-set lifestyle. Anytime he wished to see me, he had to pay her a small fortune."

Her lips parted with shock. His mother had made his father *pay* for the privilege of seeing his son? "Oh, Vin…"

"When I was ten, he finally was able to stop loving her. He married another woman, Joanne."

"A wicked stepmother?" Scarlett guessed.

He snorted, then sobered. "Not at all. She was kind to me. I spent Christmas with them when I was fifteen, when my mother was partying with her boyfriend in Ibiza. It was the best Christmas of my life, with them and my new half sister. Maria was barely more than a baby then. When I had to leave, Giuseppe and Joanne said they wanted me to come live with them full-time."

"So did you?"

Vin's gaze was unfocused as he stared ahead. Then he shook his head. "My mother refused to let me go."

Scarlett's heart broke a little at the thought of a young

boy, simultaneously ignored and used as a bargaining chip by his own mother, losing his chance to be in a stable home, safe and loved. No wonder he was so determined to be a good father to his own son.

"It doesn't matter." His voice changed. "My mother died shortly after that, and I moved to New York to live with an uncle."

"I'm sorry about your mother." She frowned. "But why didn't you go live with your father after she died? There was nothing to stop you then."

"It was all a long time ago," he said grimly.

"But—"

"Drop it, Scarlett."

She wanted to push, but something in his expression warned her. "Okay. For now." She took a deep breath. "But if we're driving by his house, can't we just stop by so I can meet him? Just for ten minutes?"

"We're on a tight schedule."

"Please…"

"They might not even be at home."

"I promise if we stop, and they're not home, then I'll quit talking about it the rest of the way to Rome."

Vin stared at her. Then, with a sigh, he picked up his phone and told the bodyguards in the SUV behind them they'd be taking a detour.

The night was growing dark as they drove through a wrought-iron gate in the Tuscan countryside. The moon was full over the trees and fragrant fields. Vin seemed to grow progressively more tense as they drove down the long, dusty road, edged on both sides by cypress trees.

At the end of the road, Scarlett gasped when she saw a gorgeous three-story villa with green shutters and yellow stucco lit up by warm golden lights in the dark night.

When they reached the top of the hill, they saw at least

forty cars parked around the circular drive and stone fountain.

"Looks like they're having a party," she said awkwardly.

Vin parked the car right by the front door and turned off the engine. For a moment he didn't move. His handsome face looked strangely bleak. She reached for his hand.

"Two minutes," he said, pulling his hand away.

"We agreed we'd stay for ten—"

At his look, she decided not to press her luck.

Moon laced through clouds, decorating the October night like bright pearlescent lace across black velvet. He walked toward the front door, looking like a man going to the guillotine. The bodyguards, after doing a quick eyeball check of the perimeter, hung back respectfully. So did Scarlett.

At the door, Vin glanced back at them, then set his jaw. He reached for the brass knocker and banged it heavily against the wood. For some moments, no one answered.

Then the door was thrown open, and light and music from inside the villa poured out around them. Scarlett saw a dignified gray-haired man standing silhouetted in the doorway.

"*Buona sera,*" Vin began woodenly, then spoke words in Italian that she didn't understand.

But she didn't need to. He had barely spoken a sentence before the man in the doorway let out a gasp and, with a flood of Italian words, pulled Vin into his arms with a choked sob of joy.

Vin was furious.

He hadn't wanted to come here. He felt manipulated, backed into a corner. Exactly how he'd promised himself he'd never feel again: like someone else's puppet, under their control.

But Scarlett had made her threat clear, with her pointed insinuation, twisting her engagement ring, that she might change her mind about their marriage if he didn't do this. He'd barely contained his fury during their drive up the cypress-lined road. *This* was the thanks he received for striving to take good care of his pregnant soon-to-be wife, letting her have her way in everything? It still wasn't enough? Now Scarlett wanted to put her spoon into his heart and stir?

He hated her for this. Up till the very moment when he'd banged on the door.

Vin had been prepared for a servant to answer, or someone he didn't know, as there seemed to be a party. But he instantly recognized the man in the doorway.

Giuseppe Borgia had aged twenty years, with more lines on his skin and gray in his hair. But he'd known him. His father.

No. The man Vin had *believed* to be his father for his entire childhood. The man whose heart would be broken if he ever knew the truth.

The last time they'd seen each other, at his mother's funeral, Vin had been hostile and cold. Nothing like he'd been the week before, during the happy Christmas he'd stayed at this very villa, believing he'd found a place to call home and a real family who loved him.

But when he'd returned to Rome after Christmas and asked his mother if he could permanently live with his father, she'd barked out a cruel laugh.

"You're not even Giuseppe's son," Bianca Orsini had said. She'd taken a long drag off her cigarette. "It's time you knew. I got pregnant after a one-night stand with a musician I met in a bar in Rio." She smiled her brittle, hollow smile. "But I needed Giuseppe's money. So I lied."

"I have to tell him," Vin had choked out.

"Do it, and for reward, he'll just stop loving you." Her

fingers tightened around the shrinking cigarette. "Did you really think I'd let you go live with him and that British woman and give up my only source of income?"

Ironically, Bianca hadn't needed that income for long. She'd died a few days later, when, while distracting her current boyfriend with caresses of an intimate nature—at least that was what the police believed—she'd caused him to accidentally swerve his convertible off a cliff, killing them both.

Vin had barely been able to face Giuseppe and Joanne at the funeral a few days later. They'd tried to hug him, to console him, telling him to pack up and come home with them. But he'd known if they realized he wasn't really Giuseppe's child, how quickly they would have given him up. Especially since they had their own child, an adorable little girl of four, who actually deserved their love.

He couldn't wait around for them to reject him. Better that he do it first. So he'd gone to live with his mother's brother in New York, a lawyer who worked eighty-hour weeks and had little to offer his grieving, lonely nephew except his example as a workaholic.

Now Vin stared at Giuseppe in the doorway of the villa. The man he'd once believed to be his father, whose hair had since gone gray. They'd both changed so much over twenty years. Would Giuseppe even recognize him now?

"Good evening," Vin said haltingly in his native Italian. The language tasted rusty on his lips. "I apologize for the interruption. I'm not sure you'll recognize me—"

Giuseppe's lips parted. Then his eyes suddenly shone with tears.

"Vincenzo," he choked out. "My boy, my boy—you've come home at last!"

The old man's arms went around him, and he felt the force of his father's sobs. A stab went through Vin's frozen heart, as if it had painfully started beating again.

Giuseppe pulled back, wiping his eyes, and called out loudly in Italian. Suddenly there were more people at the door, including two dark-haired women, one young, the other older, both pretty and smiling.

His stepmother, Joanne, and…could that be his sister, Maria, now a young woman of twenty-four? They both hugged him with cries of joy, and Giuseppe, weeping openly, hugged all three of them in his vast arms.

Vin blinked fast, feeling like his soul was peeling.

His father. His *family*. He longed to love them again. But he didn't have the right. And if they ever knew the truth, their love would evaporate.

"But who's this?" Giuseppe said in Italian, looking past Vin's ear. He saw Scarlett fidgeting shyly behind him in the gravel driveway. Heavily pregnant and still in the same casual khakis and jacket she'd worn in Gstaad, she looked incredibly beautiful, with her red hair, chewing her pink lower lip, her green eyes uncertain.

Vin took her hand.

"This is Scarlett, Papà," he said quietly in the same language. "She's carrying my child and we're going to be wed."

His father gasped, and all the new people now flooding around them—only a few of whom he confusedly recognized—immediately began crying out their welcome and approbation.

"You brought her home to meet us?" Reaching out, Giuseppe patted her cheek.

Vin said drily, "She insisted."

"Then she is already beloved by me," the old man said.

"Scarlett doesn't speak Italian."

He smiled. "She understands." And indeed, she had a bright, joyful smile as she looked between him and Giuseppe. She thought she'd brought Vin and his father back together.

If only it was the truth. If only it were even possible.

But in this moment, surrounded on all sides by love, Vin could not fight it. He pushed away his shame about the lie. As the Borgias whisked them into the villa, it was easier to just pretend, for just a short while, that he really was their long-lost son, their long-lost brother. Easier to pretend he was actually deserving of their love and care.

"You came to my engagement party!" His dark-haired young sister said happily, slipping her arm around his as she led him through the grand hall toward the courtyard outside. "You have made this a party to remember!"

"You are engaged, Maria?" he said incredulously. "You were a toddler last time I saw you! Do you even remember me?"

Her smile broadened. "I confess my memory is not perfect, but I know you from your picture." Her smile faded. "Our father often cried over it."

"Maria…"

"But all is forgiven now you are here." Brightening, she motioned across the decorated courtyard, her eyes sparkling. "That is my fiancé, Luca."

Luca barely looked old enough to be out of college, Vin thought. Or maybe he himself was just old. Outside of Manhattan most people did not wait until they were thirty-five to be wed. And even in New York, no one waited that long to fall in love.

"Forgive me for interrupting your party. If I'd known—"

"Vincenzo, having you here is the best engagement present in the world! Did you see Papà's face? He's prayed for this. When we sent you the invitation, we never dreamed you would accept."

Vin hadn't gotten the invitation, because he'd instructed his assistant to toss anything from the Borgia family straight into the trash. "Um…"

"And now you are engaged as well, and expecting a child," Maria said, her eyes shining. "Our family is growing!"

Beneath the fairy lights of the large courtyard, guests were dancing to the music of a small band. It didn't even feel cold, with the heat lamps. A beautiful evening party, with a panoramic view of the moon-swept Tuscan countryside.

He looked back at Scarlett, already sitting at a table near the dinner buffet, a plate of food in front of her as she talked to Giuseppe and Joanne. Amid all the elegant suits and gowns, she was still wearing the same casual clothes she'd worn on her morning walk in Gstaad. But it didn't matter. Just looking at her, Vin felt a flash of heat that blocked out all other thoughts and feelings. A welcome distraction.

As if she felt his stare, Scarlett turned. Their eyes locked across the crowd, and electricity thrummed through him, as if they were the only two people in the world.

Then his stepmother rose from the table, gesturing her to follow. Finishing a last bite of dinner, Scarlett rose. Lifting her eyebrow at him with a mysterious smile, she turned and disappeared inside the villa.

It was as if clouds suddenly covered the moonlight. Clearing his throat, Vin turned back to Maria, trying to remember what they'd been saying. "Ah… I hope you'll both be very happy."

"You, too, brother." Her smile broadened. "But since you're in love, getting married and having a baby, something tells me you're about to be happier than you can even imagine."

Ten minutes later, Scarlett was staring at herself in the full-length mirror.

"Thank you," she breathed, looking at herself in the

borrowed floaty knee-length dress with charming bell sleeves. "Oh, thank you so much!"

Vin's stepmother, Joanne, beamed back at her. "It's vintage, darling. Haven't worn it in years. I'm just glad I had a dress with an empire waist!" She glanced fondly at Scarlett's belly. "How wonderful it will be——" she sighed happily "——to have a new baby in the family. Now I don't even have to pressure Maria about children for a while, because you're making me a grandmother!"

From the moment Scarlett had met Vin's parents, they'd treated her like family. While talking with them in the courtyard, Scarlett had shyly mentioned she felt woefully underdressed for the party, in wrinkled khakis.

"Your bodyguards just brought in your suitcase," Joanne had said helpfully, but Scarlett shook her head, looking down at her casual clothes with regret.

"All my clothes look like this."

"Don't worry!" Joanne had said suddenly. "I know just the thing!"

Scarlett had immediately liked the dark-haired British woman, with her obviously kind heart. Now, blinking back tears, she reached out and impulsively hugged her. "I'm so glad we're going to be family."

"Me, too, darling." Joanne smiled as she drew back, her eyes glistening with tears. "I can't remember the last time I saw Giuseppe so happy. You've put our family back together and added years to my husband's life. Now——" she shook her head briskly, wiping her eyes "——we just need to find you better shoes. I think Maria has some sparkly sandals about your size…"

After Scarlett was dressed, she brushed out her red hair and put on a bit of lipstick. Feeling nervous as Cinderella, Scarlett went back out to the noisy courtyard to join the party.

She'd hoped for a family reconciliation, but she'd never

imagined a family like Vin's—so loving, so warm, so ready to welcome Scarlett and their coming baby with open arms!

Vin's father, Giuseppe, smiled at her as she returned to the festive tables on the edge of the courtyard. He said in accented English, "I'm glad you're here. I can see the love between you and my son."

Scarlett blushed and let the remark pass. She could hardly tell Giuseppe that she and Vin had gotten pregnant by accident. They didn't love each other.

But she wanted to love him.

Yes, Vin was ruthless. But he was also honorable, determined to do the best he could—as he saw it—for their baby, and for Scarlett, too. He'd repeatedly put her needs in front of his. Agreeing to drive, instead of fly. Agreeing to introduce her to his family. Most of all, agreeing to marry her without a pre-nup! She could only imagine how his shark lawyers would have their heads blown off at that one.

"When is your wedding?" Giuseppe asked.

"I'm not exactly sure. Sometime soon in Rome. We haven't really planned it yet. But I do hope you'll all be able to come…"

Her voice trailed off as Vin saw her across the courtyard. He started pushing through the crowd toward her.

Her body felt the rhythm of the music, the beat of the dancers' pounding feet against the flagstones. But she was unable to move, unable to even breathe, captured in his dark hungry gaze.

He was breathtakingly handsome. His muscled legs were barely contained by well-tailored black trousers and his broad shoulders seemed to expand the sharp white shirt with the top button undone. But it wasn't the broadness of his shoulders or sharp line of his jaw or even the intensity of his black eyes that shook her. His sex appeal was obvious to anyone with eyes.

This was more.

Scarlett felt like she knew a secret. Something no other woman had been privileged to see. Something he hid from the world and would deny to the death if ever accused of it.

Beneath the layers of slick designer suits and hard brutal muscle, Vin secretly had a good heart.

"Scusi," he said now to his father, who smiled indulgently.

"But of course, you want to be with your future bride."

Reaching out, Vin pulled Scarlett away. Beneath his touch, her body flashed hot, then cold. As they stood together on the crowded dance floor of the villa's courtyard, as the fairy lights swayed above them in the moonlit night, her heart was pounding.

She suddenly couldn't meet his eyes. She focused on the curve of his neck. On the hair-dusted forearms casually revealed by his rolled-up sleeves. The hard edge of his unshaven jawline. The upturn of his cruelly sensual lips.

Blood was suddenly rushing in her ears. Her knees felt weak. What was happening to her?

"Cara," he said softly. "You look so beautiful in that dress." He pulled her into his arms. "Dance with me."

The slow dance was pure torture for Scarlett as she felt his hard, powerful body brush against hers. His muscles moved against her breasts and belly, and his hands slowly traced down her back.

Her full breasts felt heavy, her nipples tightening, aching to be touched. Even the barest brush of him against her was almost too much—and yet not nearly enough—Agonized desire flowed through her, twisting deep, deep inside her. She ached for him to kiss her, to stroke her naked skin, to thrust inside her, fill her fully, stretch her wide—

Her breaths came in gasps. She tried to hide her desire. She couldn't let him know that such an innocent slow dance, while surrounded by his family and friends at an engagement party, was making her insane with need. How could she be so wanton? What was wrong with her?

The song finished, and she exhaled. "Um, thanks…"

But as she tried to leave the dance floor, he held her tight, murmuring, "Don't go."

His large hands moved slowly from her hips to her lower back. He pulled her back against his body, crushing her breasts against his hard chest. Dizzy with need, she looked up at him.

He smiled down at her. Powerful. Sure of himself.

There was a lull in the music. His expression changed, became dark. Hot. His lips slowly lowered toward hers—

"Vincenzo!"

They turned as Giuseppe's voice called across the courtyard. Vin's father beamed at them, his arm around his wife's shoulders, with Maria smiling beside them.

"My son," he announced, "there is no sense in you getting married in Rome, with strangers." He gesticulated wildly. "We have decided you and Scarlett should be married right here."

"Say yes," Maria begged.

"It would make us so happy," Joanne added warmly. "What do you say?"

Having her wedding at this beautiful Tuscan villa, surrounded by Vin's family? Scarlett wanted it instantly. Holding her breath, she looked hopefully at Vin.

But his expression was strangely shut down. Scarlett didn't understand why he seemed so tense at the idea. But whatever the reason, she knew he didn't want to do it. She sensed he'd been pushed as far as he'd be pushed. But he remained stubbornly silent, forcing Scarlett to be the one to give his family the bad news.

Biting her lip, she forced herself to say apologetically, "Thank you, but we want to be wed as quickly as possible—"

"All the more reason to do it here," Joanne pointed out. "What is the point of getting married in Rome? It will just take longer to get all the paperwork done. Here, it will be quicker because Giuseppe is mayor—"

"*Sì*, mayor," he repeated proudly.

"And he'll make sure all the necessary documentation is completed as fast as humanly possible. You're both American citizens now—" Joanne glanced humorously at her stepson, as if to say *What a fool you were to trade away this beautiful country* "—so no banns are necessary."

"Please!" Maria clutched Scarlett's hands. "I'll arrange a beautiful wedding for you. It'll be good practice for planning my own. Why shouldn't you get married here? It's your home now, too, Scarlett!"

Put that way, it was impossible to refuse. Scarlett looked desperately at Vin.

He scowled. "I have connections in Rome. It can be done quickly enough."

Giuseppe snorted. "Amid strangers! What about your family? What about your bride?"

Vin's jaw tightened. "I don't—"

"Please," Scarlett whispered.

He stared at her for a long moment, then sighed.

"Va bene." His shoulders looked tense. "We will have our wedding here, since my bride wishes it." As Maria clapped her hands together with joy, he added fiercely, "But I must be in Rome within five days."

"No problem!" Joanne said.

"Easy!" Giuseppe said.

"You will see," Maria chortled. "I bet we can do it in three!"

Vin's expression said he feared three days would last an eternity. Why? Scarlett wondered. What could possibly be making him so tense? Was it cold feet? Had he changed his mind about wanting to marry her? The thought caused a shiver of nervousness to go through her. Because she was starting to not hate the idea of marrying him.

"Perhaps it's not an entirely bad idea," Vin murmured, looking down at her. His arms tightened. "If we're staying, that means no more driving tonight. Which means," he whispered, "I can take you to bed now."

Fire flashed through her, and she almost tottered on her borrowed strappy sandals. Her heart was pounding so hard and fast she felt light-headed.

Her whole world shrank down to the sensation of his body near hers, his hand supporting her arm. Did he intend to seduce her? No, surely not. She was eight and a half months pregnant. Not exactly a sexpot. She wanted him. Definitely. But she was surely imagining the dark fierce smolder in his eyes.

And part of her was afraid of what would happen if he made love to her. How much of her soul he might take, along with her body…

"My fiancée is tired," he said abruptly. "I am sorry, but we must cut our night short."

"Of course, of course," came the chorus around them in English and Italian. Everyone looked at her belly and smiled. Everyone loved a pregnant woman.

"Where can I take her to rest?"

"Follow me," his father said, waving them along. He took them through the beautiful villa, up the sweeping stairs to the quieter second floor, then triumphantly through double doors to a huge, luxurious bedroom.

"But there's only one bed," Scarlett whispered to Vin in consternation. His father heard her and chuckled.

"There is no reason for you to pretend you do not share a bedroom," he said with a laugh, eyeing her belly. "We are not so old-fashioned as to need that deception. Or so stupid as to believe it! Do not be embarrassed. We wish you only to be comfortable."

Refusing to meet Vin's eyes, Scarlett said stiltedly, "Perhaps other rooms could be found—"

"Yes, of course." His father nodded, but before she could sigh with relief, he finished, "The villa is full of party guests, but we did find rooms for your bodyguards. I appreciate your concern for them," he said approvingly. "You've chosen the right woman, Vincenzo. So thoughtful and kind. Look." He nodded toward her duffel bag and his sleek designer suitcase, stacked neatly on the closet floor. "Our staff already unpacked your clothes for you. We were hoping to convince you to stay. So now there is nothing—" his eyebrows wiggled suggestively "—to prevent you both from having a good night's sleep."

Giuseppe left, shutting the double doors behind him.

Alone in the shadowy bedroom, standing next to the enormous bed, Scarlett and Vin looked at each other.

"What now?" she whispered, shivering. "What should we—"

Before she could finish her sentence, before she could even finish her thought, Vin pulled her roughly into his arms. Claiming her lips as his own, he twined his hands in her long red hair, kissing her with deep, ferocious hunger that could not be denied.

CHAPTER SIX

VIN HADN'T FELT so emotionally out of control for a long, long time.

All night, he'd been forced to endure feelings he'd ignored for twenty years, since he'd left Italy and closed the door marked "love and family" forever in his mind.

But that door had been wrenched open. He was out of practice dealing with any feeling but anger, so staggered by conflicting emotions.

Right now, there was only one thing he wanted to feel.

This. Kissing Scarlett, Vin stroked his hands up her arms, feeling the silky fabric of her empire-waist dress slide beneath his fingertips. Feeling the warmth of her body beneath. He could be sure of this.

And this. He deepened the kiss, teasing her with his tongue.

Her sigh was soft in his mouth, like a whimper, but he felt the way she moved, her belly hard against his, her breasts swollen and soft.

This was all he wanted to feel. What he could physically grasp. What he could hold.

Scarlett.

Distantly, he heard the raucous noise of the party downstairs in the courtyard. But here in the hush of the darkened bedroom it felt strangely private, even holy. This was a place out of time, belonging to them alone.

Vin felt her tremble against him. Her lips parted beneath his, open and ripe for the taking. The rational part of his brain disappeared. It was like he'd never kissed anyone before.

He caressed her cheek, running his hand down the back of her neck, through her long hair tumbling down her shoulders. He drew back, looking at her. She was so sexy. So impossibly desirable. Beneath the silk bodice of her dress, he could see the hard nipples of her swollen breasts.

His body was screaming to take her now, take her hard and fast.

He exhaled, forcing himself to stay in control. She was heavily pregnant with his child, so he'd have to be gentle. She would need to be on top. To set the rhythm.

Plus, she was nervous. He felt that in her hesitation, in the way she'd shyly asked for separate rooms. She was afraid of what their lovemaking would start between them.

She was right to be afraid.

He intended to use every weapon he had to make her fall in love with him. To make her acquiesce to his every desire, and give him total command.

He needed to lure her slowly. Until she wanted him so badly that she was the one pushing him back roughly against the bed, and climbing on top of his naked body, easing her soft, wet core around him, driving him hard until they both screamed, clutching each other—

He shuddered with need. Patience, though a virtue, wasn't his strong point.

But he was starting to suspect that the torture of wanting her, and waiting for her, would make this conquest the single most spectacular sexual event of his life. For that, it was worth a little self-control.

If he could keep himself from losing it…

He gentled his kiss, making his lips seductive and soft. She leaned her body against him, reaching up to twine her hands in his short dark hair, pulling his head down harder against hers. Her rough, savage kiss made him feel so, so good, his body taut, his blood rushing and pounding and spiraling with need—

With a silent curse, Vin pulled away. She wouldn't be able to resist now if he drew her to the bed. He saw that in her sweetly mesmerized face. She wasn't the problem.

He was.

He couldn't lose control. Not now. Not ever. He needed a new strategy to force himself to slow down.

Scarlett's big eyes gleamed in the shadowy room as she looked up at him, dazed with desire. Cupping her cheek, he said in a low voice, "You have had a long day, *cara*. You need some comfort. Let me take care of you." Her forehead furrowed, then smoothed as he ran his hand gently along her shoulder. "I saw a marble tub in the en suite. Shall I start you a bath?"

"A bath?" she said, sounding bewildered, and he couldn't blame her.

"A deliciously sensual bath." He smiled. "One you'll want to linger in."

"That would be lovely—if you're sure you don't mind?"

She was already sighing in anticipation. She *had* had a stressful day, he thought. Considering she'd woken up that morning a single mother, a cook working in a Swiss chalet, and now was in Italy, Vin's fiancée, the proven mother of his child, with a ten-carat diamond on her finger. She'd met his family and was about to share his bed. That was a lot of change for anyone. And more was soon to come.

He smiled down at her. "It will be my pleasure."

And it would be.

Going into the luxurious en suite bathroom, Vin turned on the water, then looked around quickly. How to make it even more romantic? Pulling fresh roses from a nearby crystal vase, he crumpled rose petals into the warm running water. But he wanted more. Digging through the bathroom cabinet, he found expensively perfumed bubble bath and triumphantly discovered four candles and a box of matches in the bottom drawer.

"Can I come in?" she called.

"Not yet." He carefully placed the candles around the white marble bathroom with its elegant silver fixtures. He checked the water temperature—not too hot—and added a few more rose petals over the bubbles for good measure. He lit the candles, then turned out the lights. "Now."

Scarlett came into the bathroom, then stopped, her mouth agape. She looked at him, her own beautiful face suddenly nervous. As well she should be, he thought smugly.

"For you, *cara*," he said innocently. "I'll leave you to it."

He did leave the bathroom. He was that much of a gentleman. In the bedroom closet, he found his clothes unpacked in a drawer and pulled off his formal white shirt and tailored black trousers, exchanging them for just one article of clothing that would be easy to take off—low-slung sweatpants. When he heard the water slosh in the bathtub, heard her sigh as she descended into the warm, fragrant water, he gave a single knock on the bathroom door and pushed it open.

The white bubbles covered Scarlett's naked body modestly in the flickering candlelight. Only the tops of her breasts and a small bit of belly protruded as she looked back at him in surprise.

Her long red hair was piled high in a topknot, but tendrils of hair fell down her neck. Her cheeks were flushed pink, her full lips red and parted.

Vin had braced himself for seeing her naked, but the image still hit him low in the gut. Very low. It wasn't like he could hide his desire, either, in the low-slung sweatpants. His chest was bare, showing his shape from hours burning off energy and rage in the boxing gym and martial arts dojo. His hard flat belly was dusted with dark hair, like an arrow pointing down to the center of his desire.

So be it. Let her look.

Let his intentions be clear.

"What are you—" Her voice came out a croak. She swallowed, then looking up at his face, she said in a steadier voice, "What do you want?"

"I told you." He came closer, giving her a sensual, heavy-lidded smile. "I want to make you feel good."

"You made me this bath."

"I can do even better," he said silkily. "If you'll let me."

For a moment, she seemed to hold her breath.

"What did you have in mind?"

Vin sat behind her, on the tiled edge of the enormous marble tub.

He knew he could reach down, turn her face to his and claim her lips. Claim all of her. But he forced himself to take it slow. To seduce her, bit by bit.

"Let me show you," he said softly.

With agonizing slowness, he lowered his hands to her naked shoulders peeking out above the bubbles. Amid the flickering shadows, he sucked in his breath at the sensual shock of feeling her warm, slippery skin beneath his fingers, and knowing that she was naked beneath the rose petals and bubbles, there for his pleasure, just waiting for him to claim her.

Closing his eyes so he wouldn't be tempted by the soft sway of the water visibly caressing her round breasts, he began to rub her shoulders. His massage was light at first, then gradually he increased the pressure.

Scarlett exhaled, as though the stress of months or years was melting beneath his touch. Using his fingertips, his thumbs, he rubbed the knots away from her shoulders and neck. She closed her eyes, her rosy face the picture of pleasure as she leaned against his hands, like a cat meeting his stroke.

After a few minutes, when her face was blissfully peaceful, his hands began to move differently. Slowly, he moved past her shoulders to her upper arms, then her neck. He brushed the tender flesh of her earlobes with the flicker of a caress.

By now, the bubbles had mostly disappeared, and he could see the curves of her naked body beneath the water. He had himself under control now—for the moment—but he was also only a man. Too much of this and he might dive headlong into the enormous bathtub with her, to make love to her against the hard marble, amid the slosh of the cooling water.

Lowering his head to the nape of her neck, Vin brushed the red tendrils of her hair aside and kissed her, his lips lingering sensually on her skin.

Scarlett felt the brush of Vin's lips against the sensitive skin of her neck, and it was like lightning sizzling through her. All peace disappeared.

The water's temperature had cooled, and more alarmingly, the bubbles had diminished, no longer providing camouflage. Her breasts were entirely visible now, gleaming wet and flicked with only a few tiny bubbles like decorative pearls. Her hard nipples were rosy beneath the water.

"Scarlett, look at me," Vin said in a low, savage voice.

She had no choice but to obey. Tilting her head, she looked at his handsome face. Her eyes unwillingly traced his half-naked body, his thickly muscled chest, the trail of dark hair that led downward from his belly to the low waistline of his dark gray sweatpants, and below that…!

Even in the soft candlelight, she could see the outline

of him, huge and hard for her. Involuntarily, she sucked in her breath with a whimper.

"I want you," he growled.

She swallowed. She wanted him, too, desperately. But she was afraid of what would happen if she surrendered to him completely. Would it be the start of a wonderful, loving, lifelong marriage? Or would it be the beginning of a lifetime of misery?

He was physically perfect. While she... She glanced back at her own body and her cheeks burned self-consciously. "But I'm so big..."

"Yes. You are." His hand reached down to cup a pregnancy-swollen breast, as if feeling the weight. It overflowed his hand as he tightened his fingers around an aching nipple. "And I want you as I've never wanted any woman."

The pleasure of his touch was so sharp and raw it made her gasp.

Lowering his head, he kissed her, his lips hot and smooth as silk. Fire flooded through her. She kissed him back, water sloshing around her as she placed her hand against his cheek.

"Oh, Vin," she breathed. "I want you, too..."

And she kissed him recklessly.

Abruptly, his arms plunged into the bathtub. Reaching around her, he lifted her naked, wet body from the cool water, carrying her against his hard bare chest as if she weighed nothing at all. He slowly set her down to stand in front of him, her naked body sliding against his, before her feet reluctantly touched the white fluffy rug.

She was eight and a half months pregnant, and standing naked in front of him. She was so heavy. How could he want her? How could any man find her sexy, let alone Vin Borgia, who was so handsome and powerful he could have had any woman on earth?

But he didn't love her. She shivered. If she surrendered now, would she regret it for the rest of her life?

"You're cold," he murmured. Grabbing an enormous white cotton towel, he gently wrapped her in it.

But she wasn't shivering from cold. Swallowing, she looked up at him, her heart in her throat.

"I'm not exactly your usual supermodel," she said, trying for levity, but her voice trembled around the edges.

"No. You're not." He ran his hands gently through her hair, loosening the topknot so the damp waves tumbled down her shoulders. "There is nothing *usual* about you, Scarlett. You are special. The most beautiful, resourceful, kindhearted woman I've ever known." Holding the towel, he pulled her closer. "But that's not why I want you in my bed."

"It's not?"

He shook his head. "My need for you is far more primitive than that." His fingertips traced the bare skin lightly from her collarbone to the hollow between her breasts. "You're in my blood, Scarlett." His voice lowered almost to a growl. "You belong to me, and I intend to have you."

The moment stretched out between them, threatening to snap.

Belong to him?

She couldn't belong to him.

Not when he didn't belong to her. He didn't love her, and she didn't know if he ever would.

Panic rose from her heart to her throat. "No—"

Ripping the towel from his grasp, she turned and fled, practically slamming the door behind her.

In the bedroom, she beat the world record for finding her oversize T-shirt and cotton panties in a drawer. Within thirty seconds, she was tucked into the enormous bed, the heavy bedcovers pulled tightly to her neck.

The bedroom was dark. Her heartbeat drummed in her

throat as she waited for Vin to come out of the bathroom. What did she hope to achieve by hiding in this bed? They were sharing the room. He'd just have to sleep on the sofa by the window, she thought.

But Vin Borgia didn't seem like the kind of man who would politely take himself off to sleep on the sofa. Not when he'd made such a ruthless declaration.

You've in my blood, Scarlett. You belong to me, and I intend to have you.

She jolted when she heard the door abruptly open, causing a trickle of light across the bed. She squeezed her eyes shut as she heard him blow out the candles in the bathroom, one by one. Then silence.

"Go sleep on the sofa!" she tried to say, but her voice wouldn't work. She heard the echo of heavy footsteps coming toward her. They stopped.

The mattress beneath her swayed. She felt his warmth, breathed in the scent of sandalwood. Nervously, she scooted to the other side of the enormous king-size bed. Her heart was pounding. Part of her yearned desperately for him to reach out and pull her into his arms—but she was oh, so afraid of giving him complete power over her!

He reached for her in the darkness, and without a word, slowly, he turned her to face him. She felt his fingertips tantalizingly trail the edge of her hair, her shoulder, her hip.

His hand cupped her full breast, his palm moving against her aching nipple through her thin white cotton T-shirt. His other hand moved lingeringly over the curve of her belly, moving lower, and lower still. She felt something pressing hard against her and realized he was naked.

Tension coiled deep inside her, a sweet ache of need that was starting to build beyond her control.

She'd thought she knew desire from their first night together, their night of escape and exploration and discovery. But this was something else. Something else entirely.

Pregnancy hormones had given a fierce edge to her sexual need that she'd never experienced before. Or maybe it was because she now wore his ring on her finger, she was sleeping in his bed, she was pregnant with his child and soon would be his wife.

She wanted him. She wanted *this*. All of it. A home with warmth and comfort. A family. But most of all she wanted something impossible: she wanted him to love her...

She pulled back, struggling to see his face in the darkness. Her eyes adjusted, and the scattered moonlight from behind the window blinds silhouetted the hard edges of his cheekbones and jawline with silver.

Could he ever love her? Or was he just seducing her into marriage, for the sake of their baby?

She yearned to ask but didn't have the courage. Instead, she whispered, "Kiss me."

She heard his intake of breath, then felt the hard, sweet taste of his mouth on hers.

He kissed her for minutes—or hours—until her cheeks felt abraded from the roughness of the dark bristles on his jawline. His mouth was hungry and hard, pushing her lips apart as he teased her with his tongue. She clutched his shoulders, electrified by the heat of his hard naked body, the strength and size of him against her. She gripped him tight as his hands roamed possessively over the curves of her breasts and thighs.

Breaking the kiss, he pushed her back against the bed and slowly kissed down her body, stroking her full breasts and the mound of her belly and her voluptuous hips through her thin cotton T-shirt until he knelt at the foot of the bed. Spreading her feet apart, he caressed the hollows of her feet, the tender skin of her ankle.

Then he started moving upward. He kissed and caressed her calves. He kissed her knees, and the hollows beneath them, with a sensual flick of his tongue. Moving inexorably toward her thighs, he pushed her T-shirt up to her hips, leaving her cotton panties exposed.

Stroking the outside of her thighs, he positioned his head between them, and she started to shake.

Using his large hands to spread her legs wide, he kissed and nibbled her inner thighs. His breath warmed her skin, causing prickles of heat and furious desire to spread like wildfire through her body.

He teased her, kissing her softly with little flicks of his tongue along the edge of her panties. He cupped her mound over the thin cotton, rubbing the most sensitive part of her with his palm, leaving her gasping with need.

Her hands gripped the bedsheet as her hips moved of their own accord, swaying beneath his touch.

He slowly pulled her cotton panties down the length of her legs, in a whisper of sensation. She held her breath, squeezing her eyes shut as he moved back to her.

Placing his large hands on her inner thighs, he lowered his head. She felt his hot breath full against her, teasing her, and she quivered beneath him.

Spreading her wide, he took a long, languorous taste.

She gave a soft cry at the immediate wave of pleasure. It was almost too much. She tried to twist her hips away, but he held her more firmly against the bed.

He flicked the tip of his wet tongue lightly against her, swirling around her hard, aching nub in a circular motion. Then he spread her wide, lapping her hungrily with the full width of his tongue. She felt wet, so wet. She gasped as he eased a finger inside her.

Sweet agony built inside her, higher and higher. Her hips started to lift off the bed. A low cry came unbidden from her lips as he worked her roughly with his tongue, and his expert fingers teased her. Gripping his shoulders, she screamed, blinded by the bright explosion of pleasure.

He did not wait. With a low growl, he pulled her upright and yanked off her flimsy T-shirt, leaving her completely naked beneath him.

Her body was still boneless and satiated as he fell beside her on the mattress, rolling her over him, so she straddled his hard, naked body, her belly huge between them. With her knees over the hard planes of his hips, she felt the intimate press of his rock-hard body. He was enormous.

Her swollen breasts were angled toward his mouth. Lifting his head, he suckled each one greedily in turn, causing her to gasp and arch her back with the new sweet sensation of his lips and tongue and teeth. With her legs spread wide over his hips, she slid against him on instinct, her body tightening as she felt him press against her slick core, demanding entry.

He lifted her, positioned himself, then slowly thrust inside her, filling her inch by inch, filling her to the hilt.

She moaned as she felt him push deep inside her. Her hips moved, swaying, quivering around him. He was so thick, so hard. So deep—

Hearing his intake of breath, she looked down at his face. His eyes were closed, his expression rapt, and she suddenly realized that if he had power over her, she had power over him.

Slowly, she began to ride him. As his lips parted in a soundless gasp, she rode him harder and faster, her breasts swaying with the rough movement.

Tension coiled and built inside her, even higher than before. She leaned forward, gripping his muscled shoulders with her fingertips. She felt him tense beneath her, heard his gasp. She felt him try to draw back, to slow down—

But she wouldn't let him withdraw. She rode him hard, pushing him until his body started to shake beneath her.

She heard his rising growl and felt him explode inside her. Only then did she let herself go, and as she heard him cry out, her own world exploded into a million sparkling colors, before going black with the savage intensity of their joy.

CHAPTER SEVEN

AWARENESS CAME SLOWLY to Vin. It seemed like hours later when he opened his eyes.

Blinking in the darkness, he remembered they were in the guest room of the villa. Scarlett moved in his arms, warm and soft. His woman. His hands tightened on her as she slept.

He'd deliberately teased her, intending to make her insane with desire, to make her love him. But she wasn't the only one who'd lost control.

Setting his jaw, Vin stared up grimly at the ceiling.

What if his lie about the possibility of falling for her hadn't been a lie?

Could he really be starting to care?

No, he told himself fiercely. No way. He enjoyed having Scarlett in his bed. It was sexual pleasure. That was all it could possibly be.

But this place was messing with his brain. All of it. Italy. This villa. Being around family again. It all reminded him of who he'd once been, when all he'd wanted was to have a real home, to be loved.

But Vin had toughened up since then. Smartened up. Home could be anywhere. He owned more houses than he could keep track of, mostly as investments but also for his convenience. They were all decorated the same, modern and Spartan in stark black and gray, devoid of many personal details or clutter. That was always how he liked his relationships, too. In his opinion, "love" was a fancy decoration, as tacky and inappropriate as pink flounces or Victorian chintz.

He put his hand to his forehead, feeling a sense of vertigo. He couldn't let himself return to the vulnerable, tenderhearted boy he'd been. The boy who'd actually cared. The boy who'd felt things. Who'd hungered for things that had nothing to do with money—

It was this *place*, he thought angrily.

No. He looked at Scarlett sleeping so trustingly in his arms. It was *her*.

He couldn't let himself lose his head. He had to keep it together. Stay cool. Stick to the plan.

They would be married soon, he told himself. All he had to do was make her love him enough to sign the postnup. That was all.

But it was hard for Vin to keep his vow.

It took four more days, not three, before they were able to wed. The Borgias had been wrong. Even with the town mayor expediting paperwork, even with copies of their birth certificates—Vin's listed paternity a glaring lie that set his teeth on edge—there were certain formalities that had to be completed, and not even political connections or deep pockets could completely circumvent them.

Four days.

Four days of spending every moment with beautiful, intuitive, keen-eyed Scarlett and the wonderful people who believed themselves to be his family. Four days of listening to Maria prate on excitedly about her plans for their wedding. A required visit to the American Consulate in Florence turned into a pleasurable day of sightseeing with Scarlett, gawking at the Duomo followed by lunch at a charming café in the Piazza della Signoria. Four days of taking long walks in the Tuscan sunshine, eating glorious food.

Four days of talking to Scarlett, of learning about her, of finding new things to admire. One rainy afternoon by the fire, she'd suddenly set down her book and on impulse offered to show him the intricacies of picking a pocket.

He appreciated the lesson and, in return, offered to teach her how to fight. "My dad already showed me," she said primly. "I tried my punch out on Blaise in New York."

"I bet you did," he said, grinning at her. "All right. Here's how to use your own body weight against an attacker who grabs you from behind. Bet your dad didn't teach that."

Vin still smiled, remembering how pleasurably those lessons had ended—in bed together.

Such a strange way to live, Vin thought. He wasn't accustomed to such a luxurious squandering of time. He usually spent eighteen-hour days in the office, and that was what he should have been doing now, nailing down the details of the upcoming Mediterranean Airlines deal.

Instead, he sent his assistant on to Rome without him. He told his staff to handle everything, promising only that he'd arrive in Rome for the face-to-face meeting required by the other company's CEO, Salvatore Calabrese.

He'd spent the last twenty years focused on work. He told himself he'd be justified to take a few days off, but this was no mere vacation. He had a clear goal: making Scarlett love him so she'd sign the postnuptial agreement giving him the permanent control he needed to protect his son.

At least that was what Vin told himself as he spent hours walking with Scarlett through brilliantly colored autumn fields, on footpaths laced with cypress trees, holding her hand as they talked about everything and nothing. Hours of lingering together over meals, midday picnics beneath the golden sunlight, evening dinners inside by the fire. Vin found out why Scarlett was such a bad cook. "The day after my mother died, I tried to cook a can of soup over an open stove and nearly burned the house down." She smiled. "My father declared he'd be in charge of meals for safety reasons. My job was to keep the house clean and focus on school, when I was able to go."

She smiled about it now, but when Vin broke down the many sources of pain in that sentence—her mother died, they had to cook over an open stove, she wasn't always able to go to school—he marveled at her resiliency. He admired her strength.

That didn't stop him from arguing about what they'd name their son. He wanted a simple name like John or Michael. She wanted an Italian name from his family. "Like Giuseppe," she'd suggested hopefully. Vin had shut that idea down fast.

But he was afraid his emotions were starting to be compromised after four solid days of getting to know her mind and heart. Four nights of utterly exploring her body.

He'd spent hours kissing Scarlett, running his hands over her lush curves and overheated skin, as they'd set their bedroom on fire. They'd made love in every possible way as he'd explored every possibility of giving her pregnant body the deepest pleasure.

All in all, they'd been days and nights he would never forget. He was almost regretful to see them end.

But his plan was working. He could see it in Scarlett's green eyes when she looked at him now.

Against her will, she was starting to love him.

Perhaps Scarlett would have fallen in love with him anyway, without him trying so hard. Most women did. It was not something he was vain about; it was simply a fact. They could not resist his sex appeal, his raw power and the underlying attraction of his billions in the bank. He didn't have to *try* with women. It was usually the opposite. He would be cold to them, and they stunningly and stupidly loved him for it.

Scarlett was different.

For one thing, she didn't lust for money. In fact, she was suspicious of it as a manipulative tool. That just proved her intelligence, which made her even more desirable.

Seducing her in bed had been easy. Winning her heart was a little more tricky.

He'd had to share his *feelings*.

His *regrets*.

He still shuddered a little, remembering their conversation as they'd walked beneath the cypress trees last night, in the cool October air.

"Why did you move to New York after your mother died?" She'd looked up at the villa, the windows gleaming with warm light in the darkness. "You were only fifteen. Why didn't you come live here?"

His body had tensed. He should have known she wouldn't let that go. He'd wanted to say something sarcastic, or tell her to mind her own business. But looking at her hopeful, vulnerable expression, he'd known he had to do better than that, at least until they were safely married and he had the signed post-nup. And as intuitive as she was, he couldn't tell her a lie, either. So he'd shaped his mouth into something he hoped looked like a smile and told her part of the truth.

"Even at fifteen, I dreamed of starting my own company. Building my own fortune. My uncle was a hard-driving corporate lawyer. I knew if I moved to New York he'd be able to help me."

And Iacopo Orsini had. When Vin was eighteen, he'd taken all the money he'd saved from constant work, and the untouched payout from his mother's life insurance, and asked his uncle to help him draw up the necessary papers to set up his first company. Iacopo had also led by example, showing Vin it was possible to work every waking hour, and avoid inconsequential things, like spending time with family and loved ones. Or even *having* loved ones.

"Oh," Scarlett had said, and the light in her eyes had faded as she bit her lip. "That makes sense, I guess."

"Flying makes me feel alive," he'd heard himself add. "It gives me a sense of control. I can go anywhere. Do anything. Be whoever I want to be."

"It's your idea of freedom."

"Yes."

"That's funny. My idea of freedom is being able to stay in one place, as long as I want, surrounded by family and friends. Freedom," she said quietly, "would be a real home, filled with love, that no one would ever be able to take from me."

Their eyes locked in the moonlight, and for one crazy moment he'd wanted to tell her everything. He'd been tempted to offer up not just his body, not just his name, but his past, his pain, his heart. His future.

But it was a risk he couldn't take.

"Come on," he'd said abruptly. "Let's go inside."

The memory of how he'd felt last night still left Vin feeling uncomfortable. Vulnerable. Exposed. He didn't like it. It was a situation he didn't intend to repeat.

He had to get the papers signed as soon as possible so he could get back to a life he recognized, a life under his control.

But first things first.

Today was their wedding day.

Vin looked at his bride now, as she stood across from him in the villa's courtyard with the view of the wide Tuscan fields, as Giuseppe, as mayor of Borgierra, spoke the words that would bind the two of them in marriage.

In the distance, Vin could hear the plaintive cry of birds as they soared across the bright blue sky, as they were watched by Joanne and Maria and the other friends and Borgia relatives who'd packed in around them.

Vin couldn't look away from Scarlett's beautiful face.

Her warm green eyes sparkled in the sun, shining with joyful tears as she smiled up at him. She was wearing a simple sheath dress in creamy duchesse satin, purchased in Milan, altered for Scarlett's advanced state of pregnancy. Her red hair tumbled down her shoulders, and she had a tiny fascinator with a single cream-colored feather and a bit of netting that his sister had selected. Large diamond studs to match her ring now sparkled in her ears, a gift from Vin. Maria had wanted her to hold a bouquet of white lilies, but on this one detail, Scarlett was firm: no lilies. "They're not just stinky, they're appallingly overpriced."

Vin smiled at the thought of Scarlett being worried about the price of flowers, when the diamonds she was wearing cost hundreds of thousands of euros.

Instead, she held a bouquet of autumn wildflowers. It was just like her, he thought. The vivid blooms were as bright as her hair, and the scent as sweet as her soul. But the wild roses still had thorns—little flashes of temper and fire.

Solemnly, Vin, then Scarlett, spoke the words that would bind them together as husband and wife. He didn't exhale until it was done and they were actually married. After everything it had taken to get her to the altar, it was surprisingly easy.

No man could now tear them asunder.

"You may kiss the bride," Giuseppe said happily.

Scarlett Ravenwood—Mrs. Scarlett Borgia now— looked up at him with joy suffusing her beautiful face.

Looking into her eyes, Vin felt dizzy with happiness. She was wearing his ring. Carrying his baby. Bearing his name. He hadn't felt like this since—

A cold chill went down his spine.

The last time he'd felt this happy had been in this very same villa, that Christmas when Giuseppe and Joanne had asked him to live with them. At fifteen, for the first time in his life, he'd felt wanted and loved. But within a week, he'd lost everything.

Looking at his wife's beautiful, joyful face, Vin felt a sharp twist in the gut, a darkness curling around his heart like a poisonous mist.

Letting himself be happy, letting himself care, was like asking for abandonment. For loneliness. *For pain.*

He couldn't let her change him. He couldn't let himself be vulnerable. He had to be tough. Strong. He had to keep his fists up.

"You can kiss her, son," Giuseppe repeated in English, smiling.

Lowering his head, Vin kissed her. The touch of her lips electrified him like a blessing—or a curse.

He heard applause and teasing catcalls from the loving, kind people around him. He wrenched away from the kiss. Staring at Scarlett, he suddenly couldn't breathe.

Giuseppe, Joanne, Maria and even, *especially*, Scarlett were so wrong to love him. If they only knew the truth—

As beaming family and friends came forward to offer their congratulations, Vin loosened the black tie of his tuxedo, feeling attacked by all the overwhelming, suffocating, terrifying love around him.

CHAPTER EIGHT

AS SCARLETT SPOKE her wedding vows, looking up at Vin's dark eyes, she felt like every dream she'd ever had was coming true today.

Every day had been a new dream, from afternoons spent together in the cool autumn countryside, walking hand in hand as they talked about everything and nothing, to the deliciously hot nights they'd explored each other in bed, doing things that had nothing to do with talking. He made her feel…joyful. Sexy. Exhilarated.

He'd made her feel free. Like he accepted her just as she was. Like he…cared for her.

And she'd come to care for him, to respect and admire him. She'd started to even… But the thought scared her.

After all the romantic days and nights together, gazing into each other's eyes beneath the loggia and teasing each other with hot kisses behind the thick hedges of the garden maze, today's beautiful courtyard wedding, presided over by Vin's father, was the perfect end to such perfect days.

As she and Vin spoke their vows in the courtyard, surrounded by his family and friends, Scarlett looked up at him. She'd never seen such stark emotion in his dark eyes.

Was it possible Vin might be falling for an ordinary girl like her?

Scarlett's voice trembled as she spoke her vows, but Vin's voice was calm and steady and deep. She felt his lips brush softly against hers as a pledge of forever, and she thought she might die of happiness.

Then everything changed. The tenderness in Vin's

expression hardened, turned cold. As their family and friends came forward in the villa's courtyard to congratulate them, her brand-new husband dropped her hand as if it burned him and backed away, loosening his tie, as if he could barely stand to look at her.

What had happened? Scarlett didn't understand. She felt confused and hurt as she followed him into their wedding reception lunch, held immediately afterward in the great hall inside the villa. She tried to tell herself she was being too sensitive. They'd just gotten married, with a lifelong vow. That was what mattered. Not that he'd dropped her hand after he kissed her, and his eyes suddenly looked cold.

But it troubled her as she sat beside Vin at the head table through the elegant wedding lunch.

She looked around the great hall. Maria had outdone herself. The enormous room was filled with flowers and people and music. It was so warm with love, it barely needed the fire in the enormous stone fireplace. When the staff served a lunch of pasta and salad, Vin ate silently beside her. Scarlett smiled at him shyly.

He glowered back.

Scarlett's cheeks turned hot with embarrassment as she looked away. Maybe it was the sudden tension between them, but her lower back and belly started to ache strangely. She sipped sparkling juice instead of champagne, one hand rubbing her belly over the knee-length, cream-colored satin dress.

She told herself to relax. Whatever was bothering Vin, they had hours to work it out before they left for Rome tonight. He would close the deal with Mediterranean Airlines tomorrow morning. Vin wanted to check them into a suite at the best hotel in Rome tonight, their wedding night. While he was signing the papers, she could meet her new doctor and prepare for their baby's imminent birth.

She was trying to convince him that they should skip the hotel and go directly to live in the home he'd grown up in, but he resisted.

"It's a mess," he'd said shortly.

Now, sitting at the wedding luncheon, Scarlett sighed. Pasting a smile on her face, she turned away from Vin, who was still glowering silently at nothing, and turned to chat with Giuseppe and Joanne and Maria and her fiancé, Luca. She laughed and applauded as their friends and neighbors offered champagne toasts, half of which she couldn't understand, as they were in Italian, but they were lovely all the same. She just wished her parents could have been here to see her wedding day.

Tears rose to her eyes as her new father-in-law and mother-in-law and sister-in-law all hugged her and teased her and constantly asked if they could get her anything. *She had a family again.* After all her years alone, she hated to leave them.

Rome was only three hours away, she comforted herself. She glanced at her handsome new husband. Maybe Rome would be even more amazing. The city where their baby would be born. Their first real home. It would be where their life together would begin.

Tears filled her eyes as she listened to Giuseppe's emotional toast, as he praised his son and expressed his gratitude that he'd returned to the Borgia family after so many years apart. She was still wiping her eyes and applauding at the end of his speech when Vin suddenly growled in her ear, "We need to go."

"Go?" Scarlett blinked. "But you said we could stay the entire day—"

"I changed my mind." He tossed his napkin over his empty plate. "I want to be in Rome before dark. I still have a lot of work to do. We've wasted enough time here."

Wasted? The best days of her life?

Scarlett took a deep breath, struggling not to take it personally. "All right. I understand." She was trying to understand, but her heart felt mutinous. She bit her lip, looking around. "We'll need a little time to say goodbye—"

"You have two minutes." Rising to his feet, he stalked toward the table where his bodyguards were busily flirting with two of the local girls.

Scarlett stared after him, shocked and hurt. The muscles around her pregnant belly clenched and she felt a sharp tinge in her lower back that made her leap to her feet.

"What is it?" Giuseppe said.

"I'm afraid we have to go," Scarlett said. "Vin is anxious to get to Rome. You know he has the big business deal in the morning…"

"That is a pity," Giuseppe said, rising to his feet. "You can't stay the rest of the day?"

"Thank you." Vin was suddenly beside her. He held out his hand to Giuseppe and said coldly, "It was a very nice wedding."

"You're welcome?" His father looked bemused as Vin shook his hand, then Joanne's in turn.

"You can't leave, Vin!" cried his sister. "You haven't even cut the wedding cake! I've planned activities for the rest of the day. There's a dance floor, and…"

"I'm sorry. As I told you from the beginning, I have an unbreakable appointment in Rome."

"Oh. Right." Maria looked crestfallen. Her fiancé, Luca, put his arm around her encouragingly. She bit her lip, tried to smile. "Of course, I… I understand."

Scarlett didn't understand. Why did they have to leave so soon, cutting off their wedding celebration? It seemed not just rude, but nonsensical. But she forced herself to hold her tongue.

Vin held out his hand to his sister, but the young brunette just brushed his hand aside and threw her arms around him in a hug. He stiffened, but she drew back with a smile. "We will see you soon, brother. Luca's family lives in Rome. He's trying to convince me to have our wedding there!"

"Oh?" His voice was cool.

"But we will see you sooner than that, I hope." Looking at Scarlett, she said, "Call us when the baby comes."

"Of course," she replied warmly, trying to make up for her husband's rudeness. "We will never forget all your kindness."

"Not kindness," Giuseppe insisted, patting Scarlett's shoulder. *"Family."*

She swallowed, blinking fast. "You've all been so wonderful…"

"Ciao." Vin grabbed Scarlett's wrist and pulled her away. She waved back at them, and they waved in return, until Vin and Scarlett were out of the villa and in the fresh air outside. The bodyguards were packing their luggage into the SUV.

"That was rude," Scarlett said to Vin as he helped her into the passenger side of the two-seater.

Vin's face was chilly as he climbed in beside her, starting up the engine. "You asked me to stop here for ten minutes, and we stayed for five days. What did you want, *cara*—to live here permanently?"

Without looking back, Vin pressed on the gas, driving around the stone fountain with a squeal of tires.

Twisting her head, Scarlett saw a crowd had poured out of the villa's front door to wave goodbye and cry out their good wishes. "Vin, wait!"

He ignored her, pressing down harder on the gas pedal until they were on the cypress-lined road, out of the villa's view, and all she could see were the bodyguards following in the big SUV behind them.

"What is wrong with you?" Scarlett demanded as she faced forward in her seat, folding her arms over her belly. "Why are you acting like this?"

"I'm not acting like anything. We stayed for the wedding. I thanked them for their kindness. It's time to go."

"We were rude! After everything they did for us—"

"Send them a thank-you card," he said harshly.

Gripping the wheel of the car, he made record time down the tree-lined road across the wide Tuscan fields, and they soon returned to the main road.

Scarlett was fuming. Arms folded tightly, she glared out her window, lips pressed tightly together. The interior of the car was silent for a long time, until they were back on the heavily trafficked *autostrada* headed south toward Rome.

"Stop pouting," he said coldly.

"I'm not." She continued to glare out the window at the passing Italian countryside. "I'm mad, which is something else entirely."

"Stop being mad, then." He paused. "I meant to tell you. I got you a wedding present."

Her jaw tightened, but she still refused to look at him.

"It isn't a gift that I could wrap," he continued, obviously counting on her curiosity to overcome her fury. "It's something I did for you."

"Well?" Wiping her eyes, Scarlett turned her glare on him. "What is it?"

Dodging through the increasing traffic of the highway, he said, "Blaise Falkner."

She frowned. "What about Blaise?"

Vin gave her a triumphant sideways glance. "I've ruined him." His lips spread into a grin. "He'll never be able to threaten you again. Or anyone."

Scarlett stared at Vin, feeling hollow. "What do you mean, you ruined him?"

"He's penniless, disgraced, destroyed. Abandoned by his friends. Even the Falkner mansion is getting repossessed in New York. So he's also homeless." Vin turned dark eyes on her. "I did it for you."

"I never asked for that!"

His jaw was hard as he focused on the road. "I protect what is mine."

Scarlett shivered, hearing an echo of memory.

What century do you think we're living in?

The century a rich man can do whatever he wants. To whomever he wants.

As the red car sped down the highway, she felt her belly again tighten painfully. It had been doing that with increasing frequency. Stress would do that, she told herself. It was stress. Not the early signs of labor.

She breathed, "What did you do?"

"Falkner wasn't as rich as people thought." Vin changed lanes rapidly, rather than slow down with the traffic. He gave a smug, masculine smile. "His inheritance barely covered half his debt. He refused to work and was spending thousands of dollars every night for bottle service in clubs. And women. I merely made sure his lines of credit were not extended and allowed his true financial situation to become public."

"You used your influence with the banks?"

"I'm a very good customer."

"And dropped hints to some aggressive reporter?"

He tilted his head thoughtfully. "I believe in freedom of the press."

"But how did you get his friends to abandon him?"

"Ah, that was the easiest part. Half of them only endured his company because he always footed the bill. He owed the other half money. Once he was broke—no more friends."

Scarlett might have felt bad for Blaise Falkner, if she

didn't still remember the terror she'd felt when he'd threatened to take her baby away and force her into marriage.

But still…

"Revenge is wrong," she said in a low voice.

"You're angry?" Now Vin was the one to look shocked. His expression turned hard. "He deserved it. He deserved worse."

Vin's expression scared her. He didn't look like the good-hearted man she'd come to know in Tuscany. He looked like the ruthless billionaire she'd fled in New York.

She felt tension building in her body. She put her hands on her baby bump and felt the muscles of her belly harden. Like a contraction. She took a quick breath. "You could have…just left him alone."

"I have the right to protect my family."

"We aren't in danger! We're thousands of miles away!" She took another deep breath, trying to will her body to calm down, to relax. If she could, then maybe these contractions would stop. "It was revenge, pure and simple."

"What do you want, Scarlett?" His black eyes flashed. "Should I have bought the man a pony, tucked him in with milk and cookies, thanked him for the way he threatened my wife and child? Is that what you think?"

"I think—" Her breathing was becoming increasingly difficult. She was beginning to feel shooting pains radiating from her lower spine with increasing frequency. Then—

She sucked in her breath as she felt a sudden rush, a sticky mess. She looked down at her cream satin wedding dress in dismay. At the expensive black leather seat below it.

She whispered, "I think I'm in labor."

"You—" His hard voice abruptly changed in tone. "What?"

"My water just broke."

Scarlett felt scared. Really scared. She looked at her husband. Vin stared at her, his dark eyes shocked.

Then his jaw tightened. "Don't worry, Scarlett." He grimly changed the gears of the Ferrari. "I'll get you to the hospital."

He stomped on the gas, and they thrust forward on the highway as if shot by a cannon. If she'd thought the car was going a little too fast before, now it went on wings, flying past the other cars like a bullet.

She braced herself, gripping her seat belt with one hand and her tightening belly with the other. Yet strangely, in this moment, her fear was gone.

Scarlett looked at her husband's silhouette. Through the opposite window, she saw the darkening shadows of the Italian countryside flying past in smears of purple and red. And though she had been so terrified a moment before, she suddenly knew Vin, so capable and strong, would never let anything bad happen to her or their baby. He would protect them from any harm. Even death itself...

She glanced behind them. "We lost the bodyguards."

"They'll catch up."

Scarlett held her belly as she gasped out with the pain of a bigger contraction. She felt Vin automatically tense beside her. Then she made the mistake of looking behind them again. "Oh, no—"

Vin glanced in the rearview mirror and saw flashing police lights. Scarlett saw him hesitate. She knew he was tempted to keep driving, even if every single policeman in Italy chased them.

But with a rough curse, he pulled abruptly off the *autostrada*.

The police car parked behind them. As Vin rolled down his window, the young policeman came forward, speaking in good-natured Italian. Vin interrupted, pointing at Scarlett in a desperate gesture. The man's eyes widened when he saw her sticky wedding dress, as she gripped her belly and nearly sobbed with the pain.

Five minutes later, a police car was clearing their path with siren and flashing lights as their car roared south to the nearest hospital.

Standing in the bright morning light of their private room in the new, modern hospital, Vin cradled his newborn son in his arms, staring down at him in wonder.

"I'll keep you safe," he whispered to the baby, who was gently swaddled in a soft blue baby blanket. "You'll always know I'm watching out for you."

Vin looked up tenderly at his wife, who was also sleeping. Labor hadn't been easy. She'd been too far along in her contractions to get any kind of epidural.

So her only option had been to just get through it, to breathe through each wave of agony that brought her closer to their baby being born. With each contraction, Scarlett had held Vin's hand tight enough to bruise, looking up at him pleadingly from the bed. He'd tried to stay strong for her, to hide his own anguish at seeing her pain. All he could do was hold her hand and uselessly repeat, "Breathe!"

Now Vin looked at Scarlett in wonder. She'd been so strong. He'd never seen that kind of courage. As she slept, he saw the smudged hollows beneath her eyes, dark eyelashes resting against her pale cheeks, subdued red hair spilling on the pillow around her.

He looked back down at their baby's tiny hand wrapped around his finger, and another wave of gratitude and love washed over him.

"Happy birthday," he said to his son, smiling as he touched his small cheek with his fingertips. "I'm your *papà*."

The baby kept sleeping.

Outside the hospital room window, Vin saw a beautiful October morning, a bright blue sky. He blinked, then yawned, stretching his shoulders as much as he could without disturbing the baby. What a night it had been.

Sitting down in a chair beside the hospital bed where his wife slept, Vin held the baby for an hour, watching over them. He brushed back his baby's dark, downy hair, marveling at the tiny size of his head, his fragility. Vin could never let anything happen to his wife. Or his child.

His son would have a different childhood than he'd had. Vin's own earliest memory in life was of crying himself to sleep after his nanny locked him in his bedroom when he started crying loudly for his mother. His mother hired servants based on their cheapness, not their reliability or kindness, and he was often left to their care for weeks while she enjoyed time with her latest boyfriend in St. Barts or Bora Bora.

Except on those rare nights Vin's grandfather came to stay, no one ever comforted him when he heard a scary noise in the darkness or was frightened there was a monster under his bed. Vin had learned that the only way to survive was to be meaner than any monster. The only way to survive was to pretend not to be afraid.

But now, holding his son, Vin felt real fear. Because he knew that if this tiny baby was ever hurt, it would destroy him. It made him wonder how his own mother could have cared so much more for her momentary pleasures than her own son.

Vin took a deep breath. He'd be nothing like her. His son would always be his priority. From now on, that was his only duty. His only obligation. To keep his wife and child safe. He'd have to build an even bigger fortune, to protect them from worry or care. Vin's heart squeezed. He had a family to protect now. And he would. With his dying breath.

"Vin."

He looked up to see Scarlett's tired eyes smiling up at him. She held out her hand, and he immediately took it.

"Look at our son," he said softly. "The most beautiful baby in the world."

"You're not biased," she teased.

He shook his head solemnly. "It's not opinion. It's fact—" he smoothed back the soft edge of the baby blanket "—as anyone with eyes could see. He'll be a fighter, too."

"Just like his father."

It didn't sound like criticism, but praise; and hearing that from her made him catch his breath. The golden light of morning flooded the bed and the white tile floor, casting it in a haze as their eyes locked for a long moment. Then, leaning forward, he gently kissed her.

When he pulled away, her green eyes were luminous. Then they turned anxious. "But, Vin, what about your meeting? The deal with Mediterranean Airlines?"

Vin's jaw dropped. He'd *forgotten*. He'd totally forgotten about the meeting that was so important it had been circled in red on the calendar of his mind. He looked at the clock on the wall. He'd been so determined to get to Rome, and here he was, in a hospital just north of the city. The time was nine fifteen. The meeting had started at nine.

"Maybe you can still make it," Scarlett said. "Give me the baby. We can have Larson or Beppe meet you outside. You still—"

"No." His voice was quiet, but firm.

"Are you sure?" He could see the desperate hope in her eyes that he would stay, even as she said, "I know what this deal means to you. You should go."

He wondered what it cost her to say that. Being abandoned in an Italian hospital outside Rome, exhausted and still recovering from her physical ordeal, with an hours-old baby, couldn't be what she wanted. But she encouraged him because she wanted him to have what he desired most.

But for the first time, something compelled Vin more than his business, or money, or even power.

He couldn't leave his wife and their newborn son. Not now. Not after everything he'd just seen Scarlett endure. Not when his baby was still so tiny and fragile and new.

His place wasn't in a boardroom in Rome. His place was right here, keeping watch over the ones who depended on him far more than any employees or stockholders. The ones who really mattered. His family.

And if part of him was incredulous he was making this choice, even mocking him for it, he pushed that aside. "I'm staying." He looked back at the baby. "What shall we call him?"

She looked at him with barely concealed relief, then smiled. "A name that has meaning in your family. If not Giuseppe, what about Vincenzo?"

"After me?" Vin shuddered, then shook his head. "Our baby deserves better. He must have a name of his own." He thought for a moment, then said haltingly, "My *nonno*— my mother's father—was very kind to me. He died when I was eight, but I never forgot him. He made Christmas special." His lips quirked at the edges. "He said it was his job, because of his name. Nicolò."

She considered. "Nicolas?"

Vin looked at his baby son's face and nodded. "Nico," he said softly. "I like it."

For long moments, they held hands without speaking, Scarlett propped against pillows in the hospital bed and Vin cradling their baby in the chair beside her. He thought he'd maybe never been happier, or so at peace.

But it ended too soon as Ernest, his executive assistant, burst into the hospital room. "Sir, did you turn off your phone? I have been calling."

"Obviously," Vin said tightly, "I did not wish to be disturbed. Whatever the problem, you can handle it."

"The deal just fell apart and the other CEO stormed out when you didn't appear this morning. Everything is a shambles in the Rome office…"

As he spoke, a nurse bustled in and wanted to check over Scarlett and the baby. Nico himself began to complain that he was hungry and wanted his mother.

As Scarlett eagerly took her baby into her arms, the chaos increased as Vin heard an argument in the hallway. Ernest went to check it out, closing the room's door behind him. But the arguments only got louder through the door.

"Handle your guests, please," the nurse told Vin crisply in Italian. "This is a hospital, not a nightclub."

Vin ground his teeth, then turned to his wife with a bright smile. Kissing her forehead, he excused himself and went out into the hall.

One of his bodyguards was physically blocking a slender man in glasses who was yelling and trying to push into the private room. Ernest was trying to mollify him in a low voice.

"What is going on?" Vin demanded.

"Ah. Signor Borgia." The slight man immediately relaxed and turned to him politely. "Salvatore Calabrese sent me. He wished to convey his displeasure at your disrespect today."

"No disrespect to Signor Calabrese was meant. As you can see, I was unable to personally meet him this morning to close the deal with Mediterranean Airlines because I was called away on urgent family business."

"Signor Calabrese found your lack of commitment to the business deal very disappointing. He wished me to inform you that he is father to four children and was not present at a single one of their births."

Vin wondered that any man would brag about something like that, but he said merely, "I would be pleased to reschedule—"

"That is sadly now impossible." The man pushed up his wire-rimmed glasses. "Signor Calabrese will be exploring options with your Japanese and German competitors, many of whom have larger, more established airlines than yours. He hopes you enjoy family time," the man continued politely, "as you'll soon have much more of it. Without the expansion your airline needs, you'll soon be ripe for takeover yourself." The man gave a little bow. "Good day."

As he departed, Vin stared after him in shock.

The Japanese and German airlines who also hoped to take over Mediterranean Airlines were indeed formidable and powerful. It hadn't been easy to convince Salvatore Calabrese that SkyWorld Airways was the right choice. Vin had been forced to personally meet with him in New York and London.

"All right. I'll take a gamble with you, kid," Salvatore Calabrese had told him finally. "You remind me of myself when I was young. A shark who'll win at any cost." He'd given Vin a hard smile. "Just meet me in Rome to sign the papers. I need that mark of respect. Plus, I need to know I'm selling my baby to a man who'll always put his company first."

Now Vin clawed his hand through his dark hair, thinking of the hours, money and effort that he and his team had spent, costing millions of dollars and thousands of hours, to put the deal together. This on top of the public debacle in New York of losing the Air Transatlantique deal. The snotty little assistant had been right. Vin's rivals would start to smell blood in the water.

A stab went through him as he felt the cost of making his family the priority today. Twice now, his relationship with Scarlett had wrecked badly needed business deals. And now, just when he most needed his airline to succeed, for the sake of his family, for the sake of his son's future legacy, he was facing another failure.

"It'll be all right, boss." Ernest looked at him nervously. "Plenty of other fish in the sea. Lots of ways to expand our airline. Right, Mr. Borgia?"

His executive assistant clearly expected reassurance, but Vin stared at him blankly.

For the first time ever, he didn't know his next move.

Maybe this was what happened, Vin thought numbly. When you started choosing with your heart, instead of your head.

CHAPTER NINE

"CAN'T YOU GO SLOWER?" Scarlett pleaded.

"No." Her husband sounded annoyed.

"Just a little—"

"Scarlett, this is Rome. If we go any slower, we'll be run over."

Sitting in the backseat of their brand-new Bentley SUV, she looked anxiously at their three-day-old baby quietly tucked in his baby seat beside her, looking up at her so trustingly, with those big dark eyes like Vin's.

At least, she comforted herself, he hadn't insisted on using the sports car. The two-seater had been professionally cleaned, and Vin had donated it to the highway police. "A little gift to say thanks," he told her.

Scarlett was glad it had gone to a good home, and grateful to the kindhearted policeman who'd helped them get to the hospital so quickly.

She still remembered how terrified she'd been that day, and how awful labor had been. Her body had felt ripped apart. But already, that memory of pain was starting to fade every time she looked at her baby.

Scarlett was happy to be leaving the hospital. The hospital staff had been lovely, but she was ready to go home. Ready but also terrified. Because that meant there would no longer be medical professionals hovering to give quick advice if Nico couldn't sleep at night or didn't seem to be eating enough.

But at least Scarlett knew she had one person she could rely on. One person she could trust. The person who'd never left her side, not once, even though that choice had cost him dearly. And she loved him for it.

She loved Vin for that, and so much more.

She was totally, completely in love with him. There could no longer be any question. She'd known it when, after holding her hand uncomplainingly through long hours of labor, he'd tenderly placed their newborn baby in her arms.

"Look what you've created, Mrs. Borgia," he'd said, looking down at her with a suspicious gleam in his black eyes. "You should be proud."

"*We* created," she'd corrected, looking up at him.

"We," he'd whispered tenderly.

And that was that.

She loved Vin.

Another thing that thrilled her—and terrified her.

Heart in her throat, she looked at him, in the front seat beside their driver. Bodyguards were following in the black SUV. Vin had told her he wished to remain in Rome for the foreseeable future, in hopes of patching up the deal with Mediterranean Airlines. Scarlett had been delighted. She already adored this country, this city. How could she not?

But at the moment, her husband was looking back at her, his handsome face the picture of disbelief. "Are you sure you really want to do this?"

His tone implied she was crazy. He'd asked her the same question at least six times since their driver had picked them up from the hospital.

"I'm sure," Scarlett said calmly.

"I have reservations at the best hotel in Rome. The royal suite. We'd have an entire floor to ourselves, in total luxury with an amazing view. Room service," he added almost desperately.

Smiling, she shook her head. "That's not what I want."

Vin folded his arms, his expression disgruntled. "It's a mistake."

"It's not a mistake to want our baby to have a real home, instead of living in some hotel. I don't care how fancy it is."

"You'll care tonight, when there's no hot water and the beds are lumpy. The roof probably leaks."

"You'd really rather stay at a hotel than your own childhood home?"

"It wasn't particularly great then, and I'm sure it's worse now." He turned away as the driver drove them deeper into the city. "I've rented it out for the last twenty years, and from what my staff has told me, the tenant didn't exactly improve the situation."

"Oh, come on," Scarlett said with a laugh, rolling her eyes. "It's a villa in Rome. How bad could it be?"

The answer to that question came soon, as she gingerly entered the faded, dilapidated eighteenth-century villa, set behind a tall gate with a guardhouse and a private cobblestoned drive.

Holding the baby carrier carefully in her arms—she'd refused all offers from bodyguards and her husband to carry it, as her baby's eight pounds was precious cargo to her—Scarlett went through the enormous front door into the foyer. Stepping over the crumpled trash on the floor, she went farther into the villa.

On the high ceiling of the great room, a disco ball gleamed dully in the shadows. She stopped.

Black leather furniture, zebra and leopard print pillows, strobe lights and multiple bowls of overflowing cigarette butts decorated the room. In front of the enormous marble fireplace was a bearskin rug stained with red wine... at least she hoped it was wine. Empty liquor bottles littered every corner.

Wide-eyed, Scarlett turned to her husband, who was watching her with amusement. "I told you."

"Was your tenant a playboy?" she said faintly. "From the early seventies?"

"Styles change. People don't always change with them." Vin's lips quirked. "Luigi did live here a long time. He was quite the ladies' man, for eighty-five."

"Eighty-five! So did he move, or…?" She paused delicately.

Vin shook his head with a grin. "Decided he was finally ready to settle down. Moved to Verona and married his childhood sweetheart."

"Wow," Scarlett breathed. "Getting married. At eighty-five."

"Just goes to show it's never too late to change your life." His sensual lips lifted to a grin. "He only moved out last week. So this place hasn't been remodeled yet." He tilted his head. "The suite at the hotel is still available…"

Scarlett shook her head. "No hotels. When I was young, we didn't live in any house long enough to make memories, good or bad. Don't worry," she said brightly. "We'll make this the home of our dreams!"

He snorted. "Dream—or nightmare?"

"This house has good bones," she said with desperate hope. "Wait and see."

Later, Scarlett looked back and thought the next two months of remodeling the Villa Orsini were some of the happiest of her life.

Their first night was admittedly a little rough. The bodyguards brought in the necessary supplies, then hastily decamped to a neighboring three-star hotel. Only the bodyguard who'd lost the coin toss was forced to remain, and he chose to sleep on a cot in the foyer rather than face the rats' nests of bedrooms upstairs.

So it was just Vin and Scarlett and their baby sleeping

in the great room, where the black leather sectional sofas were in decent repair, that first night.

She and Vin heated water themselves on the old stove for the baby's first sponge bath. It was almost like camping. There were no servants hovering. No phones ringing incessantly. No television or computers, even. They just shared a takeaway picnic dinner on a blanket on the floor, then played an old board game that Vin found in a closet upstairs, before they both crashed on the sofa, with Nico tucked warmly into his portable baby car seat next to her.

Her husband was protective, insisting that Scarlett take the most comfortable spot on the sofa, offering to get her anything she needed at any moment. When the baby woke her up at two in the morning to nurse, Vin woke up as well and tucked a pillow under her aching arm that held the baby's head.

"Thank you," she whispered.

"It is nothing, *cara*." His eyes glowed in the darkness. "You are the hero."

Just the two of them, she thought drowsily, regular first-time parents, a married couple in love, with each other and with their newborn baby.

The next morning, the hiring began, of designers and architects and a construction crew to start the remodel. No expense would be spared. "If you're determined to live here," Vin told her firmly, "we'll get it done as soon as possible."

As the villa was cleared out, cleaned, and slowly began to take shape, Vin suggested that they bring in permanent house staff. He wanted two full-time nannies—one for day, one for night—and a butler, housekeeper, gardeners. After their blissful night alone together, Scarlett had been crestfallen. She'd tried to convince Vin that she could take care of the villa herself. He'd laughed.

"You want to spend your every waking hour scrubbing

floors? No. Leave that to others." He kissed her. "You have a far more important job."

"Taking care of Nico?" she guessed.

His dark eyes became tender. "Being the heart of our home." She melted a little inside. Then his smile lifted to an ironic grin. "You've got your work cut out for you, married to a ruthless bastard like me."

He was joking, of course, she thought loyally. Vin wasn't a ruthless bastard. He was a good man, and in spite of his tyrannical instincts, she knew he saw her as an equal partner. After all, he'd let her make the decisions about driving instead of flying, about remodeling the villa rather than enjoying the comfort of a hotel. And most of all, he had married her without a pre-nup. As partners, they had a chance to be happy in this marriage, she thought, really happy, for the rest of their lives.

The days passed, turned to weeks. November became December. Scarlett had pictured the Eternal City as a place of eternal sunshine, but to her surprise, winter descended on Rome.

The villa had become livable. Tacky old furnishings were removed, and the walls and floors of ten bedrooms were redone. The kitchen was expanded and modernized. Bathrooms were scrapped and remodeled, and one of the extra rooms was turned into a master en suite bathroom with walk-in closet. Vin had wanted to fly in the interior designer who'd decorated his New York penthouse, but remembering the stark black-and-gray décor from the single night she'd spent there, Scarlett had refused. She wanted to make the villa warm and bright and, above all, comfortable. She'd do the decorating herself.

She loved every minute. Each morning when the baby woke her up to be fed, Scarlett woke up with a smile on her face, stretching happily in the enormous bed. She didn't get much sleep, with the baby waking her through the night, but in spite of feeling tired, Scarlett had never been so happy. Joy washed over her like sunshine.

She had the home she'd always dreamed of. The family she'd always dreamed of. The husband she'd always dreamed of. She had everything she'd ever wanted, except one thing.

Vin hadn't told her he loved her.

But soon. Soon, she told herself hopefully. In the meantime, the villa was larger than she'd imagined her home could be, so she brought it down to size. Made it homey and inviting for family and friends.

She carefully began to add household staff. Wilhelmina Stone was the first person she hired, luring her away from Switzerland as housekeeper by doubling her salary.

"You don't need to pay me so much," Wilhelmina had grumbled. "We're practically family."

"Which is why I insist," Scarlett replied happily.

Then a few other employees were added, two maids and a gardener, but Scarlett flatly refused the idea of a butler and two full-time nannies. Instead, the kind, fiercely loyal housekeeper soon became a second grandmother to Nico.

When the guest rooms became habitable, the baby's actual grandparents, Giuseppe and Joanne, came down from Tuscany for a visit in December, bringing Maria and Luca with them. They all enjoyed a weekend of sightseeing, which was ostensibly to "show the baby the sights of Rome"—as if a five-week-old in a stroller who couldn't yet sit upright would appreciate the Colosseum, the Pantheon and the Trevi Fountain.

"Of course he appreciates them," Giuseppe said expressively, using his hands. "He is my grandson! It is in his blood!"

"He can't even taste gelato yet," Vin pointed out, rather peevishly, she thought.

It was the only discordant note to the joyful melody of Scarlett's life. Vin seemed strangely uncomfortable around his family, and the more loving they were, the more he seemed to flee. Thirty minutes into their sightseeing tour, he abruptly announced an emergency at the Rome office that seemed like an excuse to leave. But Scarlett must be mistaken, because why would he want to flee his family, who loved him so?

In spite of that small flaw, Scarlett was happy and proud to share their newly beautiful home with the family that had been so kind to her. The best moment was when Maria and Luca announced they'd picked a wedding date: the second week of January, in Rome.

"A winter wedding, in Rome," Maria had beamed, holding her fiancé's hand. "It'll be so romantic."

"*You* are romantic," Luca had said rapturously and kissed her.

Scarlett had looked at Vin, but he'd avoided her gaze.

Since his parents' visit, he'd seemed even more strangely distant, spending all his time at the office, where his company was trying to devise a new offer to interest Mediterranean Airlines' CEO, Salvatore Calabrese. But the man flatly refused to have anything to do with Vin now. It made Scarlett indignant, but she knew her husband would wear him down. No one could resist Vin for long. Scarlett knew this personally.

Except she hadn't had to resist him at all lately. At least not *personally*.

He hadn't touched Scarlett in bed since their baby was born. It had been two months now since they'd last made love. At first, healing from the birth and exhausted from waking up with their baby, sex had been the last thing on Scarlett's mind. But now her body was starting to feel normal again, though she hadn't quite lost all the baby weight, and her breasts were still very full. Did he not find her attractive anymore?

She tried to ignore the feelings of rejection. She focused on the baby, who was growing chubby and starting to babble and coo. She made friends with her neighbors and started private Italian lessons with Mrs. Spinoza, a kindly widow who lived down the street. But it hurt.

Then one day while she was despondently surfing the internet, she had an idea about how to bring them close again.

According to what she read, men's needs were simple. Food. Home. Sex.

All she had to do was turn herself into the perfect wife.

Step one. Food. A man's heart was through his stomach, according to what she read online. So Scarlett learned how to cook. She started with boiling water, but within a week, she'd graduated to simple, fresh pasta dishes, which Wilhelmina tasted and pronounced, with some surprise, to be "delicious."

Vin didn't notice, of course. He generally got home late at night and would eat whatever wrapped dinner plate he found in the fridge, by the light of his computer at the dining table at midnight, usually long after Scarlett had gone to bed. But she learned new skills when he wasn't looking.

Step two. Home. A man's house was his castle. Make it warm and comfortable, and he'd never want to leave it. She looked around their newly remodeled, redecorated home. Check.

Step three. Sex.

For Scarlett, this was the hardest thing of all.

But on Christmas Eve morning, she woke up knowing that it was now or never. Today was the day.

She felt like Vin had barely talked to her in weeks. He always made an effort to play with the baby right before work, but all Scarlett seemed to get from him were cold lectures when she evaded her security detail or told her assigned bodyguard, Larson, he didn't need to follow her. Which was exactly what she was getting this morning, too.

"Stop it." Vin glowered at her, coldly handsome in his suit and tie. "I specifically assigned Larson to keep you safe. Don't make it so hard for him to do his job."

Still wearing her nightshirt and white fluffy robe, Scarlett rolled her eyes. "You seriously think I'm going to be attacked on the streets of Rome in broad daylight while I'm pushing the stroller to Mrs. Spinoza's apartment? It's silly! How am I supposed to practice my Italian with Larson glaring at her through his sunglasses? He makes her so nervous she stutters!"

"I mean it, Scarlett," Vin replied. "Either do what I tell you and let him do his job, or..."

"Or what?"

His jaw was tight. "I can't answer for the consequences."

Then he coldly left the villa, briefcase in hand. Without so much as a goodbye kiss!

She prayed her outrageous plan would solve everything. Otherwise, she was about to make a horrible fool of herself. But she had to take the chance. As her father had always said, if you want things to change, change yourself.

The moment Vin left the villa for work, Scarlett got to work, too. The enormous tree was delivered to the great hall, along with boxes of beautiful decorations. She sent the last members of the household staff on surprise vacation, leaving Scarlett and the baby alone in the villa, with her bodyguard, Larson, at the tiny gatehouse across their private cobblestoned drive.

Holding Nico on her hip, Scarlett decorated the tree herself, talking happily to her baby, singing him Christmas songs, including one in Italian. Later, she started a roaring fire in the enormous fireplace and prepared a dinner she thought Vin would love. Leaving the sauce simmering on the stove as evening started to fall, she gave her sleepy baby his dinner and bath, changed him into his footsie pajamas and tucked him into the nursery.

After Nico was safely asleep, she went into her luxurious master bathroom and started a bath. She groomed herself as carefully as a bride on her wedding night—the wedding night they'd never actually had, since she'd gone into labor on her wedding day—and moisturized her body with lotion to make her skin soft as silk. She brushed out her long red hair until it gleamed.

She didn't get dressed. Following the advice she'd read online, she left off her clothes entirely, for maximum visual impact. Not even lingerie. Not even panties. She just covered her naked body with only an old-fashioned pinafore apron.

Then Scarlett waited, terrified and breathless, for Vin to come home from work.

Tonight, she would tell him she loved him.

And then he'd tell her he loved her, too, and their lifetime of happiness would begin.

Either that, or...

She shuddered, caught between longing and terror as she waited for the door to open.

As Vin stepped out of his chauffeured Bentley into the frosted darkness of his street, he felt bone-weary.

It was late on Christmas Eve night, almost ten o'clock. He gave a low curse as he looked at his expensive watch. "I'm sorry, Leonardo," he told his driver in Italian. "I've kept you from your family. Thank you for staying."

"No problem, Mr. Borgia." His driver beamed at him. "The Christmas bonus you sent is sending our whole family on vacation to the Caribbean next month. My wife also appreciated the delicious homemade *panettone* from Mrs. Borgia." He kissed his fingertips expressively. *"Delizioso."*

Vin stared at him blankly.

"I need to thank you, too, boss," Beppe, his bodyguard on duty, interrupted. The hulking man actually blushed. "I used the bonus to buy an engagement ring for my girlfriend. I'm giving it to her tomorrow morning. And Mrs. Borgia's *panettone* was delicious. I ate the whole cake watching last night's game."

Vin was shocked. Scarlett had learned how to bake? She'd arranged Christmas gifts for his staff? And not just the practical gift of money, but a personal gift of homemade Christmas cake? "Oh. Yes." He cleared his throat. "I'm glad you liked it."

He hadn't even known. Hadn't realized.

But then, he'd been distracted lately. As his bodyguard raced ahead to enter the security code, Vin trudged to the door. He'd really thought he'd be able to convince Salvatore Calabrese to sell him Mediterranean Airlines. But the man still wouldn't talk to him. Through his skinny assistant, he'd sent Vin a single cold message: "I'm interested in selling to sharks, not minnows." And no amount of corporate diplomacy could now convince him Vin was a shark. Not since he'd put his family's needs over a business deal.

Vin felt like he was failing. At his company. At home. Working such long hours, he barely saw his baby son an hour a day. As for his wife…

Vin shivered.

He wanted to see more of her.

Much more.

They hadn't made love since Nico's birth, and at this point, all Vin could think about when he was around her was that he wanted to throw her against the wall and take her.

But he couldn't.

After what he'd seen Scarlett go through in the hospital, he didn't know when—or even if—she'd ever want him to touch her again. He didn't even know how to broach the subject. He'd never had to struggle with this before. So rather than constantly feel sexually on edge around her, like a mindless beast with only the barest thread of self-control, it was almost easier to avoid her entirely.

Looking up at the four-story elegant villa that had become a palace beneath her magical touch, and his wife the untouchable princess living inside it, Vin felt weary.

"Go home," he told his bodyguard. "We'll be fine tonight."

Beppe looked doubtful. "That's not protocol. Especially when there's the danger of—"

"It's Christmas Eve," Vin cut him off. He didn't want to think about Blaise Falkner tonight, or the fact that the man had disappeared from New York two weeks ago and couldn't be found. Another arena in which things hadn't gone to plan. "Go home. We have the security alarm. I saw Larson in the gatehouse. He'll call you if he needs you."

"If you're sure…"

"Go home to your girlfriend."

Beppe's eyes lit up. "Thank you, Signor Borgia. *Buon Natale!*"

"Merry Christmas," Vin replied dully. Alone, he pushed open the tall oak door of the villa. He went into the foyer.

Yawning, he closed the door securely behind him, turning on the security alarm. Tossing his briefcase on a table, he hung up his long black coat. Wondering if Scarlett had already gone to bed, he walked into the great room.

And he stopped.

An enormous Christmas tree, twenty feet tall, now stood in the great room by the blazing fireplace, lit up with thousands of brilliant lights like stars beneath the wood beams of the high ceiling.

Beneath the tree, he saw something even more dazzling.

"Welcome home," his wife murmured, smiling as she held out a martini on a silver tray.

She was wearing a pretty, ruffled pinafore apron tied around her waist. And beneath that…

Vin suddenly couldn't breathe.

She wasn't wearing anything under the apron.

Nothing at all.

Eyes wide, he stared at her as all the blood rushed south from his head. He couldn't think. He gaped at her.

Scarlett tilted her head, looking up at him mischievously beneath her dark eyelashes. "Don't you want the martini? It's eggnog-flavored."

He stared at her, frozen, drinking in the vision of Scarlett's long red hair tumbling down her shoulders, to the tops of her full breasts, just visible above the ruffled top of the apron. He could see the pale curve of her naked hips around the edge of the fabric.

"No? Pity." Turning, she set the silver tray down on a nearby table. He almost fell to his knees as he got the first view of her naked backside, her lush flesh swaying, each mound perfectly shaped for his palms to cup roughly in his hands. He licked his lips.

"Where's—where's Nico?" he said hoarsely.

"Sleeping upstairs."

"And Mrs. Stone?"

"It's Christmas Eve, darling. I told her to take some time off. Gave her a first-class ticket back to see her family in Atlanta."

Vin stood in the great room, surrounded by shadows and light, dumbfounded by the vision of his wife, half-naked below the enormous, brilliantly lit Christmas tree, like the gift he'd waited for all his life.

A wicked smile traced her lips as she started to walk

toward him, slowly, deliberately, her hips swaying. She stopped directly in front of him, without touching him. He could smell the faint cherry blossom of her hair, the soft floral of her perfume.

His heart was pounding. He was afraid if he touched her, he would explode.

He was afraid he would explode if he *didn't* touch her.

"I made dinner," she murmured. "Pasta. I'm keeping it warm for you." She looked at him demurely, beneath the sweep of her black eyelashes, and tilted her hip, putting a hand on her bare, creamy skin thrusting out from the edge of her apron.

Vin didn't speak. Looking down at her, he deliberately started pulling off his tie.

Scarlett's expression, which had been flirtatious and saucy, turned wide like a deer's. She took a nervous step back.

But Vin had no intention of letting her flee. It was too late for that.

Sweeping her into his arms, he pushed her roughly against the wall, gripping her wrists and holding them firmly against the cool stone. "What else have you been keeping warm?"

"Vin," she breathed, searching his gaze. "There's something I've wanted to tell you..."

But more talking was the last thing he wanted. Cutting her off, he lowered his head, plundering her mouth in a ruthless kiss. He felt her soft, plump lips part beneath his own. Releasing her wrists, he tangled his hands in her hair, tilting her head backward to deepen the kiss.

She gave a sound like a sigh as her arms wrapped around his shoulders, pulling him closer. He stroked the sides of her body, her bare skin that wasn't covered by the prim apron. He shuddered as his fingertips and palms touched the warm, silky flesh of her hips, her tiny waist beneath the apron tie, the side curve of her voluptuous breasts. She stood on her tiptoes, straining to match the hunger in the kiss. He cupped his hands over the fleshy globes of her naked backside, feeling her sensuality, her heat—

With a low growl, he lifted her up, pushing her back against the wall, wrapping her bare legs around his hips. His rock-hard erection strained between them, with only his trousers and her thin apron separating them.

Bracing her against the wall, he held her sweet backside with one spread hand—nearly gasping with the pleasure of holding her there—and yanked open the tie of the apron. Pulling the fabric off her, he tossed it to the flagstones.

And just like that, he was holding his beautiful wife, in his arms, naked against the wall of their villa in Rome.

The flicker of warm red firelight glowed against her creamy skin, against her huge breasts with taut red nipples, her long red hair. Her red lips, swollen from the force of his kiss. Red, so red. Scarlet, like her name.

As he kissed her, Vin's body shook with need. He struggled to hold himself back. It was the first time they'd made love as man and wife, the first time since the baby was born. He should go slow. Carry her upstairs to their elegant bedroom, to the perfectly appointed king-size bed. Take his time. Be gentle. Make it last…

She pulled away from his kiss. With her naked legs wrapped around his trouser-clad hips, she leaned forward. He felt the warmth of her breath, the faint brush of her lips against the sensitive flesh of his earlobe as she whispered three little words.

He realized what she'd just said. With an intake of breath, he looked down at her.

They were alone in the great room, beneath the lights of the enormous Christmas tree that stretched toward the forty-foot ceiling. But even brighter than the lights of the tree, brighter than the orange and red flames of the fire, was the blazing glory of Scarlett's eyes.

"I love you," she repeated, as if the words had been building up so long that she could no longer keep them inside. Reaching out, she cupped his jawline, the rough bristles of his five-o'clock shadow. His whole body was shaking.

I love you.

He lost his last tendril of self-control, yanking his tailored trousers so violently that a button popped to the floor. He ripped his zipper roughly apart, tearing the fabric to shove his trousers down his taut hips.

Holding her backside with both hands, he spread her wide, and with one thrust, he pushed his thick, rock-hard length inside her, filling her hard and deep.

She gasped, clinging to him. He thrust into her again, holding her roughly against the wall, stretching her to the hilt. She gripped his shoulders, head tilted back, eyes closed in fervent need.

He watched her face as he pushed inside her a third time, slowly now, his own pleasure building as he saw the ecstasy on her face. A whimper escaped his own lips. Going slow was agony, sheer masochism, when he ached to rut into her, to explode. Her fingertips gripped deeper into his tailored white shirt, into the flesh of his shoulders. Her nails cut wickedly into his skin.

I love you. The soft hush of her words still rang through his ears. Through his heart. *I love you.*

He forced himself to be still inside her. He was so close to exploding, hard and thick and aching with need. Drawing back, he filled her again, inch by rock-hard inch. He felt her hips move against him, sucking him deeper inside her, as her full, heavy breasts swayed forward. She held her breath, her muscles tense. She suddenly threw back her head, crying out his name—

As he heard her scream her pleasure, he could no longer hold himself back. He rammed into her, fast and rough, crushing her soft breasts against his hard chest. His growl rose to a shout as he exploded inside her in pleasure so violent that, as he poured into her, for a single second his vision went black.

When he regained consciousness, emotion rose in his heart, emotion stronger than he'd ever felt, emotion that would not be repressed or denied.

"I love you."

The whisper was low, guttural, achingly vulnerable. For a moment, he didn't recognize the voice. Then Scarlett, still gripping his shoulders, looked at him with the most pure joy he'd ever seen on any human face.

And Vin realized with equal parts joy and horror that the voice had been his own.

CHAPTER TEN

HE LOVED HER.

The rhythm of those words was like the beat of Scarlett's heart, the rush of her blood.

He loved her.

She'd been terrified, waiting for him to come home. More than once, she'd changed her mind and started to get dressed. What if he rejected her? What if he laughed? What if one of the bodyguards walked in first?

But that hadn't even been her biggest fear.

What if her blatant gamble to seduce her husband back into her bed, and more important, to confess her love to him, was a total humiliating failure?

Growing up as she had, Scarlett had needed to be invisible for most of her life. But somehow, loving Vin gave her the courage to be outrageous enough to reach for her dreams.

Now they'd all come true.

Christmas morning, Scarlett woke with a smile on her face, hearing her baby's soft hungry whimper from the nursery next door. She looked at her husband sleeping beside her, and her smile became a beam of pure joy.

She loved him. And he loved her.

She blessed the internet. The crazy advice had worked better than she'd ever dreamed. After he'd taken her body so roughly against the wall, after he'd told her he loved her, Vin had wrapped her shivering body tenderly in his black jacket, and they'd gone into the enormous new kitchen to eat the dinner she'd prepared, homemade bread and *fettuccine alla carbonara.* Sitting together in the shadowy kitchen, he'd smoothed a bit of sauce off her cheek, looking at her with dark unreadable eyes, and all she could think was that she'd never been so happy.

He loved her.

Vin actually loved her.

After dinner, he'd held out his hand and led her upstairs. In their dark bedroom, he'd silently taken off his clothes and pulled her into the big bed, where he made love to her again, this time with aching gentleness. This time, as he pushed into her, their eyes locked, soul to soul. No separation. No secrets.

He loved her.

Now Scarlett shaped her lips silently into the words, tasting their sweetness again and again.

Creeping out of bed quietly, so as not to wake him, she wrapped her body in a white robe and went to the en suite nursery, where she lovingly swept their two-month-old baby into her arms. Cuddling him in the nearby glider, she fed him and rocked him back to sleep in the darkness. Once he was full and drowsy, she tucked him back in his crib.

Straightening, she looked out the window at the dark frosty dawn breaking over Rome.

She'd never been so happy. She didn't know what she'd done to deserve such happiness. Her heart was almost breaking with joy. Padding back on the soft rugs over the hardwood floor, she returned to the master bedroom, into the enormous bed that she shared with her husband. Closing her eyes, she pressed her cheek against his naked back and fell asleep.

A noise woke her.

Opening her eyes, Scarlett saw by the golden light filtering through the shades that it was midmorning. She blinked dreamily, smiling. "Merry Christmas." Then she blinked. Her eyes focused on Vin across the bedroom. "What are you doing?"

"Packing," he said tersely, tossing more clothes into the open suitcase. He was already dressed, in black tailored trousers, white shirt, a black vest and red tie. His dark hair was wet from the shower.

"Yes, I see that, but packing for what?"

Vin stopped, looking at her. His dark eyes were cold, and the gorgeous-mouth that had kissed her into such uncontrollable spirals of pleasure just hours before was now pressed into a severe line. "I'm leaving on a business trip."

"When?"

"Immediately."

"What?" She sat up straight in bed. "But your parents are expecting us to drive up to Tuscany with the baby—"

"Impossible," he said flatly. "I just learned Salvatore Calabrese is in Tokyo to make a deal with another company. It's my last chance to make him sell to me instead."

"But you can't leave!" Scarlett struggled to calm her voice. She sounded like a whiny child, even to her own ears. "It's Christmas Day!"

He turned on her fiercely. "What do you expect me to do, Scarlett?" His tone was scathing. "Sacrifice my company, our son's future, just to stay here and play happy family with you over the holidays?"

Yes, that was exactly what she expected. She drew back, hurt and bewildered.

Vin stared at her for a long moment. Then he turned away to pack. "I'm not sure how long negotiations might last. It could be days. Even weeks."

"You might be gone through New Year's?"

"You'll be busy anyway. Packing for you and the baby."

"Packing for what?"

"We're moving to New York."

Scarlett's jaw dropped. Was she dreaming? She stared

at her husband in the bedroom she'd personally decorated, in the villa that, after all her devoted work, felt like home. "What are you talking about? We live here! In Rome!"

"And once we're back in New York," he continued relentlessly, "I want the baby to have another paternity test."

Scarlett sucked in her breath, feeling like he'd just punched the air out of her, falling back against the pillows. "Why would you ask that?"

He shrugged. "I want to be sure."

"Why?" Scarlett, who was not a violent woman, barely contained the impulse to leap out of bed and slap his face. "How many tests do you need? How many men do you think I've slept with? How big of a liar do you think I am?"

"It is a reasonable request. I've been lied to before."

"Not by me!"

"By others," he conceded, then glared at her. "I do not appreciate you taking this hostile tone."

"Hostile! You haven't begun to see me hostile!" Rising from the bed, she stomped across the bedroom and snatched up her white fluffy robe. Tying the belt around her, she ground out, "Nico is two months old, we've been married since October and you're suddenly wondering if he's your son?"

"Scarlett—"

"Go to hell!"

He grabbed her hands. "Stop it."

"I won't." Her breath came in angry gasps as she looked up at him with flashing eyes. "Last night you said you loved me, but now it's like you're suddenly *trying* to make me hate you. Why, Vin? Why?"

His hands tightened. His gaze fell to her lips, to the quick rise and fall of her breasts. For a moment, she thought he might kiss her. That he'd tell her what was really going on. That everything would be all right.

Instead, he abruptly let her go. "I expect you to be settled in my penthouse in New York by the time I'm done in Tokyo."

"Do you?" she retorted. "Let me guess. You already have a Manhattan doctor on standby to give Nico a few more paternity tests." She was shaking with emotion. "I'd almost think you want proof you're not his father!"

"That's not true, and you know it," he bit out. "I chased around the world to find you and my son. My intentions should be clear. I want you both in New York. We are a family." His voice was impersonal, chilly. "Furthermore, you will make sure Larson is always with you and the baby when you leave this house. I mean it, Scarlett."

"I told you, I'm fed up with having a stupid bodyguard! This is Rome! Who do you think will attack us?"

"I was attacked once in midtown Manhattan. In the middle of the day."

She exhaled. "What?"

"I was seventeen, an easy target, and the guy wanted my wallet. For twenty bucks, he sent me to the hospital." He looked at her. "When I got out, I learned how to fight. When I became a millionaire, I also hired bodyguards." His jaw was tight. "I protect what is mine, Scarlett. That now includes you and my son."

"I'm sorry about what happened to you, but that was a long time ago, and Rome is very safe..."

"I'm leaving one of the private jets for you," he continued implacably. "I expect you and Nico to be en route to New York by the end of the week."

"We're not flying anywhere!"

"Scarlett." He ground his teeth. "I own an *airline*. You need to get over it!"

Get over it?! She was quivering with rage but kept her voice calm. "No, thank you. Neither I nor my child will be getting on one of those flying death traps again."

"So let me get this straight," he ground out. "You believe the airline I've built into a multibillion-dollar business to be made entirely of *flying death traps*. You refuse to live in New York. And you intend to flout my wishes by evading the bodyguard I've hired for you, leaving both you and Nico continually at risk."

"That's pretty much it, yes."

"You have so little respect for my judgment? For my leadership?"

"Why should I listen to you, when you've made it clear you aren't listening to me?" Her arms, which had been folded angrily, fell to her sides. "I don't want to leave Rome," she whispered. "I'm learning Italian. I've made friends. Your parents live just a few hours away. Your sister's getting married here next month!"

"We can order flowers sent from New York."

"You can't be serious. She's your sister!"

"What did you think, Scarlett? That we'd live here forever?"

That was exactly what she'd thought. She'd been happy and she'd thought it would last forever. She whispered over the lump in her throat, "It's our home."

"Home?" Looking around the luxurious, comfortable bedroom, he gave an incredulous laugh. "This place isn't my home. It *was* my home, when I was a miserable child at the mercy of adults. But now, thank God, it's not." He closed his suitcase firmly. "My company is based in New York."

"I have no good memories there. None."

"You must have friends in the city."

"Blaise Falkner?"

"He's no longer in New York." His lips pressed together. "My head of security recently informed me that without money or a place to live, he's fled like the rat he is." He paused, and she got the feeling there was more he wasn't telling her. He finished, "So you have nothing to worry about."

"I know I don't. Because I'm not living there."

A knock on the bedroom door interrupted them. An unhappy-looking bodyguard appeared to collect Vin's suitcase. Scarlett whirled angrily on her husband.

"You're making Beppe work today? He was going to propose to his girlfriend!" She looked at the man miserably. "I'm sorry."

"Va bene, signora," he muttered.

Ignoring him, Vin glared at her. "I grow weary of your constant criticism."

"Oh, I see. I should just tremble and obey?"

"You're twisting my words."

"What am I, if not your partner? Am I your housekeeper? Your nanny?" Her cheeks burned. "Or just your whore?"

She had the satisfaction of seeing his eyes widen. Then they narrowed. "You're my wife. The mother of my child."

"Then how can you be so unfeeling? You said you loved me!"

Vin glanced grimly toward Beppe, now walking out with his suitcase, pretending to be deaf and blind to the whole conversation. "I am simply educating you in how it's going to be. You and the baby will fly to New York within the week. You'll be ready and willing to take the paternity test!"

Vin stalked out of the bedroom in his turn, slamming the door behind him.

Woken by the noise, their baby started crying in the nursery next door. Scarlett flashed hot, then cold. In a fury, she ran to the top of the staircase.

"We're not going anywhere!" she screamed down at him. "You can't force us!"

Vin's face was startled at the bottom of the stairs. But

he didn't answer. He didn't even pause. Just kept walking, straight out the door.

Hearing the roar of the engine as his car drove away, Scarlett slumped on the top stair, tears running down her cheeks.

How had it all gone so wrong, so fast?

Just that morning, she'd been so happy. So sure he loved her.

But he couldn't. Otherwise, how could he act like this?

He didn't love her. All her dreams came crashing down around her. Covering her face with her hands, Scarlett choked out a sob.

Then, hearing her baby's wails, she took a deep breath. Wiping her eyes, she rose from the top stair, hoping, as she went to comfort her crying child, that she could somehow comfort herself.

From the penthouse bar of his ultramodern, luxurious Tokyo hotel, Vin stared out unseeingly through floor-to-ceiling windows displaying a panorama of the city, from Hamarikyu Gardens to the illuminated Rainbow Bridge stretching across Tokyo Bay. The night sky was dazzling from the bar on the thirtieth floor.

Beautiful.

Bright.

Cold.

Vin took another gulp of his scotch on the rocks, then set it back on the gleaming bar. He leaned his forehead against his palm, feeling inexpressibly weary.

It had been two weeks since he'd last spoken to Scarlett. Two weeks since their argument. For two weeks, he hadn't seen his baby, who in his short life might already be forgetting he had a father. Vin's heart felt twisted, raw, hollow.

He tried to tell himself it was worth it. Because Mediterranean Airlines was his.

It had been a hard fight, against a worthy rival, a far larger company. But Salvatore Calabrese had been duly impressed by Vin abandoning his wife and baby on Christmas Day to spend the week through New Year's and beyond focusing only on negotiations. Vin had spent the last two weeks holed up in this hotel with lawyers.

It was fortunate the view was so nice, because other than the ride from the airport, this was all he'd seen of Tokyo.

But the deal was done. They'd signed the papers an hour ago. Mediterranean Airlines was now part of Sky-World Airways.

Vin had won.

So why didn't he feel happier?

Sitting up straight on his bar stool, he tried to shake the feeling off. Scarlett was still in Rome, stubbornly defying him. She hadn't packed a thing, according to the bodyguards, whom she also continued to evade at will. She just continued her life as before, taking care of the baby and their home, helping his family arrange the last-minute details for his sister's upcoming wedding.

His so-called *sister*.

His so-called *family*.

Vin ground his teeth. It was physically painful for him to be around the Borgias, in spite of—actually, *because of*—their love for him. If they knew the truth, that he wasn't really Giuseppe's son, that Bianca had lied to him and used him for all of Vin's childhood, they would stop loving him.

It would be subtle, of course. They'd probably claim they were "still a family." But soon they'd be making excuses not to visit. Christmas cards would grow rare. Finally, there would be no contact at all, to the unexpressed relief of both sides.

Vin was done with Rome. It was the place where he'd been forced to feel emotions he didn't want to feel.

Especially for Scarlett.

His hands tightened on his glass of scotch.

But it would all soon be over. He glanced at his black leather briefcase on the bar stool beside him.

Ten minutes after he'd left Rome, with Scarlett's hurled accusations still ringing in his ears, he'd coldly called his lawyers and had the post-nup drawn up.

He should have done it weeks ago. But after their marriage, after the birth of their son, part of his soul had recoiled from betraying Scarlett. He'd known after he tricked her into signing a post-nup, she would hate him, too. So he'd put it off, telling himself there was plenty of time.

He'd been weak. He never should have allowed himself to delay his original plan. Of course he had to make Scarlett sign the post-nup. It was the only way Vin could make sure he could always keep them safe. He had to be in control.

Without it, Scarlett would continue to blithely ignore his demands that she keep the bodyguards close.

She didn't know that when Blaise Falkner disappeared from New York, he'd left a threat behind: "You'll lose even more, Borgia."

But that was just the point. Vin shouldn't have to explain such dangers to his wife. He didn't want to scare her. He just wanted to keep her safe.

Why did she have to fight him?

He'd felt so stupidly happy in her arms on Christmas Eve, making love to her. *Stupid* being the key word.

Waking up in the cold light of Christmas morning, he'd looked down at his wife in his arms, at the sweetly trusting smile on her beautiful face as she slept. For a split second, he'd been filled with joy. Then he'd felt a suffocating panic, even worse than the day they'd wed.

Happiness led to loss. It led to pain. And the joy of love could only end two ways: abandonment or death.

He'd decided long ago that he would never love anyone. He'd never give anyone that power over him.

But had he?

I love you.

He still remembered how he'd trembled when he'd heard Scarlett say those words. When he'd heard himself say them.

I love you.

He angrily shook the memory away.

He wouldn't think of it. Wouldn't feel it. And Scarlett's love for him would evaporate, along with her trust, after he tricked her into signing the post-nup. She would hate him then.

Good.

Vin's expression hardened as he took another sip of eighteen-year-old scotch. Taking love out of the equation would make things easier all around. Safer. Because he didn't like the things Scarlett made him feel.

Desire, when he thought of her.

Frustration, when she defied him.

Fear, when he thought of a life without her.

Without even trying, his wife made him feel vulnerable, all the time, in every way. This had to end.

Staring blankly out at the Tokyo night, Vin leaned his head against his hand. He'd return to Rome, ostensibly to attend Maria's wedding, with the post-nup in his pocket. He'd get Scarlett to sign it. And then—

He'd get his life back. Well-ordered. Controlled. With Vin completely in charge, and no risk of love or being vulnerable ever again.

"Borgia. Didn't expect to find you here."

Vin was jolted by a hearty clap on his shoulder. Looking back, he saw Salvatore Calabrese, still wearing the same designer suit and bright silk tie as when he'd signed the papers selling Mediterranean Airlines.

Vin already felt like he'd spent more than enough time around the self-involved, arrogant man, but he stifled his dislike and bared his teeth into a smile. "Hello, Calabrese."

The older man slid onto a nearby stool at the glossy wooden bar and gestured to the bartender as he continued, "Glad you finally pulled yourself together to convince me you were the right man to take my airline global."

"Me, too." Wishing the man would leave, Vin looked idly down at the ice cubes in his glass, so precise and modern, as was everything about this bar, this hotel, this beautiful city.

Calabrese ordered a drink from the bartender, then sat back on the sleek leather bar stool. "You learned a valuable lesson. Never put your family ahead of yourself, kid. Take it from a man who knows."

That was true enough, Vin thought. Calabrese was supposedly estranged from all three ex-wives and his four grown children, and he'd never even met his only grandchild. He definitely didn't put his family ahead of himself.

The gray-haired man tossed some bills on the glossy wooden bar, leaving a huge tip, then glanced at Vin indulgently. "I know you'll take Mediterranean Airlines to the top."

"That's the plan." Vin wondered how to get rid of him so he could order the second scotch he wanted in peace.

"As for me, I'm going to enjoy the big payout. Take life easy for a while." He picked up his martini and looked across the room. "Maybe I'll get married again. One of those girls could talk me into it."

Following his gaze, Vin saw a trio of beautiful young

models—Asian, pale blonde, dark-skinned brunette—sitting cozily on a white leather sofa by the floor-to-ceiling windows, with Tokyo as their backdrop.

Smiling, Calabrese raised his martini glass in their direction. They giggled, rolling their eyes and whispering to each other.

"You want to get married again?" Vin said, astonished.

"Why not? A wife's cheaper than a mistress. As long as she signs a pre-nup. Always make them sign. Take my advice." He winked. "If not for your current marriage, for the next one."

Vin watched Calabrese rise from the stool, then sashay toward the young women, his martini glass held high. Vin's stomach churned as his gaze fell back on his briefcase.

He was nothing like Calabrese, he told himself fiercely. *Nothing.* Their situations were completely different.

But when Vin left Tokyo that night on his private jet, he couldn't sleep, tossing and turning on the long flight.

When he finally arrived in Rome, the January light was gray. The holidays were over, leaving only the cold comfort of winter.

His driver was waiting to drive him from the airport. When he arrived at the villa, Vin set his jaw, wondering what he'd find.

He didn't have to wait long.

"Vin!" Scarlett appeared at the top of the stairs. Her skin looked pale against her vibrant red hair, her eyes flashing emerald green. She was simply dressed in a pale silk blouse and simple trousers, but he was newly overwhelmed by her beauty. He waited, expecting her anger.

To his surprise, she rushed down the stairs and threw her arms around him.

"I'm so glad you're home," she whispered.

The feel of Scarlett's body against his, the warmth of

her, was like fresh oxygen when he hadn't realized he'd been suffocating. Vin breathed her in, inhaling the scent of cherry blossoms and soft spring flowers.

She was the one to finally pull away. Her eyes were luminous in the shadowy foyer. "I haven't been able to stop thinking about our fight. I was…I was so—" he braced himself "—wrong," she finished quietly. "I was wrong."

Her admission shocked him. Vin would never have admitted he was wrong about anything. If he ever was. Which he wasn't. "About?"

"New York." She gave him a wobbly smile. "You're right. It's your company headquarters. What am I going to do—" she gave an awkward laugh "—demand that hundreds of employees uproot their families and move to Rome, just because I love it here?" She took a deep breath, then tried to smile. "I was being selfish. I'm the one who said we should be partners. So…we should at least talk about it. I still won't take a plane, but maybe I could take a ship. Isn't marriage about compromise?"

"Yes," he lied.

"But—" Scarlett gave him a shy smile "—I'm sure you want to see the baby…"

"Yes." And he meant it.

Taking his hand, she led him upstairs. Entering the shadowy nursery, Vin looked down at his sleeping son. He heard the soft snuffle of his breath, saw the rise and fall of his chest. Nico. His precious boy. He was here. He was safe. The baby already looked different. He'd grown in two weeks. Vin hated that he'd been away so long.

Never again.

He looked at Scarlett. There could only be one person in control of his life. His home. His child. And that was Vin.

The ends justified the means, he told himself. Scarlett might hate him at first, but eventually she would thank him.

Or she wouldn't. But either way, he would get his life back. Without the chaos and messy emotion she brought.

All Vin had to do was lull her back into her previous happiness and trust in him, then once she'd lowered her guard, trick her into signing the postnuptial agreement, written in Italian, giving him every right and power over every decision.

Her love for him was her weakness.

As for his own feelings—he would not feel them. They did not exist.

The one who cared least was the one who'd win.

"I missed you, Scarlett." Vin gave her a smile so sensual that she blushed to her ears. Excellent. "I swear to you on my life," he said softly, "I'll never let us be apart so long again."

She smiled happily, not knowing his dark intentions. Taking her hand, he rubbed his thumb lightly against her palm, then kissed it, feeling her shiver.

Soon, she would be unable to defy him. His decisions would automatically prevail. She would be forced to get over her ridiculous fear of flying and travel with him when he wished. It would be good for their family. And their marriage. A flash of heat went through him as he looked down at her, at the curve of her white throat, the shape of her full breasts beneath her silk blouse.

From now on, she would have no choice but to obey. In his home. In his bed. She'd be at his command. Exactly where she belonged.

CHAPTER ELEVEN

Something had changed in Vin. As Scarlett welcomed him back from Tokyo, she couldn't quite figure out what it was.

Their last time in bed together, on Christmas Eve, had been rough and sensual and explosive. Even when he'd been tender, as he pushed inside her, his emotion had been raw on his face.

But today, since he'd returned, she felt a distance. Even as he smiled at her, even as he held her in his arms, even as he leaned down to kiss her, his dark eyes hinting at untold delights to come later—even then, there was something hidden behind his expression.

What was he hiding?

Was she imagining it?

She puzzled over it all day as they played with the baby, then got ready to go out for the evening. When she broached the subject of moving to New York, he told her he didn't want to discuss it. "Tonight, I just want to enjoy your company, *cara*."

They went out that night to his sister's wedding rehearsal dinner at a charming restaurant not too far from the Piazza Navona. Giuseppe, Joanne and Maria were delighted when he'd arrived. They'd all missed him, too. Halfway through the dinner, when Scarlett rose to her feet and publicly toasted his success with the Mediterranean Airlines deal, everyone at the table clapped and cheered.

Vin ducked his head, looking embarrassed. After all the work he'd put into the deal, his boyish humility made her more proud of him than ever. And love him more than ever.

Finally, after they returned home, after he tucked their sleeping baby into his crib, he took Scarlett to bed, too. She relished the warmth of him, the strength of him, the feel of him beside her.

She'd missed him for those two weeks.

It scared her how much she needed him now.

This time, as Vin made love to her, he held her gently, tenderly, looking deeply into her eyes. But his own eyes were carefully blank.

He touched her as if his fingertips wished to tell her everything he could not put into words. She tried to guess. He was sorry? He regretted their fight—which had been so awful, so brutal to her heart? That he hadn't lied when he said he loved her?

He made her body explode with ecstasy as he poured into her with a groan, then afterward he held her all night, snugly against his chest, in a way he'd never done before.

Cradled against him, with his strong arms around her, Scarlett felt protected. She decided she was imagining things, creating problems where they didn't exist. They were husband and wife. They were partners in life. They were in love.

She woke up smiling for the first time in two weeks. She heard a morning bird singing outside and stretched, yawning, every bit of her body feeling deliciously satisfied. How could she be anything other than happy? Vin was home at last. And today was Maria's wedding day.

Whatever conflicts arose between her and Vin, they'd work through them. Maybe they'd live in Rome for half the year, New York the other half.

She looked over at his side of the bed, but it was empty.

Scarlett started to get out of bed in her negligee, when she heard the bedroom door kick open. Startled, she saw

Vin, wearing only a towel wrapped around his trim waist, holding a breakfast tray with a rose in a small bud vase.

"You brought me breakfast?" Scarlett said in surprise. "But you must be exhausted. You traveled so long yesterday…"

"Exactly. I left you here alone to take care of Nico and my sister's wedding and all the rest. It's time I took care of you for a change." His dark eyes crinkled as he smiled, setting the tray on her lap, over the white comforter.

"By the way," he said casually as he turned away, "I've left some papers on the tray for you to sign. They're under the rose."

Frowning, Scarlett looked down. "What kind of papers?"

"No big deal." He shrugged. "Just to officially mark that you are my wife. For the Italian authorities."

She glanced at the top sheet. It was written in Italian and did seem to say something about being his wife. But her Italian language skills, in spite of her recent study, weren't strong enough to sort through the indecipherable legalese. She hesitated. "My dad always said only a fool signs something he doesn't understand. I should get it translated before I sign it."

"Sure, whatever you want," he said carelessly as he left the room. A minute later, he returned with a carafe. Coming back to the bed, he poured steaming coffee into a china cup, adding liberal amounts of cream and sugar, then put it on her tray, smiling down at her tenderly. "From now on, I'm going to take better care of you. Treat you like you deserve. Like a princess. Like a queen."

Looking up at him, Scarlett's heart twisted with love.

"Enjoy your breakfast, *cara*." He cracked a sudden grin. "I'm going to take a shower. Feel free to join me if you're feeling—" he lifted a teasing eyebrow *"—dirty."*

With a whistle, he turned away, dropping his towel to

the floor. Scarlett's lips parted at the delicious view of her husband's muscular backside before he disappeared into the bathroom. It took several seconds before she was able to focus again.

She looked down at the papers, thinking of everything she had to do today before the evening wedding. After weeks of procrastination, she still hadn't figured out what to wear. She desperately wanted to look good at the formal event, to show her respect to Maria and the rest of Vin's family. But she dreaded the pressure of scouring the chic designer shops of Rome. She always felt like a chubby bumpkin. The thought of also going to look for an English-speaking lawyer to translate and advise her felt like one unpleasant task too many.

Besides, she was Vin's wife, the mother of his child. For better or worse. If she truly believed she was his partner, why treat him like an enemy? She didn't want to be suspicious. She wanted to trust him.

So she would. End of story.

Smiling to herself in relief, Scarlett signed the papers with a flourish, then enjoyed the delicious breakfast. She polished off the almond croissant at the exact moment she heard her baby starting to fuss in the nursery. She brought the baby back to their bedroom and was cuddling and nursing him in bed when Vin came back, wrapped in a white terry cloth robe, his dark hair wet, his black eyes smoldering.

"Did you enjoy your breakfast, *cara*?"

"It was amazing. Thank you so much." She held up the signed papers. "I have these for you."

His eyes lit up with something dark and deep. He came forward. He gently took the papers from her. Seeing her signature, he kissed her on the temple and said in a low voice, "Thank you, Scarlett."

"No problem," she said, smiling up at him. Then she

sighed. "If only I could solve the problem of what to wear tonight so easily."

His own smile widened. "*Cara*, that is one problem I can solve for you."

With a single phone call, Vin solved everything. He arranged for a team of stylists to come to the villa. Beauty specialists appeared that afternoon to do her nails, hair and makeup. As Nico rolled around on the soft pad of his baby gym nearby, cooing and batting at soft dangling toys, Scarlett sipped sparkling mineral water while clothing stylists presented thirty different gowns to choose from, each more exquisite than the last.

Then she saw one that took her breath away, long and sapphire blue. When she tried it on, it made her figure look like an hourglass, especially with the lingerie underneath, a push-up bra more outrageous than she would have ever selected for herself. It made her breasts high and huge with sharp cleavage beneath the gown's low-cut bodice. The hairdresser twisted her red hair in an elegant chignon, and the makeup artist made her lips deep red, darkening her eyes with kohl. When Scarlett finally saw herself in the mirror, she gasped. She almost didn't recognize herself.

"*Bellissima,*" her hairstylist said, kissing his fingertips expressively. Scarlett blushed.

Vin had said she'd be treated like a princess, and she felt like one. She turned anxiously to Wilhelmina, who was now holding the baby. She'd become Scarlett's trusted friend. "What do you think?"

The housekeeper looked her over critically, then smiled. "Sugar, I think that husband of yours is likely to die of pride."

Scarlett prayed she was right, and that Vin didn't think she looked like an ordinary girl playing dress-up, pretending to play the role of a glamorous, sexy, sophisticated woman.

Kissing her baby's cheeks, which were getting chubbier every day, Scarlett floated out of the master bedroom, into the hall, still trembling, wondering what Vin would say when he saw her. She paused at the top of the staircase as she heard low words from below.

"Blaise Falkner…"

The voices cut off sharply as Vin and his assistant saw her. But why would they be talking about that awful man?

Her husband's eyes widened as she came down the stairs, holding the handrail carefully so she didn't trip on her four-inch, crystal-studded high heels. He met her at the bottom of the staircase.

"You dazzle me," he murmured too softly for his assistant to hear. Taking her hand, he whispered, "Forget the wedding. Let's go back upstairs…"

Her cheeks burned pleasantly, but she bit her lip. "Were you talking about Blaise Falkner?"

Vin started to shake his head, but Ernest, his assistant, interjected, "We haven't been able to track him since he left New York."

"Track him? What do you mean?"

Vin glared at his assistant, then kissed the back of her hand. Scarlett shivered as she felt the hot press of his sensual lips against her skin. "It's nothing to worry about. He's probably just too embarrassed to show his face. Drowning his sorrows in a gutter." He looked at her. "Scarlett. You are so beautiful."

Her blush deepened. "Thanks. Um. You look nice, too."

Her praise felt woefully inadequate. His black tuxedo jacket was tailored perfectly, showing off his amazing physique from his muscular shoulders to his taut waist. His dark eyes were intense in his handsome face with a jawline and cheekbones that would cut glass. But he wasn't just superficially handsome. It was more than that. Some might think he was arrogant, but Scarlett alone knew his heart, his goodness, his love for his family. That was what she loved.

Frowning, Vin tilted his head. "You just need one thing."

"What?"

Reaching to a nearby table for a flat black velvet box, he drew out a large, dazzling diamond necklace. She gasped as she felt the cold weight of the diamonds clasped gently around her throat. Then he kissed her at the crook of her neck, and she felt a rush of heat. She whispered, "Thank you."

"Now we can go," he said softly.

They kissed their baby son good-night, leaving him happily cuddled in Wilhelmina's arms, and went out into the cold night. Vin gently draped her white stole over her shoulders as they crossed their cobblestoned driveway to the waiting limousine. The gate opened on the street, and the driver, with two bodyguards traveling behind them, whisked them off to the grand *palazzo*.

Maria and Luca's evening winter wedding was sublimely beautiful, lit with candles and white flowers in the gilded receiving room of the *palazzo*. Giuseppe walked her down the aisle, tears shining on his face. Sitting nearby, Joanne cried, as well. Scarlett watched the young couple speak their vows and her heart felt overwhelmed with joy as she looked at her husband beside her and felt all the love around them.

Afterward, they adjourned to the ballroom for a formal dinner. The young bride and groom sat at a table on a dais, with their immediate families on each side of them. That included Vin and Scarlett. She hugged the bride and groom, and then Giuseppe and Joanne. She listened to the speeches toasting the bride and groom, mostly in Italian, and tried to understand. She enjoyed the freedom to drink champagne.

But the whole time, Scarlett was aware of her husband beside her, looking down at her with his darkly sensual gaze. He kept giving quick stolen kisses on her bare shoulder above the sweetheart neckline of her strapless blue gown. He kissed her on her cheek. On the lips. She leaned against him, reveling in his nearness. It was a beautiful wedding, but she could hardly wait to get home...

"We're going to miss you," the bridegroom's father, a wealthy businessman who owned this grand *palazzo*, called across the table to Vin halfway through the third course. "My son was secretly hoping your wife would give Maria some cooking lessons."

"Papà!" the groom protested.

"Luca!" The bride tossed her head in her elegant white veil, pretending to pout. "But if I learn to cook, how would we support the restaurants? One must think of helping the economy!"

But Scarlett frowned at Luca's father. "What do you mean, you'll miss us?" She looked at her husband with dismay. "Are you going on another business trip?"

"I heard you're moving to New York," Luca's father said. "In fact, I heard you've already rented out your villa here on long lease to some Hollywood actor and bought a brand-new duplex in New York for some obscene amount. I read it in the paper—was it fifty million dollars?"

Scarlett relaxed, laughed. "I'm afraid you've heard incorrectly, Signor Farro. We are talking about New York, but we haven't decided anything. We certainly haven't rented out our..."

Her voice trailed off as she saw Vin's face. Ice entered her heart.

"You wouldn't do that," she said in a small voice. "Not without talking to me. After everything I put into our home, you wouldn't rent it out from underneath me..."

Vin's expression was closed. "The decision has already been made."

"By who?" Scarlett pulled away. "By you?"

The smiles had fallen from the faces of the bride and groom. Their parents started to look anxious. Chic guests at nearby dinner tables turned to look as their voices rose.

Vin set his jaw. "Yes, by me. You were being unreasonable."

Her lips parted in disbelief. "Unreasonable?"

"I allowed you to stay in Rome—"

"Allowed!" she cried.

"—until Maria's wedding. But I already made it clear. My headquarters is in New York. Tomorrow, we will pack a few suitcases and fly there. The rest of our things can be forwarded. It's true. I have bought a brand-new penthouse close to my office, near good private schools for Nico."

Vin sat back, looking pleased with himself, as if he expected praise. Scarlett felt numb.

"We already have a home, here in Rome," she whispered.

"You'll like New York even better when we arrive tomorrow night."

"I'm not getting on a plane."

Vin's expression changed to a glower. "You have to face your fears."

She hated his patronizing tone. "No, I don't."

"You have no choice now. You—"

"Children, children..." Vin's father broke in, his weathered face anguished. "Scarlett, my dear one, I am sure my son only meant the best. But if you do not want to leave Rome, he will not force you. He is a good man. Vincenzo, my son, you must tell her that..."

Vin stood up so fast his chair fell to the floor of the dais. The noise of the crash echoed in the suddenly silent ballroom. His voice was cold as he looked at Giuseppe.

"Stop calling me your son. I am not."

Giuseppe goggled at him. Joanne and Maria both drew back in shock.

Vin's lip curled. "You wondered why I ignored you for twenty years?" he said in a low voice. "Right before my mother died, when I asked her if I could live with you in Tuscany, she laughed in my face. She told me I was the result of a one-night stand with some musician in Rio. She lied to you, Giuseppe," he said deliberately, almost cruelly, "so you'd give her money. And you paid her. Blindly. Just as you blindly loved me all those years." He slowly looked to Joanne and Maria. "So do not presume to lecture me. You are not my family." He turned to Scarlett, his eyes like ice. "And you will do what I say. You have no choice. You signed the agreement."

"Agreement?" She was still reeling from his revelation that Giuseppe was not his father. Then she realized what he was talking about, and a sick feeling rose inside her. "Those papers this morning—"

He glanced at all the people in the ballroom, then spoke too quietly for them to hear. "I always intended to make you sign, Scarlett. Either before marriage or after."

The pre-nup he'd once threatened her with. The agreement that gave him the right to make all decisions about their baby's life, and hers. The agreement that gave Vin full custody of Nico if he ever decided to divorce her. *And she'd signed it.*

Scarlett's world was spinning, crashing, on fire. Standing up from her chair, she stared at him in horror. Then, snatching her crystal-encrusted minaudière from the table, she turned away in her four-inch heels, ducking around the waiters who'd just come pouring into the ballroom with the next course. By the time she fled the ballroom, she was crying.

How could she have been so stupid?

She should have listened to her fears, not her hopes.

Don't tell him about the baby.

Don't get a DNA test.

Don't marry him.

Don't love him.

And most of all:

Always read before you sign.

Furiously, she wiped her eyes, but tears clouded her vision as she stumbled into the empty, high-ceilinged hallway. She saw Beppe leave his post outside the ballroom door and start to follow her.

"Don't even think about it!" she barked. She'd never spoken sharply to him before. She had the unhappy satisfaction of seeing him stop, his expression hurt.

Turning away, Scarlett ran past a security guard sleeping in a chair inside the foyer. She went out the front door of the *palazzo*, through the same door where she'd arrived with such happiness on Vin's arm just hours before.

Then, the exclusive Roman street had been jammed with arriving cars, gleaming and luxurious, many driven by chauffeurs. Now, the street was dark and cold and empty.

It was so cold, the drizzle of rain had turned to soft, silent snowflakes. A small dog trotted down the street sniffing at doorways. She saw a shadow of a homeless man leaning against the corner. She shivered as snowflakes melted like ice on her bare skin. She'd been in too much of a hurry to grab her white stole. But who cared about being cold?

She'd been so happy. She swallowed against the ache in her throat. With her baby. Her home. The man she loved. So completely happy.

But it had all been an illusion. Vin baiting his trap.

She had to get out of here.

Scarlett's heart pounded as she stood alone in the darkness in front of the *palazzo*. Down the street, she saw a taxi coming her direction. She could flag it down. She could rush to the villa, grab Nico and disappear. She knew how. She'd done it before.

Her heart pounded as she watched the taxi draw closer. The thought of leaving Vin, even now, and also separating him from the baby he loved, filled her with anguish.

She tried to steel herself. She told herself she had no choice. She raised her hand to flag down the taxi.

Freedom. For her entire childhood, freedom had been her rallying cry. She had to follow her dream—

Scarlett remembered the look on her father's face the day she turned eighteen and told him she'd given up her dreams of college and ever settling down. With tears in his eyes, he told her that after all their years on the run, he was turning himself in.

"What about freedom?" she'd cried.

"We were never free," he'd said quietly. "Not once. I made a horrible mistake, Scarlett. I was a coward. Running away all these years, I ruined your life, and your mother's. But no more. You will be free now." He'd taken a deep breath. "I'm doing this so you'll be free."

"Signorina?"

The taxi driver was looking at her impatiently through his open window.

Scarlett stared at him. Then, lowering her arm, she slowly shook her head. Numbly, she watched the taxi drive off.

She'd run from Vin before. If she ran now, kidnapping her innocent baby from his father, starting life as a fugitive, she wouldn't be following a dream of freedom. Not when her only idea of real freedom was to have family, stability and a real home.

"Scarlett!"

Her shoulders tightened at Vin's angry voice behind her. With a deep breath, she turned to face him.

He stopped in front of her as gentle snowflakes flurried softly to the sidewalk in the dark, cold night. "There's no point in running away," he said quietly. "The postnuptial agreement gives total control of our baby's future to me. And since I know you'll never be parted from him—" he reached out to caress her cheek "—that gives me total control over you."

For a second, she shook with fear, with regret, with rage. Then she remembered the one thing she still had.

Love.

With a deep breath, she lifted her chin, looking straight into his eyes.

"I'm not going anywhere. I'm staying right here."

Vin looked surprised. Then he caught himself and glared at her. "Good—"

"But I'm not going to let you push me around." She put her hand over his. "I love you, Vin. And you love me. That was the whole reason for this, wasn't it?"

"What are you talking about?"

"You're afraid to love me."

He dropped his hand with a snort. *"Afraid."*

"Yes, afraid. So you tried to create a wall between us." She stepped closer, until she could see the white of her breath mingle with his in the faint light. She could see the snowflakes that had fallen in his dark hair and eyelashes. "But I'm not going to let you do it. We love each other. We belong together."

"You signed it. There's nothing you can do now."

"You're wrong." Reaching up, she gently caressed his rough cheek and whispered, "I can call your bluff."

His eyes widened, and he staggered back.

"You won't hurt me," she said. "You can't. Because you love me. And I love you."

"Stop saying that—" he said hoarsely. He clenched his hands at his sides, then turned on his heel, stalking back into the *palazzo*, leaving Scarlett standing alone on the sidewalk on the dark, quiet street.

She turned her face toward the snowflakes, relishing the feel of them, soft and cold, against her overheated skin.

She had to be right. She had to be.

If she was wrong…

Scarlett heard heavy footsteps behind her. Had Vin already returned to tell her he'd changed his mind about the postnuptial agreement? Filled with hope, she turned.

But it wasn't her husband. The scruffy-looking homeless man from the corner now stood before her.

Confused, she drew back. "Can I help you?"

The man was dressed badly, his face lumpy. But when he smiled, she suddenly choked out a gasp as she recognized his face beneath the dirt.

"Yes, Scarlett." Blaise Falkner's eyes looked crazy above his evil smile. "You can."

As Vin entered the *palazzo*, his whole body felt tight, his hands clenched at his sides. He didn't even know where he was going. He just felt sick inside. Panicked. Like he had to either fight or run.

He couldn't fight Scarlett, so he'd run. He'd never run from anything in his life.

Vin ran an unsteady hand over his forehead.

When he'd told Scarlett about the post-nup, he'd expected to feel triumph, or at least a sense of calm control.

Instead, watching the happiness in his wife's eyes melt into horror, Vin had experienced a physical reaction he'd never expected. His hands had tightened into fists. He'd instantly wanted to destroy whomever had hurt her.

Except he had no one to blame—but himself.

"Vincenzo."

Vin abruptly stopped in the gilded, high-ceilinged hall-way when he saw Giuseppe waiting for him.

Just what he needed. He gave a silent curse. Another person to heap scorn on him, when he was doing a fine enough job heaping it on himself. He bit out, "What do you want?"

Giuseppe came forward, solemn in his formal tuxedo. "We have to talk."

"Make it quick."

"I always knew you weren't my biological son." He gave Vin a small smile. "Is that quick enough for you?"

He gaped at him, dumbfounded. "What?"

The older man shook his head. "Vincenzo, your mother's eyes were blue. So are mine. What are the chances we could conceive a child with eyes as dark as yours?"

After twenty years of keeping the secret, Vin was staggered. "But my mother used you for money. For years. Why didn't you tell her to go to hell, tell her I wasn't yours?"

"Because you *are* mine," he said, coming forward. "From the moment I held you as a tiny baby, Vincenzo, I was your father."

Vin thought of the first moment he'd held his own son in his arms. He knew what that felt like.

Giuseppe put his hands on Vin's shoulders. "I didn't give a damn what some DNA test might say. I loved you. You were—you *are*—my son. And you will always be."

Vin felt dizzy, like he'd gotten drunk on that one glass of champagne. The floor was trembling under him.

He'd been so wrong. He, who'd believed he could never be wrong about anything, had been wrong about everything.

He thought he'd never run away from a fight?

He'd been running for twenty years.

All these years he'd avoided Giuseppe and Joanne,

avoided emotion, avoided life. For what? For the sake of a secret that didn't matter?

His whole adult life, he'd tried to control everything, to make sure he never felt tied to anyone, so he'd never feel pain when they left. When, against his will, he'd come to care for Scarlett, it had terrified him so much he'd thought he needed to bring her to heel. To make her his slave.

Had he really thought he could rule her with a piece of paper? He was powerless where she was concerned. No pre-nup or post-nup in the world could change that.

I love you, Vin. And you love me. That was the whole reason for this, wasn't it? You're afraid to love me.

Giuseppe sighed ruefully in the hallway. "I just wish I'd known that was the reason you stayed away from us." He glanced at his wife, who'd come up behind him, followed by Maria. "We were foolish to keep silent, but we didn't want to give you more reasons to stay away."

"You knew, too?" Vin said to Joanne. She smiled, even as she wiped tears away.

"Of course I knew, darling. Giuseppe and I have been married a long time. We have no secrets."

"Well, I didn't know!" Maria cried sulkily behind her, tossing her long white veil. "No one tells me anything!"

Vin glanced at his young sister in her white wedding gown, and in that instant, his whole life came sharply into focus.

Scarlett was right. About everything.

Part of him had thought if he pushed her, she would flee, which would prove his worst beliefs and justify his actions in making her sign the post-nup.

He'd *wanted* to push her away.

You're afraid to love me. Yes, afraid. You tried to create a wall between us. But I'm not going to let you do it. We love each other. We belong together.

From the first moment he'd met Scarlett, so silly and

free in the New York dive bar, choking at her first taste of vodka, he'd been enchanted. He'd never met anyone like her, so feisty and sexy and warm.

He'd wanted her from the start, and he'd been willing to make deals to possess her—like his ridiculous fantasy that he could protect his own heart, and stay in control, by making her sign a form, or by trying to love her less, because he, the one who cared less, was the one who had the power.

But that was wrong. He saw that now.

It wasn't the one who loved less who had the power, but the one who loved more. Not because you could control the outcome, or keep from getting hurt, but because it meant you were brave enough to live without fear, hurtling yourself headlong into both joy and pain.

Being a fully alive human being, with the courage to love completely—what could be more powerful than that?

And as much as he loved his son, it wasn't the baby who'd first cracked open his heart.

It was Scarlett.

He looked at his father. "I need to go talk to my wife."

"Go, son," Giuseppe said fiercely. "Show her who you really are!"

Vin nodded, turned back down the hall.

He never should have rented their home out from under her. Another way he'd tried to push Scarlett into hating him. It had never felt like his home—until now. Scarlett had taken the sad, faded, tumbledown prison of his childhood and brought it to joyous life.

She'd done the same for him. Before they'd met, Vin had been focused on money and power, to the detriment of his own happiness. He'd been so afraid of being vulnerable that, if Scarlett hadn't shown up in the New York cathedral that day, he would have married a woman he didn't give a damn about.

If not for Scarlett, he would have turned into a man like Salvatore Calabrese: selfish, shallow and cold, too insecure to risk the only thing that mattered. His heart.

So many things Scarlett had done for him, and all she'd asked in return was for him to love her. For him to be the man he'd been born to be. The man she deserved.

Vin's walk turned into a run. Nodding at the sleepy security guard sitting inside the foyer, he pushed open the front door.

Outside the *palazzo*, the street was dark and quiet. Silent white snow fell softly to the ground. But where was Scarlett?

Then he saw her.

Still in her diamond necklace and sapphire-colored gown, her red hair looked tangled and twisted, and she had terror in her eyes.

A man was holding her. A man with a gun. A man with all kinds of darkness in his eyes.

"Vin!" she cried, struggling.

"Borgia." Blaise Falkner gave him a cold, evil smile. "I should have known you wouldn't keep away for long. You've wrecked my plan, but I'm almost glad. Now you'll see what I'm going to do to her, right in front of your eyes."

Terror ripped through Vin's heart as he looked from Falkner's face to the revolver, black as a deadly snake, held against Scarlett's forehead. For a split second, Vin's world started to go dark with fear.

Then he took a deep breath. He didn't *do* fear. Ever. And he wasn't going to start now, when his wife needed him to be strong. There was only one emotion he could let himself feel right now. He let the waves of it roll over him, like an ocean in a storm.

Rage.

CHAPTER TWELVE

WHEN BLAISE HAD pulled a gun on her in the quiet, snowy street, Scarlett had thought bitterly of how Vin had ordered her to keep a bodyguard nearby. Why hadn't she listened?

Because she'd never imagined she might need a bodyguard in the center of Rome. She'd never imagined that anyone might want to attack her...

"I've been watching your house for a week," Blaise had said, keeping his black revolver trained on her. "Hoping to get you alone."

"Why?" Her teeth chattered. "You can't still want to... to marry me?"

"Marry?" His lip had twisted scornfully as he came closer, until she could smell the sickening stench of old sweat half masked with musky cologne. "I'm way past that now. Your husband made this personal. He ruined my life. Now I will do the same to him."

Snowflakes fell softly against her skin. But that wasn't what froze her to the bone. "How?"

"He loves you."

"You heard us argue—"

"Yeah, I heard it all. It's perfect." His smile became venomous. "Now when you disappear, he'll blame himself for the rest of his life and think he drove you away. He'll always wonder. He'll never know."

"You can't!"

"Watch me." With his gun still trained on her, he snatched her crystal-encrusted clutch bag from her hand. "My car is around the corner..."

"I'm not going anywhere with you." She straightened. "Shoot me here."

"You'll go. Or my next stop will be at your house. Your baby is there, with no one but the housekeeper to protect him. Shame if they had a little accident. If the doors were blocked and the place went up in flames."

"No!" she cried, whimpering at the thought. "I'll go with you. Just leave them alone..."

"That's more like it." Blaise motioned with the revolver. "Over there, in the alley..."

But as she started to move, the front door of the *palazzo* banged open. Quick as a flash, Blaise grabbed her, placing her in front of him, holding the gun to her forehead.

Scarlett nearly cried when she saw Vin had come out of the *palazzo*. His black eyes went wide when he saw them. Then his hands clenched into fists.

"Let her go, Falkner." Vin's dark gaze focused on Blaise. "We both know I'm the one you want to hurt."

"Not just hurt. I want to destroy you. And hurting her—" he gripped into her shoulder painfully, causing Scarlett to gasp aloud "—is the best way to do that."

Vin took a step toward them. "We can talk about this. Negotiate..."

"There's nothing to negotiate, and if you take one more step, she's dead."

Vin stopped. His voice was low. "You'll die the second after she does."

Blaise gave a cackle. "You think I care? You took everything from me, Borgia. My whole life. I can never go back. And now neither can you..."

Blaise pressed the cold barrel of the revolver sharply into her skin.

Vin threw Scarlett a brief glance full of meaning. "You'd attack her from behind?"

And she remembered that rainy afternoon in October.

Here's how to use your own body weight against an attacker who grabs you from behind... She gave him a single trembling nod, and then everything happened at once.

The door of the *palazzo* banged open as Beppe and two other bodyguards rushed out. As Blaise whirled to look, Vin planted his feet, lowering his body into an instinctive crouch.

With an exaggerated sigh, Scarlett sagged as if she'd fainted. It wasn't hard at all. She was so terrified she was perilously close to fainting anyway.

Her unexpected weight broke his hold, and she fell hard to the cold, wet sidewalk.

With a loud curse, Blaise pointed the gun at her. He cocked it. She saw the deadly intention in his face.

As snowflakes whirled around her, Scarlett's life flashed before her eyes. Her mother. Her father. Her baby. All the love she'd had. And Vin. Always Vin...

As she closed her eyes, bracing herself for death, she saw a shadow fly across her field of vision. But there was no mercy. The gun went off with a jarring bang, and she flinched, gasping.

But she felt nothing.

Was this what it felt like to be dead? Scarlett's eyes opened, then she quickly ran her hands over her body. Somehow, though he'd shot her from four feet away, he'd missed her!

But Vin and Blaise were still struggling for the gun. The revolver fired once more, echoing loudly in the night.

"Die, you Italian bastard!" Blaise panted.

Vin! Scarlett scrambled to her feet, desperate to save him, terrified he'd been shot. But even as the bodyguards descended from all sides, Vin flung Blaise over his back like a sack of potatoes. For half a second, Blaise was suspended in midair with a shocked, stupid look on his face. Then he crashed hard to the concrete, where he lay still.

"The police are on the way, Mr. Borgia," Beppe said.

Scarlett heard the distant whine of a siren. She knew the steps in front of the *palazzo* would soon be covered with medical and police personnel.

Blaise lay faceup, flat on his back. Unmoving, he wheezed, "You... You..."

Vin looked down at him coldly. "You are going to prison, Falkner. For a very long time. You should pray you never get out." As bodyguards surrounded him, Vin turned to Scarlett. His expression changed. He reached for her. "Scarlett—"

"You saved me," Scarlett choked out, pressing her cheek against him. Then she drew back, frowning. "But you're wet. You..." There was a darkening patch on his right shoulder, and another on his left thigh. With a gasp, she lifted the lapel of his tuxedo jacket and saw red blooming across his white shirt, like a flower. And it was in that moment she realized why she was still alive. Vin had taken two bullets for her.

When Vin saw Falkner put his finger on the trigger, everything had become crystal clear.

He would either save his wife or die with her.

Their son would know that his father had loved his mother enough to sacrifice his own life to try to save her.

That was the best legacy any father could leave his son. The only real legacy. It had nothing to do with leaving a fortune, or a billion-dollar company. A man's true legacy was his example, of how a man should live—and how he should die. *For the ones he loved.*

"Cara." Vin pulled Scarlett into his arms, holding her like the precious treasure she was. He felt a sharp pain in his shoulder, and another in his thigh. He gritted his teeth against the pain. "He was right about one thing. If anything ever happened to you, it would utterly destroy me."

"Vin, we need to try to stop the bleeding until the paramedics…"

"Not yet," he breathed. He curved his hands around her, needing the feel of her body against his. "Everything you said was true. That's what I came to say. I was afraid to love you." He searched her gaze. "Now the only thing I'm afraid of is not having the chance to love you for the rest of my life."

She looked closely at the holes in his jacket. "It looks like this bullet went straight through your shoulder and out the back. But your leg…"

He was barely listening. "I was a coward."

"Coward? Vin, you took two bullets for me!"

"It's true," he insisted roughly. He was still shaking. It was only now that he held her, now she was safe in his arms, that he could admit how terrified he'd been. "I promised myself long ago that I'd never love anyone— never give anyone that kind of power over me. Then on Christmas Eve, after I told you I loved you, I was afraid. I was desperate to regain control."

"Control over what?"

"You, me, everything. Life."

"Oh, Vin," she whispered through cracked lips. "No one can control all that."

"I realized that today." His lips twisted as he leaned on her. He could no longer put any weight on his left leg. He wondered how much blood he'd lost. But he couldn't let her go. Not yet. "I've made so many mistakes. I just found out Giuseppe has always known he's not my biological father. He just didn't care."

"No!"

He gave a low laugh, swaying on his feet. He was starting to feel dizzy. "Control is an illusion. I understand that now. All I can control in life are the choices I make. The man I choose to be." He took her hand in his own, pressing it against his chest. "You have my heart, Scarlett. No matter if you hurt me. No matter if you leave me." Her beautiful face blurred in his vision as he whispered, "After the way I tricked you into signing those papers, I wouldn't blame you."

Paramedics and firemen and policemen were swarming the street, and inquisitive wedding guests were pouring out of the *palazzo*. But all Vin could see was Scarlett's pale, determined face.

"You listen to me, Vin Borgia," she said hoarsely. "This is something I want you to remember for the rest of your life." She took both his hands in hers. Her green eyes looked enormous. "You're safe with me, Vin. As long as I live, I'll watch out for you."

It was a strange thing to hear from a woman so much smaller than he. But as he swayed, feeling weak from loss of blood, she was beneath his arm, supporting him, the source of his strength. As he was the source of hers.

"And I know I'm safe with you," she whispered, her eyes filling with tears. "I will never leave you. I'm yours for life."

Her love washed over him like an enveloping embrace. Vin exhaled. He hadn't realized he'd been holding his breath for so long, waiting to hear those words. Years. Decades.

He breathed, "Scarlett…"

Snow fell softly in the dark January night, frosting the streets of Rome. As people swarmed all around them, Vin pulled her close. He felt new, reborn. She'd made him the man he'd been born to be.

Then he staggered back as his vision got a little hazy.

"You're losing too much blood!" She waved wildly to the paramedics. "Over here! Quick!"

The paramedics swiftly assessed Vin's injuries and worked to control the bleeding, applying pressure and bandages before leaning him into a backboard, to carry him into the ambulance. "We need to get him to the hospital, *signora*."

"Yes," she said anxiously.

"Wait." Feeling woozy, Vin looked at his wife. "We'll live in Rome."

She tried to smile. "What about the long-term lease to Mr. Hollywood?"

"Canceled. We'll stay."

She looked down at him, her tangled red hair streaked with snow and blood. "No."

"No?"

She shook her head. "That's not how marriage works. It's not my decision." Taking his hand in hers, she kissed it. "It's ours. I love you, Vin."

He looked at her, now holding nothing back, letting her see his whole heart and soul. "I love you more."

"Are you ready?"

No, Scarlett thought, biting her lip hard. She shivered, then nodded.

"Good." Vin held out his hand.

She took it and stepped onto a plane for the first time in almost a year.

"You can do this," he said.

She took a deep breath. She looked at his hand in hers, then squared her shoulders. "I know."

He smiled. "That's my girl."

The plane was tiny, a four-seater Cessna. There would be no flight attendants. Only one pilot. And only one passenger.

But it was going to be all right, Scarlett suddenly knew. Because she trusted this pilot with her life.

She sat beside him now as he pushed knobs and flicked

on switches. He moved the throttle, then glanced at her. "Maybe someday you'll get your own pilot's license."

"Ha-ha," she said, then realized he was serious.

Vin looked at her. "The best way to live is to do what scares you most. You taught me that, *cara*."

Maybe he was right, Scarlett thought suddenly. Maybe. But…

"I'll just survive being a passenger first," she said, gripping her headphones tightly.

He reached over and put his hand on her knee. "Look at my face."

She did and relaxed.

"There's no way we can crash." He sat back in the pilot's seat with an encouraging grin. "I'm safe with you, remember? You'll watch out for me."

"I meant it." She knew he wouldn't let anything happen to her, either. If anyone could keep Vin safe, it was Scarlett. If anyone could keep Scarlett safe, it was Vin.

She took a deep breath, clutching her armrests.

So much had changed in the last eight months, since the night of Maria's wedding, when he'd been shot by Blaise Falkner. Vin had spent days recovering in the hospital, where he'd also been interviewed by the police. But he'd been lucky.

"If he'd shot you a little lower in the shoulder," the doctor had told him, "the bullet would have hit you in the heart. If he'd shot you a little higher in the thigh…" He hesitated.

"I'd be done fathering children?" Vin had grinned up at Scarlett, standing by his hospital bed. "Remind me to visit Falkner in prison and thank him for his poor aim."

She didn't find it funny at all. "This is no laughing matter."

"Oh, *cara*, but it is." Vin had kissed the back of her

hand, then looked at her seriously. "One should always be joyful in the presence of a miracle."

When he finally was able to return home, he'd embraced his baby son happily swinging in his bouncy chair, who had no idea of the tragedy that had nearly taken his parents' lives. Vin had kissed his son's downy head, kissed his wife's lips, then gone straight to the study and thrown the signed postnuptial agreement into the fire.

He'd also ripped up the villa's lease to the movie star. The man had immediately threatened to sue, but Vin had solved the problem by paying for him to stay three months at a fancy hotel, and the actor quit complaining.

"Room service," Vin explained succinctly.

Vin had also insisted on paying for his sister to have a second honeymoon. It was the least he could do, he said, after ruining her wedding reception. After the young couple had returned from Tahiti, while Giuseppe and Joanne were visiting their grandson for a week, they had the whole family together for dinners and game nights.

Eventually, when Vin's wounds had healed and Scarlett felt ready, they had a farewell party to say *ciao* to Rome. They packed up what they needed most and took the train to London and, from there, a luxurious ocean liner to New York.

Scarlett had felt guilty about the six-day voyage—so much longer than a transatlantic flight—but her husband hadn't grumbled once. In fact, he'd claimed he enjoyed the vacation, and the chance to dance with his wife every night on the dance floor while Mrs. Stone kept a close eye on Nico in their lavish suite.

"In fact, I might consider a fleet of ships for my next SkyWorld expansion," he'd told Scarlett, waggling his eyebrows. She still wasn't sure if he'd been serious.

The two of them had agreed to compromise, and split their time between Rome and New York. But since they'd moved to Manhattan, Scarlett had found to her surprise that she'd come to love this rough-and-tumble city, too. Next week, when they returned to Rome, she might even miss New York. Living in their delightful two-story penthouse with a view of Central Park—which she'd decorated to be homey and comfortable—meant she often passed St. Swithun's Cathedral on Fifth Avenue.

"The place you decided to marry me," she liked to tease Vin, "in the middle of your wedding to someone else."

He grinned. "*Bella*, I know a good thing when I see her."

"I love you," she said.

"I love you more," he said seriously.

Which of them loved the other one more was, of course, not their only quarrel. They were human, after all. Sometimes Vin worked too much, or Scarlett fretted about their perfectly happy baby, who could now sit on his own and loved to giggle and was starting to talk. But even during their rare arguments, Vin would claim that Scarlett was perfect, the most wonderful woman in the world. It irritated her to no end. How could she properly fight with a man who continually insisted she was perfect?

So when Vin suggested one tiny, tiny thing she might do for his birthday, she had to listen. He asked her to take a plane ride. "I have a little Cessna parked at Teterboro. I'd be the pilot. We'd fly for fifteen minutes, tops. Short circle, totally uneventful, then we'd land." He looked at her hopefully. "What do you say?"

She hadn't wanted to disappoint him, so she'd agreed. But now…

"I can't believe you talked me into this," she breathed, as the engine noise started to build, shaking the small plane.

He grinned. "You'll love it. Trust me."

And the funny thing was, she did trust him. So maybe

he was right. Maybe she would love this. Maybe the fear that had been holding her back all this time from flying was the same one that had made him afraid to love her.

It was normal to be afraid of taking a risk. But wasn't it the point of life to find courage—even if it took a little while—and be bold enough to fly?

"Are you ready, Scarlett?" her husband asked quietly.

She felt green with fear. But she knew that if anyone could keep her safe, if anyone truly loved her, it was Vin. She took a deep breath. "Hit it."

"I love you," he said, pushing the throttle forward.

She looked at him, her heart full. "I love you more."

The Cessna started to increase speed down the runway, going faster and faster. And as the nose lifted off the ground, and their little plane soared off the runway into the bright blue sky, Scarlett knew they'd be relishing the pleasures of that argument for the rest of their lives.

* * * * *

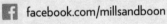